"With memorable characters and an effervescent plot that's as buoyant as it is entertaining, *Dare to Love Again* is Julie Lessman at her zestful best. Romance readers who crave a high-octane plot and a hero and heroine who take sparring to a whole new level will *not* be disappointed!"

—**Tamera Alexander**, bestselling author of
A Lasting Impression and *To Whisper Her Name*

"Nobody pens a more splendid romance than Julie! The expert on dazzling dialogue, engaging characters, and wonderful romantic plots with a twist wins my heart over every time! *Dare to Love Again* has all the elements of great story-telling—close family dynamics, love, faith, and romantic passion melded together to create another outstanding story of the McClare family."

—**Maggie Brendan**, CBA bestselling author of
Heart of the West and The Blue Willow Brides series

DARE

— *to* —

LOVE
AGAIN

Books by Julie Lessman

THE DAUGHTERS OF BOSTON

A Passion Most Pure
A Passion Redeemed
A Passion Denied

WINDS OF CHANGE

A Hope Undaunted
A Heart Revealed
A Love Surrendered

THE HEART OF SAN FRANCISCO

Love at Any Cost
Dare to Love Again

THE HEART OF
SAN FRANCISCO
· 2 ·

DARE

— *to* —

LOVE

AGAIN

A NOVEL

Julie Lessman

a division of Baker Publishing Group
Grand Rapids, Michigan

Published by Revell
a division of Baker Publishing Group
P.O. Box 6287, Grand Rapids, MI 49516-6287
www.revellbooks.com

Printed in the United States of America

Library of Congress Cataloging-in-Publication Data
Lessman, Julie, 1950–
    Dare to love again : a novel / Julie Lessman.
        pages cm. — (The Heart of San Francisco ; #2)
    ISBN 978-0-8007-2166-4 (pbk.)
    1. Single women—California—San Francisco—Fiction. 2. San Francisco (Calif.)—History—20th century—Fiction. I. Title.
PS3612.E8189D37 2014
813'.6—dc23   2013033529

Most Scripture used in this book, whether quoted or paraphrased by the characters, is taken from the King James Version of the Bible.

Scripture quotations marked NIV are from the Holy Bible, New International Version®. NIV®. Copyright © 1973, 1978, 1984, 2011 by Biblica, Inc.™ Used by permission of Zondervan. All rights reserved worldwide. www.zondervan.com

14 15 16 17 18 19 20   7 6 5 4 3 2 1

In loving memory of Leona Lessman—

a truly amazing mother-in-law who not only gave me the precious gift of her friendship and love but her incredible son as well. We miss you terribly but look forward to pinochle games in heaven with you and Ray, where I promise—I won't escape to the powder room to read *People* magazine when I lose.

May your unfailing love be with us, LORD,
even as we put our hope in you.

—Psalm 33:22 NIV

1

San Francisco, Summer 1903

Merciful Providence . . . I smell a rat! Nose in the air, Allison Mc-Clare sniffed, the unmistakable scent of Bay Rum drifting into her empty classroom of the Hand of Hope School. Although not uncommon for an antiquated Victorian house a stone's throw from the sewers of the Barbary Coast, *this* smell of "rat" was altogether different and far more frightening. She wrinkled her nose.

The man kind.

"I think you took a wrong turn, lady. High tea is at The Palace."

"Oh!" Body jolting, she whirled around at the bulletin board, almost inhaling the straight pin in her teeth. She blinked at a tall, disgruntled stranger cocked in the door of her classroom who might have been dangerously attractive if not for the scowl on his face. An unruly strand of dark hair, almost black—like his mood appeared to be—toppled over his forehead beneath a dark Homburg he obviously felt no courtesy to remove. He hiked a thumb toward the front door, his gruff voice a near snarl as he glared through gray-green eyes that seemed to darken by the moment, the color of stormy seas. "I assume that's your fancy car

9

and driver out front? Well, it needs to move to the back alley, lady, whether you're here to teach or just out slumming with the poor folks."

The straight pin in her teeth dropped to the floor, along with her jaw, as she gaped, hardly able to comprehend the rudeness of this Neanderthal who'd be better attired in bearskin and club than the charcoal suit coat draped over his shoulder. Rolled sleeves of what might have been a crisp white shirt at one time revealed muscled forearms thick with dark hair like the brainless caveman he appeared to be. It was only two in the afternoon, but already dark bristle shadowed his hard-angled jaw, lending an ominous air to a man who possessed less charm than found on the head of her pin. Her nose scrunched, the smell of "rat" surprisingly strong due to a keen sense of smell and three near misses at the altar. She fought the squirm of a smile over his high starched collar with its off-center tie—loosened as if in protest to fashionable attire he considered a noose 'round his neck.

Like the one I'm envisioning now . . .

He squinted as if she were the intruder instead of him, daring to invade his cave. "What, cat got your tongue?"

Yes, you pinhead . . . a polecat. She glared right back in silence, figuring if she waited long enough, his face would crack . . . something she'd pay good money to see. She almost wished she'd gone home with Mother and Cassie earlier instead of staying later on a Friday the week before they opened their new school. Her gaze flicked to the clock on the wall that indicated her elderly driver, Hadley, was on time to take her home. And not a moment too soon, if this barbarian was any indication of the rest of her day.

Her silence apparently ruffled his fur because his eyes narrowed, if possible, even more than before as he blasted out a noisy exhale, shaking his head as if *she* were the one with a pea for a brain. "Great—a rich dame as dumb as she is lost," he muttered, and every word his insolence had stolen from her lips marched to the tip of her tongue to do battle.

"Pardon me, Mr. Personality," she said in a clipped tone that suggested he'd just crawled out from under a rock, "but the one who is lost here, you cave dweller, is you, so I suggest you lumber back to whatever crater you climbed out of and search for the manners you obviously left behind." In a royal swoop befitting the school's new drama teacher, she snatched the pin from the floor and jabbed it into the bulletin board as if it were the backside of this unsavory baboon and every other who'd broken her heart. Before the baboon could speak—or grunt—she whirled around with a flourish, satisfied to see a sagging jaw that likely resembled the mouth of his cave. She'd obviously rendered the beast dumb. *Good—a perfect match for his brain.*

"And for your information, sir, I am the new English and drama teacher for the Hand of Hope School for girls, so I hardly need some surly wiseacre telling me I took a wrong turn. Because trust me, mister . . ." Lips pursed, she did a painfully slow perusal from the glare of those turbulent eyes miles down to laced oxford shoes that were surprisingly well polished. Her gaze sailed back up past a lean body with muscled arms and massive shoulders to settle on an annoyingly handsome face. "If I needed a compass, I'd buy one."

The grouch caught her totally off guard when the sullen slant of his mouth twitched with a hint of a smile, joining forces with a shuttered look that fluttered her stomach. "I don't care if you teach angels to fly in the wild blue yonder, lady," he said with a flip of a badge. "This is my beat, and you can't park your fancy car out front. It's an annoyance."

Yes, I know the feeling. She jutted her chin. "You don't *look* like a police officer," she challenged, eyes narrowing at the stylish sack suit he wore that appeared of high quality even if it was as disheveled as his hair.

He exhaled with a slack of his hip. "Look, lady, I'm a plain-clothes detective who's off duty at the moment, all right? And if we're going to get down to brass tacks . . ." He gave her a half-mast look that meandered from the diamond combs in her upswept hair, down the bodice of her silk shirtwaist, to her Italian kid-skin shoes beneath her House of Worth skirt. The gray-green eyes narrowed in a squint. "I'm afraid you don't look much like a schoolteacher either."

If there was one thing she disliked more than a drafty classroom in an abandoned building in the wrong part of town, it was an obnoxious police officer scowling in that same drafty classroom as if *she'd* just committed a crime. Which, given the snide look on his chiseled face, she was sorely tempted to do. She folded her arms. "Well, then, if you are an 'off duty' officer, I fail to see what business it is of yours just *where* my driver parks our car."

She stumbled back with a tiny squeak when he yanked his coat off his shoulder and barreled forward. His close proximity butted her to the bulletin board while he loomed over her like Attila the Hun. "Look, lady," he said in a tone that brooked no argument, "I'm just looking out for your best interest here." He stabbed a finger toward the front of the building, the heat in his eyes going head-to-head with the heat in her cheeks. "This is the bloomin' Barbary Coast, not a tea party on Nob Hill. A pretty debutante in a fancy car and diamond combs is an engraved invitation to trouble in a district where I work my tail off to keep crime down."

She blinked. *Pretty?*

He gouged the bridge of his nose with blunt fingers, venting with a blast of air that smelled faintly of animal crackers. "All right, okay," he said in a civil tone that sounded forced. A hint of contrition laced his words as he held out a ridiculously large hand pert near the size of a baseball glove. "Maybe we need to start over. My name is Detective Nick Barone of the 14th precinct and you are—?"

Smitten. Allison stared at his hand, then peered up at his striking face, the man so incredibly tall, it put a crick in her neck. Up close he was larger than life, older and more intimidating, the gray-green eyes such an unusual color, he might as well have hypnotized her with a watch swinging on a chain—she couldn't blink, breathe, or move. Mouth slack, she finally swallowed hard, his bold gaze and the scent of Bay Rum from his shadowed jaw doing funny things to her stomach. She tried to speak, but it was as if those incredible eyes had fused the words to her throat. Her apparent stupor actually tipped his full lips into a charming if cocky smile that sent the warmth in her face straight to the tips of her fingers and toes.

"Now, I know you can talk, ma'am, because you shot enough barbs to qualify me as a member of the cactus family, Miss—"

"Mc—" She coughed, clearing the knot of awkwardness from her throat as she tentatively placed her hand in his. "McClare—Allison McClare."

He hiked a thick, dark brow. "The McClares of Nob Hill—as in Logan McClare?"

"My uncle," she said with a shy smile, wondering how a caveman could go from heating her temper to heating her skin within four powerful strides and a smile that could thaw ice.

He responded with a sharp rasp of air through clenched teeth. The temperature in the room suddenly plummeted along with her hand when he jerked his away, his smile as stiff as an iceberg during an Antarctica winter. "I see," he said with a glacial look that broke the spell of his eyes. "A snob hill debutante used to doing whatever you blinkin' well please."

Her mouth sagged open before she snapped it shut with a plunk of hands to her hips. "Look here, Mr. Barone, when you see a sign out front that says 'no parking,' you come see me, all right, and I will make good and sure Hadley parks elsewhere." She smirked. "*If* you can read."

"It's-pronounced-'Ba-ron-ee,' long *e*," he ground out, slanting in with those mammoth hands planted low on tapered trousers. The motion parted his open waistcoat to reveal a shoulder holster with gun, stealing a rush of air from her throat. "Look, missy, I don't have time to be a nursemaid to some spoiled rich kid who doesn't have the sense God gave a gerbil. If you insist on rubbing your old man's money into the faces of every sick and starving whoremonger, cutthroat, or murderer roaming these streets, be my guest—you deserve what you get."

Gun or no, Allison stepped forward, head snapping up while she contemplated suing him for whiplash. "Well, Mr. Ba-lon-ee, long *e*, I'd like to see *you* 'long' gone from my classroom, but we don't always get what we want, do we?" She jabbed a finger toward the door like a schoolmarm reprimanding a student, eyes burning more than her cheeks. "So why don't you take your little gun and your little snide attitude right out that door, mister, because you are seriously putting a cramp in my neck." She swished her fingers under his nose as if to shoo him away. "Go—pester somebody who's actually breaking the law, you oversized bully, or I'll give you something to arrest me for."

The airheaded oaf actually stood there and laughed with a fold of arms. "Is that right? What are you going to do, Miss Mc-High-and-Mighty? Sic your butler on me? That dolt appeared as lost as you when I asked him to pull around back."

14

"He's *near deaf*, you brainless barbarian!" she shouted, his insult to Hadley unleashing her Irish temper. "Okay, that's it." She stomped to the blackboard to snatch her pointer and smacked it on her desk before waving it at the door. "Out—now!"

"Ahem . . . excuse me, miss," Hadley interrupted, "but is this hooligan disturbing you?" Straight and staunch at the door, her beloved butler stood impeccable as always in black jacket and tie, studying Mr. Pinhead with his usual air of calm. "I will be happy to escort him from the premises if you like," he said, chauffeur hat in hand and silver head tipped in question.

The buffoon laughed again, scratching the back of his neck. "Look, mister, I'd hate to break any of your bones—"

"Oh—good idea!" Allison charged forward with stick in hand. She stopped two feet away to award Hadley her sweetest smile. "Thank you, Hadley, but that won't be necessary—I'll be out shortly."

"Very good, miss," the elderly man said with a click of heels, allowing an uncharacteristic hint of a scowl at the pinhead before disappearing down the hall.

She poked the pinhead's chest. "Out—now!"

"Hey, that smarts!" he said with a laugh that bordered on a growl.

"Oh, as if you'd recognize anything 'smart,' you dimwit—out!" She prodded him toward the door without mercy while he fended her off with hands in the air, laughing so hard, she whacked him one good. "You think this is funny, mister? Let's see you laugh when I file a police report for harassment." She walloped him on the shoulder, which wiped the smirk off his face.

"Hey, lady, do that again, and I'll arrest you for assault on an officer."

"Assault on a moron, you mean—you're off duty, remember?"

She clobbered him again, and the thug promptly plucked the pointer from her hand and broke it in half with a loud crack. "Okay, sister, you asked for it—I'm going to report you to the principal of this school." He tossed the broken stick across the room with a clatter, eyes glinting.

"Good!" She slapped hands to her hips once again. "She's-my-mother, you bully . . ."

"Well, *that* explains a lot," he said with a grunt. "Another rich dame appeasing her guilt by dabbling in charity between high tea and tennis on the lawn." He stared her down, knuckles clenched on the jacket in his hand. "She'd have to be blood related to hire a sassy mouth like you."

That did it. Uncle Logan was right—some Italians were rude, obnoxious, and couldn't be trusted, an opinion he'd held since his father clashed with Domingo Ghirardelli over derailed chocolate investments. Eyes blazing, she marched right up and thumped him on the chest. "She didn't hire me," she snapped, "I volunteered." Hands back on her hips, she tilted her head, voice overly sweet. "Because rather than play lawn tennis or eat bonbons, my mother and I prefer to use our time and money to educate disadvantaged young girls so they don't grow up to be bullied by pompous blowhards like you." Chest heaving, she recharged with a harsh inhale, unleashing every bit of fury she harbored toward this dumb ox and every man just like him. "At least I have a mother and wasn't born under a rock."

His face paled. "Are you quite through?" A tic flickered in his jaw.

She elevated her chin, body quivering as all energy slowly seeped from her limbs. "No," she whispered, tears sparking her eyes. "Please leave and don't ever come back."

He might have flinched, the motion almost imperceptible, so

she couldn't be sure as he stared, the gray-green eyes a glittering vat of molten steel, smoldering hot. "Please accept my apologies for ruining your day, Miss McClare," he said softly, a tight hint of regret in his tone. Turning away, he strode for the door without so much as a glance back, his footsteps echoing down the deserted corridor before they faded with the hard slam of a door.

Emotionally drained, Allison dragged herself to her chair and collapsed on her desk, head buried in her arms as she wept over a temper she'd promised her mother she'd keep under wraps. She had no patience with men at all since Roger Luepke had broken her heart, sniping at everyone from eligible friends of her brother to the hapless young men who'd ask her to dance at The Palace charity balls. Whether potential suitors from trusted families in society or a poor courier delivering a message from the Vigilance Committee over which her mother presided, Allison begrudged every male who darkened her door. Her pain over Roger was so deep, she was quite sure each and every one were liars, frauds, or fortune hunters like the man she had hoped to marry. It seemed those type of men were to be her lot in life, and now she supposed she could add churlish civil servants as well.

She sighed and dabbed at her eyes with a handkerchief. But no matter how rude that awful man had been, she'd had no right to chastise him like she did, belittling him like he'd belittled her. He was obviously a pitiful soul who didn't know the love of God in his life and heaven knows he hadn't seen it in her. She sniffed and blew her nose before slumping back in her chair, gaze drifting into a glossy stare. "I'm sorry, Lord," she whispered, upset she'd allowed another man to toy with her emotions, causing her to lose control.

Was it any wonder she'd sworn off men since Roger, no matter how much her cousin Cassie tried to change her mind? Cassie had found the love of her life in Jamie MacKenna, but somehow Allison didn't believe there was a Jamie for her. No, she'd fallen for three phonies so far, and to be honest, she didn't trust herself anymore. When it came to croquet, badminton, or athletics of any kind, she seemed to be a natural—strength, balance, and a competitive streak fueled by an Irish temper. A deadly opponent, indeed, who seldom lost. But when it came to love? She grunted. She couldn't seem to win to save her soul, her taste in men obviously flawed. Her chin jutted high. Well, she'd just have to "save" her heart instead, devoting her life to enriching the lives of impoverished young women rather than marrying a fraud, despite Cassie's insistence she just hadn't met the right man.

Huffing out a weary sigh, she fished her reticule from the bottom drawer of her desk and rose from the chair, pushing it in. Her gaze snagged on the broken pointer strewn in the corner, and she slowly bent to retrieve the pieces, absently fingering them on her way to the wastebasket. She knew she should apologize for her tirade if she ever saw him again, but she didn't relish the thought. He was just the type of man she needed to avoid—too handsome to trust, too cocky to bear, and too pushy to tolerate. A groan slipped from her lips over a splinter embedded in her hand. "And just the type to get under my skin," she muttered as she sucked on her finger. Nope, the need to apologize or no, she hoped and prayed she never saw Mr. Ga-roan again. She tossed the broken pointer into the basket on her way out the door, releasing a wispy sigh. Because heaven knows . . . better a broken stick than another broken heart.

2

What a day. Nick Barone nudged his Homburg up and lumbered down the dark steps of the 14th precinct, grateful he could finally go home and sleep. Sleeves rolled and tie loosened, he tossed his jacket over his shoulder, wondering why San Francisco was like an infernal oven in June. For pity's sake, the locals always swore it never got above the high 60s and yet here he was, roasting in a suit like it was Chicago in July.

Of course it wasn't only the heat spiking his temperature today. Nope, he'd been in a foul mood since after lunch, when he'd stopped by the orphanage to tell Miss Penny he wouldn't be home for supper. The muscles in his jaw grew taut. Right before he'd been bludgeoned with a stick by some society dame clocking her charity time at the school next door. And not just any spoiled society dame. He kicked somebody's half-eaten apple down the street before popping the last of his animal crackers into his mouth, the acid in his stomach beginning to churn. No, this was the sassy-mouthed niece of one Logan McClare.

He wrinkled his nose as he passed an alley where rats feasted on garbage and sewage, reminding him of the bubonic plague outbreak that had fueled anti-Chinese sentiment the last two years. A plague privately blamed on Chinatown, but publicly denied by ex-governor Gage and Mayor Schmitz for the sole purpose of protecting business interests. They'd allowed the disease to establish itself among local animal populations, creating a volatile environment for the city. Nick's jaw hardened to rock. Especially for his good friend Ming Chao, whose only grandson was killed during a racial incident after the Board of Supervisors quarantined Chinatown. Chiefly Supervisor McClare, a man Nick had all but come to blows with at a board meeting earlier in the year. High-and-mighty rich men destroying people's lives for the sake of the almighty dollar. Hate bubbled in his stomach.

Just like they'd done to Mom and Pop.

Lost in his thoughts, he barely noticed the shuffle of feet from the alley. The steam pianos and gramophones blasted from dance halls where half-naked women called from windows above. No stranger to the slums, he was usually vigilant to a fault, scouring the streets and alleyways for any sign of trouble. Except for tonight, he thought with a grim press of his lips, when Logan McClare and his niece had derailed his attention.

"Aye, nice jacket there, guv'ner." A gap-toothed man strolled out from a dark corner with two slimy friends, the stench of whiskey and body odor thick in the air. "Mind if I take a look?"

Nick exhaled heavily and kept walking, in no mood to tangle with riffraff after duty. "As a matter of fact I do, boys, so why don't you just run along."

Snorts and cackles rose in the air along with a nauseating cloud of cigarette smoke. "Lookie there—he wants us to 'run along,' mates, now ain't that sweet?"

"Sure is, Hugh," a rusty voice said from behind.

Somebody flicked a glowing cigarette stub over Nick's shoulder, and he stopped, exhaling a weary sigh when Gap-Tooth stepped in his way. Fingers easing around the waistband of his grimy trousers, the hoodlum produced a flash of steel, blocking Nick's path while he grazed the blade of his knife with the pad of his thumb. He inclined his head to one of the men who stood to the right. "What say you hand that handsome jacket to my friend Stu here, guv'ner, along with your wallet, and maybe you'll live to talk about it, aye?"

Nick expelled another heavy blast of air, annoyance furrowing his brow. He jerked his badge out and flashed it at the dung heap before him. "Yeah? Well, what say you and your scum-of-the-earth chums crawl back into the sewer, pal, and you won't rot in jail, aye?"

"Well, well, now, mates, what have we here?" He peered at Nick's badge with glassy eyes. "Detective Nicholas Barone, is it now?"

"It's Baron-ee, long *e*," he said, actually contemplating changing his name. He slipped his badge into his wallet and leaned in, nose-to-nose with the half-wit. Hand perched low on his hips, he issued a near growl, stomach souring at the reeking smell of Hugh's putrid breath. "So I suggest you and your weasel side kickers take a hike before I lose my temper."

Hugh laughed, exposing yellow teeth until his smile died an ugly death. With a nasty hock of his throat, he spit a wad of phlegm on top of Nick's perfectly polished shoes.

"Oh, you shouldn't have done that," Nick said softly, never more grateful for the defense training a Japanese army friend had taught him in the Spanish-American War. With a harsh grunt, he delivered a lightning thrust to Hugh's throat with the ball of his foot, sending the knife—and Hugh—flying backward. Hugh never knew what hit him, striking the pavement with a moan before he crumpled to the cobblestones in a dazed heap. In a fluid turn, Nick challenged the other two with a hard smile, arms raised chest high. "Who's next, mates?"

A brawny one as big as Nick spit to the side and lumbered forward, circling raised fists. "I'll take you on, you blimey copper."

Nick flashed a wicked grin. "Hopin' you'd say that, guv'ner."

"Fell 'im like a bloomin' tree, Olsen," Stu cheered, easing around as if to secretly pick up the knife.

Nick struck Olsen with a palm chop to his neck, collapsing him like a bag of broken bones. He spun to counter the creeper who lunged with the knife, seizing his wrist to twist him around. Hooking his neck, he pressed the blade to his throat. "What say you, guv'ner," Nick breathed in his ear, "shall I draw blood?"

"No, please, I'm beggin' you . . ."

Nick shoved him to his knees and shackled his wrist with the handcuffs he kept in his vest pocket. The man howled when he dragged him over to Olsen, who was just beginning to stir. With a second snap of cuffs, he hooked the two together before glancing to where Hugh lay, writhing in the street. "You gentlemen have had a rough night, I know, but with a little rest, you should be good as new." He nudged the tip of the knife into Stu's neck, his whisper almost diabolical. "Get up," he hissed, "and drag that rancid sack of lard with you. I'm going to provide you gentlemen with lodging for the night."

He jerked Hugh to his feet and thrust him forward, marching all three single file to the precinct jail, wishing the blasted idiots had just left him alone. He had more than his fill of dealing with the dregs of society while he was working the beat; he sure didn't need it after a hellish day on the job. He slammed the precinct door hard behind him as he left, his lousy mood ramping up to vile. A red-banner day all around—from being beaten with a stick to threatened with a knife, and somehow he wanted to blame it all on Miss Allison McClare.

Blasting out a noisy sigh, he stormed home, finally charging into the large, well-ordered kitchen of his landlady, Miss Penelope Peel, which also served as the spacious dining area for her Mercy House Orphanage. He launched his jacket and hat onto one of twenty brass hooks he'd screwed to the wall, then stalked to the double-well sink to pour himself a drink, ignoring the wide-eyed stares of Miss Penny and her cook, Mrs. Lemp. Throat glugging, he upended the glass of water until it was gone, then slammed it onto the counter. Dishes rattled, stacked on floor-to-ceiling shelves he'd built on a better day. "So, help me, I'd rather be drawn and quartered than ever step foot in that blasted school again."

Seated at the head of the long oak table he'd built to Miss Penny's specifications, the tiny mistress of the orphanage arched a silver brow. "Excellent, Nicky," she said with a bit of the imp. "More of you to go around." A smile twitched on weathered lips that told him his rant didn't ruffle her feathers in the least. "Mrs. McClare needs a handyman for a few odd jobs around the Hand of Hope School, so I hope you don't mind—I volunteered your services."

He stared, mouth ajar, the twitch in her smile becoming a twitch in his eye. "You *what?*"

Miss Penny blinked. "Why, I volunteered you, darling boy, to assist Mrs. McClare with a few odd jobs, just like you always assist me, yes?" She laid a towel over the bowl of bread dough she'd been kneading and dusted flour off her hands. A mere sprite of a woman at five foot, the seventy-year-old dynamo was as nimble and spry as any of the ten girls she cared for at Mercy House. She approached Nick with a sparkle of affection that reminded him of his dear departed grandmother when he was growing up in Chicago. Patting a veined hand to his cheek, she assessed him through rheumy blue eyes. "What's got your nerves in a knot, Nicky?" she said gently, tone as soothing as the frail palm that cupped his bristled jaw.

He was thirty years old, but like Gram, Miss Penny had the

knack of settling his stomach like a bromide with just the tranquil touch of her hand. No matter how foul his mood after a day in the gutters and sewers, the woman could disarm him faster than a stick of dynamite in a pot of water. He'd only known her for the year he'd rented the extra room on the first floor, but every gentle stroke, every soft-spoken word told him he was important to her . . . and she to him.

Inhaling deeply, he released his frustration with a slow exhale of air. "I'm sorry, Miss Penny," he said, rubbing his temple, "but it's been a grueling day. The captain took us to task for not turning up leads on the bank robbery at Fifth and Mission, I got the runaround from the barkeep at Dead Man's Alley over a murder last night, and then some drunk takes a potshot at me, causing me to miss lunch. I get mugged on the way home and had to backtrack to book 'em, and if that isn't bad enough . . . ," he huffed out a sigh, "I find a Packard parked out front this afternoon like they own the place, just begging for trouble."

Miss Penny promptly herded him to the table where she pulled out a chair, nudging him to sit. "Now, you just rest your bones, Nicky, and I'll fix you up with milk and a sandwich."

Mrs. Lemp gave Nick's arm an affectionate squeeze. "Ah now, Nicky, it won't be so bad helping out at Mrs. McClare's school. Why, she's a gem, she is, offering me a healthy sum to clean the school once a week when I have time. A generous soul, to be sure, and she'll pay you fairly for your work as well."

Nick grunted. "Don't need the aggravation *or* the money."

"No, but you *do* need your favorite dessert, I'm thinkin', eh?" Mrs. Lemp winked. "Fixed lemon meringue pie, I did, so your evening's sure to improve."

"Thanks, Mrs. Lemp," Nick said with the seeds of a smile that helped thaw his ire.

Miss Penny handed him a tall glass of milk before heading to the counter to cut thick slices of Mrs. Lemp's bread, piling it high with slabs of leftover roast beef. "What exactly happened at the school, Nicholas, to put you in such a state?" She carried the sandwich plate to the table and slid into her chair, eyeing him with concern. "Surely the McClares' car parked out front didn't upset you like this, did it?"

Nick grunted his thanks and snatched the sandwich, chomping it with a vengeance, but thoughts of Allison McClare gave him indigestion before he even swallowed a bite. "An expensive automobile parked at the curb is nothing but trouble in a neighborhood like this, Miss Penny, and you know it. Don't you remember what happened to those fancy boys who parked their newfangled Stanley Steamer in front of The Living Flea? They were mugged and the car smashed to smithereens." The scowl was back. "Those society dames may as well post a sign out front, detailing the contents of their purses and the value of their jewelry. Parking a Packard in front is just plain stupid, especially when it jeopardizes the orphanage by luring unsavory types. And her driver outright ignored me when I suggested he move to the back."

The elderly woman quirked a brow. "Now, Nicholas, those 'society dames' as you call them are generous and God-fearing ladies of the utmost gentility. Who, I might add, have taken it upon themselves to open a school with their own funds and time. Goodness, they're risking their very safety to reach out to young women who may never have a chance for schooling otherwise, including our own precious girls here at Mercy House."

He choked on a lump of roast beef along with a hefty dose of guilt, while Mrs. Lemp jumped up to pound him hard on the back. Lunging for his milk, he immediately bolted down half of it. "Sorry, Miss Penny," he said with an awkward clearing of his throat, "it's a very noble thing Mrs. McClare is doing and I'm sure she's a lovely lady, but her daughter?" He grunted again. "I have no patience with spoiled, little rich girls who waltz into the slums so they can feel good about themselves before they scurry home to their Nob Hill mansions." He tore into another bite of his sandwich, grinding it like shoe leather on sourdough. "Especially one with a sassy mouth."

"Sassy mouth?" Miss Penny blinked. "Allison McClare? Why, I met Miss McClare several times, Nicholas, and she's an absolute delight, glowing with charm."

"Humph . . . is that what you call it?" He shoved the rest of the sandwich in his mouth and washed it down with the milk. "I find nothing charming about a smart-mouthed snob of a princess whacking me with a stick."

"Mercy, what on earth did you do?" Miss Penny stared, hand to her chest.

Mrs. Lemp chuckled. "Offered her a wee bit of the Italian grump, I'll wager."

"Now, why do you assume it was *my* fault?" Nick said, defenses edging up. "She was the one who struck *me*."

Miss Penny folded her arms, studying him with pursed lips. "Oh, and I suppose you nicely knocked on her classroom door, introduced yourself, and graciously relayed your concern over parking out front rather than back?"

Heat circled his collar. "Something like that."

"Good heavens, you didn't snap or growl at the poor girl, did you?"

He gummed his lips, refusing to answer.

"Oh, Nicky, you did, didn't you?" Miss Penny slumped in her chair, face aghast. "The Hand of Hope School is our neighbor, young man, whether you like it or not, and that includes Mrs.

McClare, her niece, *and* her daughter." She lifted a formidable chin, her tone soft even if the steel blue of her eyes was not. "You need to apologize first thing Monday morning."

"But I didn't do any—"

She hiked a brow.

He muttered something under his breath, feeling all of twelve again when Gram had washed his mouth out with soap for calling Sister Bernice an old bat.

"I heard that," Miss Penny said with another notch of her chin, "and we do not swear in this house, young man."

His jaw ground tight. *Great. A thirty-year-old police detective tongue-lashed by a silver-haired leprechaun.*

"Now, I'm sure the poor girl flew out of there either crying or vexed—"

Yeah, on a broom . . .

"—given the rants I've seen when you're out of sorts, so I'm hoping you'll make it right Monday morning with an apology to that sweet thing—"

"Sweet thing?" The veins in his forearm bulged when he fisted a hand on the table. "That 'sweet thing' near broke my shoulder with a stick, Miss Penny, and I have bruises to prove it."

"And the splintered remains of the stick, no doubt," Mrs. Lemp said with a chuckle.

The heat in his neck surged clear up to the roots of his hair.

"Oh, Nicky, you didn't!" Miss Penny moaned. "So, help me, I have a mind to take a stick to you myself—"

"Mr. Nick, you're home!" A pink-cheeked scamp raced into the kitchen with chestnut curls bouncing off her shoulders as she launched into Nick's arms with a squeal. On her heels trotted a black-and-white bull terrier that immediately bared its teeth at Nick in a low growl.

"Charlotte Marie LeRoy, what are you doing down here, young lady?" Miss Penny glanced at the watch pinned to her blouse, the crinkle in her brow now directed at the tiny six-year-old who scrambled to sit in Nick's lap while the terrier continued to snarl. "Horatio, hush!" Miss Penny said in a tone of authority that effectively bullied both man and beast. "You're supposed to be upstairs with the others while Angi reads during quiet time, Miss Lottie."

"Yes, ma'am," the little tyke said, adjusting her blue dress over her knees while she made herself comfortable in Nick's lap. Blue eyes blinked up at Miss Penny in complete innocence. "But I heard Mr. Nick's voice, so I told Angi I had to go to the bathroom, and I already did."

Nick circled Lottie's waist, the scent of baby powder and Pear's soap calming his senses.

"Are you going to spank Mr. Nick with a stick, Miss Penny?" the little dickens asked, making him smile.

Miss Penny's lips squirmed while Mrs. Lemp chuckled. The steel in her eyes melted into affection. "I'm considering it, Lottie, if Mr. Nick doesn't behave."

Turning in Nick's lap, Lottie hugged him with a husky, little grunt before she braced his face with two tiny palms, depositing a sweet peck to his lips that dissolved any frustration he had. "Don't be bad, Mr. Nick," she whispered with a gloss of moisture in her eyes that nearly wrung tears from his own. "I don't want Miss Penny to hurt you."

He released a muted sigh and tucked a curl over her shoulder, the risk of disappointing her a far greater deterrent than any piece of wood. "I'll be good, Lottie," he said quietly.

"You'll apologize first thing Monday morning, then?" Miss Penny said, tone hopeful.

Nick slid her a half-lidded gaze, prying his reply off the tip of his tongue. "Yes."

"And you'll be nice to Miss McClare and treat her with the respect she deserves?"

"The respect she *deserves*?" he bit out, eyes narrowed in threat.

"Nicholas . . . ?" The wrath of Gram stared him down.

A nerve flickered in his jaw, his gaze just short of belligerent. "Ye-s," he said through gritted teeth.

The woman had the gall to pop up and retrieve her prayer book from a drawer where she kept it for church. She thrust it under his nose. "Swear, Nicholas Barone—hand on the Bible."

He blinked, mouth slack. "For pity's sake, Mrs. Peel, that's a missal, not a Bible."

The blue eyes sparkled. "Close enough—hand on top and swear you'll be nice to our new neighbors, especially Miss Allison."

His jaw shifted while he slapped a hand on top, grinding one syllable into two. "Ye-s."

Miss Penny assessed him through squinted eyes. "And you will graciously handle any odd job Mrs. McClare or her teachers *or* Miss Allison may need to have done?"

His teeth milled so tight, he thought they might crack. "You're pushing the bounds of Christian charity, Miss Penny . . . especially with a dizzy dame like Miss La-di-da . . ."

"Ohhh . . . who's Miss Lottie Da?" Lottie peered up at Nick, eyes bright with interest. "Is her name Charlotte too?"

"One of the new teachers," he muttered, "and her name is Allison McSnob."

"Nicholas!" Miss Penny's scowl looked a lot like Allison Mc-Clare's—minus the stick.

He expelled a heavy sigh, remorse bleeding into his tone despite the press of his lips. "Her name's not Lottie Da, sweetheart,

I was just teasing. It's Miss Allison McClare, one of your new teachers."

"Oh," Lottie said, voice deflated as if she'd lost a friend who shared a name. She peeked up, brown curls askew. "So you'll be nice to Miss Lottie Da like Miss Penny said, Mr. Nick?"

"Her name is Miss Allison," Miss Penny corrected.

Nick vented with another noisy breath, gaze thinning at the twitch of his landlady's smile. "I'll try."

If it doesn't kill me first.

"You promise?" Lottie patted his jaw, gaze so penetrating, Nick started to squirm.

All resistance fled in the innocent blink of her eyes. He surrendered with a slow exhale. "Yes, Lottie, I promise."

"Oh, bless you, Nicky!" Miss Penny gave a playful pinch of his cheek before tugging Lottie into her arms with a soft kiss on the little girl's head. "And if it requires time from your job to assist with Mrs. McClare's chores, you just tell my nephew this is a favor to me, all right?"

"Yeah, sure." Nick lumbered to his feet, feeling as if he'd just been clobbered by ten of Miss La-di-da's sticks—all of 'em two by four. "But he won't be any happier about it than I am," he said, knowing full well his boss would grouse but never cross the aunt who was more like a mother.

"You let me worry about Harmon. Harold and I raised that boy to respect his elders, taking him in like our very own after his ma and pa passed on, so he'll understand. Besides, Harmon has a soft heart for good causes." She winked, setting Lottie down. "Why do you think he arranged for you to rent a room with me in the first place? He wants you to keep an eye on us." She gave Lottie a playful swat. "Run along, Lottie, and I'll be up for goodnight prayers shortly."

"Yes, ma'am." Clutching Nick's legs in a tight hug, Lottie giggled when he tickled her off his lap. Blowing kisses, she bounded from the room with hair streaming behind and Horatio hot on her heels.

Nick stared, Miss Penny's words suddenly registering. "You know? That the captain wanted me here for your protection?"

The elf of a woman bustled over to steal a couple oatmeal cookies from the large crock in Mrs. Lemp's pantry. "Of course, dear boy, I wasn't born under a rock, you know."

Nick sighed. *No, just me, apparently.*

"When Harmon called to say he had a new detective from out of town who needed a room, I knew exactly what he was doing." She handed Nick the two cookies along with a quick peck on the cheek. "And a friendship made in heaven, it was," she said with a chuckle, "just like you and Miss McClare will be, Nicky dear." She winked. "Once you apologize."

Nick bit back a groan, the image of his nemesis looming far longer than he liked. Eyes as green as grass in the spring, skin as dewy as Miss Penny's tea roses with just a hint of blush at the tips, and hair as black and shiny as the patent leather shoes Lottie wore to church. A beautiful woman. His lips went flat. Too bad she was a shrew . . . and a rich, spoiled one at that. And worse yet—related to Logan McClare. The sandwich roiled in his gut.

A friendship made in heaven? Nick grunted, thinking Miss Penny may be in need of a compass as much as the sassy Miss McClare. Because if he had his guesses right, this friendship wouldn't be made in heaven or anywhere close, especially given their heated exchange that indicated far warmer climes. He muttered his good night and strode toward the door without another word. *Heaven?* His lips took a hard slant. *Try a lot farther south.*

3

"So . . . you told me what happened between you and this police detective today, but you left out the most important thing." Alli's cousin, Cass, moved her rook two spaces, then looked up from their game of chess in the McClares' Victorian parlour. The clang of a cable car and the bleat of autos on Powell Street filtered through arched windows where sheers billowed in the summer breeze, infusing a whiff of Mother's eucalyptus and the crisp scent of the sea. Cassie's grin would have put the Cheshire cat to shame as she wiggled honeyed brows. "What exactly does this Neanderthal look like?" she said, her Texas drawl always more noticeable when she was teasing. "Besides all gussied up in animal skins and a club . . ."

Cheeks warming at her cousin's question, Alli sneaked a peek to where her mother played cribbage with Uncle Logan by the marble hearth while their bulldog, Logan Junior, lay at her feet. Her gaze strayed to her seventeen-year-old sister Meg reading a story to their six-year-old sister Maddie on the cream brocade sofa, then refocused on Cassie in a much lower voice. "Surprisingly, not as savage as you'd expect other than dark stubble on a jaw that would make a mule proud." She studied the chessboard with a scrunch of her nose as if she could smell said Neanderthal, the memory of animal crackers and Bay Rum not near as noxious as a dim-witted caveman should be. "Dark hair, almost black, clear gray eyes with a hint of green and hazel around the iris, and, of course, a height and girth to give the Flood Building a run for its money."

"Clear gray eyes with a hint of green and hazel around the iris?" Cassie's high-pitched whisper snapped Alli's attention up from the board, her mouth gaping wide. She leaned in, brows dipped low. "Thunderation, Al, just how close *were* you to this Greek god?"

One edge of Alli's lip tipped. "Close enough to smell 'animal' crackers on his breath, an appropriate snack for a cretin if ever there was. But believe me, Cass, this grump would need his scowl surgically removed to qualify for Greek god." She refocused on the board, anxious to "surgically remove" the cretin from her mind.

"Mmm . . . I don't know. Any muscles, dare I hope?" Cassie's golden hair shimmered beneath the crystal chandelier with the same sparkle as the curious glint in her pale-green eyes.

Allison nudged her pawn up one square with a grunt. "Yes, unfortunately—everywhere you look . . ." Her lashes flipped up. "Especially between his ears." She paused, alarm curling in her stomach at the sudden gleam in her cousin's eye. "Oh, no you don't—you can just get that matchmaker glow off your face right now! I'd just as soon whop the guy as look at him. Talk about oil and water—I'm kerosene and he's a lit match."

Cassie chuckled, arms folded on the game table as she perused the board for her next move. "Oh, I don't know, I'm rather fond of spontaneous combustion myself." She moved her pawn with a gloat. "Since Jamie, that is." The smile on her lips hovered. "Besides, I didn't hear you object when Jamie fanned the flames between us, and now I have a ring on my finger and a wedding six months away."

Alli's jaw sagged. "That was completely different and you know it. Jamie was already like part of the family when he started ogling you." Her lips went flat. "The only family this joker qualifies for swings from a tree." She focused hard on the board, quite sure Nick Barone was no Jamie MacKenna. "Trust me, Cass, contrary to Jamie, 'Mr. Personality' has no charm whatsoever. Besides, Jamie never insulted and bullied you from the moment you met, nor threatened you and broke any of your personal property like he did with my pointer."

Cassie's smile took a slant. "No, just my heart—twice." She huffed out a sigh. "Oh, all right, maybe 'Mr. Personality' is not a potential beau, but you'll have to get along since he's an officer of the law in that neighborhood and likely to come around again."

"Not if I can help it." Alli made her move.

"Come on, Al," Cass said softly, "you told me upstairs you regretted losing your temper and would make amends if you could."

Cassie's gentle tone pricked Alli's conscience. "I do regret losing my temper," she said quietly, "and I will make amends, I promise." Her lashes lifted while her lips squirmed to the right. "As long as I can borrow the cattle prod you always threatened to use against Jamie."

Cassie grinned. "Get your own—I have a feeling I'll be needing mine . . ."

"Hey, when's dinner? I'm hungry." Cassie's fiancé, Jamie MacKenna, ambled into the parlour with his best friends, Bram and Alli's brother Blake. Hands in his pockets and a grin on his lips, he strolled over to give Cassie a kiss on the cheek before winking at Alli. "I've worked up quite an appetite teaching these two jokers how true winners play pool."

"True hustlers, you mean," Bram said with a chuckle, perfectly groomed tawny hair a handsome match for blue eyes so crystal clear, you could almost see into his soul. "Give me a chance to even the score with a thrashing in chess, MacKenna, because my skill and finesse are in my brain, not in my hands."

Jamie bent to circle Cass from behind, whispering in her ear while he slowly grazed her bare arms with his palms. "Sometimes skill and finesse in one's hands has its advantages, right, Cass?"

The bloom in Cassie's cheeks deepened as she slapped him away. "Jamie MacKenna, you are incorrigible! Keep in mind this is exactly why Daddy insisted on a longer engagement." Her smile tipped into a smirk. "So I have lots of opportunity to call this wedding off if you don't learn to keep your hands to yourself."

He kissed the top of her head and quickly slipped the offensive hands in his pockets. "Yes, ma'am, hands to self," he said, easing into a chair at the game table. He gave her a waggle of dark brows. "Until the wedding, that is, then all bets are off, Cowgirl."

Bram straddled a chair to assess the game, his affection for Jamie clear in the tease of his tone. "Speaking of bets, Mac, just give me one game of chess, and I'll have you crying 'uncle.'"

Blake laughed, gray eyes sparkling like the silver chess pieces on the board. "So, what's new?" Alli's brother said, plopping down on a nearby ottoman. "He cries 'uncle' all the time at the firm, chumming up so Uncle Logan will assign him all the high-profile cases."

A smile eased across Jamie's face as he slid Cass and Alli a smug look. "That's because I'm a better defense lawyer than these two clowns, ladies."

"Ha! Only because of your luck in landing plum cases," Blake said. "When it comes to skills of the mind, I'm with Bram—give me retribution with chess or poker."

"Awk, ante up, ante up!" At the mention of poker, the family parrot, Miss Behave, danced back and forth on her perch, orange and black eyes dilating while she issued a favorite squawk tutored by Blake long ago.

Alli bit back a smile when her mother looked up from her game of cribbage, a wedge appearing at the bridge of her nose over Miss B.'s poker-related squawk. For the briefest of moments, her beautiful face puckered in a near-frown, clear evidence of her mother's disapproval of gambling, *especially* poker taught to her son and three daughters by her renegade brother-in-law. With rich, auburn hair piled high on her head in the loose Gibson Girl style of the day, forty-four-year-old Caitlyn McClare could have easily passed for Alli's older sister. Striking green eyes even darker than Alli's own complemented a creamy complexion that harbored few wrinkles despite the tragic loss of Alli's father to an aneurism three years ago.

Alli's thoughts veered melancholy when Uncle Logan drew her mother's attention back with a word and a smile so smitten, Alli wondered if her mother would ever realize how much he truly cared. Still unmarried at forty-six, Logan McClare was easily one of the most eligible bachelors in town. An affluent member of the San Francisco Board of Supervisors, he was also one of the city's top lawyers with his own firm. At six foot two he was handsome with penetrating gray eyes, sable hair templed with silver, and a sturdy frame that was broad-shouldered. Her lips quirked. And broad-egoed when it came to being sought after by women, no doubt. He was witty, charming, powerful, and utterly devoted to family, all valuable assets, even for a rake who turned the head of every female in society. A wispy sigh drifted from Alli's lips, heart aching for an uncle she loved like a father. All except Caitlyn McClare, that is, who seemed to keep Uncle Logan at arm's length despite his obvious feelings for her.

"Excuse me, ladies and gentlemen, but dinner is served." Hadley stood at the door in his usual regal pose, posture erect and black tails and tie as elegant as the abundance of silver hair slicked back on his head. Beloved butler to the three McClare brothers from childhood on, Hadley was as much a part of the McClare family as Alli herself, his poor eyesight and near-deaf ears no hindrance whatsoever to the affection he garnered.

"Oh, thank goodness, Hadley, I'm starving," Jamie said with a rub of his hands. He offered his arm to Cassie. "First for food, then for attention from the woman who will soon be my wife."

Alli tweaked Jamie's waist before taking her brother's proffered arm. "Unless she falls on her head first and comes to her senses."

"Hey," Jamie said with a crimp of hurt, "what'd I ever do to you, Al, but love you like a sister?"

Bram chuckled as he passed to escort Megan and Maddie in to dinner. "Wise up, Mac, you're stealing her best friend away—they won't get to chat or play chess as much anymore."

"That's not true," Blake said, joining Alli in a smirk. "He'll probably still show up every night for dinner, just like before."

"Can I help it if Rosie's the best cook around?" Jamie followed Blake and Alli into the three-story marble foyer, ignoring everyone's chuckles. "Besides, Al will get to see Cass as much as before since they'll be working at the school five days a week."

"Speaking of which . . . ," her mother hooked an arm through Uncle Logan's as he ushered her to the dining room while Logan Junior lumbered behind, "did you get your classroom set up the way you wanted, dear?"

"Almost." Allison took the seat Blake held out for her and offered a grateful smile. "Except I still need a pointer."

Cassie chuckled. "And a cattle prod," she whispered after Jamie pushed in her chair.

The bridge of Caitlyn's nose crinkled. "But I know I ordered one for each of the classrooms—are you sure it's not there? Maybe you misplaced it, darling. Put it in the storage closet or on the ledge of the blackboard."

"Or the wastebasket . . . ," Cassie offered with an innocent lift of brows.

Allison pinched her cousin's leg under the table as she smiled brightly at her mother. "No, unfortunately I had to throw it away because it had a crack that gave me a splinter."

"Oh, dear. Well, we'll just have to order you another."

"Cheese, sir?" Hadley stood ramrod straight with a small bowl in his hands.

"Yes, thank you, Hadley," Logan said, obviously not paying attention as the butler spooned a generous pile of shredded cheddar cheese into the bottom of his empty soup bowl. Placing his napkin in his lap, Logan smiled at Alli's mother at the opposite end of the table. "So, the new school opens next week, eh, Cait?" He raised his water glass. "I'd say fulfillment of your dream calls for a toast, don't you?"

"Hadley!" Mrs. Rosie O'Brien stood scowling at the door with a tureen in her hands. "For pity's sake, I said serve the tea *please*, not the *cheese!*" Short and trim in stature, the McClares' housekeeper and cook loomed tall in clout, her steely gaze aimed at poor Hadley, who obviously hadn't heard Rosie's directions clearly. Alli battled a smile when Rosie's glare shifted, her blue eyes frosting Uncle Logan before she bustled over to serve Alli's mother.

To Alli, Rosie's endearing grumpiness was as inherent to dinnertime in the McClare household as the candles glowing in Mother's silver candlesticks. Dressed in her gray uniform with a calf-length white apron, the spunky sixty-six-year-old lent as much spice to family meals as she did to her exceptional cuisine.

Unfortunately, her bristly manner was reserved for sweet Hadley, with whom she had no patience, and poor Uncle Logan for whom she had no love. Her petite frame taut with intent, she served clam chowder to Alli's mother first, continuing to ladle long after her mistress indicated enough. "It's your favorite, Miss Cait," Rosie groused, an air of authority that came from a bond forged as Caitlyn's beloved housekeeper and nanny from little on. The housekeeper's dark hair was sprinkled with silver and pulled back in a chignon as tight as the line of her formidable jaw. "You could use some meat on your bones."

"You spoil me, Rosie." Her mother nodded when Hadley approached with the pitcher of tea, awarding him a bright smile. "Thank you, Hadley—just in time for our toast."

"Yes, miss—and would you like butter with that toast?" Hadley said with a short bow, awaiting further direction.

Caitlyn's voice rose in volume, masking the chuckles that rounded the table. She quickly reached for a cracker from a nearby tray before gently patting the butler's arm. "No toast, Hadley, dear—I think I'll just have crackers instead."

"Very good, miss." He proceeded to pour the tea before disappearing into the kitchen.

Scanning the table with a broad smile that finally settled on Logan, Caitlyn lifted her goblet of tea. "Yes, I do believe this calls for a toast." She waited until everyone raised their glasses in unison, then chewed on her lip with a nervous grin. "To the Hand of Hope School, a dream-come-true long in the making, the culmination of a desire nurtured long ago between my husband and me, now fulfilled at the hands of my daughter and niece." A sheen of tears glimmered in her eyes that sparked moisture in Alli's own. Her mother's voice continued, wavering with emotion as her eyes settled on Uncle Logan once again, tender with affection. "And to Logan McClare for helping to make it all possible through his gracious and very weighty influence on the Board of Supervisors—I don't know how I can ever thank you."

"My pleasure, Cait." Gaze warm, Uncle Logan nodded with a smile before taking a drink of his tea, eyes fixed on Alli's mother over the rim of his glass while Rosie dispensed the soup.

"Whoops . . . clean out," the housekeeper said after serving everyone but Logan, "which, given your 'weighty influence,' Mr. Beware, is just as well." She whisked his bowl away with a smirk before flitting back to the kitchen. "I'll fetch more—just hope it ain't scorched."

Uncle Logan bolted his tea, gray eyes darkening to charcoal as always when Rosie picked on him. "If you want to thank me, Cait, you can rein in your bull terrier." He snatched a roll from the silver basket on the table and started buttering with a vengeance. "Sometimes I wonder why I even subject myself to dinner here three times a week."

"Because she's the best cook in the Bay Area, Uncle Logan," Blake said with a grin, opting to butter his own roll. "Same reason Jamie's always underfoot."

"Hey, watch it, McClare, I'm almost family." Jamie snatched the roll from Bram's plate while Bram chatted with Meg.

"Yes, you are, Jamie," Caitlyn said with a firm jut of her chin, "which is why you and Logan are more than welcome for dinner as much as you like." Her gaze softened in her brother-in-law's direction. "I'm truly sorry, Logan, and I will speak to her again, I promise." She nibbled on the edge of her smile, brows tented in apology. "But it would make things so much easier if you would just . . . well, take Rosie's . . . humor . . . in stride like the rest of us do."

Logan grunted. "Easy to do, Cait, when the guard dog's not chewing on *your* leg." He chomped on his roll, throat ducking when he swallowed the bite whole. "I wouldn't put it past the woman to lace my soup with something vile."

Caitlyn's smile was patient. "Really, Logan, Rosie may have a salty tongue at times, but she would never stoop to anything so devious." She cleared her throat when he started to take another bite of his bread, a smile twitching on her lips. "But perhaps we should say grace first . . . just to make sure?"

He dropped the roll to his plate, lips flat when Caitlyn bowed her head to say the prayer. Her tone was sober until she ended with a special blessing for Logan's food that carried a definite tease. "Amen." She glanced up just as Rosie returned Logan's bowl with a clunk on his plate, her tone as crusty as the bread. "Sorry . . . tail end. Not many clams left."

"Thank you," Logan said with a tic in his jaw.

"So, Allison . . ." Her mother delivered a smile, obviously hoping to steer the conversation to friendlier waters. "Did you happen to meet Miss Penny's handyman? She mentioned she might send him over to meet us regarding any help we might need."

Allison glanced up, spoon halfway to her mouth. "No, I don't think so, or at least I didn't see him."

"Well, she says he's wonderful, so I'm thrilled to find someone to help out while Mr. Bigley's out with his broken leg. The poor man won't be back for six weeks."

Cassie blew on her soup. "I feel so sorry for Mr. Bigley. Can't imagine being laid up for all that time with six mouths to feed." She sighed and sipped from her spoon. "I'm glad you plan to continue his salary while he's out, Aunt Cait, but I sure wish we could find a temporary replacement for odd jobs and general protection till he returns. There was just something so comforting about having a man in the building, you know?"

"Yes, I do," Caitlyn said with a wedge of worry in her brow. Her gaze settled on Uncle Logan, who appeared to be engaged in a serious conversation with Jamie, Bram, and Blake while Meg was busy cutting Maddie's salad into smaller pieces. "As a matter of fact, I intended to check with your uncle tonight to see if he had any recommendations for a temporary watchman we could employ for a brief time. But in the meantime, I'm grateful Miss Penny offered the services of her handyman boarder." Caitlyn sipped her chowder from her spoon slowly, eyes closed as if to savor the taste before she glanced up. "I understand he's a strapping young man who works for her nephew, the captain of detectives for the Barbary Coast."

The bite of roll Alli had just taken adhered to her throat like the butter was glue.

Her mother continued on as if hard-crusted bread wasn't stuck in her daughter's throat, depleting her air. "Apparently he moved into her spare room on the first floor about a year ago and has become like a son." She laid her spoon aside and nodded her thanks when Hadley removed her empty soup bowl, allowing her to focus on her salad. "Miss Penny claims he's a wonder at fixing everything and does it all in his spare time after his day job as a police detective, if you can imagine that."

Alli started to hack, and Cassie pounded her on the back, tone laced with humor. "No, I can't imagine that, Aunt Cait, can you, Al?"

Palms slick on the stem of the glass, Alli bolted her water before speaking, her voice a rasp. "You w-wouldn't happen to know his n-name, would you, Mother?"

Stabbing a lettuce leaf in her bowl, Caitlyn paused, eyes in a squint. "Let me see—I believe it was Mickey or Ricky or . . . no, wait—Nicky, I think she called him. Yes, that's right."

Fork sinking to her plate, Allison stifled a moan as her eyelids shuttered closed.

"Really?" Cassie said with interest, squeezing Alli's knee under the table. "His last name wouldn't be Barone, would it?"

Allison sucked in a sharp breath, pinching Cassie's hand.

"Why, yes," her mother said with a smile edged in surprise. "Only it's pronounced Ba-ron-ee, long *e* according to Miss Penny." She chuckled. "Apparently he's very particular about the pronunciation and makes no bones about it." She speared a tomato and winked at her niece. "A hot-blooded Italian, I believe she called him, and a law officer to boot—a lethal combination for anyone who crosses the line, I suppose."

Oh, Mother, you have no idea . . . Grabbing her napkin, Allison fanned her face while fire pulsed in her cheeks. *And hot-blooded?* She upended her water again, desperate to douse the heat of humiliation singeing her body. Well, at the moment, the Italian had nothing on her.

"Goodness," Cassie said with a chuckle, "detective by day, handyman by night. Does the man ever sleep?"

Her mother smiled. "Not enough to suit Miss Penny, evidently. Claims he's a demon when it comes to work, pushing himself night and day."

Demon? I'll vouch for that . . . Alli slumped back in her chair, eyes glazed.

"Goodness, Allison, are you all right, dear?" her mother asked. "You look flushed."

"Fine," she croaked, grabbing Cassie's water to down half in one painful glug.

Caitlyn reached to press a palm to Alli's forehead before gently stroking her cheek. "Well, your forehead is cool, at least." She resumed eating her salad, tone leisurely once again. "So you girls met Mr. Barone, I take it?"

"Nope, not me," Cassie said, promptly stuffing lettuce in her mouth, gaze roaming the ceiling.

"Allison? Did you?"

Alli cleared her throat, impaling the salad while thinking of a certain hot-blooded Italian. "Uh ... uh ... I think so." She avoided her mother's gaze, studying a cucumber as if it were the most fascinating of all of God's vegetables.

"Well, for goodness' sake, don't keep me in suspense, darling. What's he like? Young and strong, I hope? Does he seem like the type to tackle our antiquated building with a vengeance?"

With a vengeance? Alli gulped. "Uh-huh."

"And then some," Cassie said with a chuckle. "Al says he's younger than Mr. Bigley, maybe thirty or so."

"Really?" Her mother gave Alli her full attention, eyes glowing with curiosity. "And ... ?"

Alli vented with a heavy sigh, knowing full well her mother wouldn't rest until she had all the facts. Peering up, she wrinkled her nose as if she'd just swallowed one of the dreaded mushrooms Rosie was so fond of burying in the salad. "Oh, you know the type, Mother—tall, brawny, long on looks, short on personality."

Caitlyn blinked, her fork drifting to the side of her plate. "Oh my," she said with a hint of worry in her tone, well aware of her daughter's short fuse around men since Alli's broken engagement to Roger Luepke. "You were courteous, I hope, Allison? After all, he *is* doing us a favor stepping in to help at the behest of Miss Penny, so I hope you hit it off."

"'Hit' it off? Oh, I think that's safe to say, don't you, Al?" Cassie bumped her shoulder against Alli's with a mischievous grin.

Allison swallowed a lump the size of the cherry tomato lanced on her fork. "Uh, sure," she said and took a quick bite, smile tighter than the tomato now lodged in her throat.

Her mother released a sigh of relief that could have ruffled the sheers on the windows. "Oh, thank goodness," she said with a wide smile that matched the revelry going on among the others at the far end of the table. She squeezed Allison's hand, the relief in her face evidence of just how important it was they succeed with this school. "After all, we have the privilege of being a light in a very dark neighborhood, girls, so it's very important to make a good impression."

The tomato in Alli's throat could have been an Adam's apple as it dipped in her neck. The memory of whacking Nicholas Barone, long *e*, with her stick not just once, but three times, suddenly popped in her brain. *A good impression? Oh, you bet.* The tomato glugged as she swallowed it whole.

On both shoulders and more . . .

4

ood morning, Nicky." Miss Penny sailed into the kitchen at the unholy hour of six a.m., the smile on her face as blinding as the sunlight shafting through the double kitchen window. She promptly poured him another cup of the hot coffee he'd just brewed and kissed the top of his head. "It's going to be another beautiful day."

He grunted. *If you don't have to trudge through the Barbary Coast on foot, tracking down slime. Or apologize to a spoiled rich kid with a sassy attitude.* He tipped the mug straight up, the hot coffee scalding his throat as much as thoughts of Allison McClare scalded his temper. Eyes closed, he felt the burn all the way to his stomach.

"Thank you for brewing the coffee," Miss Penny said, retrieving a cup from the cabinet to pour some for herself. "Did you eat one of Mrs. Lemp's cinnamon muffins, I hope?"

He grunted in the affirmative, and she carried her coffee to the table to sit beside him, eyeing his empty plate that contained nary a crumb.

"Good. Busy day ahead?"

Blasting out a sigh that belonged at the end of a day and not the beginning, he rose to carry his dirty plate and mug to the counter, setting them down with a clatter. "Oh, you know—just the usual. Following up leads on the robbery, investigating the murder at Dead Man's Alley, butting heads with your nephew, groveling to a rich dame . . ."

"Nicholas . . . ?" Her tone held a warning. "Allison McClare is not a 'dame.' She is a beautiful young woman inside and out, and I expect you to treat her with respect."

Beautiful? On the outside, maybe. He slung his suit coat over his shoulder, unwilling to brave heatstroke before Allison McClare could fry his temper again. "Maybe *you* should have this conversation with her, then. The woman has no respect for the law."

Miss Penny took a sip of her coffee. "Depends on whose law you're talking about, Nicky. That of the city of San Francisco or a surly Italian at the end of a hard day." Her lips squirmed over the rim of her cup. "Or the beginning . . ."

"Only because I have your dirty work to do," he muttered, making his way to the door.

"Ah-ah-ah . . ." Miss Penny lifted her chin, brows raised in expectation. "It's not my 'dirty work,' Mr. Barone, it's that of a grouchy detective who can't hold his temper." She tapped a finger to her cheek. "Aren't you forgetting something?"

A smile twitched at the edge of his mouth, but he refused to give sway. Lips clamped in his usual frown, he returned to press a kiss to her head, the scent of lavender from her hair rinse reminding him just how grateful he was for Penelope Peel in his life.

"Could you bend down, please?" she requested, and he huffed out a loud breath, squatting before the woman who was as much a grandmother as his own. She patted his cheek, a blue-veined hand caressing him with the same affection glowing in her face. "Be nice," she said softly, "she's not an ogre like you, you know."

"Ha!" He rose and gently squeezed her shoulder. "Not to you, maybe."

"Or you either, Nicky, if you utilize some of that boyish charm you exude with me and the girls. You'd do well to keep in mind what our president says. 'Speak softly and carry a big stick.'"

A big stick. His lips quirked. Yeah, she'd probably whack him with it. "Yes, ma'am," he said to appease the smiling imp that watched him with a gleam of pride in her eyes. "And speaking of sticks . . ." He reached for the new pointer on the counter, the one he'd purchased at the Emporium over the weekend, almost afraid to give it to Miss McClare for fear of what she might do with it. He aimed it at Miss Penny with the first crook of a smile since she'd walked into the room. "So help me, Mrs. Peel, if that da—"

A silver brow shot up.

"—*woman* . . . wallops me with this one, you are footing the bill when I snap it in two, is that clear?" He snatched his Homburg from one of the coat hooks and angled it on his head.

"I guarantee you, Nicky, if you smile at her like you smile at me, you won't have to worry about her breaking anything but your heart."

"Humph." The idea of falling for a spoiled debutante was as appealing as getting bludgeoned with a stick. "No, thank you. I'd rather tangle with the sewer rats on the Barbary Coast than a rich da—"

The brow was up before he could even finish the word, and his lips ground tight. "*Woman,*" he bit out, making a break for the door. "Although *piranha* might be a better word. With any luck, she'll still be home in her feather bed, dreaming of money."

"Hate to break it to you, Detective, but she's there—saw her classroom light on from my bedroom window. She's a hard worker, our Miss McClare. Mind you, Nicholas, I expect a good report from the principal," she called when he flailed a hand in the air on his way out.

"She's not 'our Miss McClare,'" he muttered down the weed-littered steps, popping animal crackers to cushion his stomach for another encounter with the lady and her stick. What the devil was a rich dame doing up this early on the Barbary Coast anyway, teacher or no? Or at least on the edge of it, on the southeast corner of Telegraph Hill, where a large contingent of the Irish had settled along with Mrs. Penelope Peel and her family. He noted the two straggly boxwoods along the short three-foot walk to the street and made a mental note to trim and pull weeds in front of Miss Penny's three-story Victorian.

His jaw tightened. The same Victorian next to a larger one that now housed the Hand of Hope School. Unlike Miss Penny's tired-looking Gothic Revival badly in need of a fresh coat of gray paint, the Hand of Hope School had received a complete sprucing up—from the brand-new steeply pitched roof to the freshly painted scrollwork and pointed arched windows with decorative crowns. Apparently Mrs. McClare had spared no expense, even knocking out walls on the first floor to create a small but cozy theater that ran the length of the right side of the house.

He grunted as he ambled up the brick walkway lined with the pinkest roses he'd ever seen. Three newly constructed painted steps led up to a pale-yellow gingerbread house whose covered entryway was flanked with urns of trailing ivy and flowers. His lips went flat. Too pretty and too prissy for a neighborhood where peep shows, brothels, and bars dominated the streets mere blocks away. He glanced up at a large brass nameplate—Hand of Hope School—above a carved wooden door with thick double-glass panes, then yanked on the brass knob. The smell of paint and new wood and lemon oil teased his senses the moment he entered, giving him the itch to build something with his hands like he and his father used to do. To his immediate left another brass plate identified the office, a room that looked more like a library in a mansion on Nob Hill than a school on the Barbary Coast. Handcrafted oak bookshelves lined with expensive volumes flanked either side of an ornate oak desk where a Tiffany lamp perched on the far corner. A leather blotter lay front and center along with a stack of papers and an ink pen. Off to the side sat a brand-new Remington typewriter on its own table while a carved wooden credenza against the wall sported a crystal vase with flowers and wooden baskets three high.

How sweet—a touch of Nob Hill on the Barbary Coast. Nick shook his head on his way to the second room on the left where lamplight spilled across the honey-wood hall. Instantly the sound of humming put him on edge. Jacket over his shoulder, he halted at the door and cocked a hip to the jamb, fascinated by the form of one Miss Allison McClare. Stretching high on tiptoe to pin red letters that spelled "Welcome" to a bulletin board, she stood on an obscenely expensive-looking carved wooden chair with a mother-of-pearl pin box at her feet. Hershey bar wrappers were strewn across her desk along with paper-cut letters and numerals, as haphazard as the riot of ebony curls pinned at the back of her head.

In natural reflex, his eyes slowly trailed up, taking in the black hobble skirt that hugged slim hips before it belted at a tiny waist. A tailored blouse took over with puffed sleeves and high-neck collar. Stray wisps from her curly updo fluttered at the back of her neck when an early-morning breeze drifted in from a bank of three windows overlooking the alley. It ushered in the tangy smell of the bay and Fisherman's Wharf mere blocks away along with a lighter, sweeter scent he suspected came from Miss McClare.

Apparently lost in her task, she continued humming a charmingly off-key rendition of "In the Good Old Summer Time." Bending to retrieve more letters from a ledge below, she provided Nick a generous view of a backside far more charming than the lady's manner. About five foot six or seven, he guessed, she had an athletic grace about her that hinted at a formidable foe in athletic pursuits. One side of his mouth edged up. Like stick-whacking, for instance. He shook his head at how a pretty little thing could contain such a temper, and for the first time he considered just maybe Miss Penny was right. Maybe his tiff with the lady had been mostly his fault, his grouchy manner flaring in the presence of high-society dames he didn't trust. After all, Miss Penny seemed to trust her, so maybe he could too. His jaw suddenly hardened at the memory of Darla, and all humility dissipated. Nope, not after Chicago.

Hat and pointer in hand, he approached her desk, indulging in one final perusal before making his presence known. "Ahem."

"Oh!" She spun around with a little squeal, bobbling on the chair so much that he dropped both hat and stick to grab her lest she fall, hands to her tiny waist. She promptly slapped him away, saucer eyes as round as her full pink mouth, which now issued raspy heaves. Her crisp, white bodice rose and fell with every breath she took while her hand shot to her chest. "Merciful Providence, what in heaven's name are you doing?" she shrieked, the soft blush in her cheeks a nice complement to rosy lips and startling green eyes. "Are you *crazy*?"

"Apparently," he muttered, stooping to retrieve the pointer and hat. He tossed the stick on the desk with a clatter. "Must be to try and help a dame who almost bludgeoned me to death."

She stood up straight on the chair and folded her arms tight, puckering the narrow pleats of her form-fitting blouse till it drew his gaze, which was almost dead center. "Don't you ever knock?" she hissed, and his eyes flicked to her face, now burnished with a deep rose as dark as her lips. The green eyes fairly pulsed with indignation. "Or don't they knock in caves?"

A muscle twittered in his cheek. "Look, lady, I didn't come here to butt heads with you again, I came to ... to ..." He tried to get it out, that infernal apology Miss Penny was coercing him to say, but the words were like a pack of mules on the edge of a cliff, refusing to budge.

She dipped her head, the gesture quivering those green thing-amajigs dangling from her ears, which were the exact color of the emerald squint of her eyes. With an impatient flick of her wrist, she back-circled a hand in abrupt motion, as if to hurry the process. "Spit it out, Detective Ga-roan."

"It's *Barone*, long *e*," he ground out with a twitch of his jaw. He was so irked he decided to rile her with another slow scan, raking her from those pursed lips, down her bodice and skirt, and back up with a bold gaze purely meant to annoy.

It worked.

Her chin lashed up while the blush on her face nearly swallowed her whole. She slapped stiff hands to her hips. "You need to teach your eyes some manners, Mr. Long-E."

He matched her stance and stepped in with a glare, almost eye to eye. "And you need to teach your mouth some manners, Miss McClare, especially if you expect me to lift one finger to assist you or your mother with this Snob Hill academy." He splayed a hand to the front of his buttoned waistcoat, the whites of his eyes expanding. "Wait, let me guess—you're in charge of teaching manners, right?"

Whatever he said, it snapped her mouth closed, those full lips suddenly as flat as his patience. Her thick dark lashes blinked so many times, he swore he felt a stiff breeze. With a sudden sheen of tears, she whirled around on that ridiculous chair to face the wall, hugging the sides of her waist so tightly, her shoulders hunched while her head bowed to her chest.

He waited, thinking they may be able to forge a friendship yet as long as she kept her back to him all the time—the view was definitely friendlier.

"I . . . apologize, Detective Barone," she whispered, actually pronouncing his name correctly for the very first time. "I've been—" he could almost hear the swallow of pride in her throat—"unforgivably rude and I just hope . . . ," she pivoted slowly, the humility in her eyes jolting him when it heightened her beauty, ". . . you can forgive me for being such an obnoxious brat."

A leisurely smile curved on his lips. "Forgiven, Miss McClare," he said with tease in his tone, "and I sure hope apologies are on the curriculum, ma'am, because you do them so well." He extended his hand with a cock of his head. "May I help you down so we can start over?"

She drew in a deep breath and released it with a nervous smile of relief, placing her palm in his. "Yes, please." Voice as soft as her touch, she startled when the dainty tip of her oxblood kid leather shoe accidentally kicked the pin box to the floor. "Oh!" she squeaked, the crash of the pins apparently leaving her off-kilter. With a look of abject horror, she flailed in the air for several panicked heartbeats before finally thudding hard against his chest. His arms fused them together in a state of mutual stun as his hat dropped to the floor a second time.

He blinked, paralyzed by the warmth of her body, the flare of her eyes, the scent of chocolate from parted lips so lush, the fire blazing through him could have melted the candy in her bowl. As if hypnotized by the shape of her mouth, his gaze lingered there, feeling the pull . . .

"Uh, Mr. Barone?" The lips appeared to move in slow motion, their soft, pink color luring him close . . . *so* very close.

"Mmm?" Barely aware, he felt his body lean in, breathing shallow and eyelids heavy, that perfect mouth calling him home . . .

"Mr. Barone!"

Her tone could have been a whack of her stick, jerking him from his fog with the reminder that a woman still dangled in his arms. Sucking in a harsh breath, he dropped her to her feet so fast, the poor thing teetered like his sanity in even thinking about kissing a dame from Snob Hill. "Forgive m-me, Miss McClare," he stuttered in a gruff tone, "I . . . I don't know what came over me." Swallowing hard, he quickly squatted to retrieve her pin box and pins, rising to carefully place both on her desk.

"Thank you," she whispered, a heavy dusting of rose in her cheeks as she took a step back. Head in a tilt, she offered a timid smile while she frittered her nails. "So, Detective Barone, was there something you wanted?"

He collected his hat from the floor with a crooked smile. "To apologize, Miss McClare, for my despicable behavior last week, under duress by Miss Penny, of course. But I have to admit—I admire a lady who can steal my thunder with an apology of her own."

She expended a sigh, smile awkward as she reached for the pointer on her desk and absently grazed the wood with her fingers. "Yes, well, I wish I could take credit for being so noble, but it's my mother who is the true lady in this case, I'm afraid." She scrunched her nose as she held up the pointer. "She'd use this on me if she knew how rude I'd been to the gentleman who's offered to assist us around the school."

He grinned. "Move over, Miss McClare—Miss Penny already threatened me with a stick of her own if I didn't make amends first thing this morning."

Her chuckle sounded like music as she placed the pointer on

the ledge of the blackboard. "Now that would be a sight to see—a tiny, little thing like Miss Penny taking a stick to you."

His lips took a slant as he rubbed at his shoulder. "You didn't have a problem, as I recall."

She granted a shy smile, teeth tugging at the nail of her thumb. "Did I leave a bruise?"

"Only on my pride," he said, fiddling with his hat. He glanced at his pocket watch and frowned, suddenly reluctant to go. "Well, I need to get to work, but anything you or your mother need done, just give the list to Miss Penny, and I'll tackle it after work, all right?"

"Thank you, Detective—I don't know how we can ever repay you."

His lip quirked as he strolled to the door. "Keeping the stick away is a start."

She motioned to a cup of tea on her desk, her beautiful smile walloping his heart more effectively than any stick. "Can I at least offer you a cup of tea before you go? It's peppermint, you know." A sparkle lit her eyes. "Known for its calming effect . . ." She let the word dangle while she nibbled on the edge of her smile, totally captivating him against his will.

He cleared his throat. "No, ma'am, but thank you. I need to go." Annoyance pricked when those perfect pink lips broke into another glorious smile, parching his tongue to cotton.

"Well, goodness, I hope you won't be late."

He turned at the door, rubbing the felt brim of his hat. "The 14th precinct is only a few blocks away." He paused, concern wedging his brow. "I don't mean to be pushy, Miss McClare, but if your driver could drop you off and pick you up around back in the alley, that would be a lot safer than out front, across the street from the worst neighborhood in Frisco, you know?"

"Of course, Detective Barone."

He inclined his head toward the front door. "Also, I know

students will be coming and going at the beginning and end of each school day, but after classes start in the morning, I'd feel a whole lot better if you kept the front and back doors locked during the day, just as an extra precaution. That's what Miss Penny does with the orphanage."

"Certainly. I'll tell Mother."

He nodded. "And under no circumstances walk these streets after dark or alone, if you can help it, all right?"

She nodded, suddenly looking like a little girl he felt compelled to protect. He steeled his jaw. "Well, then, have a good day, Miss McClare."

"Oh, Detective?"

He turned, annoyed that this highbrow dame—*woman*—elicited such a protective response out of him. "Yes?"

"Might I ask where the nearest cable car is?"

He blinked. "Pardon me?"

The smile she gave him would have tripped his pulse if it hadn't tripped his temper first. "You see, there will be days when I'll need to work late in the classroom, and I don't want Mother to wait or Hadley to make another trip." Her chin notched up with a hint of the stubbornness he'd seen on their first encounter. "So I plan to take the cable car home."

He cocked a hip, jaw dropping while his voice rose. "Excuse me, Miss McClare, but have you ever stepped foot in a cable car before?"

The green eyes tapered the slightest bit. "Well, no, there's never been a need—Hadley drives us everywhere."

Head bowed, he shook his head, then peered up beneath tightly knit brows. "You obviously aren't aware of this, ma'am, but the closest line is two blocks south at Jackson and Montgomery, in the heart of the Barbary Coast."

Her brows lifted. "So?"

His jaw started to grind. "So, it's no place for a lady, Miss Mc-Clare, especially one who's been carted around town in a Packard."

Her chin rose to new heights. "It's-public-transportation, Mr. Barone," she bit out, dropping his title along with her previously humble manner. "And-I'm-part-of-the-public."

His grip tightened on his hat, fingers crushing the brim. "No, ma'am," he said in a clipped tone, "you're part of the upper crust that think they can go off half-cocked and do whatever they bloomin' well please."

She swiped the pointer and slapped it on her desk. "Go—I hope you're late!"

"And I sure hope you're smarter than you sound, lady, because if you think it's safe for a fancy dame in diamond combs to sashay through the worst part of town to sightsee on a bloomin' cable car, you are *way* too stupid to teach in a school."

Crack! He actually winced at the sound of wood on wood, thinking Miss McClare may just have a vocation—she and the nuns at St. Patrick's had a lot in common.

"No," she said through clenched teeth, the smile suddenly nowhere in sight, "'stupid' would be an ill-mannered cretin who thinks he can bully people with insults and bad manners."

A nerve popped in his jaw. He stepped forward, fingers itching to snatch that stupid stick and splinter it till he could toss a fistful of toothpicks in her pretty face. "If you want 'ill-mannered,' I suggest you look in the mirror, sweetheart, because I've seen better manners from the floozies on Morton Street." His statement froze her stiff to the spot while the roses in her cheeks faded to chalk. He immediately regretted his words. "Look, Miss McClare, I'm sorry I riled you again, but if you would just listen to reason—"

With a sharp suck of air, she shot forward, eyes blazing and stick flailing. "Reason?!" Two circles of bright pink bruised her creamy cheeks, clear indication he had effectively triggered her ire—*for the umpteenth blessed time.* "There *is* no reasoning with a brainless bully like you," she shrieked, voice so high-pitched, it hurt his ears. "Oooooo, you are simply the most infuriating man I have ever had the misfortune to encounter—out!"

He put his hands up to fend her off. "If you would just hear me out—"

Whoosh! The stick nearly sliced his ear before he dodged, snatching it from her fingers so fast, it hit the wall before her gasp hit the air. He loomed over her, temple throbbing. "One more stunt like that, lady, and I'll arrest you for assault with a deadly weapon."

"I'll give you assault!" She hiked a heel and stomped his foot, further singeing his temper when she marred his freshly polished shoe.

He gaped at the half-moon indentation on the tip, hardly able to believe what the little brat had done. His ire swelled while his head lashed up. "Okay, lady—*nobody* scuffs my Italian leather oxfords."

"No?" Whirling around, she grabbed a wooden ruler off her desk and jabbed it toward the door. "Out—*now*—or I'll be scuffing more than your shoes."

He stared open-mouthed, hands on his hips. "What is it with you and sharp instruments, anyway—your tongue isn't enough?"

"Oh, you . . . you . . . !" Green eyes glittering, she flew at him with stick raised, promptly popping him with the ruler.

"That's it," he muttered, and shoving his hat up, he wrenched the ruler from her hand and snapped it in two before hurling it away. He yanked his waistcoat closed and buttoned his vest with fingers as thick as the insults on the tip of his tongue. "I'm warning you, Princess, for your own good—stay off both the cable car and the streets by yourself on the Barbary Coast, especially after dark, understand?"

She scrambled for the blasted yardstick again, holding it out with two hands as if to prevent him from coming anywhere close.

Ha! No problem there.

"I understand that you're not only rude and obnoxious, you're also a bully, you, you—"

"Yeah, yeah, yeah." He glared, cauterizing her and her stick with so much heat, he was surprised one or both didn't go up in flames. "Suit yourself, lady," he said with a press of his jaw, "but don't say I didn't warn you." And yanking his hat on too hard, he strode down the hall and slammed the door behind him, a style of departure that was quickly becoming a habit where Miss McClare was concerned.

"Brainless female," he muttered, stalking down the street into the city's own personal hell, where the dregs of society would swallow a society dame like Allison McClare whole before chewing her up and spitting her out. A schoolteacher without a lick of sense who was oblivious to the fact he was only trying to warn her. Scrounging for a handful of animal crackers in his pocket, he slammed them down while passing a drunk sprawled on the sidewalk in a pool of vomit. The stench of it—alcohol, urine, and body odor—immediately roiled his senses. He shook his head. But some people were too thick and too stubborn to heed advice, and the high and mighty Miss McClare was obviously one.

Head down, he ignored the flurry of lewd comments and invitations from scantily clad women in the brothels above, hands in his pockets while his anger simmered and stewed. Jaw taut, he jerked the precinct door open and exhaled a weighty sigh. Yes, indeed, she was one of those poor, unfortunate souls in life destined to learn the hard way. He slammed the door behind with a grunt.

Like me.

5

"Jumpin' jaybirds, Miss Alli, this is fun!"

Allison glanced up from her desk at tiny Lottie LeRoy, the sweet six-year-old orphan from next door. She smiled at the little girl whose chestnut curls bounced with every crank of the pencil sharpener bolted to the wall, eager to please with whatever task she could do.

"I'm glad, Lottie, because I sure wasn't looking forward to sharpening all those pencils by myself, so you're really helping me out."

The little girl beamed, the glow in her blue eyes bringing a prick of tears to Alli's own. How she wished she could take the little darling home to play with her younger sister. Although Maddie had just turned six, Mother wasn't ready to send her to the Hand of Hope School just yet, opting to tutor her instead until the school was more established. But Allison was sure Maddie would love meeting the children at Mercy House, especially Lottie. "I'll say one thing, Miss Lottie—you are a very hard worker, young lady."

"That's what Mr. Nick says," Lottie said proudly, testing the point on a pencil she just sharpened. She giggled. "I help him pick weeds and build things."

The pen in Allison's hand stopped mid-scrawl, leaving an unsightly blot of ink on one of her student's papers. She grated her lip, voice casual. "Do you . . . like Mr. Nick?" she asked carefully, half hoping the little sprite would confirm what a terror the man was.

"Oh, gee whiz, you bet—Mr. Nick is my favorite person in the whole wide world, 'cept for Miss Penny and now you, a course."

Allison's smile sloped sideways. *Well, two out of three's not bad . . .*

"Mr. Nick reads a story to us almost every night afore I go to bed, me and the others," she said staunchly, the grind of the sharpener unable to hide the worshipful tone in her voice. "Except those nights he's gotta work, a course." The sharpener paused while she inserted another pencil, her wispy sigh carrying across the room. "When I grow up, I wanna marry somebody just like him 'cause he's so nice, handsome, and smells good too."

Allison issued a silent grunt. *Again . . . two out of three.*

"I love Mr. Nick a lot 'cause he makes me feel warm and safe inside . . . like one of God's archangels, ya know? And everybody knows angels are beautiful, right?"

Allison blinked, pen stalled on the paper once again. "Uh . . . sure . . . I guess." *As long as the "harping" they do is music related.*

Lottie's little shoulders suddenly slumped, an air of dejection settling on her features as softly as the wood shavings that settled on the floor. "Only thing is, Mr. Nick cain't be no angel 'cause he don't like God."

"What do you mean?" Allison said, her renegade thoughts about Mr. Nick screeching to a shameful halt.

She shook her little head, curls skimming her shoulders, as limp as her tone. "He reads bedtime stories to us a lot, sure, but he always leaves when we say our prayers. I asked him why one time, and he just said he ain't on speakin' terms with God no more." A weighty sigh shuddered her tiny body. "Miss Penny told us Mr. Nick is mad at God and we need to pray they'll make up. She says Mr. Nick just needs our love and prayers to show him that God really does care about him." A brilliant smile suddenly broke through her malaise, lighting a heavenly glow in her eyes. "So that's what I do, Miss Alli, yesiree, Bob—I love Mr. Nick just like it's God ahuggin' him through me."

Allison blinked, suddenly feeling lower than the shavings on the floor. She gulped when Father Burton's homily from last week came to mind.

Except ye become as little children, ye shall not enter into the kingdom of heaven. Her eyelids shuttered closed. *Oh, Lord, forgive me . . .*

The sharpener started grinding again, and Allison vowed she'd try to show Christian love and kindness to Nick Barone if it killed her. After all, if a sweet, little cherub like Lottie liked him, then maybe he wasn't so bad . . .

Silence fell when Lottie halted her task to peer up with another serious face, her eyes void of their usual sparkle, just like before. "And I'm so sorry, Miss Alli, but I don't think Mr. Nick likes you very much."

Oh, now there's a news flash for you. Allison bit her lip, turning away so the little girl couldn't see the blush on her face. She schooled her voice to hide a prick of hurt. "Oh? Why do you say that?"

Lottie's wavering sigh lingered in the air. "'Cause Miss Penny said she'd take a stick to him if he didn't treat you nice."

Allison couldn't help it—she smiled—glad to have reinforcements in her war against Nicholas Barone. "Well, maybe it would do him good," she said with a hike of her chin, grading the last paper with a satisfied sweep of her pen.

"I don't think so," Lottie said. "Mr. Nick's too big and strong for the stick."

Don't you bet on it, sweetie . . .

The little girl suddenly giggled, pudgy fingers to her mouth. "But that Mr. Nick sure is funny. Told me your name was just like mine, but then he said he was only teasing."

Allison looked up. "Like yours?" A crease popped above her nose. "What do you mean?"

Blowing off the last sharpened pencil, Lottie chuckled again, the sound as sweet as a baby's giggle. "He called you Miss Lottie Da, and Miss Penny got a little mad, but I think Lottie's a pretty name, don't you?" She finished her task and carried the cup of pencils to Alli.

Allison's mouth dropped open. She snapped it shut. *Better than Mr. Pain-in-the-Nick, I suppose.* "Thank you, sweetheart." With a gentle stroke of Lottie's curls, she took the cup of pencils from her hand, choosing to ignore Lottie's last remark in the name of Christian decency. *Like I wish I could do with the man.* "Ready for me to walk you next door?"

"Sure." She tipped her head up, her eyes meeting Alli's with a sweetness that made Alli smile. "What's a 'dizzy dame,' Miss Alli?"

Uh-oh. Allison blinked, cheeks suddenly hot. "W-why do you ask, Lottie?"

Sadness shadowed the little girl's face. "Because Mr. Nick called you that, and if I get dizzy, it means I'm sick." Her eyes were glossy with concern. "You're not sick, are you?"

Only of Mr. Nick. "Of course not, darling." Allison took the little girl's hand in hers, anxious to steer both the child and the conversation in another direction. "We best get you home before Miss Penny comes a hunting, shall we?"

"Goodness, what a wonderful day!" Alli's cousin Cassie hurried into the classroom and halted, gaze landing on Lottie. "Well, hello, Lottie—how was your first day of school?"

Allison could almost feel the tingle of excitement in the little girl's hand. "Just swell, Miss Cassie! 'Course Miss Penny always taught us afore and I liked that, truly, but holy moly, this was fun! I like learnin' with lotsa kids instead of just those at the orphanage, ya know?"

Cassie laughed. "Yes, as a matter of fact I do. Back in Texas, Mama taught me at home for a while, which was fine. But then she took me with her to the reservation school where there were all kinds of kids my age, and goodness—it was like a whole new world opened up for me."

"Exactly," the little girl said with a sound thrust of her pert, little chin, sounding so much older than six that Alli grinned. "And guess what? I made two new friends!"

Cassie bent to give Lottie a hug. "I'm so glad, because we love having you here, Lottie. And I can already tell that you're going to be one of my best students, young lady."

"Gee, really, Miss Cassie?"

Cassie tapped her nose and chuckled before she winked at Allison. "You bet, sweetheart—you've got a keen mind."

"Gee, thanks!" She looked up at Allison. "Did you hear that, Miss Alli—I have a 'keen mind.' I cain't wait to tell Mr. Nick."

"Mister Nick?" Cassie mouthed to Allison, fighting the squirm of a smile. She leaned to gently tug on one of Lottie's curls. "Do you like Mr. Nick?" she asked sweetly.

"You bet!" the little girl said with way too much enthusiasm for the man with less charm than a rock. "Everybody likes Mr. Nick."

"Uh-huh, I'm sure they do." Cassie winked . . . either that or she had a twitch in her eye.

"Miss Alli?" Lottie glanced up, face screwed in thought. "Can I ask a favor?"

"Absolutely!" Alli stooped to brush a curl behind her ear. "What is it, sweetheart?"

Hope literally glowed on the little tyke's face. "Could you call me Miss Lottie Da like Mr. Nick calls you? I like the sound when he says it."

Alli bit her lip, slipping a tentative peek Cassie's way.

"Miss La-di-da?" her cousin mouthed again, angling a brow.

A sigh feathered Allison's lips. *If you're trying to get my attention, Lord—good job.* "Yes, sweetheart, I'll be happy to," she said quietly, praying Cassie wouldn't mention it to Mother on the ride home. Not after the fuss her mother made over making a good impression on Nick Ga-roan. "Come on, sweetie, I need to get you home." Allison steered her toward the hall, gaze flicking over her shoulder. "You better hurry, Cass—Mother and Hadley are waiting in the car, and I'm sure Miss Merdian and Miss Tuttle are long gone too."

Cassie stifled a yawn as she followed Allison out. "Yes, Miss Merdian had to practically carry poor Miss Tuttle out." A wry grin tipped her lips. "God bless Miss Tuttle, but I'm not sure a retired teacher with a tic in her eye is up to handling twenty rambunctious girls."

"At least it's not all at the same time," Allison reasoned, ushering Lottie down the hall to the back porch, where she stopped to give her cousin a side hug. "I'm sorry I'm not joining you tonight for the dress fittings and dinner, Cass, but I have so much to do, I wouldn't be much fun. Besides," she said with a bit of a smirk, "my bridesmaid dress already fits perfectly."

Cassie pinched her waist. "Yes it does, you little brat, but don't stay too late, you hear?"

"I won't." Alli steered Lottie down the steps and through the yard to Miss Penny's. "I promised Mother I'd leave well before dark."

"Good. And lock the door when you get back," Cassie called,

tossing a smile over her shoulder on her way to the back alley where the Packard was parked. "Good night, La-di-da!"

"Good night, Miss Cassie." Lottie waved, then chatted on and on about Allison's least favorite subject—Mr. Nick—forcing Allison to stifle a groan. *Really, Lord, could you be any more obvious?* Guiding Lottie around the neatly trimmed boxwoods that lined a short flagstone walk, she sucked in a deep breath. With a square of her shoulders, she mounted the wooden steps to Miss Penny's screened porch that led to the kitchen, praying Mr. Nick was nowhere in sight.

"Miss McClare—hello!" Miss Penny herself answered the door with a bright smile while an elderly bull terrier stood behind her, apparently sizing Alli up. The mouthwatering smell of beef stew bubbling on the stove caused Allison's stomach to growl along with the dog. "For goodness' sake, Horatio, Miss McClare is a friend." The old woman tugged them inside for a warm hug while two older girls bustled in the kitchen with Mrs. Lemp. "I appreciate you allowing Lottie to stay and help. I hope she wasn't any trouble."

"Oh, absolutely not, Miss Penny—Lottie was a godsend, I assure you." Allison stooped to embrace the little girl before kissing her cheek. "Thank you so much, sweetheart, for all your help today. Goodness, I'd still be sharpening pencils if you hadn't volunteered."

Lottie preened, her little chest puffed out like the "pouter pigeon" Gibson Girl blouses both Miss Penny and Allison wore. "I know," she said with a serious nod.

Alli couldn't resist another hug. "Well, I guess we'll see you tomorrow, then, Miss Lottie. Good night, Miss Pen—" She paused midsentence when Lottie tugged on her skirt.

"You forgot to use my new name, Miss Alli," she whispered loudly.

Allison gulped, eyes flitting from Lottie to Miss Penny and

back. "Oh." She forced a smile. "All right, then, I'll see you, tomorrow Miss ... ," her throat bobbed again, "La-di-da."

Lottie beamed like the sun while Allison's face felt just as hot. She avoided Miss Penny's eyes as she hurried out the door. "See you tomorrow, then!" Practically vaulting down the steps to escape, Allison froze midair at the sound of Miss Penny's voice.

"Miss McClare ... may I have a word with you, please?"

A groan clotted in her throat as she slowly wheeled around. "Yes, Miss Penny?"

The old woman scurried down the steps, sympathy soft in her gaze. She placed a frail hand on Allison's arm. "He's really quite harmless, you know."

Allison blinked. "Pardon me?"

"Mr. Nick, as Lottie likes to call him. Or as the rest of us have fondly dubbed him ... ," the blue eyes sparkled with mischief, "Mr. Cranky Pants."

Allison grinned outright. "So it's not just me?"

"Oh, heavens no! Nicholas is one of the most consistent human beings you will ever meet, Miss McClare." Her mouth crooked in a wry smile. "He treats everyone poorly at first."

"Ah ... so there's hope," Allison said with a soft chuckle.

The old woman issued a snort. "Not much, mind you, but some." She cocked her head, studying Allison with a keen eye. "It may help to know, however, he's made veiled references that lead me to believe he was badly hurt by a wealthy young woman from high society."

A glimmer of comprehension dawned as Allison nodded. "So that explains his disparaging remarks about me and my wealth."

Miss Penny winced. "Yes, I'm afraid so, including Lottie's innocent reference to Miss La-di-da. But all grumpiness aside, Nicholas is a good man, more like a son than a boarder and the apple of our eyes, albeit a sour one at times." Her face softened into a tender smile. "Especially Lottie's, because other than my nephew, Nicky's the only man she's been exposed to." Her eyes sparked with moisture as her gaze wandered into a faraway stare. "The rest of my girls—ages eight to twenty-two—were abused in some way by men, most in brothels, so you can only imagine how leery they were of Mr. Cranky Pants in the beginning." A raspy chuckle parted from her weathered lips as they tipped in a sad smile. "But Lottie came to us as a baby when her mother died giving birth, so she had no fear, loving Nicholas unconditionally until he had no choice but to love her back."

Allison quietly swallowed the shame in her throat.

Miss Penny looked up then, the melancholy disappearing in a flash of a smile. "Now he loves all of us, and we love him, so you see, Miss McClare—he really is quite harmless."

Allison arched a brow. "Unless you're a wooden stick, then run for the hills?"

The old woman's chuckle floated in the air. "Precisely." She paused. "He did apologize for his rude remarks and give you the new pointer, yes?"

"Yes, of course."

"Good. You be sure to let me know if he gives you any further trouble, Miss McClare—"

"Call me Alli, Miss Penny, please."

"All right, Alli. Well, you need to get home, and I need to help with dinner, but if Mr. Cranky Pants steps over the line again, young lady, you have my express permission to whack him alongside the head with that brand-new stick, do you hear?" The old woman bustled back up the steps before Allison could even respond, pausing long enough to shoot a sassy smile over her shoulder. She winked. "After all, three times is the charm."

6

*H*ands clasped to her chest, Allison whirled around to survey her brand-new theater, a warm sense of satisfaction pervading her soul as few things ever had. A lover of the arts like her, Mother had provided the best of everything—from a brand-new baby grand to the newfangled electrical system with dimmers and spotlights overhead. Scarlet drapes flanked a curved oak arch, a perfect match for rows of polished oak folding chairs in the long, narrow room that now occupied half the first floor.

Prior to the opening of the school, it had taken months to transform the old house into the Hand of Hope School, removing walls and converting the parlour, dining room, and study into the theater, office, and several classrooms on the first floor alone. Mother had even expanded the kitchen so it could serve as a dining room for the girls and teachers as well.

A sigh of contentment breezed from her lips as she drank in the rich surroundings. Cherrywood-paneled walls gave the theater an air of elegance and refinement so foreign to the poor students who would attend. Gilded paintings depicted various forms of artistic expression, from dance and drama to music and literature. Allison closed her eyes and imagined the sounds of music and laughter and speech filling both the halls of their new school and the hearts of their students. When the stage area wasn't being used for plays, recitals, and assemblies, it would serve as a gymnasium for indoor games, parties, and gatherings of all kinds. It seemed almost too good to be true—the Hand of Hope School was up and running, hopefully to offer both a hand and hope to the disadvantaged girls of the Barbary Coast.

Casting a quick glance at the large clock over the door, she gasped. Her gaze darted to the windows at the front of the theater facing the street, where the pink glow of dusk was just beginning to bleed across the wood-planked floor. "Oh, drat, it's getting dark!" she muttered. She quickly slipped her cashmere shawl over her shoulders and pinned her plumed hat, then retrieved her reticule and doused the lights. Letting herself out the front door, she carefully locked it behind her, nerves humming with excitement.

"Now, you won't stay too late, will you?" Mother had asked, reluctance lacing her tone over allowing Allison to work late at all.

"Of course not, Mother, and there are plenty of taxis I can call," Allison had assured her, although she had no intention of taking a taxi at all, not when her very first cable car ride awaited a few blocks away. A sliver of guilt prickled at misleading Mother, but she shook it off, the thrill of independence trumping any worry she might have had. Wasn't it Mother who had encouraged her independence in the first place, insisting Allison go to college to become a teacher? She adjusted her hat with a jut of her chin, then smoothed her black gabardine skirt with sweaty hands. For goodness' sake, she was a twenty-two-year-old working girl now, a licensed educator and a self-sufficient woman. If she wanted to take the cable car home, then by gum, she'd take the cable car home!

"If you think it's safe for a fancy dame in diamond combs to sashay through the worst part of town to sightsee on a bloomin' cable car, you are way too stupid to teach in a school."

Her lips compressed. Besides, she needed to prove to herself and her family she was a responsible adult *and* prove her mettle to Mr. Grunt-and-Ga-roan as well. After all, this was only two measly city blocks hundreds of people walked every day of their lives, including the infamous Mr. Nick, right? And she'd bet not one of them carried a hat pin as large as hers.

Head high, she skittered down the front steps to the cobblestone street, the thrill of adventure tingling her skin. She paused to squint the length of Jackson Street, swabbed in purple shadows that deepened by the moment, then set out according to Nicholas Barone's directions—two blocks south at Jackson and Montgomery. Adrenaline pulsed as the sounds of nighttime on the Barbary Coast grew stronger. The tinkle of steam pianos and the tinny sound of gramophone music drifted in the air along with the pungent smell of gasoline and manure. Laughter floated her way as men and women staggered out of a bar several blocks down, and she slowed her pace when vile shouts and curses erupted. A fight broke out among the group, and Allison halted, grateful she was only four houses from Miss Penny's. A surge of gawkers spilled into the street from the bars lining her route, obviously anxious to watch the fray. She waited until the ruckus broke up, dismayed that the sky had darkened to pitch by the time it was over. Ominous streaks of purple slithered into the horizon while the noisy swarm of people slithered back into the bars.

Eyes trained straight ahead, her breathing accelerated when several shadows between the buildings seemed to move. The sporadic gas lamps offered little illumination to allay the uneasiness that now prickled her nerves.

"Oh!" Frazzled by fear, she misstepped on a crack in the sidewalk and fell down, skinning her palms while her reticule and hat flew into the cobblestone street. "Thunderation," she muttered, dusting dirt from her shawl and her skirt as she lumbered to her feet. After hobbling to pick up her purse and hat, she was just about to pin her hat on when she froze at the faint shuffle of footfall behind her. She whirled around, her stomach plummeting at the sight of two unsavory men.

"Needin' a bit of help, are you, sweet cheeks?" One of them offered a lazy grin, the smell of whiskey and sweat turning her stomach.

"N-no, th-thank you," she said weakly, sweaty fingers carefully skimming the brim of her hat for the pin.

The second man grinned while he scratched the side of his bristled face, his lurid gaze traveling her body. "Now, sure you do, little missy. What kind of gentlemen would we be if we didn't come to the aid of a damsel in distress, eh?"

Despite the chill of evening, a bead of sweat trickled beneath her high-collared blouse as Allison backed up, heart thundering. "I'm f-fine, gentlemen, truly," she stuttered, relief flooding when she grazed the knotted head of the fourteen-karat-gold hat pin Uncle Logan had given her for Christmas. "I just need to catch the cable car, so if you'll excuse me please—"

"Blimey, miss, we don't mind escortin' you none." The first man tucked his thumbs in the tattered suspenders of his dirty shirt, rolling back on his heels while the other slowly circled her from behind. "Matter of fact, we know a shortcut, don't we, Floyd?"

Her Irish temper surged. "If you gentlemen don't leave me in peace by the count of three, you will sorely regret it."

"Is that so?" the leader said with a putrid grin that churned the egg sandwich she'd eaten for dinner into bile that rose in her throat.

"Yes, sir, it is." She thrust her jaw while her grip tightened on the pin. "One."

Cackles shivered her spine when the men's laughter rolled into the air. "Ooooo, help me, Pug, please," the one man mocked from behind, "I'm askeered the hoity-toity rich gal's gonna hurt us bad." His eyes lighted on the reticule dangling from her wrist. "Why don't you just toss your purse this way, darlin', and we'll be on our way."

"Two." Her fingers began to sweat, pin slick in her palm beneath the fold of her wrap.

"You ain't too friendly, are you, darlin'?" Pug reached out to trail a grimy finger down the cashmere shawl that hugged the sleeve of her blouse.

"Three!" Heart in her throat, Allison stabbed his hand. The man's shriek of fury and pain bit the air while she whirled to brandish the pin at the other.

"Why, you little . . ." Curse words peppered the night when Allison bolted past the wounded man, fleeing for Mercy House with her skirt hiked to her knees.

Someone ripped the shawl from her back, wrenching a cry from her throat, and she picked up speed, eyes fixed on Miss Penny's door just a house away.

"Gotcha!" Brutal hands circled her waist like a vice, unleashing her bloodcurdling scream when the ivory busk of her corset gouged into her skin.

"Feisty little wench, ain't she?" a voice sneered as a foul-smelling hand cut off her air.

Cries muffled, she thrashed wildly in her assailant's arms while fear iced her skin. She heard the rip of her sleeve, and cool air rushed into the hole that gaped at her shoulder. Somehow she rammed the pin into the man's thigh, and he dropped her with a roar of agony, tumbling her to the cobblestones with a grunt. She scrambled up, and he grabbed her again, hat pin flying when he tore hat and hairpins from her head. Curls spilled down her back while tears spilled from her eyes. "Help me, somebody, please!" she cried, pummeling the man in a frantic attempt to flee.

"Oh, no you don't, missy." Pug yanked her toward the alley with a fistful of curls. "Time to pay the piper."

God, help me, please . . .

Pain seared her body as bile climbed up her throat. She kicked and slashed with unbridled anger, finally biting the noxious hand clamped over her mouth. Her scream rent the air along with the crazed howl of the man she bit, curses defiling the night as she tried to lunge away.

Ka-boom! A gunshot stilled the blood in her veins. "I suggest you vermin scatter before I do it for you."

Three sets of eyes darted to the stoop not twenty feet away. There stood Miss Penny in an apron with a shotgun in her hands, cocked and aimed and dusted with flour.

"Get inside, old lady, this don't concern you," Pug growled over his shoulder. His beady eyes settled on Floyd with a sharp nod in Miss Penny's direction. "Get the gun."

Floyd took a step forward, and a curse hissed from his lips when bits of cobblestone exploded at his feet. He jumped back while Miss Penny cocked and reloaded in the space of a heartbeat, flour dusting both her nose and her cheeks. "Now those were warning shots, you snake-belly scalawags. The next two are going to nick a little more."

"That old bat's crazy, Pug! I ain't stayin' around so some old hag can drill us with holes." Floyd backed up, hands in the air. "You're on your own," he shouted before hightailing it down the street to disappear around a corner.

Pug shoved Allison hard, and she stumbled to the ground with a cry. Moving toward Miss Penny, he absently rubbed the bloody hole in his hand. "Now, come on, ma'am," he said, voice gentle, gaze hard. "You and I both know you're not gonna shoot me . . ."

Chest heaving, Allison scanned the street for her hat pin, heart lurching when it gleamed in the lamplight just a few feet away. She snatched it up along with her shawl and hat and, not daring to breathe, tiptoed behind Pug with blood in her eyes, aiming straight for his rump.

Words Allison never heard before burned her ears when the man vaulted in the air with a screech that would have curdled his whiskey. Obscenities spewed as he kneaded his backside, mouth gaping and eyes bugging out of his head.

A deadly click drained the blood from his face.

"Now, I suggest you crawl back into whatever sewer you slithered out of, mister," Miss Penny whispered, squinting down the flour-dusted barrel of her gun, "before the two of us put any more holes in your worthless hide."

Carefully raising his hands, Pug slowly backed away, finally turning to limp all the way to the far end of the next block before vanishing into the crowd.

The air in Allison's lungs whooshed out, depleting her energy while hot tears sprang to her eyes. "Oh, Miss Penny," she sobbed, rushing into the old woman's arms. "I was so scared!"

"There, there, Allison, it's all 'behind' us now." Her touch was gentle as she patted Alli's back. She pulled away with a glint of tease in her eyes. "Especially Pug."

Alli's giggle erupted into another sob as she clung to the elderly woman.

"Goodness, child . . ." Miss Penny kneaded Alli's shoulder. "What in heaven's name are you doing out here alone this time of night?"

Alli sniffed, lip quivering at the enormity of danger she'd been in. "I-I w-was working late and m-meant to leave b-before it got dark, b-but I lost track of t-time."

"Merciful heavens, you should never wait outside for your driver, especially after dusk."

Alli pulled away. "I . . . wasn't waiting for Hadley," she whispered with a touch of heat in her cheeks. "I was . . . walking to the cable car."

Two silver brows peaked high. "At Montgomery and Jackson—in the heart of Barbary?"

All Alli could do was nod, suddenly aware that Nick Barone was right—she was too stupid to teach in a school. A frail sob broke from her lips, and Miss Penny gave her a hug.

"There, there, young lady, the worst is over, so what say we calm you down with a cup of chamomile, all right?"

She nodded again, and the older woman ushered her inside, bolting the door before she steered her down the hall into the kitchen where their pet bull terrier Horatio lay asleep by the back door. His nasal snores coaxed a smile to Alli's lips. The homey smell of fresh-baked bread calmed her as much as Miss Penny's gentle hand on her back, steering her toward the potbelly stove. With a final quivering heave, Alli dropped into a nearby chair, clutching her shawl tightly around her. Brushing disheveled curls over Alli's shoulder, Miss Penny gave her a gentle squeeze, then bustled over to the pantry. She dislodged the shells from the shotgun before tucking it high on a shelf.

"Goodness, Miss Penny, do you really know how to shoot?" Allison asked, fear giving way to fascination with this tiny woman whose gumption was as big as her heart.

Chuckling, Miss Penny bounded to the sink to pump water into a kettle. "You better hope so, young lady, or you wouldn't have been the only one shaking in her boots out there." She set the kettle on the gas stove with a wink, then pulled two cups and saucers from massive white shelves lining one wall and plopped them on the large wooden table covered with flour and a ball of dough. "My nephew is the captain of detectives for this district, you know, and we went 'round and 'round about whether I'd be allowed to stay with my girls on the edge of the worst part of town. But when I refused to leave, he bought me a shotgun and taught me to shoot, which seemed to appease him somewhat." Her lips skewed in a wry smile. "That and the fact I agreed to let one of his best detectives rent a room."

She retrieved cream from the icebox and set it on the table along with sugar and two spoons, her smile dimming considerably. "This is not a neighborhood for the fainthearted, my dear, especially at night." She paused to gently cup Alli's chin with her hand. "Promise me, Allison, that you won't wander out alone after dark anymore." Moisture glossed her eyes. "I shudder to think what might have happened if I hadn't opted for a few moments alone to bake bread while Mrs. Lemp gave the younger girls their baths."

A knot near the size of the ball of dough dipped in Alli's throat. "I promise, Miss Penny—from now on, home before dusk." She paused. "But surely catching the cable car during the daylight hours can't be all that dangerous, can it?"

Miss Penny sighed while she plucked pot holders from the counter to remove a loaf of bread from the oven. "Walking the Barbary Coast alone is always a risky venture for a woman, my dear, but definitely safer during the day." A gleam lit her eye. "Especially with a hat pin the size of yours." Her low chuckle made Alli smile. "Old Pug won't be sitting easy for a while."

"Good." A tremor rippled through Alli as she leaned toward

the fire to ward off the chill of the night and the memory of the attack. Her eyes flicked up. "Miss Penny?"

"Yes, dear?"

"Would it be okay if we . . . ," Alli gulped, "you know, kept this unfortunate incident between the two of us?"

Miss Penny turned, washing her hands at the sink before drying them with a towel. "Goodness, Allison, why? Your mother needs to be aware of the danger you were in tonight."

"And I'll tell her, I promise—soon. It's just that . . ." She swallowed hard, eyes fixed on her bruised and dirty palms as they lay face up in her lap. "Mother has so much on her mind right now with the opening of the school, and she's so excited that I'd hate to dampen it for her." Her gaze lifted, along with her hope at the kind of independence Miss Penny had achieved as a woman in a world ruled by men. "And to be honest, Miss Penny, I long for the freedom to come and go as I please, to be able to teach young women to fend for themselves like I hope to do." She drew in a stabilizing breath, praying Miss Penny would understand the need to survive and succeed on the Barbary Coast like so many of her students. "And I know this sounds silly, but for me, that means taking the cable car home whenever I work late instead of relying on Hadley."

A smile tipped the edge of Miss Penny's mouth. "It doesn't sound silly at all," she said softly. "I said much the same thing to my Harold once, not long after we married. I was a middle-class young woman who was fortunate enough to acquire a teaching degree, you see, and he wanted me to give it all up to be a lady of luxury." Her smile was melancholy. "Which I did, of course, when my son was born, but I refused to give up my independence and adventurous spirit," she said with a chuckle, "which I fear pained him a great deal." The smile faded as her eyes trailed into a faraway stare. "But God knew it would serve me well after he and my son—"

The whistle of the teapot interrupted her reverie, and she scrambled to retrieve their tea, but Allison didn't miss the moisture in her eyes. Mother had told her that Miss Penny lost both her husband and son to diphtheria years prior, and Allison's respect for this resilient woman had grown even deeper. She marveled at how Miss Penny had salvaged her own life by salvaging the lives of others.

Miss Penny glanced at the clock over her sink before she poured Alli a cup of tea. "Well, it's getting late, so we'll need to call Hadley to pick you up while I doctor your hands."

Allison nervously picked at her nails, ignoring the sting of her palms. "Actually, Miss Penny, Hadley is with Mother, Cassie, and my sisters at a late dinner, so I'll just call a tax—" The word froze on her tongue at the jiggle of a key in a lock.

"Ah—perfect timing!" Miss Penny said with a bright smile, setting the kettle back on the stove. "Nicholas can see you home on the cable car."

Oh, Lord, no, please . . . Allison's eyelids sank closed.

The front door opened and shut, and with the final click of a lock, heavy footsteps echoed in the foyer, rousing Horatio from his sleep. The terrier's low growl rumbled through the kitchen, merging with a deep chuckle from down the hall. "Mmm . . . I smell bread."

And I smell trouble . . . Bracing herself with a tight tug of her shawl, Allison sat up straight in the chair, hands shaking as she took a sip of her tea.

"Oh, Horatio, hush!" Miss Penny said with a chuckle, hurrying over to welcome Nick home. "Just in the nick of time, young man, pun intended." She perched on tiptoe and pressed a kiss to his bristled cheek while Horatio bared his teeth with another nasty snarl. "We have company."

"Hello, Mr. Barone," Allison managed, far fewer tremors in her tone than in the hands that quivered her cup. She forced a bright smile. "You're working late."

"It's *Barone*, long *e*," he said in a clipped tone, ignoring Horatio until the terrier toddled out of the room. "And I could say the same for you." His eyes narrowed as they flicked to the clock and back. "Shouldn't you be home in your mansion?"

"Now, now, Nicholas," Miss Penny said with a pat of his hand, "be a good boy, or you'll have the Hand of Hope School calling you Mr. Cranky Pants too."

"But what is she doing here?" he asked with a scowl, directing his attention to Miss Penny as she doused a clean rag under the pump and rubbed it with carbolic soap.

She scuttled over to Allison with the rag, squinting to study her skinned palms. "Miss McClare had a little accident and scraped her hands, so I'm cleaning them up before you escort her home." Ignoring his searing gaze, she swished impatient fingers toward a fresh-baked loaf of bread on the counter. "Have a slice of bread while you wait, so you're not growling like a bear."

Allison chanced a peek and wished she hadn't. His jaw looked like rock peppered with dark bristle, making the slits of his eyes all the more ominous. "What kind of accident?"

"Just never you mind," Miss Penny said, gently swabbing the dirt from Allison's hands to reveal red palms scraped free of skin. "It's been taken care of and it's none of your business."

———

"The devil it isn't." Nick hurled his coat over the hook by the door and strode toward the princess, a muscle pulsing in his cheek as he eyed the shawl she now pinched with bloodless fingers. Beneath its gauzy weave, he spied a hint of skin peeking through what looked like a gape in the shoulder of her sleeve, and a flash of fury curdled his stomach. He took one look at the beautiful disarray of black curls tumbling down that remarkable shirtwaist stained with dirt, and his gut turned over. His gaze flicked up to a pale face that only emphasized startling green eyes, and the nervous tug of teeth on those full, pink lips told him this brainless beauty had done exactly what he warned her not to do. He bit back the outrage that teetered on the tip of his tongue and singed Miss McMule with a scathing glare. "I-repeat. What-kind-of-accident?"

Miss Penny released a heavy exhale, giving Miss McClare's arm a final pat before she turned to face him, a plea for compassion glimmering in her eyes. "She's had a traumatic night, Nicholas," she said quietly. "She doesn't need you to add to it."

Normally he relented where Miss Penny was concerned, but the idea of anyone laying a foul hand on this stunning, albeit senseless, creature boiled his blood. The tic in his cheek joined forces with the one in his jaw. "Are you going to tell me what happened, or will I have to—"

"I was accosted, all right?" The creature literally groaned the words, fingers quivering as she brushed a glossy black curl away from her ashen face. The green eyes, usually shooting sparks where he was concerned, actually melted into glistening pools of apology that completely bewitched him. "I . . . owe you an apology, Mr. Barone," she whispered, one of the rare times she actually pronounced his name correctly. "You were right—I am too stupid to teach . . ."

Miss Penny's head whirled, her wide eyes inflicting the same level of guilt his grandmother had whenever he stepped out of line. "You actually *said* that?"

"No, it's true, Miss Penny," she continued in a rush, heating his face with an ardent defense he in no way deserved. "Mr. Barone tried to warn me, but I argued with him, stubborn to the core, doing exactly what he said I would do—part of the upper crust who thinks they can go off half-cocked doing whatever they bloomin' well please."

The gape of Miss Penny's eyes matched that of her mouth. "Nicholas Barone!"

He slid a sweaty finger inside his collar to loosen the chokehold from Miss McClare's praise, wishing she'd stop defending him and just whack him with a stick instead. "Look, I didn't mean it exactly that way ..."

"No, you didn't," Miss McClare said quietly, the candor in her tone disarming any temper she may have provoked in the past. Her eyes locked with his, completely void of any guile. "I'm learning, Mr. Barone—slowly, mind you, because I'm not all that bright," she said with a hint of jest before those green eyes deepened with true sincerity, "that you're just a very frank person who hates to see people so oblivious to harm."

He blinked, wishing they could just go back to insults. He was pretty sure anger was a lot safer than this dizzy heat whirling inside, leaving him tongue-tied.

"Nicholas?" Miss Penny lifted her chin. "What do you say?"

He mauled the back of his neck. "Uh ... okay, I guess."

"Oh, for heaven's sake, Nicky," she said with a fold of her arms, tone stern despite a bare hint of a smile. "You say, 'Thank you, Miss McClare, and I'm sorry for being so brash.'"

He swallowed the foot in his mouth, eyes on Miss McClare as he inclined his head toward Miss Penny. "Yeah, what she said." His momentary awkwardness gave way to a clench in his gut over the danger this woman encountered tonight, nearly becoming another statistic. His face calcified along with his tone. "I'll take you in to file a police report."

"Oh, no, I can't!" she cried, the distress in her face bleeding into her voice. "I mean I . . . I don't want to alarm my mother, Mr. Barone, and I still have my purse and person intact, so I assure you, no harm's been done."

He made a rude point of scanning her slowly, from the haphazard tumble of curls and stained bodice, to the dust and dirt embedded in her form-fitting skirt. Anger hardened his gaze as it trailed back up to settle on a milky complexion now as ruddy as her chafed hands. "No harm done?" he repeated coolly, the spasm in his cheek a perfect complement to the twitch in his hands that wanted to tear her assailants apart, limb by limb. "You could have been violated, Miss McClare, or worse—"

"But I wasn't," she insisted in a rush, the blush in her cheeks now fading to chalk.

"No, you weren't." His lips cemented into a thin line. "But the next victim might not be so lucky when the scum you refuse to report try it again."

Her face bleached as white as her rumpled white blouse.

"Really, Nicky, don't you think we've had enough melodrama for tonight?" Miss Penny slipped a protective arm around Miss McClare's shoulders.

He pierced Miss Penny with a hard stare. "You're in agreement with this?"

She hovered over the woman with a firm jut of her chin. "Allison has her reasons for not divulging this just now, Nicholas, and we must respect her wishes. Besides, she promised not to attempt walking outside by herself after dark again and plans to inform her mother of this soon."

His facial muscles went slack. "And you believe her? For blimey's sake, look at her, Miss Penny! The woman has as much common sense as one of those confounded dainty cups those blue bloods use to sip their blessed tea."

"That is quite enough, Nicholas." Miss Penny stared him down, hands lodged on Miss McClare's shoulders like an undersized archangel ready to wage battle. "I will not stand here and allow you to berate a guest in my home. Please apologize."

Shades of his grandmother revisited, unleashing a trail of heat up his neck that scorched all the way to his cheeks. Gram had been the one human being he'd respected and admired enough to curb his temper. His lips gummed tight. *No, make that two . . .*

"Nicholas?" The chin notched up.

"I-apol-o-gize," he ground out, the words distorted by the clench of his teeth.

The silver-haired imp had the nerve to cock her head with a squint of blue eyes. "I don't believe I quite understood that, Allison, did you?"

Miss McClare's lashes fluttered wide, green eyes dancing as a giggle actually broke from her mouth, perfect pink lips annoying him to no end. "No, I don't believe I did. It sounded more like a strained grunt to me, although I suppose it could have been an apology in another language or dialect." She scrunched her nose as she studied him, a gleam of trouble in her eyes. "Early Neanderthal, perhaps?"

Between the two, Nick found himself totally disarmed and dropped his head to pinch the bridge of his nose, humor threatening the hard bent of his lips. He huffed out a sigh and looked up, the stiff planes of his face relaxing into a shadow of a smile. "All right, okay—you've made your point, ladies, and I apologize, Miss McClare, for losing my temper—*again*."

The smile the woman gave him spiked his temperature at least twenty degrees, causing the skin under his collar to break out in a sweat. "So, Mr. Barone, long *e*," she said with an extension of her hand. "Shall we try this again—one more time?"

Resigned, he shook his head and laughed, a slow grin sliding across his lips. He reached for her wrist rather than inflicting pain on her sore palm and pressed his thumb to her pulse, grateful it felt as erratic as his. "As long as there are no sticks involved, Miss McClare."

"Or hat pins," Miss Penny said with a proud smirk. "Those two ruffians are sporting more holes than my best colander, I can promise you that."

Nick jagged a brow. "Two?"

Miss McClare grinned, the glow of pride in her eyes as blinding as Miss Penny's. "I actually poked them both, and I do believe I drew blood a number of times."

"Is that a fact?" Slipping his hands in his pockets, Nick lowered his head to emit a soft chuckle, wondering if maybe he hadn't underestimated the little spitfire. Pulse finally calming, he glanced up, shooting her a shuttered smile that toasted her cheeks. "Good to know."

7

Allison hurried to keep up with Nick Barone's long strides down the trash-littered sidewalk of Jackson. Her heart pumped with excitement from strolling through the devil's lair—as Miss Penny called it—as much as from the detective's breakneck speed. Athletic by nature, she usually had no problem keeping up, easily outdistancing Blake or Jamie in summer games of tag. But Nick Barone was a mountain of a man with less patience than her, evidently, when it came to achieving a goal or reaching a destination. Hands buried in his pockets, his trademark scowl was firmly in place, and she almost wished those two hooligans would chance a repeat encounter. She prided herself on being a strong woman who could take care of herself, but never had she felt so safe, so protected, so free as she did now, with him by her side.

He'd said precious little since they'd left Miss Penny's, apparently still miffed over his failed attempt to get her to file a police report once Miss Penny wasn't around to defend. But Allison stood her ground, explaining her burning need to explore independence in her new life as a teacher, something that would be squashed in a heartbeat if her family found out about the incident right now. She was determined to keep it to herself until she could prove the cable car was safe. As long as she took it before dusk, that is, which she fully intended to do. Or at least until she could talk Mother into acquiring a firearm, something Miss Penny felt was advisable in a neighborhood on the edge of the Coast.

Mouth compressed as stiff as his manner, Nick had allowed her to chatter ad nauseam for several blocks, his brooding gaze continually sweeping the doorways and alleys of the bars they passed. Occasionally he'd answer a question with a sideways glance and a faint smile, as if he found her amusing, but in no way did he afford her the courtesies she was used to with most men. Not the offer of his arm to escort her, the attentive interest of a suitor, or even the polite banter employed in social situations. Which was just as well, she supposed. Judging from the time she'd spent with him thus far, he was nothing more than a prettier, grumpier rendition of the type of men who tended to break her heart.

Eyes straight ahead, he remained silent at an intersection to allow a horse and buggy to pass, giving Allison a chance to catch her breath and study him unaware. Without question, he was one of the most handsome men she'd seen, although his manners and short moods dispelled any attraction, at least mentally. But physically? A lump bobbed in her throat. When his thumb had grazed her wrist, she was sure the leap of her pulse would bruise both her skin and his. He'd seemed little-boy awkward when Miss Penny scolded, but the moment he'd touched Allison's arm, pinned her with those hypnotic eyes, she sensed a confidence and control that bordered on cocky, as if he were used to the approval of women. Her lips squirmed. *Cave women, no doubt.*

"Does 'Sin City' amuse you, Miss McClare?" he asked, sliding her one of those veiled looks that made her think he could read every thought in her head, despite the fluff between her ears, of course. "Or does that shadow of a smile mean you're laughing at me?"

Heat scorched her face at his perception, and she quickly looked across the street, not a smart thing to do. The fire in her cheeks raged out of control over near-naked women in the doorway of a bordello, issuing lewd remarks to Nick as they passed by. Swallowing hard, she forced her gaze straight ahead, her good humor suddenly as depleted as the smile on her face.

His husky laugh blended perfectly with the ragtime and ribald revelry that filled the night air along with the stench of whiskey and smoke. "What exactly did you expect to see on the Barbary Coast, Miss McClare—gentlemen with manners and ladies dressed for tea?"

She glanced up to deliver a sharp retort and stopped at the sobriety in his eyes, sensing a compassion that seemed to fly in the face of all she knew him to be. Her ire drifted out on a weary sigh lost in a rash of profanity and slurs from men who whistled and raked her with salacious stares. "No, but I . . ." A knot of pride shifted in her throat and she gulped it down whole, suddenly ashamed of her naïveté. "Wasn't expecting this," she said faintly, embarrassed over the wealth and privilege that had blinded her to the plight of the lost and forgotten.

For the first time, he took her arm and gently steered her to the corner of Montgomery where a motley group of people waited for the cable car. "It's another world here, Miss McClare." His voice was quiet as he laid a protective hand over hers. "One I'm glad you're not privy to."

"But there are so many lost souls," she whispered, unable to stop the tears in her eyes.

"Yes, but lost by choice." His voice held a bitter edge.

"Not all," she said softly, remembering several little girls who'd attended their first day at Hand of Hope School, daughters of women who worked in the brothels, according to Miss Penny.

He glanced at her then, the hard line of his jaw softening just a hair. "No, not all."

Clang, clang, clang!

Allison looked up, the sight of a cable car chugging down the rails of Montgomery dissolving her melancholy mood. A thrill surged and her heart began to pound while a tiny giggle slipped from her lips. She fought the inclination to squeal, barely aware of the fingers she dug into his coat sleeve. "Oh, my very first cable car ride," she breathed. "Can you tell?"

His mouth crooked. "Only by the bruise on my arm."

Her giggle was almost decadent. "Oh, don't be such a baby, Mr. Barone. This thrilling adventure may be ho-hum to you, but it's a dream come true for me." She sighed. "Mother never let us ride the cable car—too many germs."

He surveyed the disreputable crowd waiting to board, nose wrinkling, no doubt, from the rank smell of unwashed bodies, stale alcohol, and burning wood from the cable car brakes. His smile took a wry twist. "Wise woman, your mother."

The rumble of wheels and the click of rails stole her attention as the bright-red California Street cable car ground to a stop, its shiny wood benches facing out like an invitation to adventure. The small crowd moved forward while Mr. Barone held her back, allowing the others to funnel in first. When it was her turn to mount the single step, he assisted her up, then pressed a nickel into her hand. Adrenaline coursing, she promptly handed the fare to the driver before taking the last of two seats on an outer bench. She absently skimmed a hand to her abdomen, as if she could calm the flutters at the prospect of her first cable car ride.

"You gettin' on or not, mister?" the driver said, and Allison glanced up to see Nick Barone standing stock-still before the platform step, eyes glazed and body stiff.

"Mr. Barone? Are you all right?" She ducked her head to peer into his ashen face, the stubble of late-day beard all the more apparent against his bloodless skin.

His Adam's apple jerked as he nodded, fingers gripped white on the pole by the step while he remained rooted to the cobblestone street as firmly as the cable car rails.

"I don't got all night, mister," the grip man said in a growl. "Either get on or get off."

Huffing out a sigh, Allison jumped up and pried his fingers from the pole, tugging on his hand as if yanking a mule. "Mr. Barone, please! You promised Miss Penny you'd see me home."

His gaze slowly lifted, as if in a trance, and the muscles in his throat convulsed again. "All right," he whispered, voice a strangled rasp, "but it's only fair to warn you . . ." He appeared to stifle a belch while he remained inert, feet fused to the sidewalk and skin suddenly matching the green in his eyes. "I get . . . seasick."

"Oh, for heaven's sake." The schoolmarm surfaced when Allison tugged on the lobe of his ear, forcing him into motion as she dragged him up the step and onto the bench.

"Ouch, that hurts," he snapped, the pain obviously breaking through his stupor.

She slapped his hand when he tried to bat her away. "It's a cable car, Mr. Barone, not a frigate. Now, you sit right there until I pay the man, do you understand?"

His jaw began to grind. "You are one pushy dame, you know that?"

"And you are nothing but a big baby," she said with a menacing glare, digging a nickel from her reticule. She handed it to the driver, then wiggled into the tight space between the oversized sissy and a pie-eyed man who actually gave her a wink. Inching closer to Mr. Barone, she decided the green tinge of his face was less threatening than the lurid look of the other man.

The cable car lurched to a start, and Allison squealed, forgetting all challenges to her peace of mind as a breeze lifted the stray curls at the back of her neck. "Oh, this is so much fun!" she said with a giggle, craning to see down the street.

She spied the four-story Montgomery Block, one of the largest buildings in the West, and nearly swooned as always over one of her favorite landmarks. "Sweet bliss, I just read a wonderful article about the Montgomery Block!" She shook Mr. Barone's arm, hardly believing he had his eyes closed. "Oh my goodness, did you know Mark Twain met a San Francisco fireman named Tom Sawyer in the Montgomery Block sauna and used his name for his novel *The Adventures of Tom Sawyer?*"

Fingers welded to the pole arm of the seat, Mr. Barone's eyes opened long enough to sear her with a dazed stare. A grunt escaped his pale lips when the cable car bell rang, eyelids sinking closed again as the car eased to a halt. The grip man called out the next stop, and Allison's sympathy rose when Mr. Barone stifled a heave. "You're taking your life in your hands," he said with a groan, lunging for his handkerchief as the car began to glide.

"That seems to be a trend in your company, Mr. Barone." A soft smile tugged at her lips.

"It's Nick," he said, jaw clamping when the car jolted from a particularly hard jog on the rails. "Yeah, well, this time I may ruin your dress instead of your stick."

"I'll take my chances, Mr. . . . Nick," she said quickly, relishing the independence of calling him by his Christian name. "Something I'm realizing one must do with a man of your ilk. And, please—call me Allison."

One eyelid peeled up. "A man of my ilk?" he repeated, rag to his mouth to ward off the threat of what appeared to be the rise of his last meal.

She scrunched her nose, biting back a smile. "You know—cranky."

His lips pinched even tighter than before, obviously thinner than his patience. "You'd be cranky, too, lady, if your stomach was churning like San Francisco Bay during a squall."

"Goodness, does this happen every time you ride a cable car?" she asked, wondering how the man kept anything down while riding public transportation.

"No idea," he said with a growl that faded into a moan. "First time."

Her head wheeled to face him, eyebrows tented in shock. "What? This is your first time on a cable car? Then how on earth did you know you'd be sick? Do you get sick on boats?"

"No." It was a croak as he smothered what could have been a belch.

She squinted. "Then I don't understand. If you don't get seasick, then why—" Her eyes went wide. "Wait—you're afraid, aren't you?"

Well, that certainly helped his color. Blood gorged his cheeks. "Don't be ridiculous," he snarled, singeing her with a glare.

Oh, good—familiar territory! "Sweet mother of mercy, you *are*, aren't you?" She clamped a hand to her mouth to smother a laugh, the idea of this mammoth, gun-toting grouch afraid of anything delighting her more than it should. She forced a serious demeanor, noting from his ruddy color that their sparring had apparently taken his mind off the ride. "For heaven's sake, it's nothing to be ashamed of, Nick," she said sweetly. She tilted her head, attempting to contain the chuckles that bubbled up in her chest. "Unless, of course," she whispered in a voice hoarse with restraint, "you're afraid of mice too . . ." Her laughter broke free in a glorious swell of giggles joined in by the sloshed man beside her.

The gray-green eyes narrowed over the handkerchief he held to his mouth. "Don't tempt me, Miss McClare—I had kippers for lunch."

"Oh, look!" she cried when the cable car coasted to a stop. "There's the Golden Era Building!" She jumped up to seize the brass-plated pole, hand holding on to her hat as she bounced on the platform. "I read a wonderful article in *The San Francisco Examiner* about its fifty-year anniversary." She whirled around, breathless with excitement, shouting to make herself heard over a steam piano from a passing melodeon music hall. "Mr. Barone!"

His eyelids snapped up. "What?" he croaked, wincing when the grip man bellowed the next stop.

"This is history and culture at its finest, I'll have you know. Why, that was home to *The Golden Era*," she explained with a waggle of her purse in the building's direction, "the city's most important literary journal. Goodness, Mark Twain was a frequent contributor and so was author poet Bret Harte, who not only worked as a typesetter there, but penned his first poem in that very building." They passed the Golden Era Building, and she dropped back onto the bench with a heady sigh, hands clasped on the leather purse in her lap. "Good gracious, do you have any idea how thrilling this is for an English teacher?"

He stared through glossy eyes, mouth gaping. "Not a clue."

She offered a sheepish smile. "You think I'm crazy, don't you?"

His lips quirked in one of the few smiles she'd seen on his face all night. "I think that was established when I broke your stick, Miss McClare."

Her smile faded to shy. "Allison," she whispered, suddenly painfully aware of his muscled arm pressing against hers and those long legs sprawled so close to her skirt. She peeked up beneath her lashes, able to see every dark whisker peppering his hard-chiseled jaw. "It appears some of the color has returned to your face, Mr. Barone. Are you feeling better, I hope?"

"Nick." His whisper was almost intimate as his eyes locked with hers, their intensity draining the air from her lungs. His gaze lowered to her lips for a stutter of a heartbeat before it rose again, tumbling her stomach with his faint smile.

She quickly averted her gaze, deflecting the heat in her cheeks with nonstop chatter as the car rumbled on the rails. "California Street!" the grip man shouted, and Alli shot to her feet. "That's m-my s-street," she muttered, wobbling as the cable car slid to a halt.

Heat scalded her skin when Nick braced her with a firm hand. "Steady there," he said, face suddenly pasty as he peered up the steep and ever-climbing blocks of California Street that led to her home on Powell. "We have a ways to go—especially since we're going to walk."

"Walk?" She whirled around on the step of the car. "But this is the best part—scaling those wonderfully steep hills via cable car. Why, it's almost as exciting as the roller coaster at Ocean Beach!"

"Yeah? Well, this isn't Ocean Beach, Miss McClare, it's a rickety cable car jerking up the hill, rattling my bones every time it jolts to a stop. No, thank you. If I'm seeing you home, we'll scale by foot." He hooked her arm to help her down, then sucked in a deep breath when his feet hit the sidewalk, exhaling slowly while a grin inched across his face. "My first—and last—cable car ride, unless somebody puts a gun to my head."

Giving a little skip, she laughed and twirled on the sidewalk, head back and arms free as she spun, reveling in the glow of the melon moon overhead. "Oh, come on, you big sissy, it wasn't that bad, admit it."

He arched a brow, hands buried in his pockets. "So we're back to that again, are we? Maybe I'm not the juvenile delinquent you are, Miss McClare, ever think about that?"

"And maybe you spend so much time being a grouch, Mr. Cranky Pants, you don't enjoy things like wind in your face or a sky heavy with stars glittering over the most beautiful city in the world." She hugged her shawl close, breathing in deeply as she walked backward to face him, eyes drifting closed. "Or revel in the intoxicating scent of jasmine as it drifts by on a sweet breeze from the bay."

She stumbled on a crack in the walk, and he lunged to grab her, stabilizing her with two hands to her waist. "Speaking of intoxication," he said softly, hands lingering while his voice lowered to husky, "I believe the jasmine may be making you tipsy, Miss McClare."

"Sweet mother of mercy," she rasped, grateful no streetlamp was close enough to illuminate the hot flush in her face, "I best keep my eyes on the sidewalk, I suppose."

"And your hand on my arm," he added with a dry smile, crooking his elbow.

"Thank you . . . Nick." She glanced up, studying him through curious eyes. "I didn't mean to make fun of you, you know, about being afraid of the cable car. I just find it rather curious that an armed officer of the law would be afraid of something so harmless."

He slid her a sideways look with the barest of smiles. "Harmless to you, maybe, but you weren't pushed down a steep street in a pram by a wicked cousin at the age of two."

Her mouth fell open. "Oh, Nick, truly?"

"Yep. Flew through the air like a trapeze act gone awry, limp as a rag doll and bloodied up good. To this day I refuse to ride anything that can careen down a hill. Near broke my skull."

"Merciful heavens, you fell on your head?" She paused, palm splayed to her chest and eyes warm with mischief. "So *that's* what happened!"

His gaze narrowed, but it didn't hide a spark of humor. "That explains my fear of cable cars, Miss McClare, but not your sassy mouth."

She tilted her head, eyeing him with a smirk. "I'm afraid that's nothing more than raw, unadulterated talent, sir, laced with a bit of temper." A sobriety settled as she averted her gaze to the street, her voice suddenly softer than before. "But I do apologize, Nick, for treating you like a pompous, pigheaded, overbearing baboon."

His laughter was low and gruff, the sound warming her body more than the shawl. "And I apologize for treating you like a spoiled, stubborn, simple-minded snob."

Her smile bloomed. "Well, see? Then I guess we were both wrong."

He grunted. "Not about the stubbornness, I suspect," he said with a droll smile.

"Mmm . . . you may be right." She closed her eyes to breathe in the familiar scent of the sea and the faint charred smell of cable car brakes. "Oh, I just adore San Francisco," she whispered, drawing in a whiff of something she'd never noticed before—sweet, like the incense at church. "Oh my, that smells nice, what is it?"

Nick's mouth crooked. "Opium, Allison, more addictive than food."

"Oh," she said weakly, a knot shifting in her throat. Her gaze snagged on a street sign, and instantly her focus shot down a narrow cobblestone road. Adrenaline rushed through her veins as her eyes expanded wide. "Stockton Street? Wait—that's Chinatown!" she breathed, heart thudding in her chest. "Oh my, I've always wanted to visit Chinatown, but Mother never let us." Heels skidding to a stop, she whirled to face Nick, a plea in her tone. "Oh, Nick—do you think we could stroll through, just once, so I can see what it's like?"

His profile stiffened along with his grip on her arm. "Forget it—your mother was right. Chinatown is no place for a naïve woman from the upper class. It's not a pretty place."

"But I wouldn't be 'naïve' if I had the chance—"

"No," he said with stern emphasis, his halt on the street so abrupt, she wobbled on her feet. "Or don't you know what that means?"

Her eyes narrowed. "I know what it means out of the mouth of a pompous, pigheaded, overbearing baboon."

His broad shoulders rose and fell with a heavy sigh as he slacked a hip, dropping his hold to gouge the bridge of his nose. "Look, Allison," he said, his manner considerably softer, "I promised Miss Penny I'd see you safely home as quickly as possible, and I assure you, a detour through one of the worst neighborhoods in this city is neither safe nor quick. Not to mention the fact that it's well after dark and you are already late getting home."

It was her turn to sigh, disappointment lacing her tone. "I suppose," she whispered. Her gaze darted down Stockton where a beehive of people buzzed and milled on a cobblestone street lined with tall, ramshackle buildings. Groups of men dressed in dark shift-like jackets congregated in front of storefronts with wooden awnings and massive glass lanterns, their strange dress and exotic faces enticing her to explore. Another wispy sigh left her lips. "I've read all about it in books, but I've so longed to see it for myself."

"Well, this is its border, so take a good, long look, Miss Mc-Clare, because it's likely all you'll ever see as long it's one of the highest crime areas in the city."

She picked up her pace as he tugged her on, his words sending a shiver down her spine. The comforting sound of a church bell suddenly pealed in the air, and her gaze flicked to the old St. Mary's Cathedral looming just ahead. Its Gothic brick bell tower rose like a beacon of hope. "'Son, observe the time and fly from evil,'" she said softly, the inscription under the clock face imparting new meaning. "I suspect that was aimed at those tempted to frequent the bars and brothels in this area."

"No question about that." Nick's voice took on the same hushed note as hers, as if the presence of a cathedral amidst this down-trodden section of the city demanded a reverence that even sin couldn't deny.

They walked in comfortable silence for a while, their breathing more labored as they climbed the steep hill. Closer to Nob Hill, block after city block of meticulously manicured homes began to appear, their lush yards edged with trees and shrubs. Lamplight cast an ethereal glow while locusts and tree frogs provided a summer symphony backdropped by the fading music of the Barbary Coast. A sudden longing arose in Allison to explore this city she loved by night. To stroll the streets on foot rather than peering from the backseat of the Packard. A thrill surged at the thought of doing just that down Market Street, with its imposing wall of skyscrapers like the twelve-story Flood Building or the historic Palace Hotel. An adventure all her own where she could be an integral part of the sea of pedestrians who darted to and fro, oblivious to the blare of horns and clang of cable cars. Or even to revel in the beauty of Union Square by moonlight, one of her favorite places in the entire city. Her excitement rebounded as she tugged on Nick's coat. "Do you know how Union Square got its name?" she asked, a schoolteacher quizzing her student.

"No," he returned, that secretive smile back in place. "How did it get its name?"

"It was built and dedicated by San Francisco's first American mayor, John Geary, in 1850, named for the violent pro-Union rallies that took place here before and during the Civil War."

"You're quite a history buff."

She tipped her chin and offered a shy grin, certain she was glowing more than the streetlamp overhead. "And, I'll have you know, I sat in the very first row when the Dewey Monument was dedicated by President Roosevelt in May."

"My, my, but we do rub shoulders."

She giggled. "Well, Uncle Logan is on the San Francisco Board of Supervisors, of course, so naturally we all sat up front."

"Naturally," he muttered, his tone sharper than before.

She glanced up to see a nerve flicker in his cheek, and for some reason, it dampened her mood. Shaking it off, she continued, trying to make light out of his obvious disdain for her uncle. "Goodness, one would think you bear a grudge against either the president or my uncle."

He grunted. "Well, not the president, that's for sure. I served under him in the war."

The whites of her eyes grew. "You fought in the Spanish-American War?" she whispered.

He slid her a sideways glance. "First U.S. Volunteer Cavalry."

The hinges of her jaw dropped again, Nicholas Barone apparently full of surprises. "Oh my stars—you were with Teddy Roosevelt and the Rough Riders?" she breathed, his stature suddenly soaring as high as the ninety-seven-foot naval monument in the middle of Union Square. "Sweet heavenly days—the Rough Riders are legendary!"

The plane of his handsome face softened with a hint of sadness as he studied her through somber eyes. "No, Miss McClare," he said quietly, "just angry men who hate injustice."

Angry men. Allison fought the inclination to shiver, thinking that described Nicholas Barone a little too well and wishing she knew why.

"Well, you're not breathing too hard," he said, neatly changing the subject when they reached Powell where she lived. "That is, for one who just scaled one of San Francisco's tallest hills." He nodded behind where the city sprawled out before them in an inky sea of lights that matched those glimmering on San Francisco Bay. "But then I guess heights don't bother you living all the way up here on Nob Hill, not with these stunning views."

"No, they don't," she whispered, quite sure that when it came to heights, she could handle Nob Hill and more. But Nicholas Barone? She peeked up at his chiseled profile, his towering frame putting a crick in her neck while her stomach did a little loop. She swallowed hard, well aware she'd be wise to protect both her head and heart when it came to the handsome detective. Because despite the stunning views, she knew all too well—heights like *that* could make a girl dizzy.

8

"Rich dames," he muttered, shooting a narrow gaze over his shoulder at the fancy glass door of the three-story mansion where he'd just dropped off Allison McClare. Cuffing the back of his neck, he issued a harsh grunt and lengthened his strides, desperate to escape the spell of a pretty schoolteacher he had no desire to know better.

Liar.

Okay, okay, desire, maybe, but definitely the wrong kind, prompted by green eyes that sparkled and hair as black as night. His mind strayed to her lush pink lips and that sassy little mole that hovered so very close—like he craved to do—and knew he needed to put as much distance between Miss McClare and himself as humanly possible. His mouth crooked as he bounded down the patterned brick steps flanked by roses and boxwoods. Distance, right.

Like another state.

His legs and fingers twitched as he waited at their curb for a Mercedes-Benz motorcar to pass, determined not to go down *that* road again. A nerve flickered in his jaw. Not the one that led to Nob Hill—the one that led to getting mixed up with a spoiled society princess used to getting her own way. Nope, he'd already learned that lesson the hard way and wasn't interested in another crash course from some la-di-da teacher. The Mercedes chugged by, and Nick loped across the cobblestone street that might as well have been paved with gold for all the wealth lining its curbs. True, Allison McClare didn't strike him as the type of spoiled daddy's girl who'd betrayed him back in Chicago, but Nick was in no mood to take any chances. Miss McClare may pose as a caring philanthropist, deigning to reach out to the disadvantaged and poor, but he knew better. Society dames like her never gave anything of themselves without ulterior motives. His lips took a twist. *Except grief and plenty of it.*

"Barone!"

His muscles calcified to stone when his shoe hit the sidewalk across the street. Nerves taut over the mispronunciation of his name, he peered over his shoulder at an imposing silhouette looming in the doorway of the McClare mansion, light blazing around it like the second coming.

"I need answers," the shadow said in a near growl, "*now.*"

Choking back colorful commentary, Nick didn't know so many muscles could twitch in a body at one time, but if there was anyone who could set his teeth on edge, it was Logan McClare. And quite frankly, after a grueling day, he just flat out wasn't in the mood. He kept walking.

"Another step, Barone, and I'll have your badge."

Nick halted, the urge to spit in McClare's eye so strong, saliva pooled in his mouth.

"*Swear to me, Nick, now—that you won't rock the boat. We can't afford to tip our hand—the payoff is too big . . .*" Nick's eyelids weighted closed at DeLuca's parting words, causing a cramp in his side. *Blast you, DeLuca . . .*

"Inside, now!" The command hung in the air like a threat long after McClare slammed the front door. Nick sucked in a heavy dose of air, fists clenched as he exhaled his fury in a questionable word muttered beneath his breath. Gouging the back of his neck, he stalked across the street, taking his time to mount the steps to the burlwood and glass door he would have bludgeoned with his fist if the archaic butler hadn't opened it first.

"Good evening, Mr. Barone," the man said with a polite nod of his head, no ill feelings evident in his tone or manner from that first day they'd sparred at the school.

"Matter of opinion." Nick strode into the foyer. "And it's Barone, long *e*," he snapped, jerking his hat off his head.

"Right this way, sir." The butler—Hadley, was it?—offered a courteous smile.

"Thanks," Nick mumbled, feeling a prick of guilt over his curt tone. After all, it wasn't this poor joe's fault that Logan McClare was a pompous idiot.

"Mr. Barone," Hadley said, pronouncing his name with a dignity few people ever did.

Hat in hand, Nick charged in, well aware of Allison sitting ramrod straight on the edge of a love seat, eyes downcast and cheeks blooming bright red while she fiddled with her nails. He honed in on Logan McClare, who stood bent over the fireplace to light a cigarette, his back to Nick. "What do you want, Mc-Clare?" Nick bit out, his temper as hot as the tip of McClare's cigarette.

The supervisor turned, exhaling a rush of smoke that filled the room with the scent of wood spice and chocolate, and Nick instantly craved one of those Turkish cigarettes Darla had given him for Christmas. Too deuced expensive for his tastes—like Darla had been. He glared at McClare with as little civility as possible. *Figures.*

"My niece tells me you escorted her home," he said smoothly, assessing him through eyes that glittered with as much suspicion as Nick's. "Thank you."

Nick refused to respond and Logan nodded to the empty sofa while he settled into a cordovan easy chair, his manner cooler, calmer than Nick tended to be when the two butted heads. "Have a seat, Mr. Barone, please. I assure you, I'll make this brief."

"Ba-ro-ne," Nick ground out. "Long *e*."

Logan ignored him with a deep draw of the cigarette before resting his arm on the chair, studying Nick through a curtain of smoke. "Why so late and why did you escort her at all?"

Nick stared. "Excuse me?"

"Uncle Logan, I already told you, I lost track of time and—"

"I understand, Allison," Logan said in a far softer tone, the concern in his eyes obvious. "And you also explained that instead of calling a taxi, you opted to board a common cable car in the worst part of town, something I can hardly believe your mother would allow."

A knot shifted in her throat before she met her uncle's gaze with a repentant one of her own. "She doesn't know," she whispered.

Logan glanced at the clock on the mantel. "Yes, well, she will soon—Rosie tells me they'll be home shortly. But that's not my chief concern at the moment. It was a foolhardy decision to take the cable car—"

"Uncle Logan, please, let me explain—"

The tenderness in his eyes cooled a degree as he halted her with a look. "There will be time enough when your mother walks through that door, young lady, but right now, my concern isn't with you taking the cable car or even Mr. Barone escorting you to the cable car stop in the worst part of town." His eyes frosted to ice as they returned to Nick, tone scathing. "What I want to know, Mr. Barone, is why my niece's usually meticulous appearance is so disheveled?"

Allison's gasp echoed in the room while Nick shot to his feet, blood blasting his cheeks. "Just what are you accusing me of, McClare?"

Logan rose to meet him, jaw to jaw, the tic in Nick's temple keeping time with the one in McClare's cheek. "Why don't you tell *me*, Mr. Barone, since my niece's hastily pinned hair and disheveled shirtwaist suggest she's been manhandled—"

"Uncle Logan, no!" Allison thrust herself between the two, facing her uncle with palms to his chest. "My shirtwaist got soiled when I fell outside the school, and the cable car blew my hair into disarray, that's all—"

"No, that's *not* all," Nick spit out, determined somebody in this hoity-toity household should know the truth. Heaven knows someone needed to keep an eye on Allison McClare, because she obviously couldn't be trusted to take care of herself. "Your niece was—"

She wheeled to face him so quickly, he caught the scent of lilacs while she pleaded with her eyes, hands folded to her chest. "Too clumsy for words," she said in a rush, her wide stare imploring his silence. "Poor Miss Penny had to clean me up and enlist Mr. Barone to accompany me home, so we owe him our gratitude, Uncle Logan, not our accusations."

Logan gripped her shoulders, pivoting her to face him. "You're telling the truth?"

She nodded, black curls bobbing in affirmation.

Nick's gaze trailed from those lustrous locks chaotically reclasped with a gold hair clip, down a shapely silk shirtwaist and fancy cashmere shawl, and knew she was nothing but a magnet for trouble in the streets of the Coast. Oh, she'd hate him if he spilled her secret, no question, but that was for the best anyway because he sure welcomed the distance. He ignored the twinge in his gut that told him he was making a mistake getting involved with this family, but it was clear somebody needed to save Allison McClare from herself.

He steeled his jaw, pretty sure enmity with a rich dame who raced his pulse was far safer than friendship. "She's lying through her teeth," he said calmly, boring into Logan's eyes to make sure he knew he was telling the truth. He ignored her gasp when she whirled to glare, and continued to speak in a curt tone. "She was accosted by two men outside the school who, I assure you from daily reports at the precinct, would have raped, robbed, and left her for dead if Miss Penny hadn't intervened. And if you don't believe me, tell her to take off her shawl."

Tears glittered in her eyes. "How could you?" she breathed.

"Allison?" Her uncle's voice was sharp. "What's he talking about?"

"Nothing," she cried, lips quivering as she seared Nick with a look.

Tired of her games, Nick blasted out an impatient sigh and jerked the edge of her shawl, prompting her shocked cry when he yanked it clear off her shoulder to reveal the torn sleeve. "She was mere seconds away from being raped, *Mr. McClare*," he said, his statement as harsh as the look in his eyes, "and somebody in her family needs to be aware of that."

Wet fury glinted in her eyes. "You promised!"

"I didn't promise anything, Princess," he said, his words a near snarl. He forced himself to be hard and callous in the face of an attraction he knew would bode him no good. His lip curled in a sneer. "I just let you talk your fool head off, so you never even noticed."

Another gasp rent from her lips right before she hauled off and stomped on his Italian oxfords, gaping his jaw. "Get out!" she screamed, raising her heel to bludgeon some more.

"Enough!" her uncle shouted. He spun her around, hands gripped to her shoulders while a nerve pulsed in his temple. "Is this true, Allison? Were you accosted?"

"I . . . I was, Uncle Logan, but I fended them off with the hat pin you gave me for Christmas, I swear!"

Nick's laugh was not kind. "Sure, right after Miss Penny chased them away with her shotgun." He faced Logan dead-on, turning a deaf ear to the ragged breaths that sputtered from his niece. "Face it, McClare, your niece is a loose cannon who needs to be kept on a chain."

"Oooooooh, that's it—where's my hat pin . . ." She rushed to retrieve her hat, fumbling wildly to remove the pin while her face was as red as the scarlet rose that bobbed on top.

She lunged for Nick, and Logan whisked her away with a hook of her waist before she could inflict damage. "Behave, young lady!" Logan said sharply, flinging the pin in her hands onto the coffee table while the little brat flailed and pleaded to poke Nick just once. "I suggest you take your leave, Mr. Barone," he said, his demeanor decidedly cool, "before I unleash my niece. Your honesty is appreciated, but your insults are not welcome here."

Nick grunted and slapped on his Homburg. "Don't have to ask me twice, because pardon my rudeness, but I want nothing to do with either you or your niece." He stormed for the door, halting long enough to toss one final insult over his shoulder, hoping to ensure Allison McClare would hate him for life. "She's nothing more than a spoiled brat who needs a firm hand," he called, punctuating his statement with a hard slam of the door. He plunged his hands in his pockets and descended the steps, grateful to close the door on any chance of a relationship with another society dame.

A firm hand. He issued a grunt that might have been laced with a smile if he wasn't so riled, then grunted again. Or better yet, firm handcuffs.

Preferably without a key . . .

<hr />

"I knew something like this would happen," Logan muttered, soothing his sobbing niece with a gentle caress of her back while she wept in his arms. "Shhh, Allison, it's all right now . . ."

She lunged away, face blotchy and eyes rimmed red. "No, it isn't, Uncle Logan—he's ruined everything!"

Logan fought the twitch of his lips as he braced Allison's arms, her penchant for drama always making him smile. He ducked his head to peer in her eyes. "Barone? As much as I'd like to saddle him with the blame, he did the right thing by telling me about the attack." He lifted her chin with a finger, gaze intent. "Why did you lie, sweetheart?"

"I didn't lie exactly," she whispered, avoiding his eyes, "just postponed the truth a bit."

He exhaled and lifted her jaw. "Look at me." Her eyes slowly raised to his, and his heart constricted at the tragedy in her face, reminding him once again just how fiercely he loved his family. "Then why did you postpone the truth?" he whispered.

Fresh tears swam in her eyes as she nibbled at the side of her lip in that endearing way her mother often did, softening his stance. "Oh, Uncle Logan, you wouldn't understand—you're a man who can come and go as you please, completely free to do whatever you want."

Whatever I want. A dull ache thumped in his chest at the irony of her statement. *Except make your mother fall in love with me.* He released a weary sigh and tugged her over to the sofa, making her sit before he settled back, scooping her close. "And what is it exactly, Allison, that you so desperately want to do?"

She sniffed and burrowed into his side like she so often did as a child. "I want to be free to make my own decisions and live my own life. To give back some of the blessings I've received by reaching out to disadvantaged young women." Her body shivered, and he instinctively tightened his hold. "And to be independent and not beholden to a man . . . ," she whispered, her voice trailing off.

His eyelids weighted closed. *Roger Luepke. Of course.* Guilt stabbed anew that he'd ever allowed his neighbor's apprentice to court his precious niece. What had he been thinking? He hadn't, apparently, given the pain that charlatan wreaked in Allison's life. No, he'd been too consumed with other things—Cassie and Jamie's roller-coaster relationship and his growing feelings for Cait—to pay closer attention to the type of man with whom he allowed his niece to fall in love. The type of man who severed her trust and stole her confidence, making her heart bleed until it was raw. Just like her mother had done to him a lifetime ago when she'd broken their engagement and married his brother . . .

Only I'd deserved it and Allison did not . . .

Expelling a weighty breath, he pressed a kiss to her hair, vowing to keep her safe no matter the cost—both at the Hand of Hope School and in the affairs of her heart. He pulled back to stare in her swollen eyes, tenderly pushing ebony tendrils away from her face. "This is about Luepke, isn't it?" he whispered.

Her chin quivered as she nodded, the heartbreak in her eyes twisting his gut. "I don't trust myself anymore, Uncle Logan, too afraid to take a chance, too scared I'll get hurt. Don't you see? I just can't live like that anymore." She swiped at her eyes with a hint of anger, chin jutting as if to prove her point. "And I won't. Which means I need to strike out on my own as much as possible, maybe even moving into my own apartment closer to the school."

Alarm curled in his stomach. "Allison, no—"

She clutched his hand so tightly, he could almost feel the desperation coursing her veins. "Not right away, mind you, but someday soon down the road, after I build my confidence and earn my independence. But I can't do that with you and Mother holding my hand every step of the way, too afraid for my safety to let me out of your shadows and try my own wings."

"Your safety is nothing to balk at, young lady." His voice held a harsh tremor that exposed his silent fear, that anyone might harm even a hair on the head of those he loved.

"And I totally agree, truly. But please, Uncle Logan, let me learn to defend myself. Give me the freedom to take care of myself while I teach at the school or ride on the cable car."

He sat back against the sofa, his jaw as stiff as the arms he folded across his chest. "And how do you propose to do that, young lady? With nothing more than a hat pin?"

"Yes, but a sharper and larger hat pin, easily accessible in my pocket or pinned to my dress." Her hands clasped in a plea. "And a firearm like Miss Penny has and maybe boxing lessons from Jamie or even carrying that perfume atomizer bracelet you gave me last year."

"Perfume," he said in a flat tone.

She jagged a brow. "Have you forgotten the day you rushed me to the hospital with Daddy when I sprayed Mother's perfume in my eye at the age of eight? Burned like the dickens and blurred my vision too—which, with the surprise factor, would temporarily disarm any attacker."

He shook his head, a smile tugging at his lips. "Only you, Allison." The smile faded into a scowl. "But a gun? I don't think so."

"Miss Penny told me a firearm is a must for any household in the vicinity of the Barbary Coast and that her nephew, the captain of detectives for the 14th precinct, actually taught her how to shoot. Claimed it was the only way he'd allow her to stay in her home—if she promised not to go out after dark and learn to use her husband's old shotgun, which she did."

Logan's lips compressed. "Yes, Harmon and I are close friends, which is the only reason I allowed your mother to purchase that property in the first place. He assured me his aunt's house was on the edge of the Coast, away from the fray, and promised to beef up patrols."

"'Allowed'?" Allison smiled, her eyes finally sparkling with something other than tears. "As if you could have stopped her. You know Mother when her heart is set on something."

"Yes, I know," he said with a faint smile. *Painfully well.* His hand covered hers. "But I'm not sure about a firearm or even Jamie teaching you to box—both are dangerous."

"So is the Barbary Coast, and yet that's where our school is."

"Against my wishes," he said with a grunt.

Allison cocked her head. "Well, I have been reading up on something else that might work," she said carefully, the excitement in her eyes too obvious to miss.

"I'm sure you have." His stern look couldn't mask his affection.

She scrambled to hike a leg beneath her skirt, hands folded like a prayer of hope. "You see, I've been researching this new form of self-defense that originated in the Far East . . ."

His smile crooked. "Chopsticks?"

Her giggle made his heart soar.

"No, silly, something that doesn't require anything but my hands and feet."

"Really." He couldn't help the skepticism that crept in his tone. He held up her hand and then pinched the toe of her tiny shoe. "Pretty small weapons, sweetheart."

Mischief laced her smile as she wiggled her brows. "Not if you know jiu-jitsu."

"Jiu-jitsu?" He squinted, trying to recall where he'd heard the word before.

"Don't you remember Teddy Roosevelt's secretary telling us when we had dinner with him in May how the president's been practicing jiu-jitsu? He said the president brought a Boston jiu-jitsu master to the White House last year to teach him the Japanese art of self-defense and told us that even women and children can learn it."

Logan chuckled. "He also told us Teddy has a habit of skinny-dipping in the Potomac during the winter, young lady, but I'm not sure that's something to emulate."

She nibbled on the edge of her smile, an innocent blush dusting her cheeks. "Uncle Logan, really—I'm serious here. Why, I've even read that some states are encouraging their police officers to learn jiu-jitsu as an excellent means of self-defense."

He drew in a deep breath and slowly released it again. "Well, I'm certainly in favor of anything that can restore your confidence *and* protect you in the process . . ."

She lunged into his arms. "Oh, Uncle Logan, I just knew I could count on you—"

"But . . . ," he said with a firm grip of her shoulders, holding her at arm's length while he gave her a firm look, "there will be conditions, and the biggest obstacle will be convincing your mother—" He glanced up at the sound of the front door and quickly tugged Alli's shawl up over her shoulders. "And mark my words, young lady—*that* won't be easy," he whispered in her ear.

"Oh, yes it will! Mother respects you more than anybody. If you really put your mind to it, you can sway her on just about anything."

No, not everything . . .

"Thank you, Hadley." Caitlyn's voice drifted in from the foyer, and Logan's pulse automatically skipped a beat, picking up pace as always when Caitlyn McClare entered a room. He squeezed Alli's shoulder and stood, stomach looping when Cait paused in the parlour door. "Logan—what a nice surprise. What are you doing here?" Her gaze lighted on Alli, and her smile instantly dimmed as it darted back to him. "Is everything all right?" she asked, a flicker of concern in her beautiful green eyes.

"Relax, Cait, everything's fine. I came by to collect the wallet I left in your billiard room last night when your boys fleeced me in a pool tournament. But Alli, you, and I do need to talk."

"Uncle Logan!" Maddie shot past Cait, Cassie, and Meg to barrel into Logan's waiting arms, swelling his chest with love for this family he adored. Why had he wasted all those years chasing other women when everything he wanted was right here? His eyes met Cait's over Maddie's riot of curls, and he wondered if she felt the spark he always did when their gazes converged. He forced himself to look away to deposit a kiss on Maddie's nose before he set her back down. "How are my girls?"

"Jeepers, Uncle Logan, you should see my dress," Maddie said with a giggle, holding her skirt out as she twirled in a circle. "Cassie says I look like a princess."

"Indeed," Cassie said with a tweak of Maddie's neck. "As does Meg, who, I might add, is growing into a lovely young woman."

"I'll second that." Logan's response prompted a soft blush in

Meg's cheeks. The self-conscious duck of her head made him want to swoop her up like he had Maddie and tell her just how beautiful she really was, but he didn't dare. At an extremely shy seventeen, Meg would only be embarrassed by any attempt to counter her mistaken belief that a full baby face and eyeglasses made her plain and plump. Not to mention the gold dental braces she wore that he'd talked Cait into, touted by a dentist friend as the latest miracle cure for crooked teeth. Cait had decided to send her middle daughter to Paris for her senior year, and Logan was grateful, hoping it would lift her self-esteem and spare further ridicule from cruel students at school. He gave Meg a wink. "You mark my words, Megan McClare, you are on your way to becoming a real beauty." His gaze flitted to Cait's and held. "Just like your mother."

"Well, I certainly concur with Meggie becoming a beauty," Caitlyn said with a self-conscious blush of her own. She gave Meg a tight squeeze, then pressed a soft kiss to her daughter's pale red hair. "Would you be a dear and help Maddie get ready for bed, darling? I need to talk to Uncle Logan and your sister, but I'll be up soon to kiss you both good night."

"Sure, Mother," Meg said with a kiss to Caitlyn's cheek. She extended a hand to her little sister. "Come on, Maddie. You can snuggle with me till Mother comes up."

The little girl gave a short little hop. "Really? And will you read to me from *Jane Eyre* like you did last week?"

"Sure, peanut." Meg led her to the door, sending a tired smile over her shoulder as she stifled a yawn. "Good night, everyone."

"G'night, Megs," Cassie called along with the others. She ambled over to plop down alongside Allison on the sofa. "So . . . did you miss us? Jamie, Blake, and Bram surprised us by treating us to dinner at The Palace, so I bet you're real sorry you didn't go now, aren't you?"

114

Allison's gaze met Logan's, and a lump bobbed in her throat despite the crooked smile that surfaced on her lips. "You have no idea," she said with a playful bump of her cousin's shoulder. She squeezed her hand. "But I was able to get a lot done, so I'm grateful."

"Good." Cassie leaned to give Allison a hug before lumbering up. "Well, I have some class preparations of my own waiting upstairs, so see you in the morning. Good night, all." She hurried over to give Logan a hug and then her aunt before the click of her heels echoed across the marble foyer.

Caitlyn wasted no time. With a faint air of urgency, she immediately shut the double burlwood doors and hurried over to sit beside her daughter on the sofa, arm bracing Allison's waist. "Something's wrong, I can feel it," she said with an uneasy glance in Logan's direction. "What's this all about?"

He released a quiet exhale and settled into his easy chair, the one he claimed when he came for dinner three times a week, which wasn't near as often as he liked. He perched on the edge, arms straddling his legs and hands loosely clasped while he employed the same calm and confident demeanor he exercised in the courtroom. "I think it would be wise to hire an armed watchman until Mr. Bigley returns."

Cait blinked, color effectively draining from her face. Her voice broke on a crack as she clasped Allison's arm. "Why? What's happened?"

Exchanging a quick glance with his niece, he softened his tone. "Cait, Allison is fine, but she did have a minor problem tonight that we need to make sure doesn't happen again."

Cait shifted to face her daughter, hand trembling as she touched Allison's arm. "What kind of problem," she said quietly, her tone almost casual in an obvious effort to remain calm.

"A minor incident, Mother, really," Allison assured with a tentative smile, pulling her shawl tightly about her. "I lost track of time, you see, so it was after dusk when I . . . well, I . . ."

"Spit it out, Allison," Cait said with an impatience seldom displayed. "When you *what*?"

Tendons shifted in Allison's throat. "When I was stopped by . . ." Her voice trailed to a whisper while her face leeched as pale as her mother's, as if the trauma was just now sinking in.

Rarely had Logan seen Cait more taut. "For sanity's sake, Allison, tell me this instant!"

"She was approached by two men," Logan supplied, his tone both gentle and firm. "On the street outside the school, but she managed to fend them off with a hat pin until Miss Penny chased them away."

What color had been left in Caitlyn's cheeks swiftly siphoned out as she stared, horror etched in her face. She clutched her daughter's arms, panic edging her words. "Sweet mother of mercy, were you hurt or . . . or—"

"*Nothing happened*, Mother, I assure you, other than a few scrapes when I stumbled on the cobblestone street."

"Good heavens, Allison, you ventured outside after dark?" Cait's voice rose several octaves. "You know better than that! Why didn't you wait for the taxi to ring the bell?"

"Because I . . ." Her eyes flitted to Logan's and back before she lifted her chin the slightest degree. "I decided to take the cable car instead of a cab."

"What?" Caitlyn shot to her feet, almost teetering as she splayed a hand to her chest.

Allison rose to grip her mother's arms. "Mother, I'm almost twenty-three years old, for heaven's sake, a certified educator with a mind of my own. I can take care of myself."

"Apparently not if you wandered out in a dangerous neighborhood after dark." Caitlyn's fingers shook as they fluttered to the hollow of her throat. "Tell me what happened," she rasped, slowly sinking back onto the sofa while Allison painted a picture of a near-harmless robbery attempt. By the time she finished, the look of horror in Cait's eyes sparked into anger. "Merciful Providence, Allison, whatever possessed you to take such a risk?"

Logan cleared his throat. "I suspect the same thing that possessed you, Cait," he said quietly, pinning her with a probing gaze, "when you opened a school on the Barbary Coast against my advice. An independent spirit and a stubborn streak longer than the cable car tracks that brought our girl home." His smile was wry. "After all, she is your daughter, Mrs. McClare."

A blush stained Caitlyn's cheeks as she jutted her chin with the same obstinacy she'd obviously passed on to Alli. "Don't be ridiculous, I'm an adult, charged by God to be the head of this family."

Allison's voice was tender as she cupped her mother's cheek. "Yes, Mother, but you don't seem to realize I'm an adult too, charged by God to follow my heart, just like you."

Logan's chest constricted when tears pooled in Cait's eyes.

Seizing both the opportunity and her mother's hands, Allison softened her appeal. "Mother, please—all I'm asking for is the freedom to become the woman you want me to be."

Logan watched as the same iron strength of character he loved in Caitlyn slowly emerged in her daughter, back straight and shoulders square. "And the woman I need to be," she said quietly, tears shimmering that matched those of her mother's. "Especially now."

Caitlyn's heart fisted as she stared, seeing herself in the thrust of her daughter's chin, the quiver of her lips . . . the pain in her eyes. Pain caused by betrayal and deception at the hand of a man she loved, and a pain Caitlyn knew all too well. She had been but seventeen when the fiancé she loved with all of her heart—Logan McClare—betrayed her with another woman and then she, too, had taken immediate action. Breaking the engagement, she had determined to become a teacher and fend for herself, unwilling to trust her heart to a man ever again. But her dearest friend at the time—Logan's brother Liam—had altered the course of that decision, wooing her with kindness, friendship, and a gentle love that had deepened and ripened over twenty-six years of marriage. She closed her eyes as more tears welled, but these were for the father of her children and the godly spouse she'd lost to an aneurism almost three years ago. A keen sense of loss and loneliness suddenly overwhelmed her. *Oh, Liam, I miss you every day . . .*

"Mother, do you understand what I'm saying?" Allison said, and Caitlyn's eyelids lifted, the blur of her daughter's face coming into focus despite the tears in her eyes.

She forced a trembling smile, reaching to stroke the worry from Allison's face. "More than you know, darling," she whispered, well aware of Logan's gaze and the regret she'd most likely find there if she dared to glance his way. "And I will respect your wishes, Alli, but only if we can come to terms on ways to keep you safe."

Logan cleared his throat. "Allison has actually come up with some pretty creative ideas, Cait, and I have lunch planned with Captain Peel on Friday as well, so I planned to solicit his help in finding the temporary watchman you mentioned the other night. I think between an armed off-duty law official on the premises and Allison's ideas, we can secure her safety."

"Ideas?" Cait offered Allison a wary look. "What kind of ideas?"

Cheeks flushed with excitement, Allison jumped in before Logan could even respond. "Well, I suggested a firearm—"

"A firearm?" Caitlyn's voice rose on a squeak.

"But I told her that was out of the question," Logan said quickly.

Allison scooted to face Caitlyn, looking more like twelve than twenty-two as she tucked a leg beneath her skirt and tied her shawl in a loose knot at her chest. "Then I suggested an even larger stickpin that I could carry in my pocket or pin to a dress or coat. You know, Mother, like that decorative pin you gave me for my birthday with the lovely gold fleur-de-lis head? Goodness, the point on that is as big as a skewer and just as deadly."

Caitlyn winced at the mental picture.

"Then remember the perfume atomizer bracelet Uncle Logan gave me for Christmas? Well, I promise to wear it at all times, warding off evil with a spray in any attacker's eyes."

Caitlyn blinked, stunned at her daughter's shrewdness with gifts.

"But I've saved the best idea for last," Allison continued with a grin that all but lit up her face. "Remember when Teddy Roosevelt's secretary was telling us about how the president was learning a new art of self-defense called jiu-jitsu?"

Bracing herself, Caitlyn gave a slow nod.

"Well, I've done lots of research, and they say jiu-jitsu moves are so easy and concise that anyone can learn them and guess what?"

Caitlyn worked hard to maintain her serious demeanor, heart swelling with love for this vibrant little girl who was now a woman. "What?" she said, fighting a smile.

Allison all but preened. "Success with jiu-jitsu is not dependent upon size, strength, or speed, which makes it the perfect self-defense mode for both women and children."

"Is that so?" Caitlyn allowed a hint of a smile, tone cautious. "So you can't get hurt learning this jiu-jitsu? There's no danger for the person taking lessons, I hope?"

"Absolutely not," Allison said, green eyes sparkling more than Caitlyn had seen in a long, long while. She wiggled her brows. "Only for the poor scoundrel who raises my ire."

Caitlyn's mouth crooked up. "I'd say that's three-quarters of the male population these days, darling." She sucked in a deep draw of air and expelled it again. "Well, it sounds like we need to find someone to teach you jiu-jitsu then, doesn't it?"

Her daughter's squeal nearly broke her eardrum when she thrust herself into Caitlyn's arms. "Oh, Mother, I love you so much!"

"But—" Caitlyn held Allison at bay—"I want your promise you will never walk to the cable car alone or even step foot on the streets in that neighborhood after dusk, is that clear?"

Allison gave an eager nod.

"And if for some reason you do need to work late, you will let me know and we'll arrange with Mr. Bigley or his replacement to escort you, understood?"

"Yes, ma'am," Allison said, hands clasped to her chin and a squeal imminent, no doubt.

"Well, then I guess it's settled. Let's go to bed." Giving her daughter a hug, Caitlyn rose and sighed, glancing at Logan with a slant of a smile. "And since you helped with the arm twisting, Mr. McClare," she said with a pointed gaze, "I think it's only fitting you round up an instructor who can teach this determined young woman the art of self-defense."

Logan laughed, the husky sound following them to the door. "Me? Twist *your* arm?" The tease in his tone chided her into turning around. "I'd say it's the other way around most of the time, Cait, and I've got the bruises to prove it."

Better a bruised arm than a bruised heart. She hiked her chin, answering his teasing tone with one of her own. "Be that as it may, I'll expect information on both a temporary guard and a jiu-jitsu instructor soon or I just may enlist Rosie to inflict a bruise or two."

"Ouch." Logan grinned before he reached for his fedora and made his way to the foyer. He pressed a kiss to Alli's cheek as his eyes converged with Caitlyn's. "Threat heeded, Mrs. McClare," he said with a formal bow of his head, humor still twitching on his lips. Strolling to the front door, he shot them a smile while he placed his hand on the knob. "I'll start the hunt tomorrow and hopefully have everything arranged by next week. So you can keep your bull terrier on a chain, Cait. Good night, ladies."

"Good night, Uncle Logan," Allison called, "and thank you for your help."

Caitlyn's heart tripped at the look of love in Logan's face as he watched his niece head up the steps. "For my girls? Always." His gaze veered to Caitlyn and held, annoying her when it fluttered her stomach. "And I'll see *you* tomorrow night." Giving a salute, he opened the door.

"Logan!" Her cheeks warmed when her voice echoed in the marble foyer. "Do you . . . do you think the lessons will work?" she asked, looking for reassurance of Alli's safety.

His lazy grin sped up her pulse instead of calming it down. "Mark my words, before we're through, she'll be able to protect herself from any man alive."

Any man alive. Caitlyn swallowed hard and nodded. "Good," she said with a shaky smile, his handsome face lingering in her thoughts long after he closed the door. *Then perhaps I should take lessons as well . . .*

9

"Okay, that's it—too rich for my blood. I need to go home and put my humility to bed." Tossing several dollars on the brass-plated pool table in the billiard room of Caitlyn Mc-Clare's home, Bram Hughes replaced his cue stick in the rack while giving Jamie a wry smile. "Good thing you're marrying a pool shark like yourself, Mac. Somebody who can hustle *you*, or you wouldn't get your head through that door."

Jamie grinned, grateful he could demoralize Bram, Blake, and Logan in pool to make up for the loss of pride when Cassie trounced him on a regular basis in a game in which they both excelled. "Yeah, humility's not too bad as long as you can maintain your pride with your friends, I always say." He chalked his cue with a broad smile, gaze honing in on Blake. "You're next, McClare—payback for beating me in chess the other day."

"Oh, no you don't, MacKenna—I may be lousy at pool, but I'm not stupid." Blake hopped off one of the leather and chrome bar stools he and Logan had dragged over to watch the game. "I'd rather give my money to Duffy at the Blue Moon than line your pockets with a sure win." Lugging his stool back over to the bar, he snatched his suit coat off the counter and slipped it on. "Anybody up for a nightcap? I'm buying."

"Count me in." Bram buttoned his jacket. "I think I'll nurse my pride with a tall ginger ale."

Blake adjusted the sleeves of his coat with a wicked grin. "Nurse it? You mean kill it, don't you, Padre? What you need is a tall, stiff one, my friend. How 'bout you, Uncle Logan—care to join us?"

Logan slid from his stool and began rolling the sleeves of his crisp, white shirt—as casual as he ever got when playing pool with the boys, his perfect four-in-hand tie still in place. "Sorry, Blake—I think I'll take a shot at the hustler tonight. Not because I'm in the mood for a thrashing, mind you, but because I want to pick his brain about something."

"Pick his brain?" Blake gave Jamie a wink. "Why? All you'll find there is puffed pride and hot air."

Bram chuckled as he strolled for the door. "Yeah, but don't forget pride goeth before the fall—Jamie's pride, Logan's fall." He shot a grin over his shoulder as he opened the door. "Followed by Jamie's fall when Logan assigns him the Preston case out of pure spite."

Strolling over to select a cue, Logan laughed and slapped Jamie on the shoulder. "That's certainly a consideration, my boy, so you may want to take it easy on your old employer or I just may do that and more." He tested the weight of the cue with a wink. "Like reassigning Blake's despised Kilcullen case to you."

"Hey, I'm all for that," Blake said, following Bram to the door. He slung an arm over Bram's shoulder as the two of them stood there grinning. "I'd like to see Pretty Boy handle a woman scorned in the divorce debacle of the year."

"No thanks." Jamie smiled and rolled his neck, flexing one hand and then the other. "When it comes to women scorned, your reputation makes you the most qualified, 'Rake,'" he said, emphasis on the nickname he and Bram "Padre" Hughes had assigned the best friend who tended to womanize.

Blake cuffed Bram's shoulder. "I guarantee you, Mac, 'scorn' never enters in, not with the Padre along to lend a shoulder to cry on for any heartbroken ladies." He offered a salute. "Break a cue, Uncle Logan—preferably over Mac's head. G'night, all."

"Good night, boys—see you tomorrow," Logan called while chalking his cue.

Grateful for time alone with Logan, Jamie set up once again, rolling the balls until the cluster was nice and tight. When he finished, he twirled the cue in hand, giving his employer a cheeky grin. "Just so I don't look too eager for the Kilcullen case, boss, how about we forgo the coin toss and I let you have the break?"

Logan chuckled and moved to the head of the table, taking careful aim with his cue. "Wise move, counselor," he said with a focused squint, apparently sizing up the angle of the shot he wanted to take. Stance casual, he leaned over the end of the table with an open-hand bridge, breaking the balls with a loud crack.

"Holy cow," Jamie muttered when three balls spun off into pockets so fast, his jaw dropped along with his confidence. "Where did you learn to shoot like that?"

Humor twinkled in Logan's eyes. "From your fiancée, Mac, who's getting tired of being the only one who can put you in your place." He rechalked his cue and studied the table, obviously assessing his best angle. "Cassie's been teaching me some of her shots."

A grin slid across Jamie's face as he shook his head. "Has she now? Well, then, I'm going to have to have a little talk with your niece, sir, to put an end to these treasonous tendencies of hers. Especially once we're married."

Logan chuckled and took another shot, sinking two balls in the process. "I suspect she's just looking for ways to keep you humble since you seem to conquer everything you set your mind to." He peered up from where he stood bent over the table, cue stick in position. "I know you show no mercy in the courtroom, billiard room, and in the boxing ring, Mac, but what do you know about jiu-jitsu?"

Jamie blinked when Logan put away two more balls. He glanced up, eyes in a squint. "Jiu-jitsu? You mean the self-defense technique President Roosevelt's been touting?"

Logan cocked a hip, both hands resting on the standing cue before him. "Yeah—what do you know about it?"

Scratching the back of his head, Jamie gave it serious thought. "Well, I've heard talk of it at the Oly Club, of course, but I don't really know much about it nor anybody who does. Why?"

Logan finished off the eight in a neat, clean swish and stood up straight. "Because I promised Cait I'd find somebody to teach Allison for extra protection when she works late at the school."

Releasing a low whistle over Logan's easy win, Jamie proceeded to dig the balls out of the pockets, making a mental note to speak to his fiancée about teaching trick shots to anybody but him. "Nice game, sir—care to go two out of three?"

"That may be stretching my luck, Mac, but I'll give it a whirl."

Jamie racked the balls once again, then stepped aside to let Logan take the winner's first shot. "What about boxing? Alli hounded me awhile back to teach her to box, so I showed her a few steps, although I didn't take it too seriously. But if you want me to, I will."

Another crash of ivory echoed in the room on Logan's next break, pocketing only two balls this time. "Thanks, I appreciate that, but I'm looking for something where she can defend herself from anyone bigger and stronger should the need arise, and where the element of surprise is a key factor."

Jamie grinned. "Pardon my saying so, sir, but 'surprise' is always a key factor with Alli. She near broke my leg when she hauled off and kicked me in the shin after I refused to teach her any more than I did."

Bent low over the table, Logan took his next shot, managing to sink another ball. "Yes, she's a feisty one and a lady you don't want to cross if you can help it." He let loose with a noisy sigh as he rose to his full height, kneading the bridge of his nose. "Not unlike her mother, I'm afraid."

"Or her Texas cousin," Jamie said with a chuckle, thoughts of Cassie warming his heart. He perched on the corner of the table with cue stick in hand and studied Cassie's uncle, the man who had become both mentor and friend and whose approval he craved more than any other. Jamie paused to draw in a deep breath, hesitation in his voice. "And speaking of Mrs. McClare, sir, . . . have you . . . given any thought as to when you might tell her?"

Logan glanced up, eyes suddenly intense. "Close the door, Jamie, will you?"

Hopping up, Jamie promptly did as he was told, returning to prop himself on the corner of the table once again, waiting for Logan to speak.

With a heavy exhale, Logan returned to his stool, shoulders slumped and both hands gripped to the vertical cue as it stood slack between his legs. A muscle flickered in the chiseled lines of his cheek, a key indicator just how difficult this subject was for him. "I have, Jamie, and just when I think the time might be right, something derails me—burdens on Cait like a recent incident at the school or Megs leaving in two weeks for a year in Paris." His shoulders rose and fell with another weighty sigh that suddenly seemed to sap his good mood and energy. "I don't want to add to her troubles at a time when she needs my strength, not news that will deplete it, so I've just been biding my time."

"I understand, sir."

Logan cuffed the back of his neck, his body suddenly sagging as if the weight of his long-held secret would destroy him too. "Of course, she has no idea just how vested I've been in various establishments on the Barbary Coast either, which is another fly in the ointment that's sure to upset her. Especially now that certain members of the Vigilance Committee are pressuring her to escalate the timetable on phase two in the cleanup of the Coast. So timing and favor with Cait is critical right now to forestall any heavy restrictions on taverns that offer gambling like the Blue Moon."

Jamie's pulse thudded to a stop. His heart clenched at the thought of anything affecting Logan's investment in the tavern that provided jobs for Jamie and his mother over the years and where his mother still worked as a cook. "They wouldn't close Duffy down, would they, sir?"

"Not if Cait sticks to the schedule she convinced me to present to the Board of Supervisors last year, which gives us enough time to go after the primary offenders such as the brothels and dancing halls instead of legitimate businesses like Duffy's." Logan slashed fingers through his usually meticulous hair, further evidence of his emotional stress. The man was always cool and controlled in the courtroom and out, his appearance as deadly calm as his words. But not this time. Jamie released a slow, wavering breath. Not when it came to Caitlyn McClare.

Venting with another weary exhale, Logan rose to his feet, meeting Jamie's gaze dead-on, his love for his family as clear as the gray of his eyes—transparent pools of deep affection and honest regret. "I promise you, Jamie, I will do everything in my power to protect Duffy and your mother's job before the truth comes out, but it will come out, you have my word."

Jamie's heart swelled with love and respect for the man before him, the man who'd been everything to him since he'd first met him at the Oly Club in college—friend, role model, mentor, teacher, employer ... and as close to a father as a man could get. His throat thickened with emotion. "I trust you, sir, in any decisions you choose to make."

A sheen of moisture glimmered in Logan's eyes for the briefest of moments before he quickly looked away, rechalking his stick with a vengeance. "Thank you, Jamie," he said in a gruff voice that betrayed the emotion he seldom displayed. "That means the world to me."

He circled the table to survey his next shot, finally positioning his cue with a hand as steady as his voice, which was now back in control. Slanted low over the far edge, he paused, glancing up to give Jamie a crook of a smile. "*Now* ... whether I'm lucky enough to ever beat you at pool again or not, if we can just get Mrs. McClare to follow suit on the trust factor?" He cut loose with a shot that hit dead-on, his smile veering toward dry. "I'll be the luckiest man alive."

⚬⚬ ⚬⚬

"Barone—the captain wants to see ya—*now!*" One of the new crop of freshly scrubbed officers stuck his head in the interrogation room where Nick and his partner were a hair's breadth away from coercing Jimmy O'Toole to rat on a friend.

Nick glanced over his shoulder with a scowl. "Tell him I'm busy on the Dead Man's Alley homicide and I'll be there when I'm done."

"Sorry, Lieutenant, but the captain said this can't wait."

Venting with a near growl, Nick gouged the bridge of his nose with blunt fingers before pushing away from the table, the wooden chair groaning in protest. Blast it all, Friday afternoons were hard enough in the Barbary precinct with a week of felonies and misdemeanors piled high and a weekend of carousing looming ahead. He sure didn't need the captain pulling rank this close to cinching a case. He rose and snatched his jacket off the back of the chair, tone as threatening as the look he gave the pimple-faced punk slouched with his head in his hands. "I'm out of patience, slimeball. If you haven't spilled what you know by the time I get back, we'll toss your sorry hide in the cage and book you for manslaughter, you got it?"

Nick banged the chair in with a grunt. "You can waste your time if you want, Flynn, but the punk's yellow and I'm through pussyfootin'. I'll have the paperwork to toss him in the cage when I get back." He stalked out of the room and slammed the door. The show of temper was no act as he stormed down the hall to the captain's office, bumping the shoulder of some baby-faced recruit he passed who looked younger than O'Toole. Not bothering to knock, Nick hurled the captain's door open, quivering the wood and opaque glass frame as it ricocheted off the wall. "What's the all-fire hurry, Harm?" he said, taking advantage of their friendship. "I thought Dead Man's Alley was a priority." He glared at his superior, not giving a whit about the bigwig in a tailored charcoal morning coat in one of the captain's worn leather chairs.

Lips compressed in the barest of smiles, Captain Harmon Peel assessed Nick with the same patient air as always when his top detective came crashing through his door. Easily fifteen years Nick's senior, Harmon Peel had proven to be not only an honest and able police official, but a good friend as well, one of the few Nick could trust in a precinct where cops on the take were as common as fleas in the jail. Despite a black handlebar moustache and stocky build, hints of Miss Penny's features could be seen in blue eyes that sported an abundance of wrinkles. The smattering of gray at his temples seemed to have grown since Nick joined the precinct a year ago, but that was to be expected in a district where prostitution, gambling, drugs, and alcohol were primary modes of survival. Harmon waved a hand at an empty chair in front of his scarred wooden desk. "Close the door and take a load off, Nick, I have a proposition for you."

"No thanks, Captain—the only proposition I'm interested in is stringing up the lowlife who snuffed out Sadie Merton's life."

The planes of Captain Peel's affable face hardened into a tight smile as taut as his tone. "It wasn't a request, Barone, it was an order. *Sit*."

Nipping the colorful retort straining on the tip of his tongue, Nick heaved the door closed, vibrating both the glass and the wall this time before he dropped in the leather chair next to the dandy already seated. Exhaling a noisy breath, he gave no more than a cursory glance at the man beside him, but it was more than enough. He shot to his feet, knuckles white and palms flat as he slanted forward on Harmon's desk. "A proposition with *him*? Not on your life, Harm—I want nothing to do with a high-rolling board member who votes with his bank account."

Harmon Peel silently rose like impending doom, the flicker in his jaw matching the one in Nick's cheek. His voice was lethal and low, a level he usually reserved for the baby-fuzz patrolman fresh on the beat. "Another word and you'll be directing traffic and policing cable cars for pickpockets, Barone, right after a stint in the cooler, is that clear?"

Grinding a stinging retort into his tongue, Nick chose rigid silence over vaulting the desk.

"I said—is-that-clear?"

Nick's temple was throbbing so hard, it could have been Morse code. *"Yes,"* he bit out, the word sounding more like a curse than a response.

"Now sit down and shut up, Nick, and listen for once instead of going off half-cocked like a loaded gun in the hands of one of those squeaky-voiced goggle-eyes I just hired."

Twitch in his cheek, Nick made him wait before he finally dropped back in the chair.

Harmon drew in a deep breath and released it again. He slowly reclaimed his seat with a steel-edged authority as sharp as the cold knife of threat Nick felt lodged in his back. "Logan McClare is not only a presiding member of this city's top government author-ity but one of my closest friends, in addition to being a highly respected member of this community. In the future, Detective Barone, you will address him as 'Supervisor McClare' in a tone worthy of his status, understood?" He paused, obviously expecting Nick's consent, which came in the form of a grunt.

"Good." Huffing out a weary sigh, the captain leaned back with a squeal of his chair. "Sorry about that, Logan, but he hails from Lower Manhattan—Little Italy—where civil discourse is appar-ently extinct." He folded his hands on a barrel chest, ignoring Nick as if he weren't singeing him with a glare two feet away. "Hired him as a favor to a friend of a friend a year ago, but for all his surly disposition, he's the best and toughest cop in this precinct."

"Only after you, Harm," Logan said with a warmth Nick didn't know the man possessed. "I just hope you're tougher than he is because we'll need something to keep him in line."

A nerve pulsed in Nick's face. "Excuse me, *sir*, but I'm not deaf, dumb, and blind."

Harm's gaze finally veered to Nick with a smile. "Well, not

deaf anyway," he said with a chuckle. He turned back to McClare. "Yeah, I'm tougher than him, but only because he needs to eat. But I gotta be honest, Logan, I hate to lose him as a detective even for a short time. He's first-rate and has solved more crimes in the last year than the rest of my staff put together. But if you can overlook his crotchety manner, well, then I guess he's your man."

Logan shifted in his chair to face him, and his cool smile told Nick he was enjoying the upper hand despite the hard line of his sculpted jaw. With a casual confidence that got on Nick's nerves, he appeared to be the ultimate solicitor, inside the courtroom or out, unruffled and in control. Not a strand was out of place on thick dark hair peppered with gray at the temples, and the near-cavernous cleft in his chin and easy good looks explained his reputation as one of the city's most eligible bachelors. Nick's facial muscles stretched taut. Yeah, that and the fact he was filthy rich and politically connected.

He assessed Nick through cool eyes the color of iced pewter. "I'd like to commission your services, Mr. Barone."

Nick slid him a sideways sneer. "To put a leash on your scatterbrained niece so she doesn't get in trouble again?"

"Barone . . ." Harmon's tone held a warning. "One more slur and your next paycheck is mine."

Better than working for an arrogant blue blood. The tendons in his neck felt ready to snap. "Yes, sir."

A faint smile played on Logan's lips as he relaxed in his chair with arms folded across a meticulous silk waistcoat and crisp linen shirt. "You're more astute than you appear, Detective, although I prefer the term 'high-spirited and adventurous' when it comes to my niece." Genuine affection flickered on his face for a split second while slate-colored eyes trailed into a faraway stare, his eyes as soft as his tone. "Allison is a remarkably rare young woman."

Nick buried a grunt. *And it's a good thing, the way she wields a stick.*

"But," he said with a lift of his chin, a counselor in control once again, "your disdain for me and my niece is exactly why I believe you're the perfect candidate for what I have in mind."

Candidate?? Nick gritted his teeth to contain all further insults. *"Victim" is more apt if your niece is involved.* He felt the captain's stare drill a hole in the side of his head, forcing his words past the clench of his teeth. "If I may be so bold, *sir*, perfect candidate for what?"

Logan grinned as if what he was about to say gave him great satisfaction. "Why, the perfect guardian, teacher, and handyman for the Hand of Hope School, Mr. Barone."

Nick stared, jaw slacking into stupor mode. "In case it's slipped your notice, *Supervisor McClare*, I already have a job."

The grin faded into a formidable smile. "Yes, Mr. Barone, I know—working for me."

Nick shot to his feet, palms strained flat on Harmon's desk once again. "What's he talking about, Captain?"

"Sit down, Nick," Harmon said with more patience than Nick would possess in a lifetime. He nodded to Nick's chair and waited for him to comply. "After the incident where the supervisor's niece was accosted, I'm sure you understand his concern to make sure it doesn't happen again."

"Yeah, but the solution is so simple, a moron could figure it out." Nick cocked his head. "Tell her to stay inside after dark on the Barbary Coast, *Supervisor McClare*, all cozy-comfy and safe."

A chuckle parted from Logan's lips as he absently scratched the back of his neck, gaze on the floor. "Well, I'm afraid nothing is 'simple' when it comes to my niece, Mr. Barone, or with her mother, for that matter." He glanced up, affection lacing his smile once again. "Beautiful women both, but cut from different cloth than most. Fragile hearts and hard heads, independent and stubborn to the point of feisty, but as soft and gentle as newborn kittens." The grin was back. "But you'll want to steer clear of the claws if you step on their tails."

One side of Nick's lip angled up. "Yeah, and I got the scars to prove it."

"Well now, see there, Nick?" Logan reached to slap him on the shoulder with a low chuckle, an action meant to disarm him, no doubt. And it was working—a realization that steeled Nick's jaw all the more. "You and I have something in common after all, eh?" He sat back, arms on the chair and eyes squinted in calculation. "So . . . I came to see the captain today because I need a watchman and handyman for the school until Mr. Bigley returns."

Nick's gaze flicked to Harm and back, forehead bunched in annoyance. "No offense, Supervisor McClare, but why me? Any officer with a firearm can provide protection and most are handy enough. Some might actually enjoy working with a time bomb like your niece."

Logan chuckled. "Yes, any officer can supply armed protection and handle odd jobs, I suppose, not to mention jump at the chance to double his salary working with beautiful women for a brief span. And who knows—maybe even aspire to snag the heart of a wealthy young girl in the process." He crossed his arms, then propped one fist to his mouth, assessing Nick through pensive eyes. "But Captain Peel assures me no one but you possesses the unique skills I need to ensure my niece's physical and emotional safety as well as my peace of mind."

Nick quirked a brow. "The ability to step on her tail?"

A slow smile inched across Logan's face. "Partially."

"Come again?" Nick's gaze thinned.

"You just made the point yourself, Nick. You can't abide my niece and she can't abide you. It only took thirty seconds to see the discord between you two, which is exactly what I need." A granite-like hardness settled over the supervisor's features, marking him as a formidable foe—obviously out of the courtroom as well as in. "Or what *Allison* needs, actually, at least right now. Regrettably the girl's had her heart stomped on more times than I care to admit, and I'm looking for someone with no interest in either her or her money."

Nick grunted. "Well, that shoe certainly fits."

"Yes, it does, Mr. Barone, but the most important reason I want to hire you makes you the perfect fit all around, head to toe."

"And what would that be, Supervisor?" Nick said with a stiff smile, playing nice before he told him what he could do with his high-priced patsy job.

"I want you to teach my niece jiu-jitsu."

Nick blinked. "Pardon me?"

"Jiu-jitsu, Nick," he said with an easy stretch of his arm over the back of the chair. "Harm tells me you picked it up in the war and have trained several of the officers here."

Nick actually smiled. *Teach a woman? Jiu-jitsu? The man is out of his mind.* He shook his head, certain McClare was as loony as his cockamamie niece. *Runs in the family, apparently, probably from generations of intermarriage.* He cleared his throat. "Uh . . . I appreciate your confidence in me, sir, but I don't teach women jiu-jitsu."

Challenge gleamed bright in Logan McClare's eyes like new-minted money. "Not even for triple your salary?"

Nick bolted up, teeth clenched so hard, he had to pry them open just to bite out the words. "Not-even-for-triple-*your*-salary, *sir.*" He stood to his full six-foot-four height, once again infuriated at the gall of wealthy men like McClare who thought they could buy people to do their bidding. Like ex-Governor Gage and Mayor Schmitz obviously bought the Board of Supervisors with the Chinatown quarantine, ultimately costing his friend Ming Chao the life of his grandson. He singed Logan with a withering glare. "Unlike some people, Supervisor, I can't be bought."

"Okay, Barone, that's a week's salary to the police fund," the captain snapped. He arched a brow. "Care to make it two?"

Nick gritted a response through his teeth. "No."

"Good, because I'm not giving you a choice here, Nick—it's either commit to working for the supervisor or turn in your badge—it's as simple as that."

Nick gaped, facial muscles slack. "You wouldn't do that, Harm."

The captain scratched the front of his neck, expression steeped in regret. "Wouldn't want to, but this precinct owes Supervisor McClare a debt of gratitude. He's our biggest ally—"

"And *your* friend . . . ," Nick spit out.

The captain vented with a heavy blast of air and leaned back in his chair, hands folded on his chest while he peered up with a tired expression. "Yes, Logan and I are good friends, but more importantly, he's an influential member of our governing body, Nick, and a man I respect and admire. Just like I respect and admire you. But when I agreed to hire you, I was assured you were willing to start anywhere, do anything—"

"And I have," Nick shouted, slamming his fist on Harmon's desk. He'd give anything to just walk, but DeLuca's warning grafted his feet to the floor. *"You have no choice but to lay low, Nick, till our guns are loaded and ready to fire."*

"Yes, you have, and you're a good detective, but I need a man who can follow orders, and if that's not you, then there's the door."

It took everything in him not to spin on his heel and leave both of them in his dust, but Nick knew that wasn't an option. Not if he wanted the payoff, and he and DeLuca had worked too hard to get this far. Blasting out his frustration, he glared at Harm, ignoring McClare altogether. "One month, and I still work my cases while school is in session during the day."

"Two months," Logan said calmly.

Nick all but scorched him with a scowl. "Six weeks, Supervisor— take it or leave it."

Harmon glanced at McClare, who gave a short duck of his head. Logan's eyes locked on Nick in unspoken threat. "If six weeks is enough time to teach Allison what she needs to know."

"It is." Nick stared him down, a tic pulsing in his cheek like the one in McClare's jaw.

The supervisor studied him with cool deliberation. "Good, and you're responsible for escorting her home after jiu-jitsu lessons three times a week." His tone softened as the barest hint of a smile shadowed his lips. "I think you'll find Allison an able student, Mr. Barone. As a little girl, she tended toward the tomboy. A competitive streak and an almost reckless thirst for adventure that's given more than one gray hair to her mother and me, I can tell you that. She's fiercely athletic, and if she were a boy, she'd give you a run for your money."

Nick grunted. "Already has."

Logan's tone turned crisp. "As far as the school, you're on duty first thing in the morning, during lunch recess outside, and back before the last class ends, remaining until everyone is home safe and sound, including my niece. And, of course, all handyman projects must be completed in a timely fashion to Mrs. McClare's satisfaction."

"Agreed." Nick met his gaze with a hard threat of his own. "For ten times my salary—"

The captain launched to his feet. "You're out of your mind, Barone—"

Logan interrupted, an edge of challenge in his voice as he slowly rose to his feet, his demeanor as cool as his tone. "No, Harmon, let him set the terms—my family is worth it. If Mr. Barone is willing to agree to six weeks' employment as the school's watchman, handyman, and jiu-jitsu instructor for my niece come Monday, then he's worth it too." He faced Nick head-on, assessing him through narrow eyes. "That is, if he's willing to provide extra protection for Allison whenever she's on the premises or on her way home."

A nerve flickered in Nick's jaw before he finally nodded his consent.

"Good." Logan folded stiff arms across his chest. "Then I suppose there are only two conditions yet to be met, Mr. Barone, and I'll need your word on both."

Nick's lip curled in sarcasm. "What, I can't use a leash?"

Logan actually chuckled. "No, Mr. Barone, although I understand how that might make your job easier." He sat on the edge of Harm's desk with a faint smile. "You can't let her know."

Shifting his stance, Nick stared, head dipped. "Pardon me?"

"You see, independence is very important to Allison," Logan said calmly, "and I don't want her to know part of your job at the school is to keep an eye on her, to protect her so to speak, escort her home after jiu-jitsu or follow her unaware on nights she chooses to work late."

Nick's face screwed in a squint. "And just how am I supposed to keep that quiet, *sir*, when I'll be shadowing her wherever she goes?"

"You're a bright man, Nick, figure it out. Convince her you're a gentleman who refuses to allow a lady to walk home or use a cable car by herself."

Cable car? The very words jammed in Nick's throat, churning the acid in his gut.

Logan smiled. "Although my second condition will definitely make the first a challenge."

Nick remained silent, unable to speak for the blockage of air in his lungs.

Any semblance of humor on Logan's face faded away . . . along with Nick's peace of mind as the supervisor's gray eyes took on a steely glint. "You are under no circumstances to ever lay a hand on my niece except in those cases necessitated by jiu-jitsu lessons, is that clear? And I want your word *and* your signature that you will not make advances."

Nick started to hack, acid choking in his throat as much as the thought choked in his mind. *Advances? To Allison "Whack 'em Till They Weep" McClare?* "Are you crazy?" he sputtered. "I may be a lot of things, *sir*, but suicidal isn't one of 'em."

Logan remained unfazed by Nick's flippant manner. "Glad to hear that, Nick, because suicide is an apt description if I even suspect a glimmer of romantic interest between you two."

A grunt rolled from Nick's lips. "Yeah, well it's not me you have to worry about, Supervisor, but I take no responsibility for any featherbrained ideas rolling around in her head."

Logan's lips pressed thin. "You better take responsibility, Barone, because I want Allison to despise you as much as you despise me."

Nick seared him with a hard look. "Not possible, sir, but I promise it'll be close."

"Good." The edge of Logan's mouth tipped. "Much as I hate to say it, you're the type of man who turns women's heads, so I'm asking you point blank to . . ." A grin inched across his lips as he kneaded the bridge of his nose. "Hang it all, I can't believe

I'm even saying this, but ..." He glanced up, a glint of humor in his eyes. "Keep any 'charm' you may possibly possess under wraps around Allison because she seems to have a weakness for smooth talkers."

"Come on, Logan, you even know this guy?" The captain grinned. "He speaks in grunts."

Logan's eyelids narrowed, assessing Nick as if he could peer into his very soul. "You know, Harm, my gut tells me one of Mr. Barone's greatest assets is the fact people underestimate him. They see this crusty, hard-nosed cop and assume he's a half-wit, but in my line of work, I've learned not to assume anything. So I'm asking again, Mr. Barone ..." He offered a handshake, challenge in his eyes. "Do I have your word you won't make advances to my niece?"

Nick stared at the hand before him, visions of Allison Mc-Clare's ebony hair, angelic face, and inviting lips flitting through his brain, twitching his nerves. Steeling his jaw, he gripped Logan's hand with more force than necessary, quite sure he'd never be in agreement with the man more. "Carved in stone," he said, tone clipped, "or so help me, you can cut out my tongue."

Logan laughed. "Don't think I won't." Reaching behind him, he shoved a two-page document to the front of Harmon's desk. "But to safeguard us both, I've taken the liberty of drafting a contract outlining the terms we've just discussed." He removed an expensive ink pen from inside his jacket and scratched in the revised salary on both sheets before initialing them and offering the pen to Nick. "Hopefully this document will ensure I won't have to."

Nick snatched the pen and then the paper from the desk. "Lawyers," he muttered, scowling as he read every single line. He slashed his signature in the appropriate place and tossed the pen on top. "I bet you draft a contract for everything you do, counselor. Meticulous to a fault to ensure your payback is secure."

"As a matter of fact I do," Logan said with an easy swipe of his pen into his coat pocket. "Except with my family." His eyes hardened like gray quartz. "With them, payback is never necessary because they mean the world to me, and I will do anything or destroy anyone to protect them." He handed the second sheet to Nick. "Your copy of our agreement, Mr. Barone."

Jerking it from his hand, Nick glanced at Harmon. "Are we through here?"

"Almost." Logan glanced at his watch. "Since this is late Friday, you'll start Monday morning, eight sharp, which is when Mrs. McClare arrives with my nieces. But I'd like you to stop in tonight to introduce yourself after school lets out, which I believe is in twenty minutes." He peered up, arms folded once again. "Have you had the pleasure of meeting Mrs. McClare?"

Pleasure? Nick's lips went flat. *Not if she's anything like her daughter.* "No."

Gaze averted to the floor, Logan's professional air softened with the flicker of a smile. "Caitlyn McClare is one of the most remarkable women you'll ever meet." The smile faded as quickly as the kindness in the man's tone when his eyes lifted to Nick once again. "My sister-in-law and her daughters and niece are the only women alive who have my ear, Mr. Barone, so I suggest you tread lightly and see to it there are no complaints."

Nick's mouth took a hard slant. "Even from your 'independent' niece?"

The smile was back. "No, I expect plenty of complaints from Allison, but they best be about your lack of charm, Detective, and not your teaching skills." He stood and extended a hand. "It's a pleasure doing business with you, Nick."

Nick ignored the gesture and adjusted the sleeves of his coat. "Well, that makes one of us, counselor. And if it's all the same to you, I'd like half my salary now, delivered to the station Monday before the end of the day, then the rest after the last lesson."

Tone casual, Logan folded his copy of the contract in thirds and slipped it inside his coat. "I think that can be arranged." His lips curved in a smile. "Afraid I won't pay?"

"Not at all, Supervisor," Nick said on his way to the door, thinking Logan's money wouldn't make up for Ming Chao's grandson, but it'd be a start for his grieving old friend. "You'll pay all right." He never bothered looking back, slamming the door behind him.

Through the nose and more.

10

"eepers, Miss Alli, you really mean it? We're gonna have a real,
honest-to-Pete play?" The whites of Heidi Abbott's blue eyes
grew as big as her two elbow patches, both as faded and worn as
the dirty calico dress they held together.

Allison laughed, her excitement equal to each of the giggling
girls in her English/Drama class. Sunlight streamed through the
shiny windows that Mrs. Lemp kept spotless, spilling across the
polished wood floor while excited chatter spilled from the lips
of each of her eight students, ages six to sixteen. The rumble of
footsteps overhead reminded her school was now at an end, and
Allison couldn't help a tinge of regret. She'd come to love the ragtag
band of students who tromped through the halls, always regretting
when Mother rang the bell at the end of each day. Throughout
the course of their first week, word of mouth had caused their
ranks to grow, and now thirty-two eager young women attended
Monday through Friday, thirsty to learn, including Miss Penny's
ten. Shocked and delighted with the numbers, Mother had already
begun her search for an assistant principal to help out in the office
when Vigilance Committee duties called her away. Allison had
never seen her happier. Like a schoolgirl herself, Caitlyn McClare's
cheeks bloomed with the soft blush of purpose and pride, and
Allison had to admit—the glow was catching.

"Of course I mean it," Allison said with a chuckle. She closed her brand-new copy of *Shakespeare's Comedies, Histories and Tragedies* and stood to her feet, rounding her desk to hand out homework. "After all, what good would it be studying Shakespeare's plays if we didn't at least attempt one of our own? Especially with such a fine theater, right?"

"Right!" The class of eight shouted in unison.

"Can I be in it too, Miss Alli, please?" Lottie bounced in her seat, bobbling the cinnamon-colored curls on her head.

"Of course you can, La-di-da. Everyone who wants to play a part certainly can."

"But who will watch the play, Miss Alli?" Ten-year-old Shannon Murphy blinked, serious brown eyes wide with concern amid a sea of freckles. She slapped a chestnut pigtail over her shoulder. "If we're going to have a play, somebody has to watch."

Allison paused, aware that most of the girls in the school were either orphans or the daughters of women who worked in the brothels, neither of which allowed for an abundance of family members to invite. "Well," she said with a chew of her lip, thoughts scrambling to come up with live bodies, "not everyone in the school will be in the play, of course . . ." The seed of an idea suddenly sprouted and she caught her breath, a grin inching across her face. *But if the play were a fundraiser and Mother invited people she knew . . . ?* A giggle broke loose and she clapped her hands. "I have an idea that just might bring in an audience, but I'll need to discuss it with Mrs. McClare first, so let's just see what happens, okay?"

"Yay!"

"But what play will we perform?" asked Angi Griffis, the shy sixteen-year-old beauty who'd lived with Miss Penny since the age of six, after her mother was murdered in a brothel.

"Well, since comedies are more fun than dramas," Allison

said, "how about what we're studying next week—*A Midsummer Night's Dream?*"

"But I liked what we studied this week, Miss Alli," Kara Grant said with a crimp of brows. "*Taming of the Shrew* was funny, so can't we do that instead? Please, please?" Hands clasped in prayer, the little dickens begged with her eyes.

"Yes!" The consensus came back in an outbreak of squeals.

"But there are boy parts," ten-year-old Denise Hogan said with a scrunch of her nose. "I don't like boys—they're nothing but pests and they smell bad."

"Denise Therese Hogan!" Allison said with a cock of her brow, fighting the squirm of her lips. "That is *not* a nice thing to say." *Except about Nick Barone.* "And they do *not* all smell bad, young lady," she emphasized with a lift of her chin, thoughts of Mr. Ga-roan pinking her cheeks. *Unless you have an aversion to Bay Rum and animal crackers . . .* Pushing thoughts of Mr. C.P. from her mind, Allison pursed her lips. "Besides, all of Shakespeare's plays have men in them and since we don't have any men here, some of you will just have to play the boys' parts."

"What about Mr. Nick?" Lottie suggested. "Petruchio's handsome, and so is Mr. Nick."

"Oh, yes, he's gorgeous!" Angi said with a dreamy sigh. "And perfect."

Alli's smile went flat. *Yes, a natural bully.* She cleared her throat. "I think we need to stick with something a little lighter like *A Midsummer Night's Dream,*" she said loudly, hoping no one would notice the fire in her cheeks over mention of the Neanderthal who'd broken his promise. And he called *her* a loose cannon— ha! Oh, if only she were! She'd have promptly blasted that nasty look off his handsome face when he'd called her a liar in front of Uncle Logan. She stifled a grunt, thinking the barbarian would make a perfect Petruchio—browbeating Kate into submission with his club. Clapping her hands to get the girls' attention, she raised her voice over both giggles and whines. "I'll have copies of *A Midsummer Night's Dream* for each of you next week so we can get started, all right? Class dismissed, and don't forget your homework is due Monday," she called after them, "and, Angi, you'll help Lottie with hers as usual?"

"Yes, ma'am," Angi said with a smile. She held out her hand at the door. "Come on, Miss La-di-da—Miss Penny needs our help shelling peas."

"But Teacher needs me to sharpen pencils, don't you, Miss Alli?" The little tyke whirled around with a plea in blue eyes that melted Allison to the spot.

"Yes I do, as a matter of fact," she said with a wink at Angi while collecting pencils from the groove in each of the desks. "I'll walk her next door when she's done, Angi, all right?"

"All right, Miss Alli. Good night."

"Come on, little girl," Allison said with a tweak of Lottie's neck. "I'll put you to work." Squeezing her hand, she led her over to the pencil sharpener where Lottie perched upon a polished wooden stool handmade by Mr. Nick himself, for her birthday, she'd proclaimed proudly. Alli hadn't the heart to deny her when she'd asked if she could bring it to school to sit on it while sharpening pencils, since that was her job. Alli watched as the sweet little thing fondled the inscription with chubby fingers before arranging her faded, hand-me-down dress over it with loving care.

"I just love my new stool, don't you, Miss Alli?" She sighed again. "Mr. Nick is the nicest boy I know, don't you think?"

Nice? Allison issued a silent grunt. *If you're six years old.* She handed Lottie the pencils and bent to kiss her cheek, wondering for the umpteenth time how someone as cantankerous and annoying as Nick Barone could be so loving and kind to a little girl. She studied the perfectly crafted furniture that bore Lottie's initials in equally perfect scrollwork and tried to imagine the same hateful man bent over Lottie's stool with chisel and knife. Burnished with a rich mahogany stain, the stool bore the mark of a master with Lottie's initials relief-carved in graceful script that clearly indicated talent and artistry. And yet this was the very grouch who'd betrayed her confidence without batting an eye. The pencil sharpener ground along with her teeth. "Ha! Nick Barone, nice?" She muttered under her breath, reluctant to admit a heart might actually beat in the Neanderthal's chest. With a twinge of guilt, she blew a stray hair away from her eyes. "Well, who knows—maybe there's hope for the cretin yet . . ."

"What's a cretin?" Lottie asked, face upturned in innocence.

"W-what?" Allison blinked, painfully aware the pencil sharpener had stopped. She pressed a hand to her cheek. *Goodness, did I really say that out loud?*

"You said, 'Maybe there's hope for the cretin yet,' and you said Mr. Nick's name." She tipped her head in question. "Does that mean you think he's nice too?"

"Of course I do, sweetheart," Alli said with a squeeze of Lottie's shoulder. *Nice and cranky.* "I'll let you finish up here while I erase the blackboard, okay?"

"Goodness, Al, what a week, huh?" Cassie all but limped into the room, dropping into one of the desks to massage her ankle. "I'm going to have to talk to Aunt Cait about letting me wear my cowboy boots instead of these awful button-up shoes. I'm telling you, God did not intend for women to wear three-inch heels."

Allison grinned and lined up the desks, pausing to lift her skirt for Cassie's benefit. "Tell me about it. I made the mistake of wearing these brand-new kid slip-on heels, thinking they'd be more comfortable than my awful lace-ups." She scrunched her nose as she continued to straighten things up. "Now I have blisters on both feet."

"Well, at least you can slip yours off under the desk," Cassie said with a moan, attempting to knead the toe of her leather shoe. "I may never walk again."

"And I may never breathe again." Palms flat to the front of her whalebone corset, Alli sucked in a deep breath—or tried to—wishing she were as free-spirited as Cassie, who'd conveniently left her corset at home. "At least you're not wearing that new whalebone S-curve Mother bought for us," she whispered loudly, sneaking a peek at Lottie as she blissfully sharpened away. "I may just follow your lead and leave it at home, at least when I teach."

"Oooo—shocking!" Cassie's green eyes sparkled like emeralds. "The adventurous tomboy finally surfaces in the well-bred Allison McClare, defying convention at last." She blew several honey-blond strands out of her eyes from her Gibson Girl pompadour. "I knew I'd make a country girl of you yet." Glancing at the watch pinned to her pale-yellow shirtwaist, she shot to her feet. "Ooops . . . forgot Miss Tuttle sent me to fetch you for an impromptu meeting with Aunt Cait." The sharpener stilled, and Cassie shot Lottie a grin. "Hey, no fair—I don't have anybody to sharpen *my* pencils."

"I'll do it for you, Miss Cassie," the little girl said with a sweet smile over her shoulder. She blew on the tip of the last pencil she'd sharpened and carefully bundled them in a cup.

"Oh, no you don't, Cassidy McClare—Miss La-di-da's *all* mine!" Alli swooped down on the tiny angel and gave her a monster hug that sent little-girl squeals bouncing off the walls. "Come on, honey bun—I need to take you home." She glanced up at her cousin. "What's the meeting about, Cass, do you know?"

Cassie stretched and made a sad attempt at stifling a yawn.

"Well, it's the last day of our first week, so I'm guessing Aunt Cait wants to powwow over what worked, what didn't, et cetera."

"Probably." Alli took Lottie's hand. "Will you tell her I have to take Lottie home first?"

"Sure." Cassie tweaked Lottie's neck, coaxing a giggle. "See you soon, Miss La-di-da."

Steering Lottie out, Alli made their way to the kitchen, Lottie's contented sigh floating down the hall. "Jeepers, Miss Alli, I sure hope I grow up to be a teacher like you and Miss Cassie someday."

"Well, if you study real hard, you could very well be, as smart as you are, young lady."

"Gee whiz, that'd be swell!" She glanced up as Alli led her across the flagstone walk in Miss Penny's backyard. "Do you like being a teacher, Miss Alli?"

Alli smiled, joy swelling inside over the satisfaction she experienced as an educator. "Oh, yes, Lottie, I love it. I think being a teacher is one of the most noble professions a person can have."

"Me too," she said, face beaming. Lottie's little shoulders suddenly sagged. "I'm sad for Mr. Nick, though, 'cause he'd like to be a teacher too, but boys can't be teachers, can they?"

Alli frowned. "Well, some are, of course, but not at our school." She paused, brows knit as she put a hand on the knob of Miss Penny's kitchen door. "Mr. Nick is a police detective, Lottie—whatever makes you think he'd like to be a teacher?"

Lottie looked up, gaze innocent and as soft and serene as the blue sky above. "'Cause he told Miss Penny he'd like to teach you a thing or two, but she said he couldn't."

Heat stung Allison's cheeks. "I see." Lips pursed, she squatted to give Lottie a hug. "You have a wonderful weekend, Miss La-di-da, and I'll see you on Monday, all right?"

"Yes, ma'am." Returning her hug, Lottie slipped inside to

join the fray in the kitchen while Alli quietly closed the door. "Teach me a thing or two," she muttered, storming across the lawn. "Humph . . . how to be rude and grumpy, maybe."

Good mood considerably dampened, Allison hurried in the school's back door and rushed down the hall, her new shoes pinching as much as her pride. "Oh, enough!" she muttered, screeching to a stop midway. She removed her heels, refusing to endure both the pain of shoes and insults from Nick Barone. After all, all the students were gone. Her silk stockings glided the glossy wooden floor that Mrs. Lemp kept buffed to a shine, and Allison's outlook suddenly improved. She took a run to slide the last twenty feet to Mother's office, bad mood forgotten. Giggling, she skated past the door, arms flailing and feet skidding.

Boom! The ceiling stared back at her and she blinked, heat storming her cheeks as she lay flat on her back in front of Mother's door. Mortified, she scrambled to her feet and snatched her shoes from the floor, praying no one had noticed as she tiptoed into the room. "My apologies for being late," she said, tone breathless, "but I had to take Lottie home."

Her mother blinked. "Good heavens, Allison—are you all right?"

"Fine, Mother, really, just a little stunned."

Her mother's saucer eyes did a quick scan from Alli's disheveled hair down her partially untucked shirtwaist to her navy silk stockings that peeked out beneath her now-wrinkled linen skirt. "What on earth were you doing, young lady?"

Alli took great pains to smooth her skirt as well as she could with her shoes still in one hand. "I was . . ." She chewed on her lip, not daring to look at anyone but Mother lest she break into laughter from the hidden grin she was certain twitched on Cassie's face. "Skating."

"Skating." Her mother's tone was as flat as the bottom of Alli's stockinged feet as they fused to the floor, toes curling beneath the hem of her skirt. Mother's shocked gaze flitted from a renegade curl spiraling down Alli's shirtwaist to the confounded shoes she now pinched in her hand. "In your stockings," she whispered, as if she couldn't quite believe what she'd seen.

Alli offered a sheepish shrug of her shoulders, lowering her voice as she leaned in. "Well, these new shoes hurt like the dickens, Mother, and after all, there's nobody here but us."

Caitlyn cleared her throat and stood, shoulders square and voice resuming its usual self-possessed air. "Put your shoes on, Allison, and tuck in your blouse, please. We've already covered most of the meeting, but at least allow me to introduce you to a new member of our staff."

New member of our staff? Her shoes slipped from her fingers and clunked to the floor. She fought a gulp. *Sweet mother of mercy, caught skating the hall in my stockings! And in front of a stranger, no less.* Cheeks aflame, she dared not look anywhere but down while she grasped the edge of her mother's desk with bloodless fingers to shimmy on first one shoe and then the other. With a hard swallow, she carefully retucked her shirt and slowly straightened with as much dignity as humanly possible after landing on her backside in the hall. Leveling her shoulders, she turned to acknowledge the new employee with a deep ingest of air. And promptly hacked it back out again in a coughing spell that sounded like she had the croup.

Her mother quickly skirted the desk to pat her on the back, arm scooping her daughter's waist as if to shore her up in her moment of humiliation. A gentle apology laced her tone even as her fingers laced Allison's own. "I believe you've already met Mr. Barone, Allison?"

Yes—way, WAY too many times. Allison sucked in air like sustenance, dizzy from the lack of blood in her brain—it was all in her cheeks.

His gray-green eyes held a trace of humor held in check only by the clamp of lips in a stiffly polite smile. He inclined his head toward Allison, a muscle flickering in his shadowed jaw as he assessed her with a cool gaze. "I trust you're well, Miss McClare?"

Her chin ascended several degrees. "Fine, Mr. Barone, thank you," she replied, purposely dropping the long *e*.

Mother patted her waist and nudged her toward the last free chair in the room—right next to his. "It's Barone, darling, long *e*. Apparently Mr. Barone's people hail from Sicily."

Allison nodded in feigned interest as she slid into her chair with a silent grunt, hands knotted in her lap. *Yes . . . cave country, I believe.*

"Allison is our English and drama teacher, Mr. Barone," Mother continued. "Which along with my niece Cassidy teaching arithmetic and music, Miss Mary Tuttle teaching science and geography, and Miss Sophie Merdian overseeing our art and reading program, rounds out our core curriculum." Mother resumed her seat, the picture of grace and poise as she folded slender hands on her desk with a touch of a twinkle in her green eyes. "And, I'm happy to say, I've been able to coax my beloved housekeeper and cook, Mrs. Rosie O'Brien, into teaching the girls culinary skills once a week as well." She offered a bright smile in Mr. Long-*e*'s direction. "So you see, Mr. Barone, having you aboard the next six weeks as watchman and handyman in Mr. Bigley's absence, no matter how brief, is the final piece of the puzzle for a school we hope will be a blessing to many."

Excuse me? Allison's jaw dropped before she could stop it, the sharp intake of her breath causing her to choke once again. A firm hand clapped on her back as she coughed, and she quickly fended it off, inching to the far side of her chair. "Thank you, but I'm fine, truly."

Or will be in six weeks or so . . .

"Goodness, Allison, do you need a drink of water?" Mother stared in concern.

"No, Mother, I'm fine, really," she said, her voice akin to a croak.

"Well then, as I was saying, starting Monday, Mr. Barone has graciously agreed to step in during Mr. Bigley's absence despite a demanding workload as a senior detective for the 14th precinct. He will be on premises before and after school, during lunch recess, and as needed during the day for odd jobs or projects, so if you have any security or safety concerns or odd jobs, please see me. I will provide Mr. Barone a docket of tasks each day, and he has offered to devise a sound security plan for us as well." She glanced around the room. "Any questions?"

"How is Mr. Bigley faring, Mrs. McClare, do we know?" Miss Tuttle asked, the snow-white bun on top of the elderly woman's head more off-kilter than usual. Gnarled hands rested in the lap of her serviceable black skirt while she picked at her nails, the tic in her eye particularly active after a full week of teaching high-spirited girls.

"Thank you for asking, Miss Tuttle. He's doing well, although Mrs. Bigley claims he's a wee bit grumpy because it's such a slow process. Says he'd rather be doing his job than sitting idle in a bed or chair." Caitlyn smiled. "I told her to let him know how much we miss him."

Alli shifted. *You have no idea, Mother . . .*

Miss Merdian raised a bony hand, the natural scowl on her thin, angular face reminding Alli of Mr. Personality on a good day. "We discussed outings with the children such as the de Young Museum and Sutro Baths—will Mr. Barone be available to accompany us on such excursions?"

Mother nodded. "Yes, Miss Merdian—excellent question. I've had the pleasure of conversing with Mr. Barone for the last half hour before you ladies arrived, and he assures me he is more than willing to assist in any way needed, including a fine arts excursion to de Young or a field day for the children at Sutro Baths. Isn't that correct, Mr. Barone?"

Mr. Personality actually smiled, his civil response as courteous and gracious as the most respectful of gentlemen. "Yes, ma'am— it's an honor to assist you in any way I can."

Allison gaped at his smiling profile, her jaw distended for the second time that day.

"Thank you, Mr. Barone. I cannot adequately express our gratitude and appreciation for your services." Caitlyn glanced at the watch pinned to her dress. "Well, then, I've taken enough of everyone's time, so thank you for a truly excellent first week, ladies, and we'll see you all on Monday." She rose to her feet, head cocked in Cassie's direction. "Cassie, would you mind telling Hadley we'll be right out? Mr. Barone and I need to speak with Allison privately for a moment."

Privately? A lump glugged in Allison's throat. *Surely he hadn't complained to Mother . . .*

"Certainly, Aunt Cait." Cassie rose and offered a handshake. "It's good to have you aboard, Mr. Barone. No matter how brief your tenure, your presence is a huge relief."

Nick stood to shake her hand, his tone almost warm. "Thank you, Miss McClare. It's nice to know I can offer some peace of mind."

Allison bit back a grunt. *Humph . . . I'd like to offer some piece of mind . . .*

"Please call me Cass. As a former Texas girl, I don't stand on formality all that much." Her gaze veered to Alli with a definite sparkle. "And with two Miss McClares in the building, it might make things a bit easier, right, Al?"

No, "easier" would be if he weren't here at all . . .

154

"Then I insist you call me Nick," he said, his congenial tone starting to get on her nerves. "That's what my friends call me."

He has friends? Allison fought the squirm of a smile.

"Then see you Monday, Nick. Take your time, Aunt Cait—I've been tanning Hadley's hide in an ongoing game of gallows, so we won't mind the wait." Cassie passed Allison with a swish of her skirts, sliding her a wink before she sauntered to the door.

Cassie closed the door, and Alli sat up straight, ready to defend herself against slander.

"Allison," her mother began with a crisp fold of her hands, "I want you to know that I am not overly thrilled with your intention to work late after school some afternoons or take the cable car home, but I realize your need for independence, so I respect that." She lifted her chin, the barest flicker of a smile on her lips. "But, you've expressed an interest in learning jiu-jitsu, so Uncle Logan and I are willing to do whatever it takes to help you remain safe. To that end, I am happy to say that we have found you a jiu-jitsu instructor."

Alli caught her breath, the thrill of learning jiu-jitsu almost enough to dispel her rancor toward the man in the chair beside her. Scooting to the edge of her seat, she clasped her hands to her chin, giddy with anticipation. "Oh, Mother, you won't regret this, I promise. You have my word I'll be the most diligent student ever. When do I start and where?"

"You'll start Monday after school, and Mr. Barone feels the gymnasium is the best place since there's plenty of room for the rubber mat he'll bring from the precinct."

White spots danced before her eyes. "Mr. B-Barone?" she whispered, her voice a rasp.

"Yes, darling, of course." Her mother flashed a bright smile. "I had my doubts that your uncle could secure a jiu-jitsu instructor in the city at all, much less so quickly, but apparently Mr.

Barone is a skilled instructor who has trained a quarter of the 14th precinct in the art of jiu-jitsu." She glanced in his direction, positively beaming. "Goodness, sir, we are so blessed to find one man who can provide so many services to our fledgling school—thank you, again."

Yeah, blessed. Alli swallowed hard, dread pasting her tongue like glue.

"So, Allison, your first class takes place on Monday. You'll need to bring your bicycling outfit with the bloomers to change into after school. Mr. Barone tells me there are kicks involved and other fast movements that your teaching attire will impede."

Alli nodded, unable to speak for the lack of moisture in her throat.

"You'll work together Monday, Wednesday, and Friday for the six weeks that he is here, and you'll meet in the gym at four o'clock sharp, which should give you enough time to tidy up your classroom after the final class of the day, all right?"

Breathing shallow, all Alli could do was bob her head up and down.

"Mr. Barone," her mother said, "is there anything you'd like to add before we conclude?"

Allison allowed a sideways peek, and for the first time, Mr. Personality met her gaze, almost a dare in those gray-green eyes despite the polite tenor of his tone. "I'd just like Miss McClare to be fully aware jiu-jitsu is not just a skill of self-defense, but an excellent means of strengthening balance, self-esteem, and hopefully, if a student applies herself . . ." He paused for effect, his meaning clear in the press of his smile. "Self-control and respect for authority as well."

A hot rush of blood blistered her cheeks, causing her chin to thrust up several degrees, lips matching the same mulish bent as his. "And will you be teaching the self-control portion of this class, Mr. Barone?" she asked sweetly. "Or will that be handled by someone more skilled than yourself?"

"Allison . . ." Her mother's voice interrupted with a quiet authority that commanded her attention. "I am well aware from talking to Miss Penny that you and Mr. Barone have gotten off to a rocky start, for which I have already apologized to him on your behalf. As your mother and principal of this school, I am asking you to lay your differences aside and give him the respect and civility due a teacher and fellow co-worker, is that clear?"

Alli nodded, blinking several times to clear the moisture that pricked in her eyes. "Yes, Mother," she said quietly, gaze fixed straight ahead.

"Good." Caitlyn's heavy sigh filled the room. "I apologize again, Mr. Barone, for my daughter's unfortunate remark. As our drama teacher, Allison tends to have a bit of the Sarah Bernhardt in her, I'm afraid, not to mention inheriting my mother's Irish temper. I'm sure she'll benefit from anything that enhances both self-control and respect for authority." Her mother's eyes softened as she smiled at her daughter, her affection more than evident. "But . . . I'm happy to say she's a quick study and a good girl who has always made me proud." The barest hint of humor crept into her tone. "However, just in case . . . my door is always open if you have any problems on either score, all right?"

"I appreciate that, Mrs. McClare," he said, no mistaking the jest lacing his own words as he slowly rose to his feet. Turning his back on her mother, he gave Allison a polite bow of his head, lips twitching with a smile that could only be construed as a smirk. "But as long as she leaves her stick at home . . ." He actually had the audacity to give her a wink before his lips eased into a superior smile. "I think I can handle Miss Bernhardt just fine on my own."

11

"Goodness, is there anything better than family?" Caitlyn sighed and nestled into the thick cushions of her wrought-iron chaise on the stone patio in the backyard, hugging herself in the silky feel of her pashmina shawl. The joyful laughter of her family filled the dusky air with a noisy game of croquet on her lush lawn in the fading pink light. Contentment flowed through her at the sight of Cassie and Alli teasing Jamie and Blake while Bram assisted Meg and Maddie with their shots. Summer's scent filled Caitlyn's senses, the lingering fragrance of honeysuckle merging with that of her roses and the tangy smell of the sea, making her wish this moment could last forever.

"No, there isn't," a husky voice responded, and she jolted, cheeks warming when she realized she'd spoken out loud. She glanced up, and Logan's tender smile sent the heat in her cheeks coursing straight to her toes when he sat beside her. His arm grazed her shoulder while he draped it over the back of the chaise. "Family is everything," he said quietly, the smile on his lips dimming as he watched the others play. "Something I realized all too late."

Desperate to calm the erratic beat of her pulse, Caitlyn angled to face him, striving for nonchalance as she carefully butted close to her side of the chaise without appearing to distance herself.

"The most important thing, Logan," she said with a gentle touch to his arm, "is what a wonderful uncle you've been to my children over the years and still continue to be." Her gaze drifted to the horseplay in the yard even as a gentle sigh drifted from her lips. "Other than their own father, no man could love or support them more, and for that I will always be grateful."

Her breath stilled when his palm covered the hand she'd placed on his arm. "Nothing in my life is more important than my family, Cait—nothing." As if sensing her discomfort at his touch, he pulled away and hunched forward, arms loose over his knees and hands clasped. He peered at the children while a muscle flickered in his jaw, his chiseled profile as sharp as his gaze. "I would do anything in my power to make them happy," he said, the husky sound of his voice skittering her stomach. He paused before unsettling her further with a sideways glance. "And that includes their mother and aunt."

Muscles contracted, both in her throat and her stomach, reminding her of that painful night last year in Napa when he'd declared his love two years after Liam's death. *I love you, Cait, and the fact is, I always have.* Their easy friendship had nearly been destroyed in the altercation that followed. *Until* she'd learned months later it had been Logan's secret vote on the Board of Supervisors that saved her Vigilance Committee proposal to clean up the Barbary Coast. Her gratitude had prompted her to restore her friendship with the brother-in-law who stirred her heart more than he should, pleading for friendship and nothing more. *"Friends forever, Cait,"* he'd promised, setting her mind and body at ease until he'd uttered those final two words. *"For now . . ."*

Her lips trembled into a smile. "I know that, Logan—you've proven it time and time again with both me and my children, and I am eternally grateful for your friendship." She didn't miss the almost imperceptible press of his jaw before loud squeals drew both of their attention to the conclusion of croquet.

"Mama, Mama—Bram and I won!" Maddie said with a squeal, launching into her mother's arms while the others ambled toward the patio, laughing with mallets and balls in hand. The six-year-old shimmied into the narrow space between Logan and her, easing Caitlyn's pulse considerably. "And Uncle Logan, guess what?" She wiggled into his lap, giggling when he snuggle-monstered her neck. "The girls are gonna play against the boys in charades 'cause Jamie says they have to teach the girls a lesson."

"Is that a fact?" Logan's deep laughter warmed Caitlyn's heart, his rapport with her youngest daughter as close as if she were his very own. *And she might have been had I not broken our engagement.* She released a silent sigh, wondering if she would ever be free from the hurt of Logan's betrayal to let thoughts like that go. He cradled Maddie like a baby, playfully nuzzling her neck while she giggled in his arms. "That means it's me against you, Miss Madelyn McClare," he said in a gruff voice, tickling her until she squirmed off his lap.

"And against Mama, too," she said with a thrust of her pert little chin, chubby hands on her hips, "because you're a boy and she's a girl."

"You're certainly right about that," Logan said with a roguish grin, unsettling Caitlyn with a sly wink. "Except I've learned the hard way not to go up against your mother."

"Ice-cold lemonade and fresh-baked cookies in the parlour," Rosie called from the kitchen window, and Caitlyn grinned at the shrieks and giggles that filled the summer night. Blake and Jamie wasted no time racing Alli and Cassie to the French doors of the conservatory while Meg's lilting giggle drifted in the brisk night air. A surge of warmth seeped through Caitlyn's chest at the sound of her seventeen-year-old daughter's laughter as Bram ushered her inside. She watched him playfully tweak Megan's neck before he opened the door for her, and for surely the thousandth time, Caitlyn silently thanked God for the gift of Bram Hughes in their family.

Without question, Bram was more brother to her son Blake than distant cousin and certainly more of a son to her than a nephew who spent most of his time at their house. But without doubt, the greatest gift he'd given her over the years was the special attention he lavished upon her middle daughter, helping to counter the cruel ridicule of peers who mocked both her weight and thick eyeglasses. With his tender heart, easygoing manner, and deep affection for Meg, Bram had done more to heal Meg's wounded spirit and damaged self-esteem than all the stellar grades in high school, awards for exceptional writing or art, or top honor roll feats. Exhaling a wispy sigh, Caitlyn couldn't help but worry how Meg would cope in Paris without Bram, when she left for her senior year abroad in two weeks.

"Hurry, Mama, or Jamie and Blake will eat all the cookies." Maddie's pleas interrupted Caitlyn's reverie as her youngest daughter tugged on her hand.

"Well, we can't have that, now can we?" Laughing, Caitlyn rose to her feet, halting only when she felt the touch of Logan's hand to her arm.

"Can we talk for a moment, Cait?" His tone was casual as the shadows of night obscured his handsome face. "Privately?"

"All right," she said slowly, pulse tripping over what might be on his mind. She scooped Maddie up in her arms and gave her a tight squeeze, depositing a kiss on her cheek before she set her back down. "Darling, will you run inside and make sure Jamie and Blake don't steal all the cookies, then save me a place right next to you, all right?"

"Yes, Mama," the little girl called, tearing into the house like a shot.

Buffing her arms more from trepidation of Logan's need for privacy than the cool shadows of dusk, Caitlyn turned and offered him a tentative smile. She suddenly shivered, the trill of tree frogs and the bite of the crisp evening air harkening back to that summer night in Napa when Logan had kissed her. "What is it?" she whispered, almost afraid to ask.

His low chuckle took the chill off when it caused heat to pulse in her cheeks. "You can sit down, Cait, I won't bite." He twined his fingers in hers to tug her back to the chaise. Then as if to put her at ease, he shifted to his end of the settee. The sleeve of his dark linen suit draped over the back like before, but thankfully far from where she sat perched on the edge, arms clutched to her waist. He smiled. "I want to talk about Allison."

"Allison?" She faced him square on, instantly forgetting any nervousness she may have had. "What about Allison?"

He chuckled again, eyes twinkling in the glow of the shaft of light that spilled from the conservatory. "Nothing's wrong, Cait, so no need for that look of panic in your eyes. I just wanted to discuss Allison's quest for independence and what I've done to secure her safety."

All of Caitlyn's concerns drifted out on a frail exhale of air. "Oh, Logan, I can't thank you enough for referring Mr. Barone to fill in for Mr. Bigley—he's absolutely perfect."

Logan's smile went sour as always at any mention of the Italian officer. "I know," he said with a flat press of his lips, absently scratching the back of his neck, "in more ways than one."

Caitlyn relaxed in her seat, grateful for Logan's assistance. "Indeed—what are the chances of finding one person with the skills to fill in as both watchman and handyman and then teach

162

Allison too?" She leaned forward, her smile warm. "I can't thank you enough."

"Yes, you can, Cait—you can let me foot the bill."

She sat straight up. "Oh, no, this is my school and my expenditure."

Logan exhaled and pinched the bridge of his nose. "Yes, but I need control of Barone because the stakes are higher than you know."

The cool night air clogged in her throat. "What do you mean?"

He stilled her with a steady gaze. "I didn't just hire him as temporary watchman and handyman for the school, I hired him as a bodyguard for Allison without her knowledge."

"What?" Caitlyn blinked. "Why?"

He studied her for a moment before he released a heavy sigh. "Because of the details of what happened the night she was accosted, and I intend to see it never happens again. And Allison is as stubborn as you when it comes to the Barbary Coast. She wants to come and go as she pleases, and Barone will make that possible."

"The details of the night she was accosted?" Her voice was weak. "What details?" she whispered, then jutted her chin when she realized what else he had said. "And I am not stubborn when it comes to the Barbary Coast and neither is Allison."

He hiked a brow. "I presented you with countless opportunities to open your school anywhere else in San Francisco, Mrs. McClare. But you insisted on doing so in the most corrupt and dangerous part of town, against both my counsel and request." The edge of his mouth tipped, lightening the sobriety of his tone. "You put the fear of God in me, Cait, worrying about you and my nieces day in and day out."

Her lips quirked. "Well, somebody needs to put the fear of

God in you, Logan, because heaven knows a dose or two wouldn't hurt." She gave him a sideways squint, bristling at his propensity to try to run her life. "And you don't need to worry about me—I'm perfectly capable of taking care of myself."

He shook his head, his smile flat. "And you wonder where Allison gets it."

"You're dodging my question—what details of the night she was accosted?" she repeated, her corset suddenly too tight.

His jaw ground the slightest bit as he assessed her, as if considering how much he should reveal. He finally exhaled loudly, then fixed her with a sobering gaze. "It wasn't a mere purse-snatching as Allison led you to believe. According to Barone, she was thrown down on the ground by some lowlife who ripped her blouse and scuffed her up pretty good before Miss Penny wielded her gun."

Caitlyn felt the blood drain from her cheeks as she stared, finding it difficult to breathe. Her eyelids flickered closed at the thought of her daughter in harm's way, and all because her mother was too stubborn to consider the risks of opening a school on the Barbary Coast. Tears pricked, and she put a hand to her eyes, fingers quivering along with her stomach.

A single sob broke from her throat before she could choke it back, and Logan instantly pulled her into his arms, soothing her with a gentle rub of her shoulders, his words soft against her hair. "I debated telling you the details, Cait, because I knew it would jolt you, but you need to understand just why I've commissioned an armed officer like Nick Barone to watch over you and the girls, the school, and especially Allison."

"B-but s-she m-made it s-sound so matter-of-fact." Caitlyn squeezed her eyes shut to stem the flow of more tears, the familiar smell of lime shaving soap and a trace of wood spice providing more comfort than it should. "Why would she lie?"

Julie Lessman

She shivered when he kissed the top of her head, his palm sweeping her back in steady motion. "She didn't lie, Cait," he said with a soft chuckle, "she just left out a few pertinent details she thought might upset you enough to forbid her from ever taking the cable car home."

She jerked away, eyes burning from the anger that seethed inside over Allison's deception. "Lies, omission of the truth—it's all the same thing, Logan, and you know it. She did nothing but whitewash the truth, leading me on to achieve her own end."

"My thoughts exactly . . . ," he whispered, lifting her chin to capture her gaze with his own. A mix of humor and affection sparkled in his eyes. "Not unlike you when you found the 'most perfect Victorian' for your new school 'just down the street from a lovely neighborhood.'"

Heat burnished her cheeks as she pulled from his hold. "It *is* close to a lovely neighborhood," she insisted, warding off the truth of his statement with a tight fold of her arms.

His rich laughter burst the bubble of her pride. "As are most of the neighborhoods in our fair city, Mrs. McClare, only this one happens to border the worst." He shook his head and reclined against the settee, his arm straddling the back once again. "Face it, Cait—Allison is a chip off the old block, and you're not going to be able to stop her from going wherever she wants any more than I could stop you."

She turned away in a huff, chin high as she stared into the manicured backyard now bathed in moonlight. His throaty chuckles coaxed a reluctant smile to her lips and she pursed them to thwart it, head cocked as she studied him through narrow eyes. "I hate it when you're right," she muttered, wishing her stomach didn't flutter when he grinned at her like that.

"I'm right about more than you know, Mrs. McClare," he

whispered, his grin fading into a tender smile as he grazed a thumb against the silk of her sleeve. "You just don't know it yet."

She shivered and backed away, arms folded in emotional barrier against Logan's affection . . . and the annoyance of her growing need for his touch. "So now I know why the stakes are high, but I still don't know why you need control of Mr. Barone."

The pin-striped silk of his waistcoat rose and fell with a heavy breath, his four-in-hand tie slightly off-kilter for the meticulous Logan McClare. His gaze held hers for several seconds, quickening her pulse. "Because I had to bribe and bully the man to take the job."

"What?" She sat up, shocked that the affable detective she'd chatted with in her school office for over an hour needed to be bribed to take a job he seemed more than willing to take on. "I don't understand—Mr. Barone was most agreeable to any task I'd assign."

Logan's lip quirked. "I credit you with that, Cait, because the man not only hates me, but he despises anything associated with wealth." He paused to give her a half-lidded stare. "And that includes my wealthy niece from Nob Hill."

Caitlyn blinked, the notion of anyone despising Allison too foreign to comprehend. Full of life and drama, her beautiful daughter had always been popular at school and within social circles as well, sought after equally by both suitors and high society. "But if he doesn't like Allison, why on earth would you want him to teach her jiu-jitsu?"

He exhaled a harsh breath, the steel glint in his eyes matching the iron clamp of his jaw. "Because he's just what we need—strong, tough, and bullheaded enough to deal with Allison, and yet angry enough at the upper class not to be a threat."

"A threat?"

His mouth leveled into a thin line. "The last thing we need is some penniless womanizer cop who breaks hearts for a living falling in love with Allison and breaking hers too." His gaze shifted to the backyard where moonlight spilled across the lawn, the set of his jaw clear indication he blamed himself for Allison's heartbreak over Roger Luepke. "Barone is safe because he's all we need him to be—protector, teacher, and the one man other than Roger who Allison can't abide any more than Barone can abide her."

Caitlyn frowned. "Allison can't abide him? Goodness, she barely knows him."

He turned back, his lips slanting into a hard smile. "Oh, she knows him all right, and she's carrying a monumental grudge because he spilled the truth about the attack, which, I might add, she had no intention of telling either of us about, at least not right away." He sat back and huffed out a sigh. "So between Allison's grudge against Barone and his grudge against me, Allison, and anyone who lives on Nob Hill, they're a perfect match for our purposes."

"But I live on Nob Hill, and Mr. Barone was perfectly charming to me," she said with a crimp of brows, reflecting on how gruff Nick Barone had been when he'd first arrived at her door, a scowl so deep she'd felt sure it was permanent. And then somehow the conversation had strayed to how much she loved Miss Penny and her girls, and what a blessing it was to have them as neighbors. Before she'd known it, her usual decorum and calm had bubbled into excitement over working in tandem with Mercy House to provide love and opportunity for needy young women. In the twitch of a muscle in his sculpted cheek, Nick Barone's near sneer had slowly dissolved into a faint smile that eventually grew as warm as his eyes when he talked about Miss Penny and her girls.

The man clearly had a soft heart beneath that crusty exterior, something that had impressed Caitlyn far more than his police credentials or other skills.

"Everyone's charming to you, Cait," Logan said with a wry smile. "For one of the wealthiest and most influential women in the city, you are the kindest and least pretentious human being I know, so I'm not surprised Barone responded well to you."

She peered up, nose in a scrunch. "I like him, but I get the sense you don't. Why?"

Logan exhaled a weary breath, the question seeming to sap his strength. "Barone and I butted heads in a Board of Supervisors meeting over a misunderstanding with Chinatown awhile back. I think he blames me for the death of a young boy during that spate of riots that broke out when the quarantine was in place."

Caitlyn nodded. "I remember the incident well," she said quietly, grateful the quarantine of Chinatown had been lifted and strides were being made in containing the plague. She looked up. "But you had nothing to do with that—that was the Board of Health's decision."

"That's not how Barone sees it. He blames the Board of Supervisors—and me in particular after we clashed in that meeting. Accused me of being in Gage's hip pocket and supporting both the quarantine and Gage's denial of the plague."

"But you and Henry Gage aren't even friends anymore."

"That doesn't seem to matter. In his eyes, I'm as corrupt as Henry by association, even though I've never agreed with his politics." He huffed out another sigh as he kneaded the bridge of his nose. "I've tried to clear the air, but he's worse at holding a grudge than Allison, and you know how angry she is at men right now, especially after that last debacle."

A feathery sigh withered on her lips as her gaze trailed into a stare. Yes, she knew. After several failed engagements to men who lied and cheated, Allison's vendetta against men had grown bigger than her heart, it seemed. She glanced up at Logan, her stomach clenching at the guilt that weighted his shoulders. "You're not responsible for the pain inflicted by Roger, you know," she whispered, well aware Logan blamed himself for introducing the two.

His chest rose and fell with a heavy exhale. "No, but I am responsible for safeguarding my family—both at Liam's request and because of my deep love for each of you, making sure the men who come courting aren't charlatans and frauds." His eyelids lifted to pierce Caitlyn with a telling resolve. "Never again will I allow my nieces to court a man unless I know everything about him and his intentions."

"I'm glad," she whispered, her heart lighter at the thought. "You're a good uncle and a dear friend, Logan, and I don't know what we'd do without you."

His smile returned. "Well, I don't intend for you to ever find out, Cait. I'm here for the long haul—friends forever, remember?"

A smile lifted the edges of her mouth. "Yes, friends forever." She breathed in a heavy dose of the cool night air, so very grateful for Logan's intervention on behalf of her daughter. Her mood turned melancholy, and she buffed her arms as if to chase it away. "I won't lie, though—it's been painful to see Allison so wounded and bruised these last six months. It's not who she is, and it breaks my heart."

He squeezed her hand. "She'll rebound, Cait. She's like her mother, remember?"

Glancing up, her eyes met his, and reading between the lines of his statement, she knew full well that Logan regretted his betrayal years ago as much as she. Maybe more, she realized, seeing a familiar hint of sorrow shadowing his gaze. "I believe that," she said with a slow nod of her head. "And sometimes all it takes is the right man to heal the hurt, like Jamie with Cassie."

"Or Liam with you," he said quietly, his voice thick with regret.

"Yes, like Liam with me." Her eyelids drifted closed as she thought of the man who had healed her heart and eventually made it his own. "We were good friends, your brother and I," she whispered, aching at the sweet memory of all they had shared. "Friendship was the perfect prelude to a lifetime of joy."

Logan stood to his feet and extended his hand with a tender gaze, his firm hold helping her to rise from her seat. "Well, that's certainly my hope as well, Mrs. McClare," he said softly as he offered his arm, his veiled reference to the future quickening her pulse. She thought she'd made it clear last year that there was no hope for them together as man and wife. But she sensed Logan clung to the idea that friendship would eventually lead them there, and a shiver skittered her body despite the warmth of his hand. He seemed to have forgotten her primary reason for turning him away when he'd asked her to marry him that night in Napa.

"I swear to you Cait—I will be faithful."

"No, Logan, you can't. A man of your habit and ilk can't be faithful without God."

"I believe in God, Cait."

"No, you believe in yourself first, God after. There's a difference."

Now, in the dark of night, she peeked at his profile as he chatted and escorted her to the door, and despite his intense loyalty and attentiveness to her and her family, she knew that very difference still stood in the way. *An insurmountable difference*, she thought with a sharp pang of regret as he ushered her inside. And the very reason she'd never give Logan McClare the chance to betray her again.

12

Why the devil did I say yes?

Nick scowled, pausing in his restless stride across the Hand of Hope gymnasium to gouge the back of his neck. *Because I had no choice—McClare put a gun to my head.* He muttered and continued to pace, wishing he could teach the supervisor a few lessons in jiu-jitsu instead of his powder-keg niece, whose fuse was lit every time Nick opened his mouth. But no, the telegram DeLuca sent had been clear: bide your time—payoff is coming. He grunted. And a far bigger payoff than McClare could ever dole out, that's for sure. A heist bigger than anything the society bigwigs had pulled off, robbing them just like they'd robbed him. And then he'd finally be free to start over somewhere else, far from the tentacles of crime that kept him bound and gagged and shackled to the likes of Logan McClare.

And his beautiful pain-in-the-posterior niece.

He glanced at his watch and huffed out a noisy breath, wondering how long it took for a society dame to change into something "suitable." Speaking of which . . . He peeled off his coat and four-in-hand tie, tossing both over a stack of wooden chairs he'd cleared away at the front of the stage, then loosened the top two buttons of his stiff, high-collar pin-striped shirt that had once been crisply

171

laundered and ironed by Miss Penny. Rolling up the sleeves, he strode across the rubber pad in his dark socks, warming up with squats and lunges that helped loosen muscles sore from nights on the beat and a long day at the beck and call of the Hand of Hope School. Flynn had been none too happy to lose his partner most of the day and forced to work more nights than he liked, but Nick wasn't exactly euphoric either, although he suspected working for Caitlyn McClare would prove considerably easier than dealing with her daughter.

It wasn't difficult to see why Logan McClare's manner had softened considerably when he'd called her "one of the most remarkable women you'll ever meet." In some ways she reminded him of how Gram might have been as a young woman—gentle, serene, and yet with a quiet spunk that indicated a spine of steel lay beneath that beautiful façade. During their first conversation last Friday, he'd noticed this breathless, little-girl quality about her when she spoke of her dreams for the school or how her eyes lit up when students had peeked in to say goodbye. Throughout the day, he'd watched her giggle and tease with the children as they tromped through the halls, as if she were a little girl herself. He shook his head with a faint smile. Or how she'd all but glowed in his morning meeting with her as if nothing were more important than chatting with him. Like she was a student herself rather than mistress of a school catering to the poorest of the poor.

She kept him busy most of the day with ongoing tasks, but always asked with humility and grace. Never ordering or demanding as he'd expected given the high-society matrons he'd known and despised. No, Caitlyn McClare was a rare woman of privilege who treated others with dignity and respect no matter their station, an assessment that put him in the unlikely camp of Logan Mc-Clare on one point at least—she truly was a remarkable woman.

As is her daughter. His mouth skewed. Remarkably stubborn, remarkably rude, remarkably bad-tempered, remarkably big chip on her shoulder . . .

And remarkably pretty? His lips clamped tight. Unfortunately, yes. He could deal with the rest easily enough, but the attraction he'd felt since the moment they'd clashed on that very first day grated on his nerves, making him skittish. Especially since he'd made the mistake of nearly kissing her senseless a few weeks back, although she was already most of the way there on her own with her foolhardy notions. *Stupid, stupid move, Barone.* Now whenever he'd seen her in the hall today or worked on an odd job in her classroom, his gaze would stray to the fullness of those maddening pink lips or the glint of sunshine against lustrous black curls. He hated how those wispy tendrils teased the back of her neck, leading his gaze astray with a silk bodice that tapered into a tiny waist before it flowed into the gentle curve of her hips.

No! He dropped to the mat and started pumping some push-ups hard, muscles straining as he counted out loud, racking them up to keep from thinking about *her.* Society dames were nothing but poison, and this one was the absolute worst. She'd beat him to death with her stick, no doubt, then poison him with her lies just for good measure.

Probably worse than Darla—

"Ahem."

He paused mid-push, arms bulging from the weight as he stared, wishing he had time for about a thousand more. Especially the way she looked right now.

Her cheeks glowed a soft pink at his bold gape, and she chewed on the edge of her lips. Nervous fingers tugged at the poufed skirt of her bicycle bloomers, as if desperate to stretch it below the knee all the way to her blue-stockinged ankles. It was a serviceable navy-blue bicycle outfit with long sleeves, belted at the waist with a double-breasted bodice—all the rage with the upper class who'd taken to bicycling like ducks to water. He bit back a smile at the pert straw hat with matching band atop her head and slowly rose to his feet, fighting to maintain a stern expression as he perused her head to toe, hands on his hips. "Take the hat off," he ordered, refusing to teach jiu-jitsu to anyone wearing ribbons and straw.

"Pardon me?"

He nodded at her head. "The hat—we're not bicycling through Union Square, Miss McClare, we're learning self-defense. You need to be unencumbered for freedom of movement."

She blinked, a long sweep of black lashes fanning her face. "But . . . but . . . I'll always be wearing a hat, won't I?" she said in a rational tone. "I mean, if the need for self-defense should arise?" He could almost feel the flutter of lashes. "Shouldn't I learn the same way?"

His jaw started to grind. "Not in my class, lady. Take it off."

Her jaw elevated at least an inch. "Not unless you ask nicely."

He kneaded his temples with his fingers, counting to five slowly before finally peering up. "Take it off, Miss McClare—*now.*" He forced the next word through clenched teeth. "Please."

"Certainly," she said with a bright smile, unpinning the hat from her head. She carefully laid it aside and turned to face him, hands clasped behind her back. "Shall we begin?"

His gaze dropped to her flat leather shoes. "You'll need to take off your shoes as well."

She arched a brow.

"Please," he said sharply.

"Why?"

Lowering his head, he pinched the bridge of his nose, smothering a groan. "Miss McClare," he said, glancing up through tired eyes, "we both have had a long day, and I have a long night ahead. It would go so much easier for both of us if you would simply defer to me as the teacher in this class just like your students do with you."

"But even I tell my students why, Mr. Barone," she said softly.

He drew in a deep breath and exhaled slowly. "All right, Miss McClare, point taken." He slacked a leg, hands low on his hips. "Whenever I teach a class to the officers within the precinct, I ask them to remove their shoes to avoid wear and tear on the mat, which is very expensive, you see, and socks or stockings help to keep it clean."

"Well, now, see?" she said sweetly, promptly slipping off her low-heeled shoes. "That makes perfect sense, doesn't it? Thank you."

Yeah, perfect sense. He issued a silent groan. *Unlike this class.*

She carefully tiptoed over and tested a toe on the rubber mat like she was taking a dip in a lake before slowly inching in to stand before him, hands clasped behind her once again.

He stared down at her as she peered up, her green eyes calm for the moment as they peeked up beneath a heavy sweep of lashes. In her stockinged feet, she barely came to his shoulders, and he shook his head, a smile inching up on one side of his mouth. "Blue blazes, woman, you're a little mite of a thing, you know that?"

She arched a brow, the barest semblance of a smile shadowing her lips. "But big enough to whop you with a stick, Mr. Barone."

"Don't remind me," he said with a short bow at the waist. "I guess I should be grateful you didn't bring it."

She returned the bow. "No need, it's right down the hall."

"Thanks for the warning." His lip curled as he took a step back. "First we limber up with warm-up exercises, loosen those muscles, if you will." He demonstrated with his hands on his hips while he performed several squats. She followed suit nicely as they continued to a count of twenty. Next he ran her through the paces with leg lunges and several sprints around the room.

Ten minutes later she was leaning against the wall with a palm to her chest, huffing and puffing. "I . . . already . . . know . . . how . . . to . . . run, . . . Mr. . . . Barone," she said in between breaths, a hint of irritation in her voice.

With a jerk of his head, he motioned her back to the mat, grinning when she huffed out a sigh and shuffled over, lips compressed as she stood before him.

Tempering his smile, he folded his arms and gave her a half-lidded gaze. "Basic rules," he snapped. "No striking, punching, or kicking unless part of the exercise. And no eye gouging, hair pulling, twisting, or grabbing fingers, understood?"

A hint of a smile twitched on her face. "Sure, take away all my fun."

The corner of his mouth hooked. "And no sticks, though I know that'll break your heart."

"You have no idea."

"Oh, I think I do," he said with a swerve of lips before his eyes turned serious. "All right, ma'am, instead of a regular class where I teach you all the basic moves like I would with the officers in training, I'm going to focus on instructing you in various threatening scenarios. Since the most likely advance of danger will come from an arm choke from behind, I'm going to teach you a series of moves to counter it, all right?"

She nodded, eyes wide as she fiddled with her nails.

"First off, I'll show you the steps by having you choke me from behind, which," he said with a teasing jag of his brow, "should thrill you to no end." He grabbed one of the chairs from a nearby stack and placed it on the mat, then tapped the back of it. "Hop up here."

Her lips thinned.

"Please," he said quickly, quite certain she'd have him trained *way* before he trained her.

Carefully placing her palms on the seat, she positioned a tiny stocking-clad foot on the edge of the seat and made a shaky attempt at rising with dignity, taking so long that Nick blew out a noisy breath and plucked her up by that tiny waist to plop her on top. She spun around and slapped hands to her hips. "I am perfectly capable of scaling a chair, Mr. Barone."

"I'm well aware, Miss McClare, but if it's all the same to you, I'd like to finish sometime tonight." He slowly turned his back on her, never more grateful she didn't have a stick. Limbs loose at his sides, he butted up to the edge of the chair. "Now choke me from behind with one arm, okay?" His voice veered toward sarcastic. "And try not to enjoy it."

He waited. Nothing. Nerves twitched everywhere in his body until a lightbulb went off in his brain as if Miss McClare were dangling it overhead herself. He huffed out a sigh. "Please." A slow smile curved on his lips when a blue sleeve cautiously curled around his neck, then instantly froze at the press of her body against his. The scent of lilac water and Pear's soap wreaked havoc with his pulse, and he gulped, hoping she couldn't feel the jerk of his Adam's apple. *Focus, Barone.* He cleared his throat. "Good. Now the first thing you want to do is grab the attacker's arm around your neck with both hands and pull down like this." He tugged, then proceeded to softly jab her with two elbow thrusts to her side, grinning at the mouse squeak that feathered his ear.

"First step, pull down, second step, a double elbow to the attacker's side . . ." He promptly stamped his foot behind, and another squeal sounded when he wobbled her chair. "Third step, a quick stomp on the attacker's foot and then you step forward and turn . . ."

He grinned at the way her elbows scrunched to her sides and her fists pressed to her mouth, eyes as round as saucers. "You're not going to hit me, are you?" she rasped.

So far his patience was getting more exercise than his student. "No, Miss McClare—you're going to hit me, but I'll show you how as gently as possible, I promise."

The fists lowered. "You also promised you wouldn't tell my family about the attack . . ."

He shook his head and planted hands low on his thighs, opting to chuckle rather than break down and cry. "You are worse than a rabid hound with a bacon-greased bone, you know that?" He peered up, thinking he'd never seen a more stubborn woman other than Gram, only this one had a temper to match. And unless he wanted to be scalded by a glare, beat with a stick, or shamed into submission over the next six weeks, he decided the best course of action would be to simply end the feud right here and now. He exhaled slowly. "Look, Miss McClare, since you and I have to work so closely with each other over the next month and a half, what do you say we call a truce and start over?"

The brat had the nerve to wrinkle her nose. "I don't know—three's not my lucky number."

He cocked his head with a squint. "Excuse me?"

"Well, this will be the third time we started over, you know," she said with a shrug of her shoulders, "so what makes you so sure the third time will be the charm?"

He blinked, absolutely stupefied that the woman not only held a grudge, she counted them too. He shook his head again, unable to stop the grin that eased across his face. "Because contrary to popular opinion, Miss McClare, I am not a moron." Pinching the bridge of his nose, he laughed and finally held out his hand.

"I'd much rather be on your good side than your bad because I'm learning all too quickly it's a lot less painful. So, truce?"

She nibbled the edge of her smile. "If you apologize for breaking your promise."

"I did *not* prom—" He clawed at the back of his neck with a groan. "All right, okay, you win. I apologize for breaking the promise I did not make and getting you in trouble, all right?" Lips pursed, he raised both brows. "Satisfied?"

"Almost." With a brisk fold of arms, she tapped a finger to her mouth, assessing him through narrow eyes. "If you also apologize for being such a grump the day you strolled into my classroom and insulted me when I did absolutely nothing wrong."

Lips gummed tight, he stared at what was possibly the prettiest girl he'd seen in a long, long while and knew deep down that friendship with her would not be a good idea. And yet, he was equally certain that enmity would shear ten years from his life. Gusting out a sigh of surrender, he nodded his head like the dolt she believed him to be, realizing with a crimp in his pride that the woman was absolutely right. He had been a grump that day, taking out on Miss McClare his frustrations at Darla and rich women he assumed were exactly just like her. She had been absolutely correct—he was a "dim-witted moron." But not dim-witted enough to stay on the wrong side of a stick-wielding woman who apparently apprenticed under Teddy Roosevelt.

He packed up his pride and put it away, well aware it would do him no earthly good with the woman before him. "You are right, Miss McClare—I took my utter disdain for spoiled society princesses out on you the day we met because frankly I don't trust them. I had a bad experience with one, and she left a sour taste in my mouth for ladies of means such as yourself. But I was wrong for doing so because being spoiled and pampered is no reason for me to be uncivil, no matter how annoying that spoiled and pampered princess may be."

It was her turn to blink. "I'm sorry . . . was that supposed to be an apology?"

His molars started to grind before his brain even sent the signal. "Yeah."

She folded her arms and hiked her jaw. "Well, then, perhaps I should apologize as well," she said with a sincere pucker of her brow. "Please forgive me, Mr. Barone, for losing my temper with you that first day . . ." She paused and scrunched her nose. "Pardon me, make that on every day we have ever met. No matter how correct my assessment may have been, it was wrong for me to call you a Neanderthal, brainless caveman, polecat, half-wit, pea brain, cave dweller, unsavory baboon, grouch, Attila the Hun, Mr. Personality, illiterate, dim-witted moron, airheaded oaf, brainless barbarian, Mr. Pinhead, buffoon, big lummox, pompous blowhard, dumb ox, ill-mannered cretin, brainless bully, lecherous lout, rude, obnoxious, and born under a rock."

His mouth fell open while a prickle of hurt stabbed in his chest. "I don't remember you calling me all of those names."

The pink lips leveled into a tight line. "Trust me, I did. Oh, and you have animal-cracker breath, Detective Barone, which isn't awful except it makes you smell like a hooligan little boy."

The hurt bled into his tone while the heat bled into his neck. "They calm my ulcers, okay?" His eyes thinned. "Which since I met you, have more than doubled."

Her mouth squirmed enough for him to notice. "Well, you'll be happy to know that you own the honor of tripping my temper more than any person alive."

"I'm honored," he said with a swerve of lips, "and likewise, I assure you."

Her teeth tugged at the edge of what looked like the start of a smile. "I had no idea Italian tempers were as volatile as Irish ones, clearly suggesting a truce may be in our best interests."

"Indeed," he said softly, suddenly transfixed by that sassy little mole that hovered so close to her mouth. He cleared his throat and re-extended his hand. "And not just a truce, Miss McClare, but I think it would behoove us to take safeguards against our hair-trigger tempers."

"Such as?" A sparkle lit in her eyes like a little girl on an adventure.

He rubbed the back of his neck, brows beetled in thought. "Well, when one of us starts to annoy the other and we feel our temper on the rise, maybe we should have a code word or name that warns us to step back and count to ten."

"Oooo, a code word—I like that!" Folded hands to her mouth, she absently chewed on her thumb. "Maybe it can be something that will make us smile—you know, like Mr. Pinhead."

His mouth crooked. "Or Miss Snob Hill or Princess."

"Exactly," she said with a grin, as if this were a game she were playing with her students. "Then if either of us ignores the code and continues to bully or insult . . ." She paused to jag a brow as if to make clear it was his problem and not hers. "That person has to apologize on the spot within ten seconds, all right?"

"I guess that sounds reasonable," he muttered, pretty sure the fear of having to apologize to this female stick monger would be deterrent enough.

"And finally . . . ," she gave a pretty tilt of her head, the twinkle in her eye veering towards diabolical, "to ensure the offensive party *does* apologize within ten seconds, there should be a consequence if they don't. You know, something demeaning . . ."

His mouth took a slant. "You mean like the whack of a stick?"

Her giggle was so contagious, he actually grinned. "Oh, nothing so dire," she assured him. "No, we need something a bit more humbling, say, kissing the other person's feet?"

He grunted. "Don't you get enough of that as it is?"

She arched a brow. "No, I don't, Mr. Pinhead. One . . . two . . . three . . ."

"Sorry," he said in a near growl, thinking this may be harder than he thought. "At least your lips won't put a dent in my shoe polish when you kiss *my* feet." He thrust out a hand. "It's a deal, Miss McClare."

"Not quite, Mr. Barone." The little brat hopped off the chair and darted from the room, tossing an evil grin over her shoulder. "I'll be right back."

"If you bring the stick, the deal is off," he called as she disappeared around the corner. He massaged his face with both hands, wondering what on earth he'd just gotten himself into. A smile tempered his mood as he thought about the little imp, clearly a dickens in a woman's body. Heat ringed his collar. *But sweet thunder, what a body.*

"I'll just need your signature right here," she said in a breathless tone, dashing back in the room with pen and paper in hand. She placed the paper on the seat of the chair and handed him the pen with a disarming smile. "I've recorded the terms and signed my name, so it's your turn."

He stared, mouth swagging as if his jaw were broken. "A contract? You drafted a contract?" He rubbed his temple to ease a headache that was just beginning to throb. "What is it with you people and contracts?" he said, snatching the pen from her hand. He scanned it before slashing his signature across a rulered line, feeling as if he were signing his life away.

"Perfect," she said with a pleased lilt in her voice. She finally held out her hand. "You have a deal, Mr. Barone, and if I'm not mistaken, we have a legal business friendship."

"Legal annoyance is more like it," he muttered.

"Did you say something, Mr. Pinhead?" She cocked her head, assessing him through a flutter of lashes. "One . . . two . . . three . . ."

"Sorry," he snapped, whipping the pen and paper from her hand before she could blink. He tossed them both on the floor. Without further ceremony, he whisked her back up on the chair with another mouse squeak, then turned around again, determined to move this lesson along. "Quick review—with an arm choke, you yank down on the attacker's arm with both hands, then elbow him twice in the side, stomp on his foot, turn and—" he spun around and jammed first his right fist forward, just shy of her stomach—"inflict a right vertical . . ." She flinched back as he leveled another lightning punch with his left fist. "Then a fast left vertical . . ." Her breath caught when he mock slammed a fist against her right forearm. "Finishing up with an inside forearm and front kick." In a wide blink of her eyes, he jerked up to kick her abdomen, stopping a mere inch from touching her body. He steadied her when she nearly toppled from the chair. "You okay?" he asked, hands steadying her waist.

This time a lump bobbed in her throat as shallow breaths rasped from her lips. Chest heaving, she slowly peeled his fingers away. "Fine," she said while a blush bled into her cheeks.

"Sorry." He gave a gruff clear of his throat before stepping back, palms still tingling from the touch of her body. "Okay, do you think you can try it on me?" Fire crawled up the back of his neck when his voice cracked like a baby-faced adolescent.

"Sure." She hopped down and marched to the center of the mat, shoulders square and chest still heaving before she turned her back to him. She sounded breathless. "Ready?"

"Let's just go through the motions first, to make sure you have the steps down, then we'll try it for real." He moved closely behind her, once again amazed at how small she was next to his hulking frame. "When you feel my choke, I want you to say each step out loud as you go through the paces, all right?"

She nodded, and several loose curls bounced in agreement.

"Okay, here we go." He curled an arm loosely around her neck.

"Tug on arms with both hands," she said, doing exactly that, before she elbowed him twice in the side, following with a hard stamp on his foot. "Two side jabs, stomp, step and turn . . ." She whirled and punched him soundly, taking him by surprise as he issued a grunt. "Right punch, left punch, forearm . . ." Hesitating for the briefest of seconds, she finally plowed him in the stomach with her tiny foot, a satisfied smile inching across her face. "Front kick."

"Perfect," he said with a chuckle, "although I think you enjoyed that a little too much."

She clapped her hands with a short little hop on the balls of her feet like a little girl at a birthday party. "Oh, I did, Mr. Barone. That was fun!"

One edge of his mouth curled. "Not for the guy behind you if I do my job right." He steered her back around with a gentle touch to her shoulders. "Okay, for real this time, and don't hold back, okay?" Her giggle floated in the air, and he grinned as he repositioned his arm in a chokehold much tighter than before. "Go!"

She was music in motion, not missing a beat as she executed every step perfectly, sending a cheer when her final kick caused him to stumble back. "I did it, I did it!" she shouted, reminding him of Lottie when she bounced in the air with a glow in her cheeks. "Again?"

"And again, and again . . ." He guided her back around and took his position. "Only each time I'm going to choke you a little harder, dragging you backwards until we get to the point where you can deflect the type of chokehold you might encounter in an actual attack." He felt her stiffen when he gripped her neck tighter than before. "And show no mercy, all right?" His tone veered toward a tease. "You know—like when you lose your temper."

She nodded and continued with the routine, over and over, till she was breathing hard and his arms and chest were tender. He glanced at the clock over the door. "I think that's enough for tonight." He bowed when she turned around. "You're going to be a formidable opponent, Miss McClare, which as the recipient of several whacks with your stick, comes as no surprise."

Her cheeks were flushed when she returned his bow, and her breathing shallow, but there was a sparkle in her eyes that told him she thrived on this foray into independence. "Thank you, Mr. Barone, I feel like a new woman, and you can't imagine how great that feels."

He unrolled his sleeves and rebuttoned his shirt, strolling over to the stack of chairs to retrieve his jacket and tie. "Something wrong with the old one?" he asked with a cock of his head. A slow grin slid across his face. "Other than her tinderbox temper?"

Her smile was halfhearted at best. "Yes, as a matter of fact." She replaced her shoes while he did the same, a weary sigh escaping as she reached for her hat. "She was too trusting," she said quietly, as if their intimate session allowed the safety to reveal insight into the real Allison McClare. "Too wide-eyed and too willing to comply with society's dictates as to what her future must be." Bending to pick up the contract and pen, she stood with eyes downcast, absently twirling the pen in her hand. "Too vulnerable to hurt," she whispered, "but never again." Her melancholy broke with a firm square of shoulders. "I can't thank you enough for taking this on, Mr. Barone. I know I haven't been easy to get along with, tonight or in the past, and for that I humbly apologize." She offered a tremulous smile, and his gut clenched when he saw a sheen of tears in her eyes. "I'm afraid we're two of a kind, you see. Like you, I was betrayed and badly wounded as well, by a man much like yourself, and more than one, really, which I suppose gives credence to your prior claim that I am 'a rich dame as dumb as she is lost.'"

He winced. "Look, Miss McClare—"

She halted him with a hand in the air. "No, you were right—I was both dumb and lost, at least when it came to affairs of the heart, but not anymore." Her chin rose along with the steel quality of her tone. "I have no illusions about my future, Mr. Barone—it no longer rests in the hands of a man, but in the heart of this school, teaching young women to be as self-sufficient as I hope to be." She blinked several times as if to clear moisture from her eyes, but those full lashes only sent a track of tears scurrying down her cheeks. Lips trembling, she took a feisty swipe at her face. "Your efforts tonight, no matter how reluctant, are the first steps in making that possible." Her voice broke on what sounded like an unwanted heave, paralyzing him with the intensity of gratitude in those glossy green eyes. "And for that I will always be grateful."

He stood motionless except for the hard shift of a knot in his throat, not sure what to say. "I'm . . . glad I can be of assistance, Miss McClare—it's my pleasure."

A grin lit her beautiful face, tears and all. "No it isn't, but it's gracious of you to lie."

He grinned. "It would have been a lie before, but not now."

"I'm glad," she whispered, a gentleness stealing across her face that reminded him of her mother. "And, please, call me Alli. I now consider you a friend to whom I owe a great debt."

"If you agree to call me Nick and not those other names crowding your brain." He scratched the back of his neck. "Does this mean I've seen the last of your stick, I hope?"

Her laughter did funny things to his stomach. "No promises, Mr. Cranky Pants," she said with a spry jaunt to the door, turning to give him a smile that sent a warm chill all the way to the soles of his feet. "Although come to think of it, I now know jiu-jitsu, don't I?" She wiggled her brows.

He laughed, peering up as he rolled the mat. "You forget I know it too, Miss McClare."

"Alli," she whispered, her smile as gentle as her voice.

He slowly rose, mat tucked under his arm. "Alli," he repeated, the very taste of her name on his tongue giving him pause. Another chill slid through him, only this one blew ice cold, rife with warning as alarm curled in his stomach. "Get changed and I'll walk you home."

Her eyes brightened. "Oooo, can we take the cable car?" she breathed, looking so much like Lottie when she wanted to help trim the bushes that he didn't have the heart to say no.

"Sure. As long as I don't lose my supper."

She squealed before she disappeared around the corner, leaving him alone with his thoughts and an awful dread that slowly churned in his gut. The memory of their near-kiss weeks ago flashed in his mind like an unwelcome threat, and he felt the kippers he'd had for lunch begin to rise in his throat. He dove for the bag of animal crackers in his pocket, pelting the total contents into his mouth to settle a stomach—and a heart—that was moving way, *way* too fast. "Blue blazes, I hate motion sickness," he muttered, stomach cramping over the prospect of something he desperately wished to avoid. He expelled a shaky breath.

And for once, he wasn't talking about the blessed cable car.

13

"You're awfully chipper for a competitive person who hates to lose," Cassie said with a sly smile, eyeing Alli over the chessboard in the parlour. She moved her queen to capture Alli's pawn. "Especially with a sister leaving for Europe tomorrow for almost a solid year."

Alli glanced up, the reminder that Meg was to complete her senior year in high school as an exchange student in Paris suddenly sapping her smile. "Thanks for popping my good mood," she said with a scowl, dinner roiling in her stomach. "I'm going to miss her something fierce."

"Me too," Cass whispered, "but at least she'll be back at Christmas for the wedding, right? And honestly, Al, as difficult a year as she's had with all her girlfriends acquiring beaus, I think Paris will be good for her, don't you?"

"Absolutely." Alli stared hard at the chessboard, but all she could see was Meg's tear-stained face whenever she'd been snubbed at parties of so-called friends in the social elite.

"Checkmate!"

Alli's mouth gaped into a smile. "How in the world . . . ?"

Cassie leaned in to cross her arms on the table. "One of the basics of chess, Al," she said with a lift of brows, "one must be present to win—mentally as well as physically."

"Is it that obvious?" Alli grated her lip, smile sheepish.

The twinkle in her cousin's eyes turned tender. "Oh, no, honey," she said softly, affection lacing her tone as she squeezed Alli's hand. "Not to someone who's deaf, dumb, and blind."

"Oh, you are such a brat," Alli said with grin, tossing Cassie's hand away while her eyes flitted to where her mother and uncle played cribbage by the hearth. "So I'm a little distracted—"

"A little?" Cassie sagged back in her chair. "Goodness, Al, I could have been playing blindfolded and still won. Not to mention your not batting an eye over losing, and *this* from a notorious sore loser who usually barricades herself in the kitchen, commiserating with a batch of Rosie's cookies." Her green eyes honed to a squint. "You've been in a happy fog for a couple of weeks now, and if I'm not mistaken, it appears to coincide with your first lesson with Mr. Barone."

"Hush!" Alli sputtered, gaze darting to make sure Mother and Uncle Logan were still focused on their game. She leaned in, nervous that Cassie's voice might carry in a room far too quiet with everyone else upstairs cheering the boys on in a billiards competition. "My distraction has nothing to do with Nick, and if it does, it's simply because I love jiu-jitsu."

"Ah . . . it's 'Nick,' now, is it?" Cassie teased. "So, no more sticks?"

Alli chuckled. "No, no more sticks," she said with an imp of a smile. Arms braced to the table, she bent in. "'Cause *now* I get to kick and elbow him instead, which is a lot more fun."

"I'll bet." Cassie's grin faded into careful assessment, the levity in her eyes tempered by concern. "You like him, don't you?" she whispered.

"Of course I do," Alli said quickly, ignoring the heat she felt creeping into her cheeks. "Nick is helping me to gain my independence, so we've agreed to be civil."

"Just civil?" Cassie's tone was cautious with a hint of worry that Alli understood all too well. Cassie had been there when Roger had shattered her heart, offering comfort night after night while Alli sobbed herself to sleep. Even had to be restrained from sending Jamie—the Oly Club's boxing champ four years running—to blacken Roger's eye. A sad smile shadowed her lips. "Yes, just civil," she fibbed, too scared to admit even to herself that civility with Nick Barone possibly posed a much bigger threat than their prior enmity had. She shivered. "I have no desire for anything more, trust me."

"None?"

Alli hesitated, reflecting back on the day Nick had almost kissed her, not only stealing her voice, but her sleep for weeks after. She'd been caught off-guard by the desire she'd seen in his eyes, her skin shimmering with heat from the near touch of his lips. But she didn't trust him—any more than he trusted her—and that was just fine. Preferred, actually, because Alli had no faith in that glorious tingle when she'd thudded into his arms. No trust in that catch of her breath when his eyes sheathed closed with a glaze of attraction that surely rivaled her own. No, she'd been there too many times and learned the hard way a tingle could be as deceptive as a diamond ring, gouging deeper than any cold and chiseled stone.

Yes, Nick Barone provoked desire, but another far outweighed it—the desire to protect her heart, which was still badly bruised. *And* the desire to realize her dream of being the independent woman she so longed to be. Two things that would *not* happen if she let her guard down with Nicholas Barone ... *or* with her matchmaking cousin. Her gaze flicked up to Cass, who was analyzing her way too closely, and wondered how to throw her off the scent without having to lie. After all, she had *no* desire to be romantically involved with anyone right now, right? "No, Cass, no desire at all," she said with a firm lift of her chin.

The green eyes squinted. "Well then, let's just explore this a tad, shall we? When you say 'no desire,' you mean no desire for a relationship with a man right now, correct?"

"Precisely," Alli said, relieved she didn't have to fib to a bottom-line cousin with whom she'd shared every secret since the age of two. Her jaw tightened. "Or ever, if I have my way."

Arms propped casually on the table, Cassie nodded, eyes studying the board. "All right, so no desire for a relationship." Her lashes flipped up as her gaze pinned Alli to the chair. "But does that mean you have 'no desire' for Nick Barone either, as in attraction to the man?"

"No . . ." Alli blinked. "I mean yes . . ." She scrubbed her face with her hands. "Oh, I don't know what I mean because you're confusing me."

The probing look dissolved into a sad smile. "And you're confusing me, Al," Cassie whispered, a trace of hurt in her tone. "You and I are sisters more than cousins, sharing everything all the way back to our cribs." She reached across the table to grasp Alli's hand, the intensity in her eyes piercing Alli straight through. "We tell each other everything, remember? And then we settle it with prayer. But I can't do that if you close me out."

Alli swallowed hard, fighting the sting of tears that always accompanied the fears she harbored inside. Clutching her arms to her waist, she nodded. "All right," she said quietly, "what do you want to know?"

"Are you attracted to Nick Barone?"

A heavy sigh shuddered from Alli's lips. "Yes."

"Is he attracted to you?"

Her eyelids weighted closed and instantly the memory of his near-kiss invaded her brain, spiking her pulse, warming her cheeks. "Maybe . . . or sometimes I think so . . ."

"Why? A look? A comment? What?" In her typical no-nonsense style, Cassie wrangled the truth as easily as a steer on her father's Texas ranch.

Alli glanced up, her voice barely a whisper. "He almost kissed me."

Her cousin jolted straight up as if she'd been roped like one of those steers. "Thunderation, Al, and you didn't tell me?"

"Shhh!" Alli grabbed Cassie's hand and jerked her close. "I was going to tell you eventually, I promise."

"When?" Cassie whispered in a near shriek. "After the wedding?"

"Now, see? This is exactly why I didn't say anything." Steeling her jaw, Alli folded her arms, knowing full well where Cassie would try to take this piece of news. "Before I know it, you'll have me married and pushing a stroller with triplets, Cass, and that is *not* what I want."

"And what *do* you want?" Cassie demanded, following suit to lean in on the table. Her brows arched high over eyes sharp with concern.

Alli's chin rose. "You already know my aspirations—I want to be independent and take care of myself. And become the best teacher I can to help poor women be independent too."

Cassie shifted elbows to the table, head propped on folded hands. "And marriage doesn't factor in at all, I suppose?"

An involuntary shiver swept Alli. "Absolutely not. A husband will only stop me from doing what I want, and I want to teach."

"Horsefeathers," Cassie said with challenge in her eyes. "Jamie's not stopping me from teaching once we marry . . ."

Alli grunted. "Yes, well, Jamie's not most men, nor did he stomp on your—" She stopped cold at the jag of her cousin's brow, remembering all too well how many times Jamie MacKenna had, indeed, stomped on Cassie's heart before the ring was on her hand. She blew out a weary sigh. "So, what's your point, Cass?"

"My point is, that yes, there are rats in the world like Roger Luepke, but you can't let them control your life." Her eyes softened. "You can't let *fear* control your life because that's all this is. You're afraid to feel anything for any man, sure that each and every one is going to cut you to the quick like Roger, and sometimes even the good ones, like Jamie, did to me. But you know what I'm afraid of, Al?" A glint of tears sparked in Cassie's eyes, reminding Alli of just how close their bond was. "I'm afraid the cousin I love like a sister—and the one woman I've always admired for her spark of adventure—will miss out on what God has for her because she's too afraid to take a chance." Moisture pooled in Alli's eyes, and Cassie gripped her hand. "Look, all I'm saying is why don't we just pray about this and let God lead you instead of letting fear do the job, okay? Who knows? Maybe the attraction you two feel for each other will lead to something wonderful."

A shaky breath quivered from Alli's lips. "I'm not sure if Nick is even attracted to me."

Cassie arched a brow.

"Oh, okay, maybe a little," she said with a chew of her lip, "but he's been wounded by love as much as I have, and I'm pretty sure he has no desire to pursue a relationship right now."

"And that's fine if that's the way God wants it to be. But . . . if there *is* supposed to be something between you and Nick, I gotta tell you—from where I'm sitting, he seems like a pretty decent guy. I've only known him a couple of weeks now, but he's smart, hardworking, has a big heart with the kids, and I swear, Mrs. Peel reveres him like he's related to the Pope. Let's face it—the man has to be pretty special if a good woman like her is crazy about him. For goodness' sake, he even goes to church with her and her brood every week, so he obviously has faith."

Alli's lip crooked. "So did Jamie, as you recall, but you learned the hard way that his faith was pretty thin."

"Yes, I did, but we prayed about it and look—God and I got our man in the end, right?"

Alli bent in, hands clenched white to the sides of the table. "Yes, but that still doesn't mean Nick Barone is a man with the type of faith you and I both agreed we'd hold out for."

The firm lift of Cassie's chin indicated her mind was made up. "All the more reason to address this situation with prayer so God can take it where *He* wants it to go." She covered Alli's hand with her own, intensity fairly shimmering in her eyes. "Look, Al, I love you and want you to be happy, so let's just pray about it so you can unclench those fingers and let go, trusting God to fill them—and your heart—with the blessings He wants you to have, okay?"

Expelling another wobbly breath, Alli nodded. "I'll try."

"Good," Cassie said with a soft smile. "You try and I'll pray."

Clasping Alli's hand once again, Cassie closed her eyes while Alli followed suit, her cousin's quiet prayer reminding her of the deep faith their parents had instilled in each of them. A faith Alli had let slide when she'd discovered her fiancé was a fraud. Despite her many prayers for the right beau, Roger had managed to fool her and everyone else—from Uncle Logan's neighbor who'd hired him as an apprentice at his winery, to the winery's neighbors who had befriended him as well, including Uncle Logan. As handsome as Jamie, Roger had pursued Allison until she'd happily agreed to become his wife with a ring made of paste. Overnight, her trust in God became as artificial as the ring she'd proudly worn on her hand, no faith in His ability to keep her heart safe. And yet now, listening as Cassie prayed, Allison wondered if God hadn't rescued her heart after all, allowing the sizable diamond in her ring to come loose. It had been that same loose diamond that prompted a trip to the jeweler where she'd discovered her ring was as counterfeit as her fiancé. Uncle Logan wasted no time investigating Roger's past, and Alli had been shattered to learn that not only was Roger a fraud, but a man who was marrying her for her money while seeing other women behind her back.

"And finally, Lord," Cassie concluded, "please help Alli forgive Roger once and for all so she can move forward and experience all the blessings I know You have for her." With a whispered "amen," Cassie squeezed her hand, head ducked to search Alli's face. "Feel better?"

Inhaling deeply, Alli exhaled again, realizing that the heaviness she'd carried around since Roger's betrayal seemed lighter somehow. She peered up at her cousin through a blur of tears. "You know what—I think I do." She swiped the moisture away, tone steeped in regret. "Oh, Cass, why did I turn my back on God when He was the very shelter I needed all along?"

Cassie's smile was tender. "Because betrayal makes us angry, Al, and we want to lash out. When Jamie betrayed me, I couldn't rail at you or Aunt Cait or my parents, but I could rail at God, so I did—just like you. Both of us have put our lives in His hands from little on, and frankly, we expected Him to keep our hearts safe too. And in the end, He does, just like He did with Jamie and me, giving us both a love we never dreamed possible." She feathered a stray hair from Alli's eyes. "Just like I believe He wants to give you. But He never promised absence of pain, only that He'd help us overcome it. Remember last week's homily? 'In the world ye shall have tribulation: but be of good cheer; I have overcome the world.'" Wetness glimmered in Cassie's eyes that matched Alli's to a tear. "You're an overcomer, Al, just like me, but neither of us can do it without Him."

Alli nodded and dabbed her eyes with her handkerchief, sneaking a peek across the room. "Thanks, Cass—you have no idea how much I needed this."

Cassie grinned. "Sure I do—you did the same for me with Jamie, remember?"

An unladylike snort rolled from Alli's lips. "Yes, but I sure didn't want to. I wanted to slap him silly, but Bram said he was already slapping himself enough for the both of us."

"Very true," Cassie said with a mischievous smile. "I'm surprised you didn't use a stick."

"Don't think he's off the hook yet." Alli pushed her chair out and rose with a stretch. "If that man gloats over trouncing me in chess one more time, I just may."

A husky laugh escaped Cassie's lips, confirming what they all knew—Alli might be a poor loser, but Jamie MacKenna was a poor winner, wearing his victories—which were considerable in boxing and pool—like a badge of honor. "Don't worry, Al, after he wins upstairs, the boy will be in dire need of humility." She wiggled her brows, obviously anticipating matching skills at pool with the love of her life. "And I'm just the woman to teach it."

⁂

"Meg?" Alli peered out into the dark veranda of her mother's study, relieved to find her sister huddled on the far end of the wrought-iron settee. "What are you doing out here by yourself, sweetie?" She eased the French door open. "Everybody's looking for you."

Her sister glanced up, and Alli's stomach clenched when she saw her face glistening in the moonlight, slick with tears. A frail heave shuddered from Meg's lips, and Alli rushed to her side, gathering her in a tight hug. "Oh, Meggie, what's wrong?" she whispered.

"I . . . I'm so s-scared to go . . . ," Meg said, her broken whisper wrenching Alli's heart.

She pulled away to brace Meg's swollen face in her hands. "But, why? You loved the Rousseaus when we stayed with them three years ago, and you and Lily were the best of friends."

Meg sniffed and swiped her eyes with the side of her hand. "I . . . kn-know, but what if she's changed? What if she turns on me like Ann and Eva, treating me like I have the plague?"

Alli caressed her sister's face, aching at the way her sister's so-called friends had turned on her after Devin Caldwell humiliated Meg at several social functions. "She won't, Megs, I promise. You and Lily have too much in common—you're both kind and gentle young women who are at the top of your class. Frankly, I think Ann and Eva might be a bit jealous because you always excel in school and they don't." She swept a stray curl from her sister's face. "And you and I both know that's the whole reason Devin Caldwell has always picked on you like he has. The little worm can't stand you besting him over and over again."

The faintest of smiles tipped Meg's mouth. "He may be a worm, Al, but we both know he's not so little anymore." Her shoulders hunched in a cumbersome sigh. "He's as tall as Uncle Logan and just as handsome . . . the little twerp."

Alli chuckled, surprised her sweet little sister would utter a negative word about anybody. "Goodness, I never thought I'd see the day! Devin Caldwell has been a thorn in your side forever, Megs, so it's about time you call a spade a spade and a worm a worm. I'd think you'd be thrilled to go to Paris and put an ocean between you and that little brat."

Her smile faded all over again. "I am, Al, but I'm going to miss everyone so much."

"Likewise," Alli said with another quick hug. She buffed her sister's arms. "But you know what? Something deep down inside tells me Paris is going to be good for you, Megs. A chance to put your childhood behind and blossom into the woman God intends for you to be."

Tears welled in Meg's eyes. "Oh, Al, do you really think so?"

Alli squeezed her hand. "I do," she whispered, "and I have prayers to back it up."

Meg's full lips flickered into a shy smile. "That's what Bram always says, that God has a plan and purpose for me that will take me by surprise."

"He's right, you know," Alli said with a tender smile. "You should listen to him."

Meg nodded, her watery gaze fixed on the moon-striped bay. "I don't know what I'm going to do without him, Al," she whispered. "Bram's always been my best friend, making me feel pretty and feminine when other boys tore me down." Her lower lip quivered. "How am I going to survive without him?"

Alli kissed her cheek. "By the grace of God, Meggie, the same God who's loved you and shown you just how special you are through the kindness and favor of one Bram Hughes."

A gentle smile curved on Megan's lips. "He has, hasn't He?" She exhaled slowly, as if dispelling all doubt. "Somehow I've always felt God's love through Bram's friendship, and I just have to believe that when I'm in Paris, I'll feel His strength through Bram's prayers too."

"And mine as well, don't forget, and Mother's and Cassie's too." She patted Meg's arm and rose. "And speaking of prayers, we better pray there's cake left, 'cause Rosie was just delivering your farewell chocolate cake to the parlour before I came looking for you. So we best hightail it before it's all gone." She extended her hand. "Ready?"

Meg stood, shoulders square and voice steady as she clasped her sister's hand, her sweet face aglow with a shy innocence that was uniquely Meg. "You know what, Al?" she whispered, her impish smile so like a little girl on the verge of becoming a woman. "I think I am."

14

There better be cake left or else . . ." Hunger rumbling in her stomach, Alli ushered Meg into the parlour, the laughter of family helping to dispel her melancholy over a sister who would soon be gone.

"Goodie! They're back—can we have cake now, Mama, please?" Maddie whirled around on her mother's lap, interrupting a focused game of cribbage with Uncle Logan.

"You bet, squirt," Uncle Logan said, reaching to tug her pigtail while he slipped Alli's mother a grin, deftly executing a move in the game. "Especially since I just skunked your mother again."

Her mother's smile tipped as she gave Maddie a hug. "Blake, darling," she said with a glance over her shoulder to where her son was snitching a cherry off Meg's cake. "Be a dear and move Rosie's cutting knife to the far side of the table so I'm not tempted to use it." She gave Logan a droll smile. "But hand me the cake server, please, the one with the *very* sharp point."

Alli grinned along with Uncle Logan as he gave her mother a wink. "Ouch. Come on, Cait—you know you don't mean that."

"Actually, Logan, I don't know that at all," she said with a sweet smile. She kissed Maddie's head and rose. "Guess what, sweetheart? You get to share cake with Uncle Logan."

"Whoopee!" the little tyke shouted, bouncing up and down in her arms.

"Pardon me, Miss Caitlyn," Hadley said at the door, "Mr. Andrew Turner to see you."

Uncle Logan scowled. "Turner? What in tarnation is he doing here?"

"Thank you, Hadley," her mother said with a warm smile before she flashed Uncle Logan a look of warning. "Andrew is here to drop off a report for the Vigilance Committee, Logan, so I'd appreciate you keeping your comments to yourself."

Something Uncle Logan obviously didn't consider an option. "You know how I feel about Turner, Cait," he groused, "and yet here you are, entertaining an archenemy of mine."

Releasing a weary sigh, she handed Maddie to Uncle Logan with a patient pat of his cheek. "It's not entertaining, Logan, it's business, and just because you had a falling out with your best friend in college is no reason for me not to treat him with the civility he deserves. Especially as a member of the Vigilance Committee assisting me on an important project."

Logan grunted, ignoring Maddie as she attempted to crawl over his shoulder. "Monkey business if I know Turner, and I'd think you'd exercise extreme caution with a man who worshiped you from afar before you married Liam."

"Honestly, Logan, sometimes I don't know who's the bigger juvenile—you or Blake."

"I vote for Blake," Jamie volunteered from across the room.

Caitlyn ignored them to brush a kiss to Maddie's cheek. "I'll be back soon, honey, so you enjoy cake with Uncle Logan and don't worry about getting it on your dress or on Uncle Logan's clean white shirt because tonight is bath night, all right?"

"Really, Mama? Gee whiz, that's swell!"

"No, *not* really," Logan said with a pinch of Maddie's waist, eyeing her mother with a mock scowl. "Your mother's just being a sore loser."

"So *that's* where I get it!" Alli made a beeline for the cake, slapping Blake's hand when he attempted to filch another cherry. "Thank heavens the vultures didn't cut it yet."

Cassie took a sip of her coffee, giving Alli a wink over the rim of her cup. "Well, it wasn't easy reining them in because the natives were restless."

"Restless, huh?" Alli directed Meg to the seat of honor on the sofa between Bram and Blake, where her farewell cake sat on the coffee table waiting to be cut and served.

"Uh, not sure 'restless' is the right word, Cowgirl." Jamie snatched a Hershey bar from a candy bowl and tore the wrapper off, crumpling it in a ball. He bounced it off Blake's nose, then strolled over to hand a piece to Maddie.

"Oh, sure, give her more chocolate, why don't you?" Logan muttered.

Jamie strolled to the love seat and offered Cassie a piece before tossing one in his mouth. "Humiliated might be a better word," he continued, his smile edging toward cocky, "since I walloped several unlucky natives tonight."

"Hey, I'm not unlucky," Bram said. He draped a casual arm over Meg's shoulder, blue eyes twinkling as he offered a lazy smile that lit up his handsome face. "I get to sit with the goodbye girl, and I'll just bet she'll give me the first piece, won't you, Bug?"

Meg giggled, her full cheeks pink as she peeked up at Bram with adoration.

"And I get the second, right, Megs?" her brother chimed in, hooking Meg's waist. "So you won the round of pool, MacKenna, but you're clearly the loser here."

"Loser?" Jamie polished off the Hershey bar with a quick brush of palms before settling in next to Cassie. "Could you define that please? I don't believe that word's in my vocabulary."

Cassie patted his arm with a wry smile. "Neither is humility, darling, but I'll educate you later in a private game of pool."

"Mmm . . . 'private,' you say?" Jamie asked, attempting to steal a kiss before Cassie slapped him away.

The edge of Alli's lips tipped as she cut the cake, handing the first piece to Meg. "Thank goodness you're better in pool than he is, Cass, or he'd be impossible to live with."

"Hey, can I help it if I'm good at everything I do?" Jamie tweaked the back of Cassie's neck, grinning when she swatted him away.

"Not everything," Alli said with a sly smile. She handed cake off to Maddie and Uncle Logan before turning to give Cassie a wink. "How much you wanna bet I can level you flat in a sport of my choosing, MacKenna?"

A pucker of disbelief wedged above Jamie's nose. "You—Allison 'Read 'em and Weep' McClare—beat me at a sport?" He folded his arms with a dare of a smile. "That I'd like to see."

"You know, I was hoping you'd say that." She bent to cut more cake for Cassie and him, then handed his piece over with a waggle of brows. "Savor your dessert now, Jamie boy, because it's gonna turn sour when you land on the floor—both you *and* your ego." Alli gave Cassie a wink. "Right, Cass?"

A grin inched across Cassie's lips. "You're brilliant, Al, you know that? And since Jamie *is* our boxing champ—" she pinched his cheek, lowering her voice to mimic his favorite claim to fame— "tutored at the feet of Gentleman Jim Corbett himself, *he's* the perfect volunteer."

"Volunteer for what?" Jamie said, brows in a scrunch, bolting his cake.

"Oh my *yes*, he certainly is," Alli said with a wicked chuckle. She perched on the edge of Uncle Logan's cordovan easy chair with her dessert. "Aren't you, Jamie?"

"Aren't I what?" he repeated, delivering a cheeky grin to Bram and Blake as he set his empty plate on an end table. "The perfect volunteer to demonstrate skill in boxing or pool?"

"No, on how to alienate your friends," Blake said with a dry smile.

Caitlyn reentered the parlour, brows raised in her son's direction. "Blake Henry McClare—kindly remove those clodhoppers from my antique coffee table, young man. Must I remind you that you do not live in a pool hall?"

Jamie chuckled. "I'd say that's pretty obvious from the way he plays." Jamie squinted and sniffed in the air. "Hey, do I smell cookies?"

"You smell trouble, MacKenna," Alli said with a cock of her brow, "if you think you're gonna weasel out of my demonstration." She tugged him up from the couch. "Come on, Mr. Cocky, I need somebody pretty big, strong, and dumb to demonstrate my jiu-jitsu on."

Bram chuckled. "Well, we'll give him 'pretty' and 'dumb.'"

"Not to mention 'pretty dumb,'" Blake said with a grin.

Logan laughed, a sleepy Maddie plastered against his white shirt, which now sported the same chocolate frosting that circled her mouth. "Sounds like you have a reputation to vindicate, Mac."

"So, what do I have to do?" Jamie asked, rising when Cassie prodded him from behind.

"Just stand there and look pretty." Alli snatched a pillow from the loveseat.

"Which you do so well, darling," Cassie said with a sweet smile.

Alli tugged him to the middle of the room where there was

plenty of empty space and tossed the pillow behind him. "This will be easy, Jamie. All you have to do is try and attack me."

"Allison, this isn't dangerous, I hope?" her mother asked, a crease in her brow.

"No, Mother," Alli fluttered her lashes at Jamie. "At least not for me." Mouth pursed in thought, she positioned him just so. "There, now all I need is for you to try and choke me from behind."

Grinning, he shot Cassie a wink. "This is sounding better all the time."

Alli chewed the edge of her lip, eyes fixed on the single pillow behind him. "Hey, Bram, throw me those pillows beside you, will you?" she said, snatching them in the air when he tossed them her way. She laid them behind Jamie, grateful her flared dress wouldn't impede her kick.

Hands perched on his hips, Jamie eyed the mountain of pillows on the floor. "You don't really think you're going to knock me down, do you?" he asked with a dubious smile.

"Well, that's the plan." Alli gave him a saucy look while she slipped off her shoes.

"Oh, this I gotta see." Uncle Logan carefully shifted a sleeping Maddie to his shoulder before swiveling to face the action. "It's time to assess whether our investment has paid off."

"Goodness, you're not going to hurt him, I hope?" Her mother angled her chair forward.

Jamie laughed. "I seriously doubt that, Mrs. McClare. I am the Oly boxing champ four years running, you know, and considerably bigger than your daughter."

"Well, your mouth is anyway," Alli quipped, eliciting chuckles from around the room. "I will now demonstrate the defense for a rear chokehold with our 'boxing champ, Mr. MacKenna.' Ready, Jamie?"

"Have at it, Miss McClare." He looped a loose arm to her throat. "And don't hold back."

"Harder, please," she instructed, adrenaline coursing when she felt his arm tighten against her neck. "You're absolutely certain you want me to give it my all?"

He laughed, his breath warm against her ear. "Yes, Al, I think I can han—"

His voice trailed off when Ali spun into a blur. "Tug . . . jabs . . . stomp . . . turn . . . right . . . left . . . forearm . . ." She finished with a hike of her leg, catapulting Jamie onto the cushions with a swift kick. "Kick," she finished with a lift of her chin, cheeks flushed as she bowed to her family.

Logan bounded to his feet with a cheer that never even fazed the little girl asleep on his shoulder, the pride in his tone as jubilant as if Alli were his daughter instead of his niece. "That's my girl!"

"Good heavens, darling, are you hurt?" Cassie bent over Jamie with a squirm of a smile.

"Only my pride," he said with a groan, lumbering to his feet with a sheepish grin. "Gotta hand it to you, Al, you could knock the wind out of anybody with a kick like that."

"I'll say." Cassie hooked an arm to Jamie's waist. "Not to mention if somebody gets fresh." She kissed his cheek before giving Alli a wink. "I may need lessons."

"I think I need to see that again," Blake said with a chuckle. "Mac toppled so fast, I missed it."

Jamie ushered Cassie back to the sofa. "Yeah? Well, I'd like to see it again too, McClare, only with somebody more experienced at picking himself up off the floor. Let's see her toss *you* on your sorry rump."

"If you're talking '*sorry rumps*,' I vote Mr. Beware." Rosie stood at the door with a tray of fresh-baked cookies, her volume raised to cue in Miss Behave, no doubt.

"Awk, pain in the rump, pain in the rump . . ."

Alli grinned and shook her head over the pet phrase Rosie had taught Miss B. in honor of "Mr. Beware," her snide distortion of Uncle Logan's last name.

Rosie passed out cookies—Meg's favorite, to take along on the train—to everyone but Uncle Logan before depositing the cookie plate on the coffee table. She loaded the half-eaten cake onto her tray while Uncle Logan rose to pluck several cookies for himself, searing Rosie with a nasty glare. "Surprised you didn't make a separate batch for me," he muttered, "with hemlock."

"Aye," she said with a firm tilt of her chin, "but thought better of it since the family appears to be attached." One edge of her lip curled. "A wee bit like a pet leech, I suppose."

"Now, Rosie . . . ," Caitlyn said softly, the affection in her tone more than evident.

Hadley strode into the room toting a tray of coffee, lemonade, and a plate of deviled eggs.

Rosie's jaw slipped. "What in blue blazes are you doing with those eggs?" she groused.

Placing the tray next to the other, Hadley rose with a calm tug of his tailored black coat. "Why, your request for coffee, lemonade, and eggs, miss," he responded with dignity.

Rosie winced and quickly kneaded her brow. "I *said*, 'bring milk for Megs,'" she whispered loudly, "not 'bring the eggs'!" Shaking her head, she snatched them from his tray.

"Very good, miss." Hadley offered a polite bow and left, a ghost of a smile on his lips.

"He'll be the death of me yet," Rosie mumbled, pausing at the door to shoot Uncle Logan a scowl. "If *he* doesn't do me in first."

"I should be so lucky." Logan chomped on his cookie.

Alli bumped Cassie's shoulder with a grin. "Maybe that's been Hadley's plan all along," she whispered. "Other than Uncle Logan, I've never seen anyone better at riling Rosie."

Cassie chuckled. "A true talent some men seem to have," she whispered back, "getting under one's skin—like Jamie with me in the beginning." She winked. "And Mr. Nick with you."

Mr. Nick. A blush braised Alli's cheeks at the mere reminder of the man who, indeed, had a true talent for "getting under her skin," warming both her body and her temper. Her stomach instantly looped at the memory of that near kiss, confirming there was no way she could let a man like "Mr. Nick" *under* her skin. A shiver shimmied her spine as she took the lemonade Jamie offered, giving him a shaky smile. Because there was no question that once *under . . .*

She gulped, the drink souring her tongue as much as the thought.

. . . it'd be *way* too easy to slip into her heart.

15

"Red rover, red rover, send Miss Alli right over."

Nick shot a glance over his shoulder as he straddled the ladder at the back of the Hand of Hope School, where the younger girls were playing red rover while the older girls chatted beneath a massive oak. Paintbrush in hand, he watched Allison rub her hands together with a dangerous gleam in her eye before she hiked her skirt to her ankles. With a deafening war cry that coaxed a smile to his lips, she charged the opposing team like a band of wild Indians, convincing him once and for all that under that beautiful exterior, a tomboy lurked in disguise. His lips quirked when she broke through the other team's barrier, which, sadly enough, consisted only of Cassie and Lottie, whose groans were easily drowned out by the whoops and cheers from the other side.

Cheeks flushed, Alli promptly stole Lottie's hand, taunting her cousin with a gloat. "Looks like I won and you lost, cousin dear, which means *you'll* be providing candy for my girls *and* grading *my* papers for a solid week per the terms of our bet."

"Uh, not necessarily," Nick said, shocking both himself and the others when he laid the paintbrush aside and dismounted the ladder. Wiping his paint-stained hands on his old work trousers, he ambled over to where Cassie stood open-mouthed, a smile beginning to curve on her face. He gave her a wink. "What d'ya say we get your team back, Miss McClare, and teach the cocky drama teacher how to play the role of a humble teammate?"

"Hey, no fair," Kara yelled with a cross of arms. "You can't just join after we won."

"Why not?" Cassie said with a bold thrust of her chin. "As I recall, Miss Alli joined your team halfway through recess, so if *you* got to add a team member, why shouldn't I?"

"Sounds fair to me," Nick said with a slack of his hip. He glanced at his pocket watch. "Only six minutes of recess left, ladies, so I suggest we get a move on."

Alli stared, mouth ajar while the barest hint of a smile tugged at her lips. "This is nothing but a bald-faced conspiracy, you two!" Shooting a smirk over her shoulder, she sashayed back to her team, taking her place. "But we'll prove who the real winners are, won't we, girls?"

"Yeah, we'll show 'em," Denise said while the other girls cheered her on.

Alli rubbed her hands on her skirt and grabbed Lottie and Denise's hands. "Tighten up, girls, and don't let 'em through, okay? Red rover, red rover, send Miss Cassie right over."

Groans rose as Cassie broke through the weakest spot, promptly towing Lottie back over.

"Good job," Nick said, clasping Lottie on one side and Cassie on the other.

Cassie leaned close to his ear. "We're calling the cocky one over, right?"

His gaze narrowed on Alli. "Miss Smarty-Pie? Oh, you bet." He firmed his hold on both sides, taunting Alli with a cheeky grin. "Red rover, red rover, send Miss Smarty-Pie right over."

Giggles rose as the little girls squealed, hopping and dancing in circles when Alli placed a hand to her chest, brows raised in mock indignation. "Me?"

"You're the only smart mouth I see," Nick said, sliding Cassie a grin before giving Lottie a wink. "How 'bout you two?"

"No question," Cassie quipped while Lottie giggled. "Unless, of course, *Miss Alli*'s a chicken . . ."

"I'll show you chicken," she called, methodically rolling the sleeves of her pale-blue shirtwaist, eyes glinting with challenge. She shrugged her shoulders as if to loosen her muscles, then backed up several steps, seemingly oblivious to the whoops and hollers of her team. Knee bent and one foot forward, she braced fists to her sides with that same do-or-die gleam in her eye as when she focused on jiu-jitsu moves.

A grin eased across Nick's lips at her banshee cry, and with a warrior press of her jaw, she hurtled forward, skirt hiked well above her ankles while she barreled down like a bullet from a Smith & Wesson.

Whether wanting to spare Lottie a jolt or just that cocksure she could take Cassie and him down, she hit hard between them, eliciting a grunt from Cassie's lips. Holding fast, Nick grinned as Alli ricocheted like a rubber band, arms windmilling when she lost her balance with a squeal. Breath suspended, he scooped her up by the waist to keep her from landing in the grass, no oxygen whatsoever when her chest slammed against his. Momentarily paralyzed, he held her several heartbeats too long, completely derailed by eyes so green, they all but swallowed him whole. "Thank you," she whispered, and his gaze followed the husky sound to parted lips that tightened his belly.

"Ahem . . ." Cassie's interruption scorched both of their faces.

He quickly released her with a gruff clear of his throat, aware of the cacophony of groans across the yard for the very first time. "You're welcome," he said with a casual smile that belied the thrum of his pulse. "It's the least I can do for a teammate." Glancing down, he spied a splotch of yellow paint on her skirt and groaned, suddenly noting a thick glob of paint on his own pants.

Her eyes followed his, and she sucked in a sharp breath. "Oh, no—this is my favorite skirt!"

Ding-ding-ding! Miss Tuttle appeared on the porch ringing a bell nearly bigger than she, silver bun flopping as much as the bell. Alli's team vaulted in the air with deafening shrieks, evidently no allegiance whatsoever as long as they received candy from a teacher.

"Oh, my." Cassie chewed on her lip. "I'll take the children in, Al, and you tend to your skirt."

"B-but . . . how will I get it out?" she said, looking up at Nick like a little girl lost.

A fierce protectiveness rose until he reminded himself this was the woman who not only whacked him with a stick on first sight, but leveled him in jiu-jitsu three times a week. He cleared his throat. "Uh, look, I'm sorry about your skirt, but I can get it out, I promise."

"Oh, good," Cassie said with a sigh of relief. She gave her cousin a side hug, obviously avoiding the glob of paint on Alli's skirt. "Now, you let Mr. Nick take care of that skirt, Al, and I'll take care of your class, all right?" She winked. "I'm sure I'm leaving you in good hands."

Heat ringing his collar, Nick strode over to his box of paint supplies and snatched the turpentine along with a questionable-looking rag and putty knife. "Sit on the bottom step," he ordered, and she hiked a brow. A smile twitched on his lips. "Please."

Brows in a crimp, she did as he asked, shifting the paint stain so it rested flat on the plane of her thigh. She eyed the knife. "I won't need my stick, will I?" she asked with a hint of jest.

"No, ma'am, you're safe with me." *I hope.* He squatted to carefully scrape the paint from her skirt, his body humming at touching her like this. Avoiding her gaze, he focused hard on the stain, wondering why this felt so much more intimate than when they trained in the gym.

A throaty chuckle feathered his cheek and he glanced up, pulse tripping at the tease that sparkled in those perilous green eyes. "Safe? Apparently not, Detective Barone."

He grinned, and pink dusted her cheeks. "The dilemma appears to arise when I attempt to keep you safe from yourself, Miss McClare, not from me." Ignoring the warmth traveling his body, he concentrated on blotting the paint with his rag.

"Well, we only have one more week of lessons," she said in a chipper tone that made him feel hollow inside, "and then you'll turn the responsibility of my safety over to me."

"I need water," he muttered, annoyed that her statement bothered him so much, especially when it was his idea to end after six weeks. He'd already taught her as much as she needed to know to ward off an attack, and he certainly didn't want more time in close proximity with a woman who quickened his pulse. His lips tamped in a tight line. *Especially one related to Logan McClare.* He jumped up to fetch another rag, dousing it in his water bucket and squeezing it out. "This'll be cool and wet, but it's part of the process, Miss McClare."

"Alli," she reminded softly, and the very sound feathered his skin with heat.

Jaw tight, he avoided her gaze as he patted the spot once again, refusing to be sucked in. Playing games with her in a schoolyard with a gaggle of children was one thing, as were jiu-jitsu sessions in the gym after school while students and teachers still buzzed around. Suddenly, squatting this close, sponging her thigh with no one around felt too snug and too cozy to suit, a clear-cut warning he had no business reacting to this woman the way that he did.

"Do I have your word you won't make advances to my niece?"

His teeth began to grind at the memory of his response to McClare's initial request. *"Carved in stone,"* he had said, *"or so help me, you can cut out my tongue."*

That very tongue now cleaved to the roof of his mouth, drier than the paint crusted on the rim of his bucket. Sure, he'd meant it at the time, but every day in Allison McClare's presence seemed to be taking a toll, weakening his defenses with a tilt of her smile, the scent of her hair . . . Yes, he'd always noticed a tension in his gut whenever she walked in the room, but now it had more to do with attraction than anger, and the very thought scared him silly. Throughout their sessions over the last month, they'd maintained a friendship of sorts, easy banter and cautious conversation, laced with humor and a comfortable respect that made him so uncomfortable, he almost missed the blasted stick.

Lips compressed, he focused hard on removing the spot—and his growing attraction to Miss McClare—grateful his tenure as teacher was almost at an end. Lost in his thoughts, he squinted hard while scrubbing her skirt, suddenly aware he was also massaging her leg. A harsh breath seized in his throat as his fingers froze on her thigh. Heat coiled in his belly, and his gaze snapped up to hers. "You do it," he ordered, voice gruff as he shoved the rag in her hand. "Knead the paint with your fingers to remove it, and I'll get the turpentine."

You're a blinkin' idiot, Barone, he fumed, furious over an attraction that sizzled so much, it could have singed the hair on his arms. Allison McClare was off-limits, no matter how attracted he was to her, and by thunder, he'd keep his word to Logan Mc-Clare or die trying. Which, given the blood pulsing his veins at the moment, might be a distinct possibility. *Only one more week . . .* Snatching another rag, he doused it in turpentine, then wrung it out with more force than necessary, sucking in a polluted breath before huffing it out again. "Blot until the paint is gone, all right?"

She nodded, patting the stain with a wrinkle of her nose. "Goodness, this smells awful, but it does appear to be working . . ."

"It will," he said with far more assurance than he felt when it came to the woman before him. "Tonight, mix one cup lukewarm water and 1 teaspoon lye soap, then sponge it on the stain and let sit overnight. Tomorrow, just rinse in cool water and wash."

"Looks like it's gone," she whispered, handing him the rag while she awarded him a shy smile that heated his blood all over again. "Thanks, Nick, for going to so much trouble."

"Least I can do," he muttered, plucking the offensive cloth from her hand. He strode back to the ladder and tossed the rag onto a pile of others before scaling the rungs. His voice sounded hoarse as he reached for his brush. "Sorry for almost ruining your skirt."

"But not for ruining my run in red rover, I suppose?" Her teasing tone made him smile.

"No, ma'am, anybody could see you needed to be taken down a peg or two."

She glanced at the watch pinned to her blouse before those perfect lips bloomed into a smile that put another hitch in his pulse. "Well, we'll just see who de-pegs whom in the gym tonight." She gave a saucy tilt of her chin. "I've been practicing on Cassie's fiancé, you know."

"Have you, now?" He tempered his grin, reminding himself flirting with Allison McClare was *not* a good idea. Slapping the paintbrush back into the can, he cleared his throat while he stirred.

"Don't forget—cold water for the rinse—the colder the better, got it?"

She bounded up the steps with a smile. "Got it. Rinse with lots of water, preferably ice cold."

Cooling himself off with a flap of his shirt, he exhaled loudly when the screen door finally clattered behind her. "Cold, *cold* water," he mumbled, wishing he had a little ice of his own. "And you can bet your bottom dollar, Miss McClare, that I'll be doing the same."

⁂

"Cait—wait up!" Logan shook hands with the Budget and Finance Committee supervisor after the Board of Supervisors meeting ended, then strode down the hall with his hat in hand.

"Yes?" She paused half-turned at the door, affection in her eyes despite a manner always cautious whenever he was around. *Good grief, will I ever win her trust after the debacle in Napa over that stolen kiss?*

"Congratulations on passage of the addendum to phase one, Madame Chairman," he said with broad smile. "You twisted every heart in there tonight, including mine."

Her melodic chuckle floated above the din in the noisy hall, warming his heart. "I suspect I owe the victory more to a bit of arm-twisting from my very powerful brother-in-law rather than heart-twisting from a mere figurehead on the Vigilance Committee."

He grinned. "Which just proves we're a formidable team when we join forces, right?"

Her eyes softened as color dusted her cheeks. "Thank you, Logan, for your support in cleaning up the Coast. I don't know how I can ever thank you for making my dream come true."

Easy, Cait—make mine come true . . .

"And Liam's too," she whispered, the very name eliciting a hint of the guarded look she always reserved just for Logan.

He cleared his throat, awkward as always when she invoked the name of her deceased husband—the brother he'd lost her to so many years ago. Heat warmed his collar. *Wielding it like a blasted weapon to keep me away.* "What's important to you is important to me," he said, well aware that before he could win Caitlyn's trust as a man, he'd need to win it first as a friend. He nodded toward the street. "I was hoping I could give you a lift home so we can talk."

She hesitated, her smile wavering for the briefest of moments. "I'm afraid Hadley's out front and it is pretty late . . ." Her dark lashes flickered as she peered up. "It can't wait?"

He forced a casual air, thumb grazing his fedora. "I'd rather not since it concerns Allison."

Concern marred her beautiful features. "All right, but it's nothing serious, I hope?"

"Not at all." He put his hat on and slipped a hand to the back of her waist to usher her outside, making a beeline for where Hadley was parked at the curb. Leaning in the open passenger side, he offered Cait's driver a smile. "Hadley, I'll be driving Mrs. McClare home tonight."

"Very good, sir," the elderly butler said in his usual proficient manner. He nodded at Caitlyn. "Miss. Good evening to you both."

"Thank you, Hadley, I'll be home soon." Caitlyn gave a half-hearted wave.

Hooking her arm over his, Logan steered her to his black Mercedes Phaeton, fighting a smile over the way she chattered away, so uncustomary for a woman who was comfortable with silence. He'd noticed since Napa how much stiffer she'd been with his goodbye kisses on the cheek after family dinners or when he guided her to the parlour with a protective hand at the small of her back. She was clearly no longer comfortable being in close proximity, which bothered him, but it couldn't be helped. He'd learned the hard way you couldn't rush a woman like Caitlyn McClare, and he had no intention of doing so again. It would be close family ties until he could win her trust as a friend. *Before I can win her heart as my wife.*

"May I?" he asked, indicating the need to lift her up into the high tufted carriage seat, and she gave a short nod, the sudden stiffness of her body making him smile as he hoisted her up with hands to her waist. Fidgeting with her skirt, she settled in with a small purse in her lap while he strolled around and hopped up beside her. Her words about the strides they were making on the Barbary Coast were now edged with a breathless excitement typical when she harbored a passion for something. His smile took a slant as he started the vehicle. The kind of "breathless" passion he hoped to elicit in her one day, God willing . . .

God willing, indeed . . . A nerve twitched in his cheek. The same God in which Caitlyn accused him of not believing the night in Napa when she'd turned him away. His jaw firmed. So help him, he'd convince her he was a man of faith if it took every breath in his body, and he'd begun the very next week. A man of carnal appetite all of his life, he now avoided his former dalliances like the very plague that had ravaged the city two years prior. Governed by morality for the first time since he'd entered college, he'd become a homebody—Caitlyn's home, to be exact—unwilling to be seen with any other woman lest the evidence be splattered across the front page of the society papers. Where once he'd attended mass with the family only on Christmas and Easter, he now met them in Cait's pew each Sunday, after which he treated them to lunch at the Palace, his permanent residence when not at his Napa estate. Well aware of Caitlyn's teetotaler tendencies, even his drinking habits had changed, never imbibing at her home or touching anything harder than wine at dinners out and only one glass at that. No, he'd taken great pains to pursue her with meticulous planning and care, as if she were one of his court cases where life and death hung by a thread. He issued a silent grunt. Because it did—*his* life and *his* thread of hope—for the woman he longed to hold in his arms for the rest of his life.

"Logan?"

He jerked from his thoughts, glancing at Cait as he turned onto Powell. "Yes?"

A ridge popped above her nose. "Are you all right? You seem to be somewhere else . . ."

I am, Cait—in your arms. He cleared his throat. "Sorry, a lot on my mind."

"You wanted to talk about Alli?" A passing streetlamp highlighted the delicate rise of her brow while a breeze played with the tendrils of hair at the back of her neck, drawing his gaze.

"Alli, yes," he said slowly, downshifting as the phaeton slowly chugged up the steep hill. A grin tipped his mouth. "She sure took the wind out of Jamie's sails with that jiu-jitsu demonstration."

She laughed, lips settling into a soft smile as she stared over the dash. "Not necessarily a bad thing, the way that boy gloats when he wins."

A grin eased across his lips, his affection deep for a man who'd become the son he'd always longed for. "He's a cocky thing, that's for sure, but one heck of a fine man, I'll tell you that. He'll make Cass a wonderful husband." He quickly jerked the wheel to the left, deftly avoiding an oncoming horse and buggy. The smell of manure rose to his nostrils, obliterating the familiar scent of fish from the wharf. "But back to Alli," he said with a sideways glance. "How are she and Barone? Still polite enemies, I hope?"

Head tilted in question, she pursed her lips in thought. "At first, yes, but given way to a polite friendship, I believe, which pleases me. I'd rather they be friends than enemies, Logan."

"Not with his reputation, Cait. I suspect he's a womanizer, and a penniless one at that."

A wrinkle appeared above the bridge of her nose. "And how would you know that? I've seen no indication of anything to support that accusation. Did Harmon tell you that?"

His lips went flat. "No, but I can spot a womanizer a mile away, Cait, trust me."

A smile flickered at the edges of her mouth. "Oh, I see—takes one to know one?"

He peered at her out of the corner of his eye, her jest barbing more than he liked. "Regrettably, yes," he said quietly, "but that's part of my unfortunate past, Cait. My family is the most important thing to me now, and you need to know that."

She averted her gaze to the dash once again. Drawing in a deep breath, she buffed her arms in an antsy avoidance of the truth. "Well, I like him. He seems straightforward and honest."

He frowned, slowing to let a cable car pass as he approached her street. "So did Roger Luepke, if you recall." Downshifting, he took the corner and glided up to the curb, turning the engine off with a weary expulsion of air. He angled to face her, jaw tight at the memory of the charlatan he'd introduced Alli to. "Look, Cait, as long as I draw a breath, what happened with Luepke will never happen to any of my nieces again. The last thing I want to hear is that this Barone character is getting cozy with Alli. We know nothing about the man."

"But Harmon hired him, for goodness' sake—surely that vouches for his credibility?"

He tossed his fedora on the seat, raking fingers through his hair in a nervous gesture. "As a detective, yes. As a man I can trust with Alli on a more intimate level? Not on your life. Even Harmon knows nothing about him—just that he's a friend of a friend who called in a favor. When is Mr. Bigley back?"

"Next week. Why?"

"Good. I promised Barone six weeks, which is next week, and quite frankly, if he and Alli are hobnobbing as friends, I'd rather have him out of her life."

A flicker of alarm flashed in her eyes. "So he . . . won't be seeing her home anymore?"

He grunted. "Oh, he'll be seeing her home all right—she just won't know it."

"What do you mean?" she asked, two tiny ridges appearing at the bridge of her nose.

"I mean I plan to continue to pay him to be on call—and quite well, I might add—to protect her without her knowledge so she can exercise that independent streak she inherited from her mother."

Her eyes softened. "You're a wonderful uncle, Logan," she whispered, "and a wonderful friend."

His gaze penetrated hers, causing a dip in her throat. "No, Mrs. McClare," he said softly, "just a man desperately in love with his family."

She looked away then, fingers fiddling with the strap of her purse as she quickly changed the subject. "So, how is this going to work with Nick after Mr. Bigley comes back?"

He folded his arms. "That's where you come in. How often and how late will Alli stay after school, do you know?"

Creases puckered her brow. "Well, she's put together a fund-raiser play, so if I know Allison, she'll want to practice two or three nights a week after school for the next month at least. That shouldn't go any later than four o'clock or so, but I'm certain she'll find some excuse to dilly-dally well up unto dusk." A smile softened the lines in her face. "We both know the girl has no sense of time, especially when she's focused on a task." She shook her head, the smile on her lips blooming into gentle affection. "Goodness, she gives everything her all, so between that and her stubborn pursuit of perfection, she'd stay at the school until midnight if I let her."

The corner of his mouth quirked. "Mmm . . . wonder where she gets it?"

A twinkle lit her eyes in the glow of the streetlamp. "Oh, her uncle Logan, no doubt."

He grinned. "I doubt that would stand up in a court of law, Mrs. McClare." Clearing his throat, he forced his attention away from the soft curve of her lips. "As far as Alli goes, that makes it more difficult, but not impossible, although I doubt Barone will like it. But that's too bad because Harm will give him no choice. So whenever Alli stays late, you'll simply alert Mrs. Peel and she'll advise Barone. You'll need to insist Alli telephones prior to leaving, of course, and then you'll immediately contact Mrs. Peel. She'll make sure Barone follows at a distance to ensure she gets home safely."

"Oh, yes," she breathed, clasping hands together like a little girl privy to a juicy secret. "You've thought of everything! Now Alli can be independent and safe at the same time, and she need never know you've arranged for a flesh-and-blood guardian angel."

Logan's lips slanted as he hopped from the carriage seat and rounded the car. "I doubt Barone qualifies for celestial duty, but the 'flesh and blood' aspect is precisely why I want those two apart." He raised his arms to help her down, fighting a grin at the tug of teeth against her lip while she avoided his gaze. Hands to her waist, he swooped her to the ground, pulse sprinting at the feel of her body against his palms. His release was immediate, as if her very touch had singed, and in a way, he supposed it had. Touching Caitlyn McClare was not a good idea if he hoped to forge a friendship, no matter the attraction that stirred on either side. And, oh, it stirred all right. He felt it in the tension in the air, as thick as the knot that bobbed in her throat when she fidgeted with her skirt. And as warm as the blood pulsing through his veins when he offered his arm.

"No, Logan, really." She took a step back. "It's late and there's no need to walk me in."

With a firm clasp of her arm over his, he promptly ushered her up the brick steps leading to her Nob Hill Victorian, his tone as decisive as his hold. "Come on, Cait, what do you take me for, a cad? A gentleman always escorts a lady to the door."

"Yes, but I'm family," she said with a sideways glance that darted away when it connected with his. "Not one of your many ladies you escort about town."

He fisted the brass doorknob of the arched burlwood door, pausing to give her a sober stare. "Family, yes, but let's be clear about something," he said quietly. "*You*—and my nieces—are the only women I see or escort about town anymore, and I count it one of the greatest pleasures I'm privileged to have."

Her eyes rounded in surprise before she laughed, the awkward sound indicating her disbelief. "Really, Logan, an eligible bachelor like you? That must break quite a few hearts."

He opened the door with a slow push, fixing her with a steady gaze. "I hope not," he whispered, stepping aside for her to enter. "I have no desire to break anyone's heart ever again."

With a shift in her throat, she nodded and hurried into the foyer. Turning with shoulders square, she held her head high in that regal way she resorted to whenever she struggled to regain control. "Thank you for the ride and for seeing to Alli's safety. My children are blessed to have you in their lives."

With a short bow, he gave a brief tip of his head. "Good night, Mrs. McClare. Tomorrow I'll see you for dinner and cribbage." Before she could close the door, he turned on his heel and strode to his car, the faintest of smiles curving on his lips.

And tonight? I'll see you in my dreams.

16

"But I don't understand—why aren't you going to teach Miss Alli anymore?"

Nick glanced up while he rolled the jiu-jitsu mat for the last time, heart squeezing at the solemn look in Lottie's eyes. The little tyke sat cross-legged on the edge, the new blue serge "uniform" Mrs. McClare furnished sagging on her tiny frame as much as the sad expression on her face. He huffed out a sigh and continued rolling, nudging the rubber against her knees until a tiny smile crept across her lips. "I already told you, La-di-da—Miss Alli has learned everything she needs to know." He bopped her legs several times, finally rolling the mat over her knees. "Now, unless you want to be a big bump in this mat, young lady, I suggest you get up so I can give you a horsey ride."

She hopped up with a throaty giggle that made him grin, then promptly launched onto his back, clinging to his neck like a spider monkey to its mother.

"Hold tight, all right?" Tucking the mat under his arm, he rose and anchored her little legs to his chest. "Let's get you home before Miss Penny whacks me with Miss Alli's stick."

Her giggle tickled his neck. "But aren't we going to wait for Miss Alli?" she asked, digging her knees into his side to make him go faster.

"Naw—no telling how long it'll take her to change. She has a tendency to dawdle—"

"I beg your pardon . . ." Allison stood in the doorway, arms crossed and chin high while a small hobo-style purse dangled from her wrist. The lavish silk bow on her straw hat was a pretty match for a fitted navy suit that more than complemented her curves. Reticule swinging in hand, she sauntered in with a cocky air that was purely for show, her flair for drama evident in every single thing the woman did. She slapped a hand to pearl buttons that meandered down a very distracting satin shirtwaist. "And *this* from the man who took a full two weeks to paint a single coat of paint on the back of the school," she said with a plunk of hands to her hips. *Lush, slender hips, to be exact . . . leading up to a tiny waist and—*

Jerking his gaze away, he strode to the door. *Focus, Barone, and not on the dame.* Despite the heat creeping up his neck, he refused to be cowed, offering a tight-lipped smile while he and Lottie sidled past. "Only because the *drama teacher* demanded stage scenery for a small hamlet the size of Rome." His gravelly tone made Lottie giggle.

Allison spun around to follow, quickly locking the front door before racing to catch up so she could tickle Lottie, who immediately flailed heels into Nick's ribs with a loud squeal. He wasn't sure who was the bigger pain in his side, but he'd lay odds on Miss McClare. She darted past like the ruffians he'd seen in the hall before recess—skipping backward with a mischievous grin on her lips. "Come on, Detective Ga-roan," she teased, "Mr. Bigley would have had the scenery built and the house painted in the time it took you to crawl up that ladder and back." In a flash of teeth, she whirled around with her nose in the air, sashaying down the hall like she owned the place. His mouth crooked. And she did, he supposed, with as many hours as the woman put in, giving every moment of

Julie Lessman

her time and talents to the outcast children of the Barbary Coast. Lottie giddyupped his ribs with another squeal, and he shook his head, unable to stifle a grin. Holy thunder, what he wouldn't have given to have a teacher like Alli when he was a kid instead of those crusty nuns. Lively, gorgeous, caring, and fun . . . even *with* a stick.

At the back door, the little imp had the audacity to pivot and smirk, butting the door with her backside to hold it open. "But then Mr. Bigley is probably *way* younger than you."

His jaw ground despite his stiff smile. "I'm thirty, Miss Mc-Clare," he said in a clipped tone, making sure the rubber mat swatted her as he swept by. "Bigley has me by ten years."

"Only in age." Locking the door, she bounded down the steps two at a time, nipping at his heels like Horatio when Nick gave Lottie "horsey rides" at home. "As far as crotchety, you have at least twenty years on him, Mr. Cranky Pants, a grouchy old man well before his time."

Lottie giggled, bouncing without mercy. "Mr. Cranky Pants, Mr. Cranky Pants!"

Nick seared Alli with a look as she hustled up Miss Penny's back steps to open the screen door, cheeks flushed with fun. She looked so adorable, he was tempted to grin, but he settled for his trademark scowl instead. "See what you started?" he groused, brushing past her into the screened porch area while Lottie rode him like a steer rider busting a bronc. "And for your information, Miss Talk-Often-and-Carry-a-Big-Stick, I am in a good mood most of the time unless needlessly provoked."

"Excuse me, Mr. C.P.," Alli said, following him into the kitchen, "but I believe it was your permanent grouchy moods that have earned you that title, am I right, La-di-da?"

"Right!" The little cowpoke kneed him for good measure with every rib-busting bounce.

227

"What's right?" Denise asked, assisting Angi with setting the polished-oak table while Miss Penny retrieved two freshly baked loaves of bread from the oven.

"That Mr. Nick is a cranky pants." Allison gallivanted past as if she lived there instead of him, reaching for Lottie, who immediately launched into her arms. She spun the little dickens several times before setting her down. "Face it, Nick Barone—you have one mood—crabby."

A low chuckle rolled from Mrs. Lemp as she fried chicken that watered his mouth. "Oh, I don't think that's fair to say. Our Nicky has lots of moods other than crabby."

"Thank you, Mrs. Lemp," Nick said with a thrust of his chin, slipping an arm to the old woman's waist while Horatio snarled.

"There's also testy, crusty, and cantankerous, just to name a few." Peering up with laugh lines that fanned from teasing blue eyes, the cook pinched his cheek with a butterscotch grin. "Aye, but we keep him around 'cause he's so lovely to look at, don't ya know?"

Heat crawled up his neck, but he ignored it with a wry smile. "Appreciate the support, Mrs. Lemp." He went for a drumstick, only to have Miss Penny thump the back of his hand.

"Oh no you don't, young man, not before you've washed and we've said grace—"

"Hey, he's not 'young,'" Lottie said, cheeks as rosy as the bowl of apples Mrs. Lemp kept on the counter. "Miss Alli says he's an old man." She latched onto Nick's leg, giving a delighted shriek when he bounced her in the air. "What's *decrepit* mean?" she asked with a squeal.

"It's a synonym for Mr. Nick," Allison supplied.

"W-what's . . . a sin . . . o-min?" Her voice wobbled with every bob of Nick's shoe.

"You know, two words that mean the same thing, like Miss

Alli taught us last week." Denise notched her chin, freckled face beaming with pride.

Nick shot Lottie in the air with a hard thrust of his foot, swooping her up and tickling beneath her arms. "Kind of like Miss Alli and the word *trouble*," he said, smile atilt.

"All right, you two." Miss Penny tugged Lottie from Nick's arms with a smile. "We have mouths to feed, so wash up, please." Setting Lottie on the counter next to the sink, she proceeded to wash the little girl's hands with a soapy dishrag, shooting Alli a smile over her shoulder. "We'd love to have you stay, Allison, if you like—we have plenty."

"Thank you, Miss Penny, but I actually have plans tonight." Her gaze flicked to the chicken with the same look of longing as Nick before she headed for the door. "G'night, all!"

Stifling a groan, Nick snitched a drumstick on his way out. "Save me some chicken."

Alli spun around. "Oh, no you don't—your obligation officially ended with our last lesson. I am now skilled and perfectly able to take care of myself, remember?"

Drumstick lodged in his teeth, he held the screen door open with a roll of his eyes. "Not on my wasch, Mish McClare," he said, voice nearly indistinct for the food in his mouth. He plucked the chicken leg out and motioned for her to go. "Your uncle hired me to teach and see you home until the last class, and that's what I intend to do." He sent Mrs. Lemp a wink. "Keep a plate warm, if you please, Mrs. Lemp, or I'll be showing you 'crusty.'"

A chorus of giggles and goodbyes followed them out the door as Alli shook her head, skittering down the steps like a frisky puppy in dire need of a leash. "Honestly, Nick, you don't have to walk me home. All I really need are directions to Spanish Alley, and I'll be fine."

He froze on the steps—while the chicken froze in his mouth. "What?"

She turned at the bottom of the stairs, the picture of innocence. "I was hoping to visit a friend who has done our laundry for years now—Lili Chen. She lives on Spanish Alley, I understand, but she's always picked up and delivered, so I've never actually been to her shop."

The drumstick nearly crashed to the ground along with his jaw. "In Chinatown?" he rasped, choking chicken crust down before he sailed the bone into the trash barrel at the back of the yard. His eyes bulged as he wiped his fingers on his handkerchief, unable to comprehend this woman's latest harebrained notion. "Are you crazy?"

The green eyes narrowed. "No, Mr. Pinhead, I'm not, but I have my suspicions about you if you think you can dictate where I may go." The chin rose. "One . . . two . . . three . . ."

He groaned, biting back the insult that hovered on the tip of his tongue. "I'm-sorry-Miss-McClare," he enunciated in a clipped tone, careful to meet the terms of their truce, "but Chinatown is part of the Barbary Coast and far too seedy for you to go alone, remember?"

She blinked, obviously taken aback by this bit of news. She gummed her lips in thought. "Oh. I guess I forgot."

He fought a grunt with a strain of his jaw. *Oh, big surprise.*

Her chest rose and fell with a heavy draw of air before she expelled it again, tone considerably more amenable. "Well, then, if you don't mind, Nick, can I trouble you to accompany me to Spanish Alley on our way home?"

"I mind," he said in a near growl, steering her through the side alley to the front. "There's no way you can go traipsing through Chinatown on social calls this time of night, so you may as well forget it."

She balked with a dig of her heels. "And just exactly why not,

Mr. Barone?" The clipped use of his formal name gave fair warning her ire was on the rise.

He turned and parked hands low on his hips, feeling a bit of jaw-grinding coming on. "Because the sights you're likely to see at night are not pretty, Miss McClare. There are brothels on every corner where women and little girls peer at you through iron-barred windows. Poor souls sold into prostitution at a young age and exposed to harsh treatment and disease."

"Why, th-that's n-nothing short of b-barbaric," she stuttered.

He folded his arms, her rich-girl naïveté starting to rankle. "So is living in the lap of luxury on Nob Hill, Miss McClare, while children sleep in gutters with rats, but it happens." He regretted the words the moment they left his mouth when a sheen of tears welled in her eyes. Releasing a heavy exhale, he plunged his hands in his pockets, suddenly ashamed for the way he always harped on her wealth. As if she could help being born with a silver spoon in her mouth. "Look, Alli," he said quietly, "I apologize for that last remark. It was . . ."

"Rude and unfeeling?" She blinked several times as if to dispel her tears, and he sighed again, wishing she didn't elicit such protective feelings.

"Yeah, and 'testy, crusty, and cantankerous,'" he said with a faint smile, hoping to coax a similar response. "Forgive me?"

She peered up beneath dark lashes spiked with moisture, those lush lips quivering into a smile so sweet, it took everything in him not to pull her into his arms and taste it for himself.

"On one condition."

He couldn't contain the groan this time. "What?"

She tilted her head. "Take me to Chinatown, please? Just once?"

"Allison, no—"

"But I've never been there before, Nick," she said with that little-girl plea that reminded him so much of Lottie. "And I need to." Her voice trailed to a whisper. "To see the . . . degradation that some women are forced to live with so I can understand and maybe help someday." She gave him a hopeful look, compassion literally burning in those deadly green eyes. "Please . . . ?"

He mauled his face with his hands, the smell of fried chicken lingering on his fingers. *I need to be whacked with that stick of hers for what I'm about to do . . .*

"It's the last time you'll have to bother with me, I promise."

Yeah, right. His eyelids lifted to take in the glow of adventure in her innocent face, the thrill of independence in eyes that already held way too much sway . . . He huffed out a blast of air that branded him for the moron she'd believed him to be. "In and out, then home, got it?"

"Oh, yes, yes!" She launched into his arms with a hug that robbed his lungs of all air, thankfully paralyzing his body lest he respond in a way neither of them wanted.

Or needed.

She pulled away with a giggle, the flush in her cheeks a perfect complement to creamy skin and ebony hair. "You won't regret it, Nick, I promise," she said with a bounce in her step.

Already do. Clamping a hand to her arm, he all but dragged her down the street while she chattered on, unable to shake the feeling that this was a tactical error.

Her lively step kept pace with his long-legged gait, scurrying to keep up. "And after Chinatown, you have my word that I'll hop on that cable car and go straight home all by myself."

"Wrong. After Chinatown, I'll get on that stupid cable car to see you home, nausea or no."

"Seriously, Nick, you don't have to—"

"Yes, Allison, I do," he emphasized with a stern lift of his brow.

"The terms of my contract were to walk you home after each lesson and by thunder, I'll honor them." His lips thinned in disgust. "The last thing I need is your rich uncle on my back."

Her excitement dimmed as she came to a dead stop, a hint of hurt in her tone. "You don't like him, do you?" she whispered, sorrowful eyes indication she held her uncle in high esteem.

His jaw tightened as he secured her arm, tugging her on. "He's not on my Christmas card list, if that's what you mean."

"Why?" she asked, voice quiet and gaze burning his profile. "Why don't you like him?"

He shot her a sideways look, her uncle and Darla Montesino reminding him just why he didn't trust the upper class. "Because I don't trust rich men or their power-hungry families," he said with a bite in his tone, wishing he'd never drawn close to Allison McClare.

"That includes me, I suppose?" The hurt in her voice made him feel like a jerk.

Expelling a weary exhale, he glanced both ways at the corner of Jackson and Montgomery. He gripped her upper arm to practically carry her catty-corner across the cobblestone street to Chinatown. "It did," he groused, annoyed that he no longer looked at her that way. His voice softened despite the clip of his words. "But you're different. Kind. Unpretentious. Giving rather than taking." He released her arm on the other side of the street, continuing on with a brisk gait, hands shoved deep in his pockets and shoulders hunched. His eyes narrowed as he stared straight ahead into the kaleidoscope world of Chinatown—as foreign to the city as Allison was to the greedy and pompous upper class that had ruined his life. Bitterness roiled, leaving a sour taste in his mouth. "And nothing like your uncle."

She slowed him with a gentle touch, drawing his gaze when

she stopped. "You're wrong about Uncle Logan, you know," she said quietly. "He's a good man, Nick."

A muscle pulsed in his jaw. "I'm sure he is to you, but the simple truth is men with money like your Uncle Logan execute power with a sharp blade." His eyes locked with hers, ignoring the curious stares of Chinatown residents as they milled around them. "Haven't you heard the expression 'power tends to corrupt, and absolute power corrupts absolutely'?"

Her chin inched up the barest degree. "Of course I have, but Uncle Logan is not corrupt."

"Says the woman with a silver spoon in her mouth." He huffed out a noisy breath, tired of pussyfooting with a society dame who didn't know which end was up. "I don't mean to offend, Allison, but your head's in the clouds up there on that hill, totally ignorant of the damage men like your uncle do to the poor beneath their upper-crust feet." His jaw hardened along with his tone while he stared her down, hands loose on his hips. "Like my good friend whose grandson was murdered because of a quarantine *your* uncle Logan helped put in place."

All blood siphoned from her face, making her wide green eyes and coal-black hair all the more stark and beautiful. "What d-do you mean?" she whispered, her hurt unleashing his guilt.

He pinched the bridge of his nose, massaging the seeds of a headache as he exhaled loudly. "Look, Alli, that was uncalled for and I apologize." Glancing at his watch, he forced a tight smile. "It's getting late, so let's not ruin the last few minutes we'll ever spend together, okay? I'll give you a quick tour, and if you're a good girl, I'll even buy you a moon cake."

That did the trick. Nick battled a grin when her eyes circled as wide as her mouth. "Oooo, what's a moon cake?" she asked, clearly sidetracked from their clash over her uncle.

His grin broke free at her little-girl enthusiasm, pride swelling that he could be the first to introduce her to this Chinese tradition. "Don't get too excited—they don't taste all that great, but it's part of the Chinatown experience. It's a moon-shaped pastry with this awful lotus-seed paste, kind of fruity, but a bit sour in taste."

His gaze flicked to where tattered red flags of a Chinese bakery waved in the breeze, and he pressed a palm to her back to speed up her pace. Which wasn't easy. She was like Alice in Wonderland, jaw slack and reticule clutched to her chest while she gawked, drinking in every detail as if it were the green tea Ming Chao served in his restaurant.

He latched on to her arm to guide her where he wanted to go, but that didn't stop her head from swiveling to and fro, mesmerized with something as simple as a neighborhood grocery where dead ducks hung limp and greasy in dirty windows. She wrinkled her nose at the putrid smell of garbage from baskets of rotten vegetables thick with flies, tainted further by the body odor of the milling crowd. Her pace slowed when she spotted a ragged little boy chatting with a white-bearded man in front of a ramshackle store, the boy's knee-length queue snaking down his back. A cloud of sweet smoke drifted in the air, engulfing both the boy and the old man as he puffed on a long, carved pipe.

A frown marred her features as she swallowed hard, apparently no longer enthralled with the scent of opium now that she knew what it was. "Do a lot of people smoke opium in Chinatown?" she whispered.

Nick's mouth crooked. "Enough."

"Oh," she muttered weakly while a knot shifted in her throat. Her gaze strayed across the street where ten-foot wooden doors lined the front of a chipped stone building. Emblazoned with garish yellow stars and grimy windows with tarnished brass grates, it obviously intrigued her like everything else in Chinatown. "Oh my, what an . . . interesting building," she whispered, a hint of reverence to her tone. "Is that a church or a temple?"

He couldn't help it—he grinned. "It's a brothel, Miss McClare—yet another reason why you need an escort, if you can't tell a house of prostitution from a house of God."

Her cheeks bloomed with color, and he shook his head. If ever there was an innocent, it was Allison McClare, and the very thought tightened his grip on her arm.

"Oh, my." She peeked up with such an adorable smile, his heart did a flip. "You were right—this *is* too seedy for me alone, which makes me all the more grateful for your company."

He pursed his lips, unable to thwart a flicker of a smile. "Yeah, well, it's the last time, Miss McClare, so get your fill now because my days of playing escort are over."

Her chin jutted high. "Yes, they are, and I can't thank you enough for all you've done, not the least of which is allowing me to experience a part of my city I've longed to see forever." The color heightened in her creamy cheeks as she clutched his arm with a new bounce in her step. "And you have my word," she continued in a bubbly rush, "after Chinatown, I'll hop on that cable car and go straight home all by myself. Then your chore will be over and done forever."

Over and done forever? The rapid-fire tirade of a high-pitched Chinese argument interrupted his thoughts along with the tinkling of music. All at once, a man flailed through the air to land hard on the sidewalk in front of them, causing Allison to jump back with a squeak when he retched in the gutter. Nick hustled her past with a dry quirk of his lip while he stifled a grunt, returning to his former thought.

Wanna bet?

17

Clinging to Nick's arm, Alli stared in awe, head back and jaw slack, eyes as round as the gape of her mouth. Never had she seen anything so exotic, so foreign, . . . so heartbreakingly poor!

Chinatown. So close and yet so very far away. Where the air was alive with myriad smells and odors that whirled Alli's senses—roast duck and ginger and fried noodles that Nick referred to as chow mein, all mingling with the mystical scent of perfume, opium, and something smoky and sweet Nick identified as incense burning on temple shrines. Groups of men dressed in dark shift-like jackets congregated in front of storefronts with wooden awnings and massive glass lanterns, eyeing her with curiosity through narrow eyes. Silver-haired matrons hurried by with young girls in tow, each arrayed in loose black silk coats and trousers, all casting furtive glances her way. Alli caught her breath at the beauty of amber skin aglow with dark, almond-shaped eyes and shimmering jet-black hair adorned with ornaments.

"Oh my, this is fascinating," she breathed, her ears tingling from the melodic *shwish-shwish, sheee-shee* of conversations she didn't understand, or the bumble-bee hum of a musical instrument Nick confirmed as a Chinese flute. Her body buzzed with adrenaline as he ushered her through the crowded streets, eyes flaring wide at myriad three-story structures—some brick, some wood, some with metal and wood canopies sheltering the sidewalk—*all* riveting!

She listened when Nick pointed out various sights and sounds and smells, her gaze darting from faded silk and bamboo lanterns suspended from overhangs to hodge-podge balconies where large porcelain pots overflowed with spindly flowers and plants. Huge yellow flags with blue dragons held her spellbound, whipping over the rooftops in the opium-scented breeze. Impoverished yet fascinating, the fourteen-block square was as unique to the city as the people themselves.

Her initial desire to visit their laundress Lili Chen suddenly resurfaced and she spun to a stop, hands clasped in prayer. "Oh, Nick, here I am in Chinatown for the first time in my life and probably the last, and I'd give anything to meet some of its people." Her teeth tugged at her lip. "Like maybe a visit to Lili Chen's home? You know, just to say hello?"

His lips flattened into a scowl while he snatched her arm to continue on. "I already told you, you won't be welcome there, so get that idea out of your head right now. This is a tight-knit community, Alli, where privacy is paramount." He steered her safely past a parade of four laughing little boys who were waving sticks, marching single file with white and black skullcaps on their heads. "They don't need you nosing around, visitors barging in where they're not wanted. This is a city within a city for a reason—to maintain their privacy and tradition. Everything they need is right here—work, food, schools, entertainment, newspapers, education—you name it."

A cramp squeezed in her chest, as tight as the grip of Nick's hand on her arm. She slowed her pace, blinking hard to deflect the moisture that threatened over the keen disappointment she felt. Was it so wrong to want to experience the culture of this exotic place, to meet its people and learn of its customs so maybe someday she could reach out to them? Good heavens, she'd waited twenty-two years to explore this city she loved, and here she was—oh, so close!

Too close. "B-but . . . but—"

"But nothing, Miss McClare," he groused, "case closed." He slid her a look and groaned when he obviously spotted the tears in her eyes. Halting on the sidewalk, he mauled his face with his hands, a mutter under his breath merging with a loud growl from his stomach. "You are one monumental pain in the posterior, you know that?" He huffed out a sigh and angled to face her, hand slung low on his hips. "I guess you're hungry too."

She caught her breath, not daring to believe what that comment might mean. She nodded, fingers pinched white on the purse in her hands.

"Figures." Jaw tight, he snagged her arm and all but lifted her off her feet, barreling down the street so fast, she had to hold on to her straw hat.

She was winded and breathing hard when he finally came to a stop. Even so, the air heaved still in her throat as her eyes slowly scanned up. For surely the sixth time that night, her mouth gaped in amazement at the unusual sight of plaster walls emblazoned with mural paintings of exotic birds and landscapes. Interspersed throughout were colorfully clad Chinese figures depicted in various scenes. "Oh my . . . ," she whispered again, the air in her lungs slowly seeping through parted lips.

Nick nudged her from behind. "I thought you were hungry," he whispered, the warmth of his words in her ear causing her to whirl around with heat in her cheeks.

"I . . . I am," she said, suddenly in awe of another massive structure looming overhead, only this one was eyeing her with a half-lidded gaze that caused her stomach to flip.

He hiked a brow, gruff manner now edged with a smile. "So, you wanna gawk or go in?"

"Ohhhh . . . ," she whispered, clasped hands to her lips, "is this where we're going to eat?"

"It is," he said with a wry tilt of his mouth, prodding her in with a hand to the small of her back. Her body tingled, both from anticipation and the touch of his palm guiding her through a wooden door carved with a three-tailed dragon. "This is my friend Ming Chao's restaurant," he said, bending close to be heard over the magical sound of a xylophone played by an Oriental beauty with silken black hair. "Home of the best Hunan chicken in Chinatown, or anywhere else, for that matter."

Alli's heart pounded as she stepped in, her mouth watering immediately at the delicious smells that assailed her senses. The room had a decidedly intimate air that spread a warmth in her chest rivaling the glow of candles flickering on scarlet-clad tables. The soft murmur of conversations melded with the delicate tinkling of music to create a surreal effect that swept her a world away. When her eyes adjusted to the dim light, she caught her breath at the rare sight of a room crowded with well-dressed business-men in suits and ties dining with locals attired in traditional dark, boxy garb. It was a foreign country unto itself where people of all color and class defied social convention, filling her with a sense of hope that brought a mist to her eyes.

"Mr. Nick!" A small, wiry man bounded forward with arms stretched wide, flashing a toothy smile above a wispy silver beard that trailed his chest. A waist-long silver queue bounced over one shoulder of his black tunic while loose satin trousers flared in the breeze, revealing satin slippers with wooden soles. "You away too long!"

Embracing the tiny man with a hearty hold that Alli feared might crush, Nick grinned and slapped him on the back with a force that rattled the old man's rusty laughter. "Are you kidding? I'm still licking my wounds from the last time, when you humili-ated me in mahjong."

The man's high-pitched giggle made Alli smile, dark eyes thinning into happy slits as his head briskly bobbed up and down, flapping the tassel of his embroidered flat cap. "Ah, but true mark of humble man you come back, yes?"

Nick's rich laughter boomed off gold-and-scarlet water-silk-papered walls, shocking Alli when she realized she'd never heard it quite so full and so free. "For a humble man, yes. For a jaded cop from Lower Manhattan? Not so much."

Nodding, Ming Chao took a step forward, his gaze lighting upon Alli with a secret smile. Bending at the waist, he bowed in greeting, weathered eyes shrewd in assessment. "Ah, and you Mr. Nick's woman, yes?"

Heat scalded her face as she shook her head, unable to speak for the tongue now fused to the roof of her mouth.

Nick shored her up with a casual hand to her back. "Sorry, Chao, she's just a friend."

A sly smile eased across the old man's wrinkled face as his eyes narrowed. "Ah, yes, Mr. Nick, but pretty friend, yes?"

Nick's husky chuckle did nothing for Alli's composure when the scoundrel's fingers playfully nipped at her waist. "*Very* pretty," he responded with a laugh that told her he was enjoying her discomfort.

"Hello, I'm Allison McClare." She extended a hand, finally managing to speak. "It's nice to meet you . . . Mr. Ming?" she said, not quite sure which name to use.

The warm smile on his lips withered as he stared, ignoring her hand with an arch of a silver brow. "McClare?" he repeated, gaze thinning as he slid Nick a frown.

Nick's weary exhale blew warm against her head. "Logan McClare's niece, but nothing like him, I assure you." He nodded toward the back where a couple just vacated a booth. "It appears my favorite table is available, Chao, and I did promise her the best Hunan chicken in the city."

Eyes locked on Allison with a sharp stare, Ming Chao slowly nodded, chest expanding with a heavy draw of air. "For you, Mr. Nick—anything."

A chill slithered Alli's spine as the old man abruptly turned to pluck silk embroidered menus from a carved mahogany table before silently leading them to a booth.

"He doesn't like me, does he?" she whispered as Nick ushered her behind their host.

"You're a McClare, Allison, figure it out. The name doesn't exactly endear you to the people of Chinatown, especially to a man whose grandson was killed during a quarantine riot."

She whirled around, almost colliding with Nick. "Oh, Nick, no! It was Ming Chao's grandson who was killed?" Pain seared at the personal connection with the spry, old man.

The hard angles of Nick's face softened. "Yes, but Chao is a fair and courteous man who will treat you with the respect due both a lady and my friend."

A knot jerked in her throat as she nodded, allowing Nick to seat her in the dark mahogany booth with gold embroidered cushions. With a stiff bow, Ming Chao handed her a menu and in a knee-jerk reaction, she clasped his hand with shaky fingers, unable to thwart the sting of hot tears in her eyes. "I am so very sorry," she whispered, lips trembling, "for the loss of your grandson."

He froze at her touch, eyes apparently glazed with shock at the boldness of her manner, and then as moisture swelled in eyes filled with pain, he nodded with an awkward pat of her hand. Pulling back, he placed Nick's menu before him and quickly disappeared, leaving Allison to stare after him with a cramp in her chest. "Oh, Nick, I didn't offend him, did I?"

Eyes tender, Nick assessed her with a somber look. "Normally I'd say yes, because the Chinese don't like to be touched by strangers, but I think he was moved by your sincerity and grief, Allison . . . as was I." With a clear gruff of his throat, he studied the menu.

She swallowed hard, picking at her nails. "Nick?"

"Yes?" He continued reading, obviously waiting for her to continue.

She peeked up beneath half-lidded lashes, desperate to understand the source of anger he and Ming Chao bore toward Uncle Logan. "Will you . . . tell me what happened? How Ming Chao's grandson was killed?"

He glanced up, staring for several ragged beats of her heart before expelling a heavy rush of air and laying the menu down. He leaned forward to rest folded arms on the table. "Why?" he asked, gaze boring into hers as if trying to decipher the motivation of her request.

More muscles shifted in her throat as she swallowed her hesitation, determined to mend fences with a man who'd breached her own walls to become a good friend. "Because we're friends, Nick, and my heart aches if I or my family wounded you or Ming Chao in any way."

"You order?" A young man in a plain back tunic placed a porcelain teapot painted with scarlet dragons on their table along with matching cups. Offering a short bow, he stood before them with a question in serious brown eyes.

Nick looked up with a faint smile, shoving his menu to the edge of the table. "Yes, Ming Hai, thank you." His eyes flicked to Alli's. "Do you mind if I order for you?"

"Please," she whispered, relieved when he rattled off a long list of Chinese words that somehow sounded so natural from his tongue.

With another curt bow, Ming Hai departed while Nick reached for the teapot, his casual tone at odds with the somber look in his eyes. "What happened to Ming Chao's grandson," he said quietly, "doesn't make for pleasant dinner conversation, Allison, so maybe after." He sipped his tea. "I'll have indigestion enough with all the hot peppers Chao uses. Don't need to add to it."

A slow exhale breezed from her lips as she smiled with a neat fold of hands, grateful he'd sidestepped the serious question. "So . . . what exactly did you order for me, Mr. Barone—Hunan chicken seasoned with extra red pepper for all the times I've whacked you with my stick?"

A dangerous grin traveled his lips, causing her stomach to flutter. "And risk you throwing up on the cable car too? I doubt a green face would enhance your emerald eyes, Miss McClare, no matter how close a match."

She laughed, feeling the tightness in her chest slowly unravel.

"Hunan chicken, of course," he said with a lazy smile, studying her through shuttered eyes as he took another taste of his tea. "Not as hot as your temper, but enough of a wallop you'll think you've been hit with your own stick."

She arched her brows, enjoying this playful side of Nick Barone she'd only just begun to see. "In case you haven't noticed, Mr. Ga-roan, I'm a grown woman who revels in the thrill of the cable car, not a weak-kneed little boy likely to lose his supper."

His smile took on a life of its own as his voice turned husky. "Oh, I've noticed, Miss McClare, you can bet your stick on that."

She blinked, cheeks suddenly going head-to-head with the scarlet linens. Deflecting with a large gulp of tea, she upended the cup, loathe to put it back down and face him again.

His low chuckle taunted. "I'd go easy on that, Alli, you'll need it later to put out the fire."

Fire? Her cup shook as it rattled into the saucer. *Fire, indeed!* The one in her face, the one from the chicken, and the one when he looked at her like that.

He raised his cup in a toast, a sparkle of approval in gray-green eyes that warmed her more than the tea. "To the Snob Hill princess who made a liar out of me."

She grinned and sipped. "How so?"

The laughter in his eyes melted into a tender smile. "You're different, Alli, a privileged woman who gives of herself to those who are not. You seem to really care about the kids at the school." His bold gaze locked with hers, unleashing a heady swirl of heat in her belly. "You're a very special lady, Allison, and I consider it an honor to be your friend."

She swallowed hard, quite sure she was glowing more than the candles. "Me too, Nick."

Ming Hai returned with heaping plates of Hunan chicken and more tea, and never had she enjoyed a meal more. Whether it was Nick's colorful stories, the sound of his laughter when she regaled him with hers, or even the sumptuous taste of glazed chicken with scallions and red and orange peppers, never had she felt more languid and warm. She even mastered the art of eating with chopsticks, noting with satisfaction the gleam of approval in Nick Barone's eyes.

After Ming Hai delivered a plate of orange slices and her moon cake to end their meal, Alli rested her head on the back of the booth like him, both comfortable with the silence as they listened to the music with eyes closed.

And then from across the room, a clear, sweet tone arose, and for a moment Alli thought the xylophone player had begun to sing, so plaintive was the sound. Her gaze was instantly drawn to the young musician who sat in a chair, wearing a white silk embroidered jacket and matching silk trousers. She held a stick-like fiddle against her upper thigh while she slowly grazed a bow across two vertical strings like a violin, creating a sound so melancholy, it was as if the instrument were weeping. Allison stared, mesmerized.

"It's called an erhu," Nick said softly, interrupting her trance. "An ancient Chinese stick fiddle that almost wails with grief, like the Chinese people when they lose one of their own."

Her gaze returned to his, heart thudding at the emotion she saw in his eyes, as if the music mourned for him as well as Ming Chao. "It's beautiful," she whispered, "albeit haunting."

A trace of a smile—and yet painfully sad—shadowed his lips. "And starkly appropriate when tragedy strikes for those that you love."

All at once he seemed so very far away, eyes in a distant stare. She longed to reach across the table and take his hand, to offer comfort for the grief she saw in his face, but knew she could not. Nick Barone was, indeed, too far away—not only in distance across the table, but in his heart, which had been barricaded as thoroughly as her own. With a gentle caress, she absorbed the warmth of her teacup instead, conveying her sorrow with a tender look.

"How much do you know about the quarantine three years ago?" he whispered.

"Not much," she said quietly, shame warming her cheeks over how little attention she'd paid to the abuse Chinatown suffered during an outbreak of the bubonic plague. She'd been too engrossed in her own social life, school, and fancy-free trips to Europe to consider the import of these people's lives. Fragrant steam misted her face as she took a sip of her tea, the warmth of the liquid coating a throat suddenly all too parched.

She sensed he needed to talk because he spoke in a low drone, telling her of his close friendship with Ming Chao's son Lee during the Spanish-American War along with Ito Akira, the Japanese friend who'd taught them jiu-jitsu. The three were inseparable during the campaign, part of the tight-knit group known as Teddy Roosevelt's Rough Riders. Nick's voice wavered at the mention of Ming Lee's death on San Juan Hill, only the first of Ming Chao's many heartbreaks.

"The next year Chao lost cousins in Honolulu," he continued, eyes fixed on the steaming cup in his hands, "when its China-town there was burned to the ground by city officials during a quarantine for the bubonic plague. The year after, he lost his only grandson in a racial conflict during a similar quarantine here when a Chinese laborer died of the plague." His gaze lifted to hers, voice suddenly as hard as the bitterness in his eyes. "Without definitive proof, city officials strung rope and barbed wire around Chinatown in the dark of night, inflicting great hardship on an unsuspecting and gentle people."

He leaned in then, fingers gripped white on the table while his words mounted in anger. "Instead of isolating buildings in which the victim lived and worked, instead of seeking out those in which the sick man came in contact, instead of hunting the rats that carried the disease, they chose to blame all of Chinatown instead." He eased back in his seat, the flecks of gold fire in those gray-green eyes all but searing her to the spot. "Cutting them off from the rest of the city and much-needed supplies." A harsh bite infected his tone. "Except, of course, for enterprises owned by wealthy men like your Uncle Logan, which were conveniently exempt from the blockade."

Alli swallowed hard, fighting the sudden prick of tears. "I'm so sorry, Nick, for all the pain Ming Chao has had, but I don't understand why you think Uncle Logan was at fault."

The tender smiles were suddenly nowhere in sight, vanished in the twist of a sneer. "The Board of Supervisors empowered the Board of Health to quarantine Chinatown, and your Uncle Logan is on the board, is he not?"

"Yes, but he would never do anything to hurt these people—"

He grunted. "I know better. I've butted heads with your uncle more than once on issues that would aid the Chinese, not the least of which was in support of his good friend, Gage."

Allison shook her head, her own ire rising along with Nick's. "I may not know all the details, but I do know for a fact that Uncle Logan withdrew his support from ex-governor Gage long ago, well before the plague hit the city. I've heard him discuss it with Mother many a time."

He opened his mouth to speak, then closed it when Ming Hai refilled their tea, the quiet void between them as stiff as the smile on the young boy's face. When he left, Nick focused on the orange slices, silence reigning while Alli stared at her plate. The beautiful moon cake pastry he'd ordered suddenly roiled her stomach.

"What's wrong?" He peered up beneath a crimp of dark brows.

"Nothing," she whispered, "I just hate to see you so angry."

He grunted and finished off the fruit, jaw tight as he chewed and ignored her gaze.

She stared at him through a sheen of tears, this man so gruff and angry and yet so tender and kind to those he loved, and longed to know the pain he harbored inside. Pain far beyond his anger over Chao, she suspected, or Uncle Logan, or even a world where greed prevailed. She grazed an idle thumb across the smooth wood of her chopsticks. "The hurt festers deeper every day, you know," she whispered, knowing full well of what she spoke. "When you hold on to the bitterness with both hands."

Looking at him now, she saw the same distrust she'd harbored herself far too long, until Cassie had prompted her to pray and let the pain of Roger Luepke go the only way that she could— through forgiveness. A forgiveness that could heal Nick's past like it was healing her.

Her eyes softened along with her tone. "God's called us to forgive, Nick, and none of us can truly be happy or experience

His blessings until we let go of the bitterness that stands in the way." She ducked her head, a faint smile hovering. "Hasn't anyone ever told you peace comes through forgiveness?"

His head shot up while fire flashed in his eyes. "Yeah, my grandmother, but she died right before my uncle was murdered by rich men like Logan McClare."

The blood froze in her veins while tears of shock pooled in her eyes. "Oh, Nick, no . . . ," she whispered, her heart bleeding for his loss . . . but more so for the awful anger that kept him chained to the pain of his past. Swallowing hard, she tentatively reached across the table, grazing his fingers with her own. "I'm so very sorry. Please—tell me how I can help."

A tic flickered in the stiff line of his jaw, a hard veneer settling on his features that shivered her to the bone. "Forgive me for being frank, Miss McClare, but I don't want your help." He shoved his plate away, the abrupt motion jarring the teapot. He reached for the bill that Ming Hai had laid at the edge of the table. "I've had quite enough 'help' from you rich types who espouse virtue and forgiveness right before you knife a guy in the back. The only help I want is your cooperation in seeing you safely home so I can wash my hands of the lot of you."

He may as well have slapped her, given the heat stinging her cheeks. Limbs quivering, she rose, no power over the tears that slipped from her eyes. "No, please, I'll spare you the trouble. I'm quite sure I'm safer with riffraff than a man with so little regard for me or my family."

"Allison, wait—"

She ignored his command, shoving her plate across the table with a clatter when it careened into the pot. "Enjoy my moon cake, Mr. Barone, please. Not much harmony, I'm afraid. But the prospect of never seeing you again?" She thrust her chin high, her words as harsh as his before she spun on her heel. "Good fortune, indeed."

18

Nick stared, body paralyzed as Allison bolted for the door, frustration hissing from his lips when he realized what he'd done.

"So help me, I'm an idiot," he muttered, jerking his wallet from his suit coat.

He flung payment and tip on the table and gave a curt nod to Ming Chao as he flew past, hurling the wood door open so hard, it ricocheted off the wall. Several people approaching the restaurant jerked back at the sound, but he pushed past, mumbling an apology as he scanned the crowded street lit only by the dim glow of a streetlamp. He took off in the direction they'd come, sprinting down a cobblestone road rank with sewage and occasional clumps of manure, dodging a Chinese man swinging his load on bamboo poles balanced on his shoulders. Nick squinted, trying to catch sight of her amid clusters of men jabbering outside of a Chinese gambling house while white-haired ancients sat on crates, passing an opium pipe. His heart seized when he finally spotted her a block away, darting to cross the street in front of a man carting produce in a rickshaw wagon. A cramp split his side as he pursued, and he had no doubt he deserved any pain that came his way. Allison was a decent sort who didn't deserve his wrath, no matter how much he'd been betrayed by a wealthy woman just like her.

"Alli!" He kicked up his speed, heart pumping in his throat at the catcalls of several drunks when she passed a noisy saloon. Chest heaving, he gained on her in the next block, sweat licking his collar like guilt licked at his mind. "Alli—wait!"

She turned, and his heart wrenched at the sight of her face, mottled with tears. "Leave me alone," she screamed, stumbling over a cobblestone when she tried to dart from his reach.

"I can't do that," he rasped, sweeping her up in his arms before she could fall to the pavement. Body wracking with sobs, she fought him like an injured animal, clawing and kicking while her sobs shuddered his soul, but he only gripped tighter, desperate to stem her anger. "Allison," he whispered, breathing hard against the sweet scent of her hair, the clean starch of her hat, "I deserve your wrath and more, but I'm asking you to forgive me—please?" He felt the shift in her mood when her heaves quieted against his chest, his shirt now damp from mucous and tears. A rush of emotion swelled within, and he pressed his lips to her hair, murmuring his sorrow. The crowd flowed around them, like a stream around a boulder, and for the first time since Darla, Nick felt the flicker of something deep inside.

"Allison," he whispered, pulling away to cup her face in his hands, baring his soul to this woman who now held a piece of his heart. "I'm a wounded man striking out, so I'm asking you to forgive me, because hurting you is the last thing I want to do."

Swollen eyes blinked back, and he sucked in a harsh breath, the urge to kiss her so strong, he felt the air heave still in his lungs. His gaze lighted on her lips, and his belly instantly tightened at the desire that shivered his body.

"Do I have your word you won't make advances to my niece?"

His muscles tensed while Logan McClare once again stood in his way, first with Nick's hunger for justice on behalf of Ming Chao, now with his hunger for the man's niece.

"I forgive you," she whispered, full lips parted and slick with tears. "But I thought we were friends, Nick—why would you attack me like that?"

Cradling her face, he grazed her jaw with the pads of his thumbs, craving nothing more than to divulge every dark secret of his soul, but painfully aware he could not. "We *are* friends," he whispered, "but I'm a man with more than his fair share of demons and temper." He swallowed hard, socked in the gut by just how beautiful she was. "And I guess you got a little too close to both." He bent to brush a gentle kiss to her forehead before slipping his arm through hers. "Let's get you home, Miss McClare, before your uncle issues a warrant for my arrest."

"Nick?"

He glanced down at her upturned face, the glow of the street-lamp illuminating an innocence more enticing than opium. "Yes?" he said, firming his grip as he steered her through the swarming crowd to Jackson where they would board the cable car.

She nibbled at the edge of her lip, as if worried he'd snap at her again. "Have you always been this angry? Or did it happen when you lost your grandmother and uncle?"

He blasted out a heavy sigh, well aware he owed her the truth on some points at least, as to why he had turned on her so. "No, I haven't always been this angry," he said quietly, his thoughts traveling back to when he, Mom, and Pop had spent Sundays after church fishing along the Chicago River, the only day his parents took off from the grocery store they owned. Mom would pack a picnic, and Pop and he'd wage a tournament for the big-gest fish while Mom cheered them on and read her book. Nick had a fondness for church back then, his desire to please God as strong as his desire to please the two people who meant everything to him. A faint smile tipped the edge of his mouth as he guided Alli across the street to where people waited for the cable car. "Hard as it is to believe, I was a pretty happy kid and even a lead altar boy, I'll have you know." He slid her a sideways smile. "Father O'Malley was partial to me since I was one of the few boys who didn't give him any trouble."

Her chuckle eased the heaviness that always settled when he thought about Mom and Pop. "Forgive me if I find it hard to believe, Mr. Ga-roan, after all the trouble you've given me."

He tweaked the back of her neck, causing her to hunch her shoulders and giggle. "Forgiven, Miss McClare," he said with a wary eye on the cable car ahead, "although I can't say the same about being forced to ride on that blasted cable car."

"Then, let's walk instead," she said with a sassy tilt of her head. "I'd rather not risk an incident with Hunan chicken, if it's all the same to you."

His brows dipped. "You don't mind? Hoofing that many blocks?"

She shrugged her shoulders. "Not if you enlighten me as to why a sweet little boy with affection for God grows up into a grouchy man with a hair-trigger temper."

He released a weighty sigh, suddenly realizing it was time. Time to unburden himself of years of bitterness and regret . . . and maybe time to begin to trust again. But only with part of the truth . . . a part that wouldn't give him away. He studied the woman beside him and decided she'd be a good place to start. A girl who knew his failings and seemed to care nonetheless. A friend who stirred deeper feelings he longed to explore. And a woman he'd been sworn to protect, not only from danger, but from the protector himself—the man who posed the greatest peril of all.

With a noisy exhale, he proceeded to tell her a tale about being an orphan, not a complete lie since his parents died in a fire at their store the summer Nick turned eighteen. Their death was a painful part of his past that no one in San Francisco could know, lest they discover the dirty details that set him on his path of revenge. His gut tightened. A suspicious fire, to be exact, the very week Pop refused to pay for protection from thugs of a neighborhood "athletic club." No one could prove the "accidental" death of his parents had been a message sent by "the Lords of the Levee," a First Ward political machine who extorted protection money from small businesses. But Nick knew. He paused, waiting for a horse and buggy to pass before he ushered Allison across the street to Powell, the grind of his jaw evidence of a hateful vendetta he knew God could never condone. And although it wasn't an eye for an eye, it was pretty close, a plan to put a gun to some heads and make some murderers bleed . . .

"Who raised you then?" she asked quietly, sympathy lacing her tone.

"An old woman who took me in like Miss Penny takes in orphans," he lied, unwilling to divulge too much about his gram. "Insisted I call her Gram. Her son was like an uncle to me."

"How did she . . . die?" The hesitation in her whisper was obvious, conveying a concern that her question might upset him.

"Cancer." His tone was bitter and sharp, just like his life after Gram had died, taking with her any family he had left in this world. Any love, any hope. *Any faith.* He stared straight ahead, but all he saw was Gram, wasting away in that ghastly bed.

He heard her swift intake of air. "How old were you?" she whispered, her innocent query jolting him back. He blinked, his memory of those bitter days hazy like the lights glimmering on Nob Hill as the fog rolled in, but the pain as sharp as ever.

"Older ... and out on my own," he said quietly, grateful he spoke the truth and didn't have to lie on this one point at least.

She peered up beneath the brim of her straw hat. "Gram was a godly woman?"

His grunt was accompanied by the barest of smiles. "All of four feet eleven, and wielded a bigger stick than you, ready to take me to task if I missed church or ran with the wrong crowd." He fought the sudden sting of tears in his nose. "Truth be told, I still miss her something fierce."

"And her son—the man who was like an uncle—he was the uncle who was ...?" Her voice faded to silence, as if she couldn't bring herself to say the word.

"Murdered, yes." Every muscle in his body tightened at the mention of the uncle who'd protected him, fathered him.

She halted him on the sidewalk with a sheen of tears in her eyes. "Oh, Nick, I'm so very sorry. Did they ... ever catch who did it?"

"No." His voice was a hiss ... a lit fuse sizzling away in his gut as revenge spewed from his lips. "But if it takes my last breath, I'll find the slime who did it and gun him down too."

Her body went completely still, and then with no warning at all, she lunged to embrace him, paralyzing his limbs so much, all he could do was stand there inert. "You've had so much tragedy in your life, it's no wonder you're angry inside." She pulled away to cup a hand to his cheek, eyes as tender as Gram's used to be when she'd kiss him good night. The barest of smiles tipped the edges of her beautiful mouth. "Something tells me that underneath all that anger and pain, Detective Barone, is a sweet little boy so wounded, the hurt had nowhere to go."

He smiled. "Maybe, but if you expose me, Miss McClare, you'll answer to Mr. Cranky Pants."

"And ruin my fun of calling you pet names?" She hiked her chin with an imp of a smile. "Not on your life, Mr. Pinhead."

Their laughter merged in the night, making him wish the bright lights of Nob Hill were farther away. Slowing his pace, he spoke, voice suddenly husky and low. "Allison . . ."

She looked up—the trusting eyes of a girl he longed to love and protect.

"Thank you for listening," he said softly, tucking a silky curl back into her hat. "I haven't been able to open up like that with anyone since Gram." He exhaled slowly. "It feels good."

Her smile was as soft as the lips that framed it. "You're welcome, Nick, but at the risk of inciting the ire of Mr. Cranky Pants, I'm compelled to say—it could feel a whole lot better."

Scanning the street both ways, he steered her across to her elegant Victorian, lips skewed in an off-center smile. "Now, why do I feel a lecture coming that would make Gram smile?"

She scurried up the steps with the same energy with which she did everything, giving him a twinkle of a smile out of the corner of her eye. "I don't know. Maybe because people who truly care will tell you the truth?"

All but hopping onto the slate rock step beneath the marble portico, she turned to give him a tentative grin, nibbling on the edge of her lip as if worried she might offend.

He moved in close, slowly grazing her jaw with the pad of his thumb. "Are you saying you care for me, Miss McClare?" he whispered, lips curving at the vulnerable look in her eyes.

She blinked, gaze wide and lips parted. "I . . . I mean, of course I care for you, Nick," she stuttered, "we're friends, after all." Her throat muscles convulsed as she took a step back, purse clutched to her chest like a shield. "Which is why my heart aches, knowing your anger not only changes who you are, but cuts you off from the only One who can set you free from the pain."

Her innocence captured him, convicted him, calling him to be the type of man who would have made Gram proud . . . *and* his parents. It was his turn to swallow hard and he did so several times, as if to clear the sour taste of bitterness that had tainted his tongue for far too long. Drawing in a deep breath, he nodded, eyes fixed on the tips of his expensive polished shoes—a habit Gram had instilled, citing a clean shine was a reflection of a good and prosperous man.

Prosperous? Certainly, as the sole heir of his uncle's ill-gotten gain. But, good? Not unless he took the veiled advice of Allison McClare and forgave the murderers who'd destroyed his family. Something he wasn't sure he was willing to do, at least not yet. He felt his jaw stiffen as he eased away. No, he needed the hate and bitterness to follow through, to enjoy pulling the trigger on those who had pulled it on him.

She must have sensed his reluctance because she took a tentative step forward, touching a gentle palm to his face to stroke the bristled plane of his jaw. "Promise me, Nick," she whispered, "that you'll start talking to God again. That you'll open your heart and let Him back in. It's what Gram would want, and as your friend, it's what I want for you too." Her lips curved in a beautiful smile. "Because frankly, Mr. Ga-roan, although Mr. Cranky Pants may be fun to tease—" an imp of a grin eased across her face—"to coin a phrase, he can be a 'monumental pain' to be around."

He grinned in spite of himself. "That's better than a monumental pain in the posterior."

Her chin spiked up in mock indignation. "No it isn't, and we both know it." She lifted on tiptoe to press a gentle kiss to his cheek. "Good night, Nick."

She turned to go and against his will, he stopped her, staying her arm before tugging her near. "Alli," he said softly, suddenly captivated by the graceful contour of her face, the lush curve of her lips. His fingers strayed to fondle the soft flesh of her ear and as if under a spell, he found himself listing forward, eyelids drugged as he hovered over that perfect mouth he craved to devour. His breathing was shallow and raspy—like hers against his skin—an innocent invitation to taste a forbidden fruit almost too tempting to deny.

Almost.

Exercising every ounce of willpower he possessed, he pressed a soft kiss to her forehead instead, before straightening with a harsh draw of air. Fisting the brass knob of the burlwood door with way too much tension, he opened it wide, gaze guarded to deflect the desire still burning inside. "Good night, Allison," he whispered, voice husky and low, almost wishing it were "goodbye" to save both of them the danger of anything more.

She blinked, a hint of confusion in emerald eyes that wreaked havoc with his iron will. "Good night, Nick," she said, a valiant attempt at nonchalance he didn't believe for a second. "Thank you for taking me to Chinatown."

His smile was firm—like his resolve to keep a safe distance. "You're welcome." He watched her slip into the foyer, his heart as heavy as the door she closed in his face. "It was my pleasure," he said, the sound of his weighty sigh following him down the steps.

Unfortunately . . .

19

Mother, did you know the Eiffel Tower's the largest building in the world? . . .

Caitlyn laid Meg's letter in her lap. "Yes, darling, I did," she whispered, lips tipped in a melancholy smile at the memory of Liam telling her the very same thing on their honeymoon to Paris. *A lifetime ago.*

Resting her head on the back of the wicker love seat in the conservatory, she sighed, the earthy smells of mulch and loam failing to soothe as her gaze trailed from Meg's letter to the sliver of moon overhead. The panes of glass reflected her sorrow while her thoughts took her back to a time when her four precious children were only a glimmer of love in her husband's eyes. Expelling another weighty sigh, she grazed her fingertips across the surface of the soft vellum sheet scented with the perfume she'd bought Meg for Christmas, and knew her daughter would thrive in Paris. Her exuberant letter contained not a hint of being homesick, for which Caitlyn was truly grateful, although she couldn't say the same for herself, a mother deeply "homesick" for a daughter sorely missed. But knowing Meg was happy at last was one of the few comforts Caitlyn enjoyed from the absence of a shy and gentle daughter who'd always been a balm to her mother's soul.

Out of nowhere, the thought struck that Meg could possibly meet a beau in Paris and want to stay through college, and suddenly all air heaved still in Caitlyn's lungs, fear cramping her heart at the painful prospect. Tears immediately stung at the reminder that not only had she lost Liam, but someday in the not-too-distant future, she would lose each of her children as well, their loyalties and lives belonging to another instead of to her, and rightfully so. The very notion pierced her mother's heart anew, and a frail heave parted from her lips as she put a hand to her eyes, weeks of mourning a child's departure finally taking its toll.

Eyes closed and letter limp in her hand, she was grateful the house was still tonight so she could weep in private, her emotional state a bit of an embarrassment that she'd react so strongly to Megan's departure. And yet, here she was blubbering like a baby while Maddie was sound asleep. Rosie had retired early due to a headache, Cassie and Alli were out with Jamie and Bram, and Blake was only heaven knows where, a contemplation that caused Caitlyn to cry all the more. Not to mention she had begged off on a committee meeting with Andrew, the poor man at a total loss when she answered the door with red-rimmed eyes.

She laid back against the chaise, head lolling and mood mellow, the dirt-pungent smells of the conservatory usually a balm to her soul, but not tonight. Abandoning herself to a rare moment of release, she gave vent to the deep, hidden sobs that rose from within, purging her of a sadness as intermittent as the mood swings and cycle disruptions that plagued her of late. With shaky, little heaves, she fished her handkerchief from the pocket of her empire tea gown and blew her nose. She so felt like a lost little girl, body scrunched sideways on the settee, legs tucked to her chest and arms folded as she buried her head and continued to bawl.

"Cait?"

Her heart seized mid-sniffle, head jolting up. *Logan?*

"What's wrong?" he said, a fierce edge of concern in his voice and eyes glowing with an intense protectiveness that always made her feel safe. Sitting alongside, he placed a large palm over the hands she now clasped to her knees. "Why are you crying?"

She shook her head, mortified to be caught in such a pitiful state, cheeks burning from both tears and humiliation over her obvious lack of control. She grappled with the heirloom watch pinned to her dress. "W-what are you d-doing here?" she rasped. "It's well past eleven . . ."

His eyes pierced with a look of worry that embarrassed her all the more. "Blake and I came back to play pool awhile ago, but the house was so quiet, I thought everyone was in bed." He grazed a thumb across her hand. "Tell me what's wrong, Cait—please."

"Nothing," she insisted, her nasal tone branding her a liar. With a frantic sweep of legs to the floor, she hefted her chin in a valiant attempt at composure, arching a brow to turn the tables on him. "Haven't you ever had a mood where you break down and cry to clear your head?"

The edge of his mouth crooked as he studied her with tender eyes, head bowed as if comforting Maddie. "Yes, but I usually just take it out on the bag at the gym."

Issuing a rare grunt, she dabbed at her eyes. "Yes, well, that's a luxury I don't have."

"Sure you do," he said with a hint of jest, voice gentle. He scooped her close as he would any of her daughters, casually resting his head against hers. "I can easily install one in your study or even let you take potshots at me."

He gave her arm a tender pat as she'd seen him do hundreds of times with each of her children, and to her horror, a floodtide of water welled in her eyes.

His words softened to a compassionate whisper. "Why are you hurting, Cait?"

Heaven help her, that's all it took for the floodgates to open, and with a ferocious need to be held she didn't quite understand, she collapsed against him in a fit of painful weeping. Sobs wrenching her body, she clenched his silk waistcoat and promptly drenched it with tears, huddling close when his arms surrounded her with a strength that made her feel sheltered and loved. The familiar scent of lime shaving soap and wood spice both comforted and stirred, but she chose to focus on the need to be held by someone for whom she deeply cared.

Her eyelids shuddered closed. *Even if it's a brother-in-law who poses a risk to my heart.*

Cocooned in his silent embrace, she wept until her sobs trailed off into frail whimpers that finally slowed and settled into an intimate silence. The steady beat of his heart merged with her own, a beautiful harmony that was oddly comforting. Both the tension in her body and a wispy sigh seeped out with every gentle stroke of his hand to her hair, reminding her just how long it'd been since she'd allowed herself to weep in the arms of another.

She reveled in the gentle glide of his thumb to her cheek. "Whatever it is, Cait," he whispered, "you won't shoulder it alone. I'll be here for you—always."

Emotion swelled in her throat and she nodded, the clean scent of starch and lime and Logan filling her senses with a peace and security she hadn't expected in the arms of this man. "Thank you," she said quietly, finally pulling away to dab the handkerchief to her face. Her cheeks immediately heated at the abundance of water stains on the silk of his waistcoat. "Sweet heavens, but I've soaked you good," she said with a nervous chuckle, peeking up with contrition in her gaze. "If you leave it, Logan, I'll have it cleaned."

The faint tilt of his lips clashed with the sobriety in his eyes. "It's not the vest I'm concerned about, Cait." With the utmost gentleness, he tucked a loose strand of hair over her ear, the warmth of his fingers lingering far too long for her peace of mind. "What's wrong?"

She scooted back to her side of the settee, suddenly feeling quite foolish. Barricading her arms to her waist, she forced a bright smile. "Actually, it's quite silly—a grown woman making a fool of herself over missing a daughter who's merely away at school."

He settled in to face her, arm draped over the back of the settee. "It's never silly to make a fool of ourselves over those we love," he said softly, "only proof of just how deep that love is."

She blinked, lips wobbling into a smile. "Why . . . what a beautiful way to look at it, Logan—thank you."

His smile was sheepish. "Had to come up with some rationale for mutilating the bag in my gym since Megan boarded that train."

Her lips parted in a delighted chuckle, hand to her mouth. "Oh no, you too?"

"Yep, me too." He reached for her hand, giving it a gentle squeeze. "I've already told you, family is everything to me, just like it is with you. That means if one of us hurts, we all hurt. If one of us leaves, we all grieve the loss." His mouth quirked. "Of course, some of us opt for more manly ways in which to vent our frustrations."

She stared, the tumult of emotions that had prompted her crying jag now welling into a deep affection for the man before her. Overcome with intense gratitude for Logan in her family and life, she reached out without thinking to gently cup the scruff of his jaw, shocked when his late-evening beard quivered her stomach. "I don't know if I've ever told you," she whispered, "just how much joy you bring into our lives."

Logan froze, pulse thudding to a stop at the touch of her hand. *Oh, Cait, give me the chance to bring more . . .* Her words warmed his heart as much as her lips would warm his body, and he fought the inclination to swallow hard lest he betray the need to love her the way he so longed to do. But if Napa had taught him anything, it was that Caitlyn McClare was the most skittish of fawns waiting to bolt. He dare not risk tenuous months of restoration to a friendship badly damaged by a kiss taken too soon. Battling the impulse to cup the hand she held to his cheek, he offered a calm smile instead, limbs deathly still lest he scare her away. "No, Cait, you haven't, but my heart rejoices to hear it." His eyes burned with an intensity he longed to convey through his touch. "Now more than ever—I live to bring my family joy," he whispered. *And none more than you . . .*

Her eyes softened with a tender sheen of moisture as muscles shifted in her throat, and when she leaned to press a kiss to his cheek, his heart seized. Heat ricocheted at the touch of her lips, and the urge to turn his head mere inches and partake of her mouth was so strong, his body shuddered as he forced it away. Clearing his throat, he quickly stood, voice too husky and hoarse. "Up for a game of cribbage?"

The green eyes blinked. "At this late hour?"

Glancing at his watch, he grinned and extended his hand. "It's only eleven on a Saturday night, Mrs. McClare, and if it's not too late to blubber alone in the conservatory, it's not too late to get our minds off Meg with a game to lift our spirits. Besides, I think it's only fair if your son fleeced his uncle in pool, the uncle should at least have a shot at his mother, don't you think?"

The most perfect lips he'd ever seen—or kissed—curved in a dubious smile as she took his hand to rise to her feet. "I fail to see how you fleecing me in cribbage will lift *my* spirits."

Bracing her arm firmly with his own, he led her from the room with a low chuckle. "Why, I'll let you win, of course," he said, patting her hand. "After that heart-wrenching display of melancholy, Cait, how dare I do anything else?"

Her laughter warmed him inside and out, the glimmer in her eyes no longer because of her tears. "Ha! Do-or-Die McClare laying his pride aside to let someone else win? Especially his pitiful sister-in-law whom he demoralizes in cribbage each week?" She tilted her head, affording him a patient smile. "I'll believe it when I see it."

"Believe it, Cait. Whether you realize it or not, there are some things more important than my pride, the welfare of my family being one. So, yes, to bolster your mood, I may just let you win."

"Oh, now it's 'may'?"

"*Will* let you win," he emphasized with a playful jag of his brow as he ushered her into the parlour. *At cribbage, that is.* Seating her in her chair, he settled in his own with a confident air. At the game of love? He reached for the cards to shuffle the deck before offering the cut.

Not a chance . . .

<hr/>

Tweeeeeeeeeeet!
Every eye in the room focused on Alli as she blew her whistle, the cast staring back with goggle eyes and lips chewed in nervous anticipation. A grin inched its way across her lips as she and Cassie

exchanged a glance before they bounded to their feet in noisy applause. "Brava, brava, young ladies—that was simply the finest rehearsal Miss Cassie and I have ever seen, bar none."

Shrieks and giggles rose from the stage where sixteen young ladies of all ages hopped and hugged in rowdy celebration over the fund-raiser play they'd been rehearsing every day for almost two weeks. "So, we're almost ready, Miss Alli?" Shannon asked, the whites of her brown eyes as round as the footlights at the front of the stage.

Alli slid Cassie a wink before lifting her chin with a proud smile. "Almost, Shannon. Another week or so of rehearsals, and this will be one of Hand of Hope School's finest moments, not to mention raising funds that will allow a day field trip to . . ." She paused, trading another grin with Cassie that conveyed excitement over what was in store for the girls. "Adolph Sutro's famous Cliff House for lunch, with a tour of its photo gallery, art gallery, and gem exhibit."

Both Alli and Cassie winced when the small gym exploded with deafening whoops and whistles and the thunderous clomp of feet on the stage. Laughing, Alli blew her whistle again, reining the girls in. "All right, ladies, it's time to call it a day, so please collect your wraps and belongings from the classroom and *quietly* proceed to the front door to head home. Good night!"

The girls' goodbyes echoed in the gym as they filed out, and Cassie stretched her arms overhead, a gleam of pride in eyes warm with affection and approval. "Whew, I'll tell you what, Al, I had my doubts you could succeed in Shakespeare with young girls who've never been exposed to the arts, but I gotta hand it to you—they were wonderful."

"Aw, thanks, Cass," Alli said, all but glowing over her cousin's praise. "But I certainly couldn't have done it without you."

Reaching for her hat that rested beside her on a chair, Cassie put it on with a devious smile. "Or without all that wonderful scenery Mr. Nick built for you, so don't forget about him."

Forget Mr. Nick? A blush scalded Allison's cheeks as she whirled around to gather her script from the chair. *Uh, not likely.* Not after the man all but paralyzed her the night he'd walked her home from Chinatown when she thought he was going to kiss her. Her heart had seized the moment his shuttered gaze had fixed on her lips, depriving her body of all oxygen while his fingers casually toyed with the lobe of her ear. And then in a jolt of heat that shimmered her skin, he'd slowly leaned in, coaxing her eyelids closed as if she were drugged while she awaited the touch of his lips against hers. A touch that had branded her forehead instead of her lips, telling her loud and clear Mr. Nick saw her as only a friend.

A shiver scurried through her—along with a keen sense of disappointment—over how very close she'd come to making a fool of herself over one Nicholas Barone. She slid her papers into her attaché case and quickly slipped her jacket off, thoughts of Nick warming her body as much as his surly moods used to warm her temper. "Goodness, it's hot as blazes in here," she groused. "I wish Mother would get that silly radiator fixed before we all melt to death."

"Uh . . . Al?" Cassie's hand lighted on her arm, tugging her back with a questioning gaze. "It's in the low 50s outside, a record low for August, and it's downright freezing in here. So why don't you tell me why your face is as red as sunburn in the middle of a heat wave?"

"G'night, Miss Alli and Miss Cassie!" Lottie popped her head around the corner until Shannon dragged her away with a final wave.

"Good night, Miss La-di-da, good night, Shannon," Alli called, grateful for the distraction from Cassie's question. "See you to-morrow."

"Are you girls ready to go?" Her mother appeared in the door-way, pinning a modest floral hat on her head. "It's almost six, and Hadley's waiting."

Alli spun around, hand to her chest. "Oh, Mother, I can't believe I forgot to tell you, but I was planning on staying a little late to finish up a few things, if that's okay."

Caitlyn paused, obviously taken by surprise. "Oh." The lace of her high-collar blouse bobbed, indicating she wasn't comfortable with the idea, but she'd agreed to give Alli more freedom. "Well . . . I suppose that will be all right," she said slowly, unable to hide the tension in her tone. "If you promise not to stay too late." She glanced out the front windows where the late-afternoon sun was streaming in, and drew in a deep breath. "But you only have two hours of sunlight, darling, because there's no walking to the cable car after dark, remember?"

"Yes, Mother, and I'll leave before then, I promise." Alli hurried over to give her a hug, hoping to reassure that she was perfectly capable of fending for herself. "I have my atomizer bracelet and my hat pin, not to mention a pretty deadly kick, so please don't worry."

A fragile sigh parted from her mother's lips as she nervously tugged on her kid gloves. Adjusting the short, fitted bolero jacket of her tailored suit, she managed a stiff smile. "Well, we'll expect you home around 7:30 or so, all right?" Her eyes flicked to Cassie. "I'll wait for you in the car, dear, while you gather your things." With a squeeze of Alli's hand, she turned and made her way down the hall, leaving Alli feeling both guilty and more than a little excited. Breathing in a hefty dose of sea-scented air, she turned to her cousin with a skip in her pulse, hands clasped to her chest. "Can you believe it? My first official venture alone!"

"I'm thrilled for you, Al, truly," Cassie said with a wry smile as she sauntered over to where Alli stood. "But you didn't answer my question." She folded her arms and angled a brow, the semblance of an "I told you so" smile playing at the edge of her mouth. "I want to know why the mere mention of Mr. Nick's name set your face on fire a few moments ago?"

Said "fire" was back, singeing her face like a forest aflame. "W-what do you m-mean?" she whispered, reluctant to admit her true feelings for Nick to herself—much less to the cousin and best friend who longed to see her fall in love.

Cassie's smile went flat. "I mean, Allison McClare, you are keeping something from me about Nick Barone—I can feel it. Ever since your last jiu-jitsu lesson two weeks ago, you've been in a funk despite the fact you've just pulled off an amazing feat with these girls in an incredible play by Shakespeare, no less. She tapped the toe of her shoe on the gymnasium floor. "Something tells me you have feelings for him though you claim to be only friends."

Alli suddenly had an overwhelming desire to trim a hangnail with her teeth. "We are j-just friends, Cass, I p-promise," she said, spitting a sliver of thumbnail out of her mouth.

"Ah-ha!" Cassie gripped Alli's arms, giving her a little shake. "You're fiddling with your nails, a dead giveaway. You're falling for him, aren't you, despite all your babble about friendship?"

Alli stared, her nail now as ragged as her lip, which she seemed to gnaw at the mere mention of Nick Barone. Giving up the ghost of a sigh, she finally gave a short nod.

"I knew it!" Cassie announced with supreme satisfaction, lifting Alli off the floor in a voracious hug. "All it takes is you two passing in the hall, and I swear the radiator goes tilt."

A shaky sigh fluttered from Alli's lips. "Well, for one of us, anyway."

Cassie's eyes narrowed in a squint. "Oh, come on, Al, I've been watching you both for the last month—the man is smitten, and you're not going to convince me otherwise."

Alli plopped back into her chair, gaze lapsing into a bleak stare. "How about a brotherly kiss on the forehead, Cass—is that convincing enough?"

"Nope." Cassie dropped into the next chair, angling to face her. "I've seen the way Nick looks at you when he thinks no one is looking, and trust me, it's anything but brotherly."

Alli grunted. "Maybe, but even if you discount the kiss on the forehead, he admitted he's angry at God over some pretty awful things in his life." She expelled a mournful sigh, heart heavy over the pain of Nick's past. "He's an orphan, Cass, with no family of his own." She swallowed hard. "Lost his gram to cancer and then his uncle was murdered."

"Oh, Al . . ." Cassie gripped Alli's hand, the disbelief in her eyes tinged with tears.

Alli exhaled slowly, the motion all but draining her. "Suddenly it makes a whole lot of sense why Nick seems so angry at times, and I'll be honest, Cass—I almost don't blame him."

"Me either," Cassie whispered. "But you and I both know from painful experience that anger and bitterness will only rob a person of God's blessings, right?"

She nodded.

"Which means Nick is in dire need of someone who can show him how to forgive so God can heal his heart." She lifted a hand to gently stroke her cousin's cheek, love welling in her eyes. "And other than Jamie, few have learned that lesson better than you with all the hurt you've experienced with heartbreak."

"I know." Alli stared at the floor, her voice a frail whisper. "I tried to talk to him about God and forgiveness when he walked me home from Chinatown, but he didn't seem interested."

"Doesn't surprise me. So, we let God do the legwork instead." Cassie ducked to give her a smile. "With prayer."

Alli glanced up, Cassie's faith spurring her own. "You think?"

"I know, and so do you. And before God's through, Nick Barone will know it too."

Alli's chest expanded and contracted with a wavering sigh. "Oh, I hope so," she breathed, her spirits lifting that God might actually have something in store for her with Nicholas Barone.

Cassie chuckled as she gave Alli a tight hug. "Well, that's good, 'cause 'hope' is definitely one part of the equation." She peered over Alli's shoulder at the clock on the wall. "Gotta run before Aunt Cait leaves without me, but we'll pray when you get home, okay?"

"Wait—you said 'one part'? What's the rest of the equation?" Alli pulled back, forehead in a bunch.

"Why, the perfect equation, of course," Cassie said with a wiggle of brows. "Faith, hope, and love. You know—a whole lot of our faith mixed with a whole lot of your hope? And before we know it . . . ," she winked, "we may have something that looks like a whole lot of love."

20

Nick popped an animal cracker in his mouth while he waited in the bushes, wondering what in blazes a woman could do in an empty school all by herself that she couldn't do at home. He glanced at his watch, then squinted down Jackson. The glow of dusk was beginning to wash the ramshackle buildings with a surreal glow that made the Barbary Coast almost pretty. A grunt escaped as he pelted more crackers to the back of his throat. Yeah, it was pretty all right—pretty ugly, with all that went on after dark. His eyes flicked to the sliver of light that bled through the curtains at the front of the school, and he huffed out a noisy blast of air. She better wrap it up soon because she was running out of daylight and *he* was running out of patience.

"Allison's fixing to leave soon," Miss Penny informed him over twenty minutes ago after Mrs. McClare alerted them Alli had called regarding her imminent departure. Per orders from the *supervisor*, Nick would follow the independent Miss McClare all the way home without her knowledge, which meant more blasted time on that infernal cable car. The edge of his mouth tipped in a reluctant smile. At least it only entailed a bout of nausea instead of a pain in the neck too, which Allison had suddenly ceased to be. No, now the pain in his neck had traveled south to produce a dull ache in his chest over the realization their time together was over. He hadn't seen her—really seen her—in two weeks, other than the rare times they'd run into each other when she walked Lottie home or the nights like tonight when she stayed late. Nothing more than a short hello and goodbye or the back of her head when he needed to follow her home, and it annoyed him just how much he missed her. But the simple truth was, Allison McClare was now where he needed her to be—nothing more than a girl from his past, and one he needed to forget.

Soon.

Tossing the remains of the animal crackers in his mouth, he crushed the Barnum's box and dropped it in the pocket of his sack suit, figuring he'd need the whole bloomin' box to settle his stomach for the cable car. He checked his watch for the twentieth time and scowled.

What the devil is she doing, anyway? Expelling a noisy breath, he moved with the stealth of a shadow from Miss Penny's lawn to that of the school, mounting the pristine white steps with the utmost care. Pausing at the top, he listened, head cocked to catch any sound that he could.

Nothing. No footsteps, no floor squeaks, no humming. The windows were obviously closed, but even so ... Unease skittered his spine like rats skittered the alleys of the Coast, and hands cupped to the window, he peered through the crack in the curtains. Suddenly words he hadn't uttered since the war ground from his lips, eyes gaping as Allison McClare wobbled on the top rung of a ladder. Nick would have sworn she was swaying as she attempted to paint scenery—the red roof of a house facade Mr. Bigley was supposed to finish—with a paintbrush taped to the end of that confounded stick.

So help me, Allison ... Biting back another colorful complaint, he quietly made his way to the front door, silence essential so he wouldn't scare the brat half to death and risk her toppling from the ladder. Pulse hammering, he attempted to unlock the front door with the key Mrs. McClare had given him, incensed all the more to find it unlocked. "Blue blistering blazes," he muttered under his breath, easing the door open with nary a sound before silently stealing into the gym. One glance at the stretch of her lithe and curvy form confirmed proximity to Allison McClare was not a good thing. At least, not anymore. Not since the little brat had crept into his heart with her spunk and sass and passion for life, a passion that included a devotion to God he'd missed more than he realized. Apparently too focused while she hummed quietly to herself, she never even heard his approach, and releasing a silent sigh, he slowly mounted the steps to the stage. Halting twenty feet away, he prayed he was close enough to catch her if she were to fall. "Alli," he whispered, hoping the soft sound of his voice would gently draw her attention.

The humming and painting happily continued, confirming once again that this woman lived in a world all her own. Nick's lips went flat. A world in which he was becoming entirely too comfortable. "Alli," he said again, his whisper edged with annoyance this time.

"Oh!" Jerking straight up, she whirled around at the waist, body and ladder teetering so hard the paint bucket went flying, hitting the paint-stained sheet beneath her with a clunk and a splat. Nick's heart climbed in his throat when the woman herself flailed in the air as if in slow motion, limbs thrashing along with that infernal stick.

Pulse in a sprint, he sprang forward with instinct and speed honed to near perfection in jiu-jitsu, heart crashing into his stomach while Allison crashed into his arms. With a harsh catch of his breath, shock gave way to temper at the risks that she took. "What is it with you and heights, anyway?" he snapped. "You trying to break your silly neck?" Rib cage heaving, he glared, waiting for the tongue-lashing that never came.

"Oh, Nick!" Hand quivering, she gently stroked his cheek. "I've missed you so much."

He swallowed hard, the love in her eyes draining his temper along with his resistance, making the desire to kiss her more potent than all the bottles of booze peddled mere blocks away. Unable to control the impulse, he turned his lips toward her palm, eyelids shuttering closed when he captured her fingers with the caress of his mouth. Heat skimmed his body at the sound of her soft gasp and never had he craved a woman's lips more.

"Do I have your word you won't make advances to my niece?"

He opened his eyes to a beautiful face aglow with an innocent awe while she traced the contour of his mouth with quivering fingers, the longing in her gaze as obvious as his own.

The knot of his four-in-hand tie bobbed when he carefully set her down on the paint-splotched sheet, removing his hands from her person with a fierce stab of regret. "I've missed you too," he said quietly, his voice huskier than intended.

Hope glowed in her eyes when she moved in close, fidgeting with her nails as she peeked up beneath a sweep of dark lashes. "Nick, I . . . know this isn't conventional, but then I'm not a conventional woman . . ."

His lips curved in the barest of smiles. "I'd say that's an understatement, Miss McClare."

Her smile softened with that little-girl look of wonder when something surprised or delighted her. With a shuddery breath, she moved in to lay her head to his chest, tentative arms circling his waist. "I think I'm falling in love with you, Nick," she whispered, "so I need to know—do you have any feelings like that for me?"

No! His pulse slammed to a stop while his eyes weighted closed, icy shivers of shock rooting him to the floor when he realized he was lying. In one ragged beat of his heart, the truth struck hard—he was falling in love with her too. As if possessing a mind of their own, his arms drew her close while he nestled his head against hers, breathing in her scent for what he knew would be the very last time. "Yes," he whispered, weaving his fingers into the silky tresses pinned at the back of her head, "but it doesn't matter, Alli, because we can't do this."

She pulled back. "Can't fall in love? Don't you think it's a little late for that?"

He feathered her jaw with his thumb, his smile sad. "I do, but I can't act on it."

"But why?" she whispered, her voice as fragile as the innocence in her eyes.

Easing from her hold, he stepped back to bury his hands in his pockets, fixing her with a look that was riddled with regret. "Because I can't kiss you or love you the way that I want."

She shook her head, confusion furrowing her brow. "But I don't understand—why?"

His jaw automatically hardened. "Because I gave my word."

She blinked, a large blotch of white paint caressing her cheek like he longed to do. "Your word? To whom?"

"Your uncle," he said with a tight press of his lips.

The whites of her eyes nearly expanded to the size of the smudge. "What? When?"

He exhaled. "When he hired me to fill in for Mr. Bigley and to teach you jiu-jitsu." His mouth took a slant. "Even made me sign a contract."

Those lush, dark lashes twitched several times as if she were trying to comprehend. "A contract?" she whispered. "To do what— not fall in love with me?"

His gaze flitted to her mouth and back and he absently licked lips now as parched as his throat. "No. To not make advances."

Two beautiful brows bunched in a frown as comprehension slowly dawned in her eyes. "So . . . you're saying you can't *legally* kiss me?"

His chest rose and fell with an expulsion of air. "Afraid not."

Nibbling the edge of her lip, she tilted her head, brows sloped in question. "But you . . . you think you might . . . want to?" Her question was soft, tentative . . . as if afraid he'd say no.

He issued a grunt, gaze hot as it settled on her mouth. "Oh, yeah, I definitely want to."

"Really?" An impish smile inched across her face as she chewed on the tip of her thumbnail. With a shy grate of her lip, she grabbed his hand and tugged him to the ladder.

"What are you doing?" he asked, not trusting the pixie glint in her eyes.

Ignoring his question, she placed one dainty shoe to the first rung and hiked herself up, turning to curl her arms to his waist. "What am I doing?" she asked, brows arched in her most professional teacher mode. "I just told you I'm falling in love with you, Nick Barone, and you indicated you're doing the same, which means we seal our declaration with a kiss."

He scowled, willpower stretched as thin as his nerves. "I told you—I can't kiss you, Allison."

"No . . . but *I* can." A giggle tumbled out that sounded like trouble before she stood on tiptoe to warm his lips with her own.

Body pulsing, heat rolled through him while he stood there inert, his breathing as ragged as hers when he finally had the strength to nudge her away. "Alli, please, you're killing me here . . ."

Tease gleamed in her gaze like mischief gleamed on her lips, still moist from the taste of their kiss. "Oh, don't be a baby," she whispered, as if he were balking on that first step of the cable car. "Because your name may be on that contract, Mr. Ga-roan . . ."

She brushed her lips against his, her giggle soft when she pulled away to give him a wink. "But *mine* isn't."

❦ ❦

"Can I help you?"

Nick eyed the pretty secretary in the reception area of Mc-Clare, Rupert and Byington and took note of the nameplate at the front of her desk. "Yes, Miss Peabody, you can—I need to see Logan McClare—*now*—so which office is he in?"

Her eyes circled wide. "I'm s-sorry, s-sir, but do you have an appointment?"

He leaned in, hands sprawled on the front of her desk like a threat. "No, Miss Peabody, I have a beef, and either you tell me which office he's in or I'll just blast down that hallway slamming doors till I find him."

She shot to her feet. "I'm sorry, sir, but I can't let you—"

"Have it your way," he mumbled, her panicked objections trailing him as he stormed down the hall. Jaw grinding, he honed in on a brass plate with Logan McClare's name, and with a meaty fist, he pounded twice on the cherrywood door before flinging it wide.

"What the—" Pen in hand, McClare peered over wire-rim reading glasses with obvious displeasure while Miss Peabody's protests echoed behind.

Nick slammed the door in her face, his scowl going head-to-head with McClare's. Striding forward, he plucked an envelope from his jacket and slung it on Logan's desk.

"What the devil is this about?" Logan said, ignoring the envelope.

"Blood money, McClare, every filthy cent." Hands on his hips, Nick loomed over the desk like a thunderhead. "You need to know I have feelings for Alli and I plan to act on them."

A flicker of surprise registered in Logan's eyes before he eased

278

back in his leather chair, gray eyes hardening into slits of pewter. He slowly twirled the pen in his hands, the view of the bay outside his six-story window far more serene than the tension that crackled in the room. "I'm afraid you can't do that, Mr. Barone—we have a contract."

"So, sue me, counselor. But either way, I have designs on your niece."

Logan chucked his pen. "Or her money," he said, tone casual.

Nick jerked forward, palms flat on the edge of the desk. "So, help me, if you weren't Allison's uncle, I'd lay you out right here and now. As it is, I'll thank you to shut your mouth—she's too special of a woman for you to imply my interest is motivated by money."

"Yes, she is," Logan said with a fold of his arms, gaze shrewd as he eased back into his chair. "Which is why I will do everything in my power to protect her from the wrong men in her life. I let her down with Roger Luepke—you can bet it won't happen again. Which means, Barone . . ." He picked up the envelope and riffled through the stack of bills inside before tossing it back on the desk with a cold smile. "Not only am I going to pursue legal action, I plan to rattle any skeletons in your closet if I have to look under every rock to do it."

A nerve pulsed in Nick's jaw as he stared, the acid in his stomach churning along with his guilt. Never in a million years had he intended to fall in love with Allison McClare, but against his will, he was well on his way. It had taken Alli herself defying convention with a kiss, but the moment her lips had touched his, she branded his very soul, unleashing a desire buried so deep, it jolted when he realized just how much he cared. A man of his word, he'd gently held her at bay, body so tight with desire, he feared he'd give in and break the promise he'd made.

"Let me talk to your uncle first," he'd said in a strangled voice, "to tell him that our agreement is off." He'd swallowed hard then, barely able to believe the words about to part from his lips. "I want more than friendship," he'd whispered, feathering her mouth with his thumb, "and he needs to know that."

Tears had welled in those almond-shaped eyes, and when she'd lunged to kiss him again, it'd taken every ounce of willpower he owned not to give in and devour her on the spot.

The same iron will steeled him now as he stared at McClare, wondering just how deep the supervisor would dig into secrets Nick couldn't afford to share. Was he bluffing or was Nick jeopardizing the revenge he'd worked so hard to ensure? The plan for vengeance he'd promised both his uncle and himself. *And retribution for my parents as well.* Sweat licked the back of his collar as thoughts darted through his mind. Was his trail cold enough that McClare wouldn't catch the scent? Or would something trip him up, destroying his chances with Alli as surely as he planned to destroy those who had ruined his life?

As if sensing Nick's hesitation, Logan picked up the envelope and pitched it across his desk, landing it on the edge where it teetered along with Nick's temper. "I'll triple that if you cut your losses now, Barone, and stay out of her life."

"I told you, it's not about the money," he hissed, teeth clenched as tight as his fists.

"Sure it is, Nick." Logan's smile was as steely as the gun strapped beneath Nick's arm. "You're a penniless plainclothes cop who mysteriously shows up a year ago with no history, no background, and no friends. Nothing but a friend of a friend in New York who begs Harm to give you a job." His smile eased into a sneer. "Not exactly marriage material for a niece I'd protect with my life." Elbows cocked on the arms of his chair, he rested his head on the back, two fingers tented against his mouth. "I'm telling you again, Nick—take the money and run or I'll expose you and shatter you in front of my niece."

His heart thundered in his chest while he considered the risk, well aware a man of Logan's means could do that and more, sabotaging everything Nick had worked for over the last five years. His eyes strayed to a picture of the McClares on a credenza over Logan's left shoulder, and Allison's beautiful face captured his gaze. He thought of the last two and half months he'd known her—the best of his life—and knew she was worth fighting for. Knew he couldn't let another high-society kingpin win once again. He thought of Ming Chao, and bitterness tainted his tongue. *Especially Logan McClare.*

Straightened to his full height, he squared his shoulders. "Well then, I'll just take my chances, *sir*," he said with the same disdain he saw in McClare's face, praying he'd hidden his tracks well enough to keep him away from the truth. *Until I can pull the trigger. . . .*

Logan shot up, palms knuckled white on his desk like Nick had done earlier. "You're going to regret this, Barone," he said. A nerve pulsed in his jaw. "I'm going to take you down."

Nick's lip curled in a hard smile that matched the steel glint in McClare's eyes. "Sorry to break it to you, Supervisor, but money lords like yourself have already taken me down, and I doubt I can go any lower." Shoving a chair out of his way, he strode to the door.

"Barone!"

He glanced over his shoulder, hand on the knob.

"Before I'm through, you'll be so low, flames'll be licking the soles of your fancy shoes."

"Yeah?" Nick arched a brow. "And you'll be right beside me, counselor, demon director of greed, corruption, and bribes." And without so much as a look back, he slammed the door hard, already feeling the heat on his way down the hall.

21

*D*ash it all, can this day get any worse? Logan leaned back in his chair with eyes closed, kneading his temples with the pads of his fingers, hours of prep yet to go tonight on the worst case he'd taken to trial in years. He hadn't needed this—Barone barging in, threatening to woo Allison and her bank account—not on top of losing a big case to Andrew Turner last week. *And not seeing Cait in almost a week due to a horrendous workload.* He exhaled a heavy breath. "Confound it—the only way this day could get any worse—"

Knock, knock.

"Excuse me, Mr. McClare." Miss Peabody stuck her head in the door, an apology in her tone, "but the district attorney is here to see you, sir."

Yep, that would be it. Logan groaned, face pinched in a scowl. "What's he want—to gloat over the Delmonico case?"

She offered a sympathetic smile. "I don't know, sir, but he did say it was personal."

He huffed out a noisy sigh. "Tell him I have five minutes to spare and no more."

"Yes, sir."

She left and Logan studied a report until the door opened again after a knock, admitting the bane of Logan's existence. "What do you want, Turner—gloating rights?"

Andrew Turner entered and closed the door behind him, his all-American smile—the one that earned him favors from women and juries—grating on Logan's nerves. "Appreciate your time," he said, ignoring Logan's jab in that fluid, easy manner that had won him many a friend in school, including Logan, with whom he'd been inseparable. The two of them had been a formidable team in the fraternity—two handsome and wealthy heartbreakers, able to turn the head of any girl they wanted. Until the day came when they wanted the same one—beautiful Caitlyn Stewart, the woman who ruined Logan McClare for any other. And apparently Andrew as well, given his frequent visits to Cait's house of late. He nodded to the cordovan chair in front of Logan's desk. "May I?"

"Help yourself," Logan muttered, "you usually do." He tossed his pen on the desk and sat back in his chair, arms folded and smile flat. "So, what do you want, Andrew?"

Turner laughed, a sparkle in pale, blue eyes that tended to captivate the opposite sex, his wheat-colored hair stylishly slicked back as he rested palms on the arms of his chair. "That's what I've always liked about you, Logan—a bottom-liner who goes straight to the punch, whether in the courtroom or in friendship."

One edge of Logan's lip curled in a cold smile. "As I recall, you were the so-called friend who inspired the 'straight to the punch' mentality."

He laughed again, the sound not as self-assured as the man appeared to be. "Yes, well, I earned that punch fair and square, no doubt about that." Smile sheepish, he stroked his jaw with the back of his hand. "And although I've apologized over and over, I'll continue to do so till you finally believe me." The smile sobered into an intensity Logan recognized from the courtroom, when Turner was trying to sway a jury with his sainted piety—the righteous, churchgoing district attorney out for the good of man. His voice resonated with a sincerity that most people believed. Logan issued a silent grunt. Or at least those he hadn't double-crossed. "I never meant to break you and Caitlyn up, Logan, I swear. Her best friend badgered until it just slipped out."

Logan's eyes narrowed to slits. "Sure it did, Turner, and I'll just bet it broke your heart when she skittered back to tell Cait her fiancé was seeing another woman behind her back."

Turner leapt to his feet. "It did, blast you! You were my best friend, Logan, and it tore me up to lose our friendship."

"But not as much as it tore you up to lose Cait, did it, Andrew?" Logan sat up, knuckles white on the arms of his chair to keep from slamming them into Turner's face. "Especially when Liam turned the tables on both of us and married the girl of our dreams." A nerve flickered in Logan's jaw as he snatched his pen from the desk, jerking his papers forward. "Sorry, old boy—I don't believe you now any more than I did then, so save your double tongue for the juries."

Turner expelled a weary breath, mouth compressed as he straightened to his full height. "I'd rather have done this as friends, Logan, but since that isn't possible, I'll come straight to the point." His chin lifted a degree as he fiddled with his tie, tightening his Windsor knot before nervously adjusting his sleeves. "I intend to court Caitlyn and was hoping for your blessing."

Logan stared, jaw distended before he laughed out loud. "You're joking."

A ruddy color bled up Turner's neck. "I assure you I'm not. I have fond feelings for your sister-in-law, Logan, and I hope to pursue them."

Logan launched to his feet. "Over my dead body," he shouted. "Get out—now!"

"I was hoping we could be civil about this, McClare, amicable for Caitlyn's sake."

"You want civil?" Logan stormed around his desk, fists itching to take a swipe. "I'll show you civil, you lying letch. Cait and I have an understanding, so keep your filthy hands off."

Turner held two palms up and stepped back. "Look, McClare, I didn't come here to fight, I came to clear the air and advise you of my intentions in an honorable manner. Cait and I have had many a discussion, and never once did she mention any 'understanding' with you."

Logan all but singed him to the spot, his own four-in-hand tie and high-starched collar about to choke him to death. "That's because she doesn't know it yet, you clown, but she will soon. The woman was mine twenty-seven years ago and she's mine today, and so help me, I will bloody you good if you even think of standing in my way."

Anger glinted in Turner's eyes, the amiable manner suddenly as cold as their friendship. "That's Cait's decision, not yours." His smile was chilly. "Or are you afraid you'll lose again?"

Logan lurched, jerking Turner up with two fists buried in his buttoned-down suit. "I'll see you dead before I lose her again," he breathed, inches from Turner's mottled face.

Turner shoved him back, eyes glittering. "Is that a threat, counselor?"

"Consider it a warning." Logan took a step forward, hands knotted. "Now get out."

Smile hard, Turner moved to leave, head cocked and hand on the knob. "I'd rather consider it a challenge, if you don't mind," he said, his unruffled self-assurance getting on Logan's nerves. He gave a tip of his hat as he opened the door. "And may the best man win."

"Count on it," Logan shouted before the door slammed in his

face. He returned to his desk to stare out the window, body shaky but his confidence rock-solid. He and Cait were getting closer all the time, he could feel it, their friendship deepening by the day. It was only a matter of time before their partnership in loving and nurturing her family would ripen into more. He gazed across the city in the direction of Nob Hill, never more sure of a win.

"And so help me," he whispered, seeing Andrew Turner clearly in mind, "you will eat both your heart out and your words, prosecutor, when Cait returns to where she was meant to be all along." Picking up a frame, he stared at the only woman he'd ever loved, beseeching God for the only thing he ever really wanted. Mrs. Caitlyn McClare.

Wearing my ring as well as my name.

❧ ☙

"Hold the elevator, please."

Jamie stopped the elevator with a hand to the door before the operator could even flip the lever, grinning while Andrew Turner loped down the hall and slipped inside. "So that's how you condition to give us a run for our money in the courtroom, sir, sprinting for elevators."

Andrew laughed and extended his hand to shake Jamie's while the attendant closed the doors. "That and duking it out with your boss, I'm afraid." He grinned. "Something I imagine is common enough with Logan."

It was Jamie's turn to laugh as he buried his hands in his pockets, hip to the wall. "Oh, yes, sir, I guarantee every single one of us has gone a round or two with Mr. McClare, including Mr. Rupert and Byington."

"Friend or foe, he's a formidable opponent." Andrew paused, his smile warm. "And exceptional teacher, apparently, given your trial wins thus far, counselor. You seem to have his moves and mannerisms down in that courtroom, Jamie, which is a high compliment, indeed." He slapped Jamie on the back just as the elevator jolted to a stop. "If I didn't know better, I'd say you were a chip off the old block, son."

Heat thundered up Jamie's neck. "Thank you, sir—that's the ultimate compliment, I assure you. I respect and admire Mr. McClare a great deal."

"Lobby," the attendant called, and the doors creaked opened, jolting Jamie at the sight of his mother and sister waiting for the elevator.

"Jammy, wait—can we take a tour of your office—please, please?"

The district attorney smiled as Jamie's sister, Jess, bounded forward to give Jamie a hug, her black curls bouncing. "We have time, you know—our reservations aren't till noon."

"Is this your sister?" Andrew Turner offered a broad smile.

Jamie hooked an arm to Jess's waist with a proud grin. "Yes, sir, this is my little sister, Jess, who, I'm ashamed to admit, is a chess prodigy who wallops me regularly."

Mr. Turner offered his hand, and Jess shook it heartily, her bubbly personality and glowing face making her seem more thirteen than seventeen. "A pleasure to meet you, Miss MacKenna. Your brother has stolen many a case from me and my colleagues, I assure you, so it's rather nice to hear someone can trounce him at home."

Jess giggled and gave a short bob of her head. "Thank you, sir."

"And this is my mother, Jean MacKenna, with whom, it's safe to say, I argued many a case before I ever darkened a courtroom door. Mom, Jess—this is the district attorney, the honorable Andrew Turner."

Extending his hand to Jamie's mother, the D.A. paused as he stared. "Excuse me, Mrs. MacKenna, but have we met before?"

Jean MacKenna tilted her head, as if to study him with a squint of her eyes. "I don't believe so," she said openly. "This is the first time Jess and I have ever ventured to Jamie's office before, as we seldom wander too far from home." She reached for his hand to shake it with a warm smile. "But it's a pleasure to meet you, sir."

"Likewise," the district attorney said with a slow nod. "It's hard to believe you're Jamie's mother, Mrs. MacKenna, as young and beautiful as you are."

Jamie's mother blushed. "Why thank you, Mr. Turner—what a lovely thing to say."

He shifted his keen gaze to Jamie, a crimp buckling his brow. "You just graduated last year, Mr. MacKenna, so that would make you . . . ?"

"Twenty-six, sir," Jamie said with a clear of his throat.

The D.A. laughed. "Well, that settles it, then. This woman is entirely too young-looking to have a son your age, so I'm afraid no one would believe it in a court of law." He bowed. "An absolute pleasure making your acquaintance, ladies. Enjoy your lunch, and make sure Jamie picks up the bill." He gave Jamie a wink. "He can afford it working for Logan, no doubt."

"What a nice man," Jamie's mother said, gaze following Andrew Turner out the door.

Jamie tugged his mother into the elevator with a chuckle. "Yeah, he is, Mom, but not in Logan's eyes, I'm afraid." He nodded to the attendant with a smile. "I guess it's back up to six, Horace."

"Yes, sir, Mr. MacKenna," the elderly man replied, closing the doors with a clunk.

"Why doesn't he like him?" his sister asked, her curious gaze a mirror reflection of her mother's.

"I'm not really sure," Jamie said, slipping a loose arm around both of their shoulders. "But I suspect he has a good reason." He gave his sister's neck a tweak as the elevator started to rise.

And her name is Caitlyn McClare.

⚬

Alli feasted on her cioppino while her eyes feasted on Nick Barone, the man who was stealing her heart by the moment as she dined on a splintered dock at Fisherman's Wharf—formerly Meiggs' Wharf. Seated on a weathered whiskey barrel with Lottie asleep in his lap, he laughed and chatted with crusty Italian fishermen who spun tales of crabbing beyond the Golden Gate while stirring hot cauldrons of stew. Steam curled from the pots into a heaven so blindingly blue, the bay had no choice but to shimmer in response, aquamarine waters bobbing with a sea of salt-incrusted vessels, from fishing dinghies to schooners skimming the sky.

Pushing her empty bowl away on the rickety crate table, Allison perched stiff arms to the edge of her barrel stool and leaned back, eyes closed and head tilted to absorb the rays of the sun. Somewhere a foghorn bellowed while seagulls squawked overhead, in beautiful harmony with Nick's husky laughter. Allison drew in a brisk breath, inhaling sea air ripe with the aroma of fresh crab, shrimp, and mussels steeped in a rich broth of tomatoes and wine. A wharf specialty, all laced with basil and oregano that tingled her tongue with a taste she wouldn't soon forget.

Nick's hearty chuckles interrupted her reverie, and tingles of yet another kind shivered her skin. Tugging a tattered towel bib from her neck, she watched as his massive hands idly stroked Lottie's silky curls while he talked to the men. The contrast of a giant of a man tender with so tiny a child melted her heart as thoroughly as the chocolate ringing Lottie's little mouth. "I promised I'd take her to the wharf to smell and taste the chocolate at Ghirardelli," he'd explained when he'd asked her to go along, "and I promise *you* it'll be the best thing you've ever tasted."

Somehow I doubt it. Her gaze strayed to Nick's full mouth, wide in a grin over something the fishermen said, and her stomach took a tumble, confirming what she'd felt for Roger had been nothing like this. As gentle and tender on the inside as he was gruff and big on the outside, Nick Barone had a knack for making her feel cherished and safe. Just like he did Lottie, Miss Penny, and everyone else at Mercy House, who all but worshiped him as much as she. In the three weeks since they'd discovered their deeper feelings, she'd seen him almost every single day, and Alli had never been happier. Whether dinner and card games with Miss Penny and the girls or sharing a plate of Hunan chicken at Ming Chao's, loving Nick felt as natural and warm and satisfying as spicy fish stew savored on a crisp September day. And merciful heavens—his kisses?

"You didn't eat your chocolate."

She blinked, heat stinging her cheeks when she realized she'd been distracted over tasting something else. As if privy to her thoughts, he grinned, the fishermen suddenly nowhere in sight. Shifting Lottie to his shoulder, he reached across the crate to pick up the chocolate bar he'd bought for them. Eyes fused to hers, he took a bite before slowly prodding the rest against her lips, his thumb grazing her mouth along with the candy. "I don't blame you," he whispered, the glint of humor in his eyes edging toward smoky. "It's not what I'm hungry for either."

Blood broiled her cheeks and he laughed out loud, caressing her jaw with the tips of his fingers. "I'm crazy about you, Al, you know that?" He tapped her chin. "Come on, Princess, time to get you and Miss La-di-da home."

"Oh, drat—already?" Alli huffed out a sigh that was only part jest. Hopping up, she stood on tiptoe to kiss Lottie's cheek before looping her arm through Nick's and taking a step forward.

"Hey." He tugged her back so firmly, she all but bounced off his chest, his body anchored like one of the posts on the peer. "Excuse me," he said with a thick jag of his brow, "but I don't believe this little dickens bought you chocolate or cioppino, did she?"

A grin inched across her lips as she perched on tiptoe to press a sweet kiss to his cheek. "Thank you, Mr. Nick," she said in her best sing-song voice.

"That's better." He deposited a kiss to her hair and Lottie's before steering them along the dock where fishermen mended their nets. Seemingly endless rows of feluccas—Italian fishing boats—lined the wharf while snippets of Italian chatter and laughter floated in the air. The rich sound of Italian arias from Verdi and Puccini swelled in the sky like seagulls and sandpipers gliding over the bay, as sweet as the smell of chocolate from the Ghirardelli factory one block away. The sun slowly sank into the horizon, washing wooden shacks and ramshackle storefronts with a pink haze that lent a watercolor effect, causing the city she loved to glow as much as Alli herself.

Navigating the cobblestone streets in comfortable silence, Nick smiled down at Alli when Lottie snorted in her sleep. "I suppose we tuckered her out, but it's a sleep well earned as pushy as the little tyke's been, badgering me to take her to the wharf." He gently pushed a stray curl back under Alli's feathered straw hat. "Kind of like you with Chinatown, Miss McClare."

"But look how much fun we've had," she defended, peering up with a sassy smile. "Even Miss Penny says you're not as grumpy, although I beg to differ if a cable car's involved."

His lips twitched despite a stern tone. "Yeah? Well I'd like to see how chipper you'd be if your supper rolled in your stomach faster than a cable car on its rails."

She shook her head with a cluck of her tongue, sympathy

edging her tone. "Yes, well, nobody's perfect, Nick, so I'll just have to accept it as one of your flaws."

"*One* of my flaws?" He halted her beneath a tungsten lamp while a Ghirardelli horse and wagon rumbled by. "What else?" he demanded with a slack of his hip.

She stared up through a squint laced with a smile. "Well, for starters, you've gone from being a pain in the posterior to a pain in the neck now that I always have to look up."

The edge of his mouth crooked. "Pain in the neck, huh? I'd say that's payback, Princess, for all those whacks with the stick."

"And then there's that thing you do with your ear when you're hiding something."

His jaw dropped. "What thing with my ear?"

She tilted her head. "Oh, you know, when I ask about your day and you say it was fine?"

"What's wrong with that?"

She huffed out a sigh. "Goodness, Nick, you and I should be able to talk about anything, but whenever I get too close to something you don't want me to know, you tug on your left ear."

He stared, eyes gaping along with his mouth. "I do not."

She hefted her chin. "You most certainly do."

He shook his head and started walking, his long stride leaving her in the dust.

She scurried to catch up. "And you get grumpy and rude when I tell you the truth."

"*Rude?*" He halted to sear her with a glare while shifting Lottie to the other shoulder.

Folding her arms, she angled a brow, lips pursed in a school-marm manner.

Air blasted through his teeth before he mauled the bridge of his nose. "Okay, you might have me on grumpy and rude, but I am *not* afraid of the truth."

Eyes softening, she disarmed him with a gentle squeeze of his hand, twining her fingers through his. "Aren't you?" she whispered. "Like admitting you're still angry at God?"

With a grind of his teeth, he wrenched his hand free, fingers flying toward the lobe of his ear before they quickly bypassed to knead the back of his neck. "Blast it, Allison, why do you keep bringing this up? It's not important to me."

Her stomach lurched just like it always did when Nick and Uncle Logan were in the same room. Unbidden, moisture welled. "I know," she whispered, "but it's important to me, and therein, the flaw."

He flinched as if the truth of her statement made his left earlobe itch. Dropping his gaze, he expelled a weary sigh while his fingers kneaded his temple. "All right," he whispered, the steam apparently seeped from his ire. "I promise to try"—a knot ducked in his throat near the size of the fist clenched to Lottie's back—"to talk to God again." His eyes lifted to hers, and the raw love she saw in their depths twisted her heart. "But only because it's important to you."

She blinked to clear a sheen of tears, lifting her hand to caress the side of his jaw. "It's important to *me*, Nick, because it's important *for* you," she said quietly, love swelling for this unlikely captor of her heart. "I long to see you free from that haunting pain I sometimes see in your eyes." She fisted his waistcoat and tugged him down while lifting on tiptoe to brush her lips against his. "Because I love you, Detective Barone, despite the best efforts of my stick."

With an abrupt sweep of his mighty arm, he jerked her close and tucked his chin on top of her head, the sweet warmth of Lottie between them filling her with a contentment unlike any she'd known. "And I, you, Princess." His voice was a husky rasp as his fingers gently fondled the nape of her neck. "Against my better judgment and all common sense, temper, sticks, and uncles." He pressed a kiss to her nose before straightening once again. "So . . . what else?"

With another fold of her arms, she tucked a fist to her mouth, face screwed in thought. "Well, there is one last thing," she said with a scrunch of her nose, "but I don't suppose it's too bad."

He cocked a hip, prodding Alli on with an impatient wave of his hand. "And that is . . . ?"

She nibbled her lip. "You taste like animal crackers," she confessed, fighting the squirm of a smile. "You know, like I'm kissing Bobby O'Toole."

Mr. C.P. popped up with a truly vintage scowl. "And who the devil is Bobby O'Toole?"

She fluttered her lashes. "Why, the little neighbor boy two houses over, just turned six. Absolutely adores animal crackers, you know." She looked both ways before leaning in, voice lowered to a loud whisper. "I think he likes me."

He grunted, a smile working its way across his lips. "I should have a talk with the boy."

"You know, you should—you two have a lot in common." She sighed. "He threw the most outrageous tantrum last week, right in the middle of the street." She tilted her head, her smile far away as if recalling a fond memory. "Reminded me of you."

A massive shadow loomed before he tugged her in close. "You got something against animal crackers, Princess?" he whispered, gaze fixed on her mouth.

She gulped, stomach swooping like gulls over the bay. "O-only w-with B-bobby O'Toole."

"Good." He unearthed the half-eaten chocolate bar and offered her a bite before he took one of his own, slipping it back in his pocket. Eyes never leaving hers, he slowly chewed and lifted her to his waist as if she weighed nothing at all. Both her feet and heart dangled as he braced her with one arm while holding Lottie in the other. "How's this?" he whispered, lips hovering so close, the scent of chocolate on his breath made her dizzy. "I love you, Allison Erin McClare," he whispered, mouth skimming hers with the utmost tenderness before he deepened his kiss with a soft moan.

"Hey, I smell chocolate . . ."

A groggy voice rose between them, and Allison giggled. "You do, do you?" she said, wobbling so much when Nick put her down, that she clung to his arm. "Well, if you ask really nicely, Miss La-di-da, I'll just bet Mr. Cranky Pants will give you some."

"Cranky Pants?" Nick said with a growl, "I'll show you cranky." He nipped at Allison's waist with one hand while tickling Lottie's stomach with the other, unleashing squeals and laughter from them both.

"I want chocolate!" Giggling, Lottie did a little jig in Nick's arms, her chubby legs thumping against his side. "Can I have some, Mr. Nick, please, please?"

He glanced at the horizon where a pool of fuchsia seeped into the inky waters. "I suppose, but only a bite. Miss Penny will whack me with her stick for ruining your dinner."

"Ooooo . . . I hope she lets me do it instead," Allison said with dance of her brows.

He grinned. "Me too. I'm in the mood to disarm you with a chocolate kiss or two."

Lottie wiggled. "Can I have a chocolate kiss, Mr. Nick?"

"You bet, La-di-da." Breaking the chocolate into threes, he handed them each a piece before popping the last in his mouth. With care, he cupped little Lottie's face in his mammoth hand and gently pressed a sweet peck to her cheek.

"Mmm . . . you smell good!" she said with a giggle.

"How 'bout me, Mr. Nick?" Hands clasped to her back, Allison offered a saucy grin.

He gave her a shuttered gaze that made her mouth go dry. "With pleasure, Miss McClare," he whispered, dragging her close to graze her mouth with his own. Woozy from the scent of both chocolate and Nick, Allison swayed on her feet, her breathing shallow when he finally pulled away. Eyes smoky, he slowly traced his finger down the line of her jaw. "And I mean that in the truest sense of the word."

Lottie gasped. "Are you and Miss Alli gonna get married, Mr. Nick?"

"*Lottie!*" Allison's cheeks pulsed with heat.

The little girl blinked, brows in a scrunch. "Well, boys usually marry big girls they kiss, don't they, Miss Alli, and Mr. Nick just kissed you, didn't he?"

Nick cradled Allison's face, his gaze so full of love, she thought she might faint. "I most certainly did, La-di-da, and boys most certainly do." His voice was a husky whisper that shivered her stomach. "That is, if they're lucky enough to get the girl to say yes." He deposited a kiss to the tip of Lottie's nose. "But this is our secret, La-di-da—yours, mine, and Miss Alli's, okay?"

"Okay, but can I have more chocolate?" she asked.

He laughed, eliciting a giggle when he tickled her waist. "Sorry, sweet pea, but I'm clean out. Besides, that's enough sweets for tonight, don't you think?"

"No!" she said with a thrust of her little chin, a pixie grin curling her sweet lips.

"Me either," he said, loosing a squeal of delight from the little dickens when he swung her up on his shoulders. "But something tells me it is, little girl." He squeezed the tiny legs now braced to his chest. "Both for you . . ." He gave Alli a wink, grabbing her hand while they climbed up the hill. "And for me."

22

So, Mr. Ga-roan . . . this isn't so bad, is it?" Alli smiled up at Nick as they spun to a waltz on the dance floor at The Palace Hotel, being in Nick Barone's arms—and in his heart—the perfect gift for her birthday celebration. Especially since he hadn't wanted to come, not when he discovered Uncle Logan was paying for dinner and hosting dessert in his Palace suite. But he'd laid his pride aside to come—for her.

A grin eased across his handsome face as he gave her that languid gaze, the heat in his eyes warming her all the way to her toes. "Not as long as I can look at you instead of the scowl on your uncle's face," he said in a husky tone. Whirling her with a heady spin, he leaned close, breath warm against her cheek. "Although I'd pay good money to see it right about . . ." Drawing her closer than the dance allowed, he all but melted her to the spot when his mouth slowly nuzzled her ear. "Now," he said with a grin as he pulled away, and Allison giggled when she peeked Uncle Logan's way, his searing gaze as heated as the shivers Nick's kiss had produced.

"He'll come around, you'll see." She laid her head against his chest, the steady beat of his heart as comforting as Nick's attempts to make amends with her uncle over the last month, as stiff as they may have been. Alli's lips curved in a tender smile. The big lug was as stubborn as Uncle Logan, it seemed, two of the men she loved most in the world, loving her as much as they despised each other. Her eyes drifted closed while her mood drifted toward melancholy. Their disdain for each other was the only flaw in an otherwise perfect month. A month when Nick Barone had not only allowed Allison into his heart, but—after gentle coaxing for him to attend church with her and even pray—was slowly allowing God back in too.

He laughed, the sound more of a grunt that rumbled her ear as she rested against his muscled chest. "Let's hope it's before he takes me for every dime I own. I expect his courier to show up and serve me papers any day now."

Allison's head jerked up. "Oh, he won't do that, I promise. I'm sure it's all bluff."

The music ended, but Nick held her in place with palms to her waist. "He doesn't strike me as one to bluff when it comes to protecting the family he loves," he said with a thin smile, "which I have to admit, is one of the few things I admire about the man." Thumbs grazing her dress, he bent to brush a kiss to her cheek before tucking his arm through hers to escort her from the floor. "And to be honest, after all the jokers who've broken your heart, I don't blame him."

"You looked pretty smooth out there, Detective Barone," Jamie said when Nick seated Alli into her chair, "for a guy who deals with assault and battery all day long."

The edge of Nick's mouth tipped in a wry grin. "Not the least of which was at the hands of our birthday girl here, wielding a stick."

"Always knew she was a smart girl." Logan raised his glass in a toast to Alli with a nod of his head before his gaze iced Nick. "Or used to be."

"Logan, behave," her mother said with a scolding tap of his

arm as she sat beside him at a linen-clad table graced with flowers and candles. "It's Allison's birthday, for goodness' sake, and you don't always have to be such a bully."

"Uncle Logan? Behaving?" Alli wrinkled her nose in a tease meant to diffuse her mother's gentle rebuke. "Isn't that an oxymoron, Mother?"

"So, what exactly is 'assault and battery'?" Cassie asked, giving Uncle Logan an affectionate wink. "You know, so I recognize it in case we see it tonight?"

"Thought you'd never ask," Jamie said, tugging her to her feet. He turned to the rest of the table and gave a short bow, his demeanor suddenly formal despite a twinkle in hazel eyes. "Allow me." He took Cassie into his arms. "Assault, Miss McClare," he said, eliciting a squeal when he dipped her in dramatic display, "is the threat of an action of one person toward another." He demonstrated by hovering his lips close to hers, causing her to giggle. "*This* is assault, Cowgirl—the 'threat' of a kiss."

Blake lifted his wine in a toast. "And battery, Cass," he said with a wayward grin, "is when you smack him clean across that pretty mug of his."

Jamie gave Blake a mock glare as everyone laughed. "How would you know, McClare? Bram and I had to all but carry you through Old Man Slattery's Criminal Justice class."

"Yes, but he was a crack shot in Professor Tut's fraud class, as I recall," Bram said with a chuckle, matching Blake's toast with his goblet of water. "Posing as a law student, I believe."

More laughter circled the table as Jamie cleared his throat. "As I was saying," he continued, focusing on his fiancée again while he lingered above her lips like before. "That was assault, Sugar Pie, and *this* . . ." he said with a wayward grin as he dove for her lips, "is battery."

Logan shook his head, his good humor obviously restored by Jamie's antics. "A quick study, that boy, if ever there was."

"Well, he's not the only one . . ." Blake's gaze locked on two pretty women sitting alone a few tables away. He rose to his feet and adjusted his tie with a grin that spelled trouble. "I feel the need to fine-tune my skills at both bribery and fraud, convincing that young lady over there that I may just be the man of her dreams." He slapped Bram on the shoulder. "What do you say, old boy—she's got a friend who looks just as lonely. Heaven knows you need the practice now that Meggie's not here for you to step on her toes."

"You have a point," Bram said with a tug of his cuffs before rising to push in his chair. "Besides, someone has to warn that poor girl what she's getting into."

"Bless you, Mr. Hughes," Alli said, popping up to tweak Blake's neck as he passed. "Women everywhere thank you for your chivalrous protection from the likes of my brother." She bent to press a kiss to Nick's cheek. "And you, Mr. Barone, how about a rendezvous on the veranda in ten minutes while Mother, Cass, and I pay a visit to the ladies' room?"

Jamie snatched Cassie's hand. "Oh, no you don't, Sugar Pie—the music is calling and I've got more legal terms to discuss." He towed her away with a wiggle of brows.

Caitlyn shook her head. "That boy. Thank goodness the wedding is only three months away." She offered Logan a smile when he assisted with her chair. "We'll be back shortly."

"You owe me a dance," Logan called, watching Cait disappear through the crowd before his gaze narrowed on Nick.

"Excuse me." Jaw tight, Nick rose and strode in the direction of the veranda while Logan's searing gaze followed him out the door.

Bolting his drink, Logan shoved his chair in hard before making his way to the veranda, determined Nick Barone would not have the chance to ruin Allison's life. Although he'd done his best to dissuade his niece from becoming involved, she refused to heed his advice, and he hadn't been able to shake the worry that Barone wasn't all he appeared to be. His lips compressed. Hopefully now he had the leverage to force Barone to leave Allison alone without wounding her further. The danger of his niece becoming more smitten gnawed at his mind, and with what he'd learned from the detective he'd hired, he knew he had to act fast.

He pushed through the beveled glass door onto the veranda. The chill of the pungent sea breeze cooled his temper somewhat, steeling his nerves as if he were entering a courtroom to do battle. He scanned the marble terrace, spotting Barone bent over the stone wall in the far shadows, arms crossed as he studied the city below. Bracing himself for a fight, Logan approached, his voice low as he halted ten feet away. "Allison may be blinded by infatuation, Barone, but I assure you, I have no such illusions."

Barone slowly rose to his full height, back rigid as he turned to face Logan with a hard-chiseled stare. "Then I'd say it's lucky I'm courting your niece, Supervisor, instead of you."

Logan's temper itched for release despite his nonchalant air. "You're a fraud, Barone," he said in a calm tone. "I've felt it in my bones all along and soon I can prove it." He strolled forward with a tight smile, indicating an inch of air between forefinger and thumb. "My source is this close to providing an exposé that will show Allison what you truly are, so I'm offering you a final chance to make a clean break."

"Not interested," Nick said, tone curt, but Logan didn't miss the hard shift of his Adam's apple as he butted a hip to the wall.

Instincts sharpening, Logan sauntered over to lean beside him, hands loosely clasped on the balustrade as he peered down at the city. "Yes, well, you may just want to rethink that, Nick, especially when you hear my offer." He shifted to face him, the muscles in his face sculpted as tight as the marble statue in the fountain a few feet away. "I'll triple the money you gave back with an added bonus of $5,000 when you leave San Francisco for good. Just give Harmon your notice and a forwarding address."

"Keep your money, counselor," he sneered, pushing off from the wall. "I don't need it."

Logan halted him with a hand. "Well, that's just it, Nick—you will. Because if you don't leave, I'll have your job and any other you think you might be able to get in this city."

Nick flung his hand away. "Wealth doesn't give you the right to control people's lives."

"No, but the truth does." Logan adjusted his jacket. "Think about it, Nick. The truth will hurt Allison far more than you ending it tonight and leaving town. If you care for her at all—"

"Blast it—I love her!"

Logan paused, the intensity in Barone's eyes convincing him the blackguard might actually have feelings for his niece. He hiked his jaw, a tic in his cheek keeping time with the drum of his pulse. "Then leave her alone, Nick. She doesn't deserve a man lying to her again."

"Nick? Uncle Logan? Is . . . everything all right?"

He looked up to see Allison standing not ten feet away, face etched with concern. "Fine, sweetheart," he said easily. "I think Nick and I have arrived at an understanding."

The muscles in her face relaxed along with those in his stomach. "Oh, good," she whispered. "It's important to me that you both get along."

"Of course it is, darling." Logan gave her a peck on the cheek.

"And it's important to both of us that you're happy, right, Nick?" When Nick didn't respond, Logan gave Allison's shoulder a light squeeze. "We're going up for cake and presents in my suite, so don't be long."

"Oh." Allison spun to face him, a hint of worry in her tone. "Mother asked if it would be all right to take the party to our house instead. Apparently Maddie was upset when she made her stay home tonight sick, and now Mother's feeling guilty about leaving her. She thought it might be better for her to go home earlier than planned."

Logan expelled a heavy sigh. "I thought she seemed out of sorts tonight. I'll take her home right now, and the rest of you can follow later."

"No, Uncle Logan, she said she wanted you to stay and she'd call Hadley."

"Nonsense. I'll take her home and the rest of you can come when you're ready. Just ask Peter the maitre d' to retrieve the cake I ordered from the kitchen and bring it along, all right? And don't forget your presents in a bag in the hall closet of my apartment." He handed her a key from his pocket with a wink. "But don't you dare peek in the bag, understood?"

"Yes, sir." Allison grinned and perched on tiptoe to give him a kiss on the cheek, her eyes misty with gratitude. "Thank you for always being there to take care of us, Uncle Logan."

A knot jerked in his throat as he pulled her into a tight hug. "Heaven knows I try, sweetheart." His eyes connected with Barone's over Allison's shoulders with deadly intent. "Whatever it takes . . ."

23

"J can't thank you enough for taking me home, Logan—I feel like such a ninny." Caitlyn picked at her nails in the front seat of Logan's black Mercedes Phaeton, gaze fixed on the lit tower of the Ferry Building at the far end of Market. She thought of poor, sweet Maddie, cheeks burnished with fever and eyes rimmed with tears over missing the party, and guilt slashed anew. "I should have stayed home like originally planned."

"And miss one daughter's birthday party while another sleeps the night away?" Logan grunted. "The little sweetheart is probably out cold, Cait, and you're worrying for nothing."

"I hope so . . ." Her voice trailed off.

"I know so, Mrs. McClare, so relax, all right? I told Allison to bring the cake and presents along when they're ready to head home." He reached for her hand and gave it a squeeze, an action that endeared Logan McClare to her all the more. An endearment that seemed to be growing of late, she suddenly realized, a situation that didn't alarm quite like before.

"Thank you," she whispered, giving his hand a gentle press back. She studied his handsome profile, amazed at how much stronger she felt with him by her side. "I don't know what's wrong with me—I've been edgy all evening."

"Oh, really? Haven't noticed," he said with a sideways grin. "Come on, Cait—a *bully*?"

She nibbled the edge of her smile, her look sheepish at best. "Well, you do tend that way at times. Just look how you treated poor Andrew last week when he stopped by with his report."

Logan scowled, a natural reflex where Andrew Turner was concerned. Cait stifled the urge to smile. There certainly was no love lost between Logan and his former best friend from college days, especially now that Andrew dropped by more often for Vigilance Committee business. As a dedicated board member, it appeared he took the role as seriously as he did that of district attorney, his passion to clean up the Coast seemingly as strong as hers. Cait bit the edge of her lip. A "passion" that appeared to arouse jealousy in Logan. Which was not all that unfounded, she realized, given Andrew's increasing flirtations and repeated requests to take her out to dinner. She expelled a quiet sigh. But she had no more interest in becoming romantically involved with Andrew Turner than she did with Logan McClare. Her gaze flicked to the hard line of Logan's jaw, now clamped as always when Andrew's name came up. Her committee relationship with Andrew was definitely becoming more difficult given the intimate friendship she was developing with the man beside her, upon whom she seemed to depend more and more.

He shot her a look that could have singed the satin cloak on her shoulders . . . or Andrew Turner's eyebrows had the poor man been present. "Blast it, Cait, why do you give that rogue license to come by whenever he wants? I guarantee board business is not all he has on his mind."

"Oh, for heaven's sake, Logan," she said with soft chuckle. "Andrew Turner is as devoted to the cause of cleaning up the Coast as you and I, and as far as your insinuation that Mr. Turner is a rogue, I've seen no evidence thus far." She tilted her head, hoping to disarm him with a tease. "But even if I had, if that were cause to ban the man from my house, I'm afraid you might find the locks changed as well, Mr. McClare."

His gaze narrowed. "Hardly—I've abdicated the title to him in case you haven't been paying attention."

Her smile turned tender. "As a matter of fact I have, and I admit, it's quite becoming."

"Good," he said with a mock frown. "I worried it may have escaped your notice."

"Nothing escapes my notice where you are concerned, sir, which brings us back to my original comment. You have to admit—you tend to bully when family is involved."

His grin took a slant. "Last time I studied the law, it wasn't a crime to protect your family, Mrs. McClare. If it were, you and I might well be sharing a cell."

Heat dusted her cheeks at the very thought of her and Logan sharing anything that confined them to close quarters. She quickly averted her gaze to Lotta's Fountain as they passed by, the cast-iron pillar drinking fountain donated by entertainer Lotta Crabtree causing her to lick her parched lips. "And you *are* rather hard on poor Nick."

The smile on his face slid into a scowl. "'Poor Nick' is right. The man's almost as penniless as the bums he investigates on the Coast, which is too reminiscent of Luepke to suit, not to mention that other freeloader Allison almost married."

Caitlyn sighed, Logan's concern for her daughter at odds with her growing affection for Nick. "Honestly, I've gotten to know Nick fairly well these last few months, and I have to say I like the man. But more importantly, Allison likes him as well—a lot."

"We all liked Roger Luepke too, if you recall, and the man

was as phony as the warrants Henry Meiggs stole to finance the wharf."

"I suppose . . ." Her gaze trailed out her window as Logan shifted lanes to pass a clattering milk wagon before he signaled a right turn on Powell. "But Miss Penny thinks the sun sets and rises on Nick, and I certainly trust her judgment on people."

Logan shot her a hard glance before he turned onto her street. "Need I remind you Luepke had no bigger advocate than Monsignor Milton? There are some men who could fool the Pope himself, and I have a gut feeling Barone may be one."

Limbs paralyzed in her seat, Cait wasn't listening as her eyes locked on a patrol wagon outside her home halfway up Nob Hill. Her hand flew to her mouth to squelch a tiny cry. "Logan— *hurry*—something's wrong!"

Gaze flicking up to her house, Logan wasted no time, nearly colliding with a cable car before rounding Caitlyn's corner on two wheels. He ground to a stop behind the police wagon and jumped out, rushing to assist Cait who almost leapt into his arms.

"Oh, Logan, if anything happened . . ." Her voice trembled as much as her legs as she bolted up the brick steps to the marble portico, hands shaking on the brass knob when she hurled the door wide. "Rosie? Hadley?" She rushed into the foyer, panic in her cry.

"Oh, Miss Cait!" Rosie jumped up from the sofa with a limp handkerchief in hand, nearly toppling Caitlyn with a fierce embrace. The warmth of Logan's hand steadied Caitlyn from behind as Rosie sobbed in her arms. "Maddie's gone, and we can't find her anywhere."

All blood drained from Caitlyn's face as she teetered, close to fainting dead away if Logan hadn't braced her from behind. She tried to speak, but fear stole the sound from her throat.

"What do you mean 'gone'?" Logan snapped.

Rosie looked up, face blotchy from tears, unconcerned for once with her enmity toward Logan. "Sh-she was upset when Miss C-Cait left for the party and tried to f-follow her out the door. I had to run after the little m-mite and rock her t-till she fell asleep, putting her down around six. But when I checked on her not an hour ago, she w-wasn't in her bed . . ."

"Have you searched the house—under her bed, in her closet?" Logan gripped Rosie's arms, voice steady but manner tense.

Hadley stepped forward, his dignified demeanor intact except for an abundance of worry lines etched in his brow. "Yes, sir, both Mrs. O'Brien and I scoured the house top to bottom to no avail, so we called the police. Two officers are searching upstairs this very moment."

Caitlyn could barely breathe, visions of Maddie's tear-swollen face choking her air. She grappled for Logan's hand, unable to stop her nails from gouging his palm. "Oh, Logan," she rasped, "what are we going to do?"

He surrounded her with strong arms, steadying her body with a vise hold and rock-steady tone. "We're going to remain calm and rational, Cait, and think this through, step by step. She's a little girl of six, for heaven's sake—she can't have gone far. We'll find her." Her ragged breathing slowed as he kneaded her back, the confidence in his voice vibrating in her ear as her head lay against his chest. "Hadley, I assume you searched every room including the attic and cellar, calling Maddie loudly as you did so?"

"Yes, sir."

"I take it all doors were locked except for the front entrance, so did you search outside, out back, at the neighbors?"

"Everywhere, sir," Hadley said, his response bearing the faintest hint of a waver.

"And none of the neighbors saw her, heard anything at all?"

"No, sir, not one, but I only queried a house or two. And Mrs. O'Brien and I were in the kitchen finishing chores, so neither of us recall hearing anything amiss."

Logan's voice echoed in the foyer, taut with authority. "Rosie, I want you to brew a large pot of chamomile tea with mint for Miss Cait, all right? Hadley, I need you to go house-to-house on both California and Powell to ask if anyone has seen Maddie. See if they saw anything suspicious in the area, then give them Cait's number to call should any information come to light."

"Yes, sir," Rosie and Hadley said in unison, darting off to their respective duties.

"Oh, Logan . . ." Caitlyn sobbed, and Logan bundled her close. "We'll find her, Cait, I feel it in my bones, and she *will* be all right, trust me."

Trust him? Her heart lurched at the thought of Maddie in harm's way, but oh, how she wanted to trust that Logan was right!

No, trust Me. The thought, so soft and so still in the midst of her fear, immediately calmed like nothing ever could—not trust in the man who held her now or the protective warmth of his embrace. Her eyes sank closed as she exhaled a frail breath, knowing full well her trust would be far better spent in the hands of God rather than in the arms of Logan. Breathing in the sweet breath of hope, she gently pushed him away, palms resting on his gray silken waistcoat while she gazed into worried eyes very nearly the same color. "Logan, will you . . . pray with me?"

Pray? He stared, prayer the very last thing on the long list of steps his proficient mind told him to do. He needed to grill the police for information and call in reinforcements to widen the search. There was Cait to settle down and an unsuspecting family who would soon walk in that door, devastated by the news that one of their own was missing. He had a house to tear apart, brick by brick if necessary, to find a little girl who held his heart in the very palm of her tiny hand—all the while his pulse pounded and sweat slicked the back of his collar. And Cait wanted him to *pray*? The man she accused in Napa of having little or no faith? And to the very God who'd denied his many pleas for a second chance with the woman who now invoked His name? He swallowed hard, recognizing that for all his valiant composure, it was Cait's eyes that reflected a peace he desperately longed to have. Drawing in an unsteady breath, he gripped his hands over hers as they lay on his chest and gave a short nod.

Her words seared him as much as the touch of her palms as she closed her eyes, brow furrowed in pain and tears glazing her skin. "Oh, God, our hearts are breaking—please keep Maddie safe and please help us to find her. We ask for Your guidance to where she might be and Your holy wisdom to know what to do. Please, God—bring her back to me—to us—*please*."

Head bowed, Logan spotted a surge of gray out of the corner of his eye when two uniformed officers appeared at the top of the staircase and made their way down ... *without* Maddie. Squeezing Cait's hand, he approached as they descended into the foyer, offering a handshake. "Gentlemen, I'm Logan McClare, Maddie's uncle, and this is Caitlyn McClare, her mother. Have you uncovered anything to help us find her?"

The officers shook Logan's hand and apprised him of the little they knew about Maddie's disappearance. With somber faces, they assured him they would file their report and requisition a foot search through adjoining neighborhoods once they interviewed the immediate neighbors.

"Ma'am," one officer said, addressing Caitlyn, "is your daughter prone to running away or ever leaving the house?"

Caitlyn shuddered, and Logan shored her up with a protective arm around her back, causing her to lean into his embrace as if desperate for the strength he offered. "No, Officer," she whispered, her voice steadier than her body, which trembled within his hold. "Maddie is only six and a good girl who has never caused us a moment of worry before this."

"Forgive me for asking this, Mrs. McClare," the second officer said with a sobriety that quickened Logan's pulse, "and please know Officer Brendan and I think it highly unlikely, but we need to ask if there might be any reason to believe your daughter could have been abducted. A threat against you or Supervisor McClare, perchance, or suspicion over anyone who may have visited your home recently—a repairman or neighbor or someone who had access to the house?"

Caitlyn's body seized at the mention of abduction, and Logan tightened his grip, speaking before Cait had the chance. "None that I'm aware of, officers, either for Mrs. McClare or myself, and I feel certain Caitlyn would have advised me of anything suspicious."

He felt Cait nod, and the officer exchanged glances with his partner. "Well, then, sir, ma'am, if you'll excuse us, we'll question a few neighbors and then check back before we file our report and organize a search."

"Certainly," Logan said, voice crisp. "Thank you, Officers, for your time and your help."

"Not at all, sir." Officer Brendan nodded before he and his partner departed.

At the click of the door, Logan shielded Cait in his arms, resting his head against hers. His heart thudded at the prospect anyone might have actually kidnapped Maddie. Heaven knows as a key member of the Board of Supervisors, he'd made more than his fair share of enemies, but he refused to believe foul play was involved. "We need to search the house ourselves," he whispered, and he felt her nod.

The next half hour was the most excruciating of Logan's life other than the deaths of his parents and brother and the day Cait broke their engagement a lifetime ago. Room by room they searched—together and apart—the frantic sound of Cait's voice calling Maddie's name echoing through the house like it echoed in his brain. When their search was done, he held her in the parlour while she wept, every fragile heave shredding his heart.

"Why don't you drink some tea?" he whispered, stroking her hair like he'd longed to do for so many years. But not this way— not with their hearts raw with pain over the loss of a child so dear. He pulled away to cradle her tear-swollen face, grazing her jaw with his thumbs while he uttered the only words that came to mind. "We will find her, Cait," he said quietly. "I know this because we prayed. And although God isn't inclined to answer my prayers, you're a woman of deep faith, so I have no doubt He will answer yours."

She blinked, his handkerchief limp in her hands as she stared, fresh moisture welling all over again. With a trembling hand, she gently palmed the scruff of his jaw, a thread of awe in her tone. "Oh, Logan," she whispered, a single tear spilling into the curve of her mouth. "I never knew—you have faith in God after all, don't you? Just not for yourself."

His breath hitched, the impact of her statement cold-cocking his heart. Although he'd never admit it to her, she'd been right in Napa to confront him about his lack of faith, implying it hadn't been up to snuff. The truth was he didn't know if it even existed anymore because he'd had a bone to pick with God for too many years now, and her name was Caitlyn McClare. The one woman he wanted more than any other and the one woman God wouldn't let him have. Suddenly the realization that there was a flame of faith inside of him, no matter how frail or small, brought a measure of peace he never believed possible. A muscle convulsed in his throat over the very idea that *yes*, he actually *did* believe God would answer their prayers about Maddie, and the fact that this tiny seed of faith was based on God's favor to Caitlyn rather than to him mattered not a whit. All that really mattered was that he, Logan McClare, possessed a belief in God of which he hadn't been fully aware. And somehow in the deep recesses of his soul he knew—as sure as he knew he loved Caitlyn McClare—that where there was faith, there was the hope of answered prayer.

In the midst of that very thought, his heart stopped cold, seizing his lungs at the very same time. With a harsh heave of his chest, he shot to his feet. "Sweet God in heaven, please . . ."

"Logan, what's wrong?"

But he hardly heard her for the pounding of his pulse as he sprinted into the foyer, almost colliding with Hadley and Rosie as they delivered sandwiches and tea. Bolting up the stairs, he loped down the hall to Caitlyn's room, heart ramming into his rib cage as he entered the same room she'd shared with Liam . . . *and* the same room his parents had shared before them. Chest pumping, he rushed to the closet that took up half of her wall and flung the louvered doors wide, jerking Caitlyn's clothes away from the far side. The scent of Pear's soap and lavender rushed his senses, wrenching his heart and stirring his hope. "God, I swear," he whispered, throat dry as dust and sweat beading his brow, "if You answer this prayer, I will be Yours forever . . ."

"Maddie?" He dropped to his knees and crawled to the far

side of the closet, the same hiding place in which he used to hide from Liam in their games of hide and seek when they were boys. *And* the same hiding place in which he'd hidden with Maddie two winters past in a family game of hide and seek. "Maddie!" he shouted again and flailed his hand into the dark nook he'd discovered the summer he was eight, the one hidden by a jut in the wall. Nothing more than an odd little gap created by the wooden clothes chute in the hall, and one nobody knew about but him. *And* a precious little girl named Maddie.

With a wide sweep of his hand, his fingers skimmed something soft and warm and—he grinned outright—*snoring!* Laughter deep and powerful rolled through him as he lay prostrate in the dark closet, heart full and hand caressing the most precious gift he'd ever received. Even as his laughter rang out, tears stung at what God had done for him tonight . . . and Cait.

Cait.

"Logan, where are you?" Her cry sounded muffled, but panicked all the same.

"Here!" With a glide of his arm, he scooped Maddie up and slowly backed out.

"Oh, Maddie!" Tears streamed Caitlyn's face as she whisked her daughter from his arms and rushed to sit on her bed, cuddling and sobbing as if she would never let go.

"Sweet heavens," Rosie cried, face mottled from weeping. Dabbing her eyes with a sodden handkerchief, she joined Cait on the bed, petting a drowsy, little girl who was just beginning to wake up.

Not one bit ashamed of the tears in his eyes, Logan stood there soggy-eyed, his grin a mirror reflection of Hadley's as Maddie's tiny mouth expanded in a yawn.

Hovering behind, Hadley handed a clean handkerchief to

Caitlyn while laughter and sniffles filled the room with beautiful music.

"Maddie ..." Caitlyn gently brushed the tousled curls from her daughter's eyes. "Why on earth did you hide in the closet, darling? You worried Mommy so much."

"And your Auntie Rosie," Rosie said in a rusty rasp that sounded as if she'd been crying for hours. "Why would you do that, pumpkin?"

Maddie blinked, another sleepy yawn escaping before she snuggled further into Caitlyn's embrace. "I missed Mommy and couldn't sleep, Rosie, so I took more medicine."

"Medicine?" Caitlyn said with a gasp. She held Maddie at bay, eyes searching her daughter's. "What medicine?"

"The medicine Rosie gives me when I'm sick, remember?"

"Good grief, the *laudanum*? But you hate that! We have to wrestle you to take it."

A groan rattled in Rosie's chest. "Oh, blessed fog on the bog," she muttered, kneeling before Maddie. "From the cup of special honey and cinnamon tea I left atop your bureau?"

Maddie nodded, eyes somber with an innocence that plucked at Logan's heart. "It tasted so good, Rosie, I wanted more," she whispered.

Rosie stroked Maddie's hair. "Aw, darlin', how much of the cup did you take?"

"All of it," the little girl whispered, her eyes lanquid pools of innocence.

"Oh, Maddie, no!" Caitlyn's eyes sealed closed as she squeezed her daughter tightly, an expression of horror pinching her face. "Never, *ever* take medicine on your own again, young lady, do you hear? When I think what could have happened—"

"But it didn't, Cait." Logan kneaded her shoulder with a gentle touch. He squatted in front of Maddie, chucking a finger to her chin. "God heard our prayers, didn't He, munchkin?"

Her heavy eyelids fluttered while her lips tipped into a sleepy smile. "Did you pray for me, Uncle Logan?" she asked with a sweet tilt of her head.

"You bet, squirt." He deposited a kiss to her nose, then lifted his gaze to meet Cait's. "Me and your mama, but I think it was my prayers that carried the most weight." He gave Cait a wink.

Cait's lips trembled into a smile while tears glazed her eyes. "Thank you," she mouthed.

Rising, Logan gently massaged her shoulder once again, heart swooping at the love he saw in her eyes. "Always," he whispered.

She exhaled a shuddery breath as she turned Maddie to face her. "Darling, promise me you will never, *ever* take medicine on your own again."

Maddie's eyes misted as she peered up, the quiver of her lip tugging at Logan's heart. "I promise, Mama, but I just thought if I got better that maybe . . ." A little lump dipped in her tiny throat. "Hadley could take me to Alli's party."

"And so he will," Caitlyn said, crushing her in another tearful hug. "Everyone is coming here for cake and presents soon, so we best get your robe and slippers on, all right?"

"I'll take the little dickens, Miss Cait." Rosie hefted Maddie from Caitlyn's arms, placing a noisy kiss to her cheek. "We'll freshen her up with a bath so she's all ready."

"Thank you, Rosie." Caitlyn rose, swatting at a fluff of dust in Maddie's auburn curls. "That closet has left you musty, little girl, so scoot." She tucked a finger to Maddie's chin, voice gentle despite the stern look in her eyes. "No more medicine on your own—ever—all right?"

"Yes, Mama."

"Come, darlin', best hurry before we miss the party." Rosie shifted Maddie with a grunt.

"If you please, Mrs. O'Brien, I'd be honored to carry the little miss." Hadley tugged Maddie from Rosie's arms, not even waiting for the housekeeper's consent.

Logan paused, expecting Rosie to cut the butler down to size. Instead, his jaw dropped a full inch—along with Cait's—when Rosie peered up at the stately butler with a gentle expression usually reserved for Cait and her girls. "Thank you, Hadley, for your calm and your kindness tonight." The woman's chin actually quivered while a sheen of tears softened eyes prone to a glare where the butler was concerned. "I . . . I haven't had a fright like that since my Johnny was lost at sea so many years ago," she whispered, rooting Logan to the spot when a single tear trailed the old woman's cheek. "And I . . . ," she wiped the tear away with a hard swipe of her hand, back suddenly rigid in what looked to be a fierce show of composure, ". . . appreciate your strength, comfort, and cool head when I appeared to lose mine tonight."

Maddie secure in his arms, the butler nodded with the faintest of smiles. "Indeed, it was my pleasure, Mrs. O'Brien," he said in his usual crisp manner, turning toward the door.

"Mr. Hadley." Rosie's voice halted him halfway, his handsome face placid as he awaited her next command. Squaring her shoulders, she jutted her chin, tone carrying more respect than Logan had ever heard with the butler before. "It may have been years in the coming, Mr. Hadley," she said with a gruff clear of her throat, "but I believe you've earned the right to call me Rosie."

Not a muscle flickered in the serene and regal bearing of a man Logan had seldom seen ruffled by emotions of any kind, but the slow blink of his brown eyes softened enough for Logan to notice. "Very good, miss," he said with the barest trace of humor lacing his tone. "And you, my dear woman, may call me . . . Hadley." His eyes held a twinkle. "In any volume you prefer."

A slow grin inched across Rosie's face as she followed him to the door. "Hadley will notify the officers, and then we'll have this darlin' down lickety-split, Miss Cait," she called over her shoulder. "Hadley?"

Rosie waved a hand toward the door with a broad smile, indicating for Hadley to go first.

Caitlyn turned to Logan, mouth ajar as she pressed a trembling hand to her lips. "Sweet heavens above, what just happened?"

Logan chuckled and extended a hand to help Caitlyn up. "I'd say God used a little girl to heal the wounds of an age-old feud."

"I don't believe it," she whispered, shaking her head as she took Logan's hand to rise.

Hooking her arm over his, he arched a brow. "You? The woman who lights enough candles to eradicate the parish electric bill—doubts God can heal a fractured relationship?"

The green eyes misted as she peered up. "No, I believe that," she said quietly, voice trailing into a whisper that caused his heart to thud in his chest, "because you've proven that tonight." Her lips curved into the most beautiful smile he'd ever seen, and he ached to take her in his arms, but he would not make that mistake twice. The next time he kissed Caitlyn McClare, it would be *her* idea, not his, because he would *not* lose her again. But she was warming to him, he could feel it, and he could see it in her eyes, aglow with the hint of starry-eyed affection he recognized from years ago when she'd worn his ring on her finger. His body hummed as she absently caressed the sleeve of his arm, head cocked in almost a flirty tease. "What I don't believe, Mr. McClare, is that there could finally be peace in this house after twenty-six years."

Striving for nonchalance, he placed a casual hand over hers to escort her to the door. "Don't count on it," he said with a crooked smile, "unless you plan to bar me from your home."

His pulse stalled when she stopped, smile fading to soft as she studied him intently. "Not likely when you've captured the hearts of my children so completely." As if in slow motion, she carefully cupped a tender hand to his jaw and rose on the balls of her feet, grazing his cheek with a kiss that stilled the very blood in his veins. "And mine," she whispered, mouth lingering so close to his that his throat went dry.

The warmth of her words caressed his skin, weighting his eyes closed as a shudder traveled his body. *Oh, Cait—I adore you and I will love you forever* . . .

"How about a game of cribbage while we wait, Mr. McClare?"

His eyelids slowly lifted to that same teasing sparkle with which she used to challenge him to games of cribbage years ago while courting. Heavily fringed lashes flickered, framing an innocence that made him heady, as if he'd drunk too much champagne too quickly. The curve of her lips lured while those deadly lashes lowered in playful challenge. "Suddenly I feel lucky."

"Do you, now?" He gave her a half-lidded smile he hoped unnerved her at least a tenth as much as she had him. "One can only hope," he said, Adam's apple impossibly thick. He swallowed hard.

And pray.

24

"Oh, come on, Nick, don't be such a killjoy." Cassie paused in the auditorium with broom in hand, badgering Nick with a bully tease—heavily laced with guilt—that made Alli bite back a grin. "You and Alli have been seeing each other officially for over a month now, so you're practically part of the family—you need to come to Napa for Thanksgiving."

Nick's rock-hard jaw ground in a manner with which Alli was quickly becoming familiar. His smile was tight as he continued to stack chairs along the wall following the fund-raiser play. "Trust me, Miss McClare, if I show up in Napa—'killjoy' will be dead-on for both your uncle *and* me."

"Just come for dinner, then," Cassie pleaded, sweeping up cake crumbs and bits of trash from the punch reception following the play. "Then Hadley can drive you home after, right, Al?"

"Absolutely." Alli held the dustpan for Cass while she peeked up at Nick with hope in her eyes. "You can leave right after dinner instead of staying overnight, I promise."

Slinging the last of the chairs onto a pile, Nick shot Alli a dry smile, wiping his forehead with the rolled sleeve of his button-down shirt. "Had I known you two planned to harass me tonight, I would have never agreed to fill in for Mr. Bigley."

"Oh, pooh—of course you would have," Cassie argued. "Despite that obnoxious stubborn streak of yours, Mr. Cranky Pants, I have it on good authority you are a marshmallow with children, elderly women, and damsels in distress." She slipped Alli a wink. "And the damsel you've been seeing, Mr. Barone, is in distress over your potential absence for Thanksgiving."

Smile flat, Nick shook his head, displaying an impressive bulge of biceps as he hefted the scenery he'd built and headed out of the room to store it in the attic. Alli stared after him with a wistful sigh. "He is such a mule," she muttered, stooping to pick up a stray program. "Just like Uncle Logan."

"Yes, but mules with your best interest at heart," Cassie reminded, pushing a curl from Alli's forehead that insisted on bouncing right back. Her eyes softened. "They'll come to terms with each other, Al, you'll see. We've all been praying too hard for them both."

"I know." Alli blew the stubborn curl out of her eyes and squeezed Cassie's hand. "I just wish we could get them to do more than grunt at each other."

"You mean like Mr. Nick did with you in the beginning?" The twinkle in Cassie's eyes made Alli smile. Her cousin reached for the dust mop and began to glide it across the polished maple floor, pinning Alli with a pointed look. "And you won *him* over, right?"

Alli's lips took a swerve. "Yes, but it took a stick to do it, as you recall, which come to think of it, I may have to resort to with Uncle Logan as well."

"Mmm . . . now there's an idea," Cassie said with a playful crimp of brows. She hesitated when several knocks sounded at the door, heralding Jamie, Bram, and Blake's arrival. Glancing at the watch pinned to her lavender blouse, she slid Alli a wry smile.

"And speaking of a stick, we could've used one to prod these boys to be on time. Poor Nick's done all the heavy labor."

Cassie hurried to let "the boys" in. "You're late," she said with a jag of her brow.

"*Or* right on time." Blake scanned the newly swept and cleaned room as he strolled into the auditorium, Bram on his heels. Jamie lagged behind to kiss Cassie at the door.

"Sorry, Al, but Logan called a last-minute meeting." Bram bent to kiss Alli's cheek.

"Probably because he knew you planned to help Nick before we go out to dinner," Cassie said, strolling in on Jamie's arm.

"You may be right." Jamie leaned to give Alli a hug. "The minute Logan found out we were helping Nick with cleanup, he called an impromptu update."

The heavy clomp of footsteps sounded on the stairs before Nick strolled into the room, wiping the sweat from his brow. He eyed the guys all trussed up in sack suits a lot fresher than his rumpled pin-striped shirt. "Good thing the work's done—hate to mess up those pretty suits."

"Sorry we're late," Jamie said with an apology in his tone. "Logan called a meeting."

"Figures." Nick's smile was dry. "No problem—you'll smell a whole lot better for dinner at The Oakdale Bar & Clam House than I would, so just as well."

Cassie spun around. "Wait, you're not joining us tonight?"

"Sorry, Cass." Nick unrolled the sleeves of his shirt. "Got tapped for a surveillance detail, so I'm walking Alli home first, unless you can talk her into going with you." He shot Alli a sympathetic gaze before sliding his jacket on and straightening his tie.

"Al?" Cassie hurried over. "Come with us, please! You've been craving clams."

Alli sighed. "Sorry, Cass, but I'm exhausted from the play and all I really want to do is go home and curl up with a book in bed. But have some for me, okay?"

"Oh, boo—you mean I'm stuck with these three all by myself?"

Blake rolled back on his heels with a grin, hands in his pocket. "Nope, you can go home with Alli so I can take your fiancé someplace a lot more fun."

Cassie sashayed over to loop an arm to Jamie's waist, lips pursed in a threat edged with a smile. "Not unless the boy wants a jolt from a cattle prod."

Jamie stole a kiss. "Rather get a jolt from your lips, Sugar Pie, if it's all the same to you."

"All in good time, Mac," Blake said, "when Cassie brands you for life." He slung an arm over Bram's shoulder. "Come on, Cass, how devious can we get with Padre Hughes along?"

"Your one saving grace." Cassie wiggled free. "Bram's the only one I can trust."

"I beg your pardon," Jamie said in mock offense, "I only have eyes for you, Cowgirl."

Alli chuckled. "Only because she'd scratch 'em out if you didn't."

"Very true," Cassie said, snatching her coat from a chair. Jamie helped her put it on while she shot Nick a threatening squint. "All right, Detective Barone, you're off the hook *this* time, but I want details on this surveillance next time you're over. Your line of work fascinates me."

"Hey, what about mine?" Jamie asked, escorting Cassie to the door.

"Only the part about *man*slaughter, City Boy," she quipped, blowing a kiss in Alli's direction. "Good night, you two, and make him ride the cable car, Al, for begging off dinner."

Alli laughed. "Will do—my feet are killing me and unless the good detective wants to carry me, there will more than likely be a cable car in his future."

Nick groaned. "Along with a bout of nausea."

"Trust me, you haven't seen 'nausea' till you've watched Blake flirt with a waitress," Bram said over his shoulder, fending off a slug from Blake. "Good night, all."

"Good night," Alli called. She snuck a peek at the clock while lifting her coat off the stack of chairs. "Oh, drat—it's getting late." She turned to face him, brows sagging along with her smile. "Maybe I should just call Hadley to pick me up so you're not late for work."

"The deuce with work." His voice was a low growl as he drew her close, the tender look in his eyes evidence of his regret over disrupting their evening. "The derelicts will still be there after I walk you home." He wove his fingers into her hair, cupping her face. "I'm sorry, Al. I'd much rather be eating oysters with you than hiding out in an alley that smells like a sewer, and with Flynn, no less, who doesn't smell much better." His gaze turned smoky while he bent to nuzzle her ear, infusing her tired body with a fresh rush of adrenaline. "And nothing like you," he whispered, lips grazing her neck with kisses that left her as limp as the coat in her hand.

She eased him away, her breathing as ragged as her pulse. "Don't you dare make me regret going home by myself to read a book, Nick Barone," she whispered.

The deadly smile that slid across his lips told her he knew exactly how his kisses affected her. "Why not?" he said, voice husky. His thumb fondled a curl before it moved to graze the soft flesh of her ear. "Thinking of you doesn't exactly make it easy being in an alley with Flynn."

"Oh, turnabout is fair play, is it?" She darted from his hold.

His mouth crooked as he snatched the coat from her hand, promptly helping her to slip it on. "You bet, Princess, especially if you force me to ride the cable car the whole way."

"And risk resurrecting Mr. Cranky Pants?" She hooked her arm through his. "No, thank you." Her voice gentled. "Look, Nick, I don't want you to be late *or* sick. You can just safely see me to the cable car at Montgomery and Jackson, and I'll be fine, truly."

"Not a chance." Dousing the lights in the gym, he ushered her out the front door, lips compressed in a flat smile. "Never thought I'd say this, but you are well worth the indigestion."

"Why, thank you, Mr. Barone." She wrinkled her nose in after-thought. "You did mean to imply the cable car gives you indigestion, not me, correct?"

"No comment," he said with an off-center grin, locking the door behind before he escorted her to the sidewalk.

The street was shrouded in darkness except for intermittent streetlamps that lent a garish glow, and Alli found herself sidling closer to Nick. Raucous laughter and rowdy singing could be heard from various bars where the tinny music of gramophones drifted overhead like the sweet and musty haze she now knew to be opium. A bare sliver of moon hung in an inky sky as ominous as the leering shadows that milled and loitered in streets and alleyways.

A shiver skittered Alli's spine and she clutched Nick's arm all the more. The bright lights from seedy dance halls and taverns blocks away were almost a comfort compared to the gloom of alleys rife with rats and refuse and evil that lurked and threatened. "It all seems so different this late at night," she whispered, heart thudding as she peered at ramshackle bars and buildings out of the corner of her eye. Gaze straight ahead, she was afraid to make eye contact with inebriated men who whistled and called out lewd remarks as she and Nick passed by. "So very . . . ," Alli swallowed hard, "dangerous and forbidding."

Nick exhaled a weary breath, eyes scanning the street as he tightened his hold. "It *is* dangerous and forbidding, Alli, which is why I was so angry when you talked about walking to the cable car alone. This is no place for a man to walk by himself, much less a woman. Thousands of men have been shanghaied here—drugged, beaten, kidnapped—only to awaken aboard a ship halfway to China where they're forced to work for years at a time. Even my partner and I seldom work this beat alone—it's just too dangerous after dark."

Nick's pace slowed at the sight of two rough-looking characters weaving toward them in rumpled suits far too nice for this neighborhood, setting his nerves on edge. One of the men spoke, his words a slur as he flashed a grin of crooked teeth that made the jagged scar across his cheek all the more noticeable. "Say, mister, can you spare some change to buy a gent a drink?"

"I'd say you've had more than enough," Nick said, his voice dangerously low. He felt Allison shudder beneath his grip while he stared the two jackals down. A nerve twittered in his cheek. "I suggest you boys head home and get some sleep."

Their menacing laughter heightened the uneasy feeling in his gut, polluting the air as much as the foul stench of whiskey on their breath. The eyes of the man who'd addressed them almost glittered in a craggy face that resembled the toughest of leather. "Is that so?" he muttered, his words slurred and slow as he eased a hand inside his suit jacket. Nick heard Alli gasp when a long-bladed knife glinted as steely as his gaze in the dim light of the streetlamp overhead. "Now is that any way to treat a friend of Aiden Maloney?"

Nick sucked in a harsh breath, body stiffening at the sound of that name. With lightning reflex, he shoved Allison behind him and stabbed a hand inside his jacket to reach for his gun.

"Uh-uh-uh . . . wouldn't do that if I were you, mister," the second man said with a cackle, allowing a double-barreled sawed-off shotgun to peek from beneath his coat. "Willie—frisk him real good because this here boy is our bread and butter."

"Sure thing, Milt."

"What do you want?" Nick said, although he already knew. His jaw hardened to rock as the thug patted him down, grinning like a demon when he relieved him of his Smith & Wesson. The lowlife promptly tucked it into his trousers. Alli sobbed, but Nick ignored her, gaze fused on the garbage before him.

Milt let loose another unholy laugh, motioning his head toward the alley beyond. "A little insurance, Mr. *Barone*, and a great big bonus from the boss for Willie and me. Now you and your lady move real slow towards that alley there."

"Leave her out of this," Nick said, his voice a hiss. Willie moved to the side and Nick could feel the shiver of Alli's body as she clutched him from behind.

"Now you know as well as I do, Mister Barone, that we cain't do that, not unless we gouge those pretty eyes out of her head."

Alli screamed and Willie instantly yanked her away, silencing her with a hard slap across her cheek. She buckled to her knees before he jerked her back up with a knife beneath her chin.

Nick's heart pumped in his throat at the look of terror in her eyes. He started to lunge, then froze at the cock of Milt's gun.

"Now, unless you want to see ol' Willie here draw blood from that pretty little neck of hers right here in the street, I suggest you two mosey on over to that alley real quiet like."

Nick sucked in a deep swallow of air, forcing his nerves to

employ the calming techniques he'd learned from Ito Akira. *Easy does it, Barone.* His gaze fixed on Alli's, silently willing her to do the same. "Do as they say, Allison—this is just an *exercise* in patience," he said carefully, praying she'd pick up on his clues regarding the fourth defense exercise she'd learned. "Take *four* deep breaths and you'll feel calm by the time we reach the alley, understand?"

Her nod was shaky as she stared back, eyes saucers of fear. Willie goaded her forward while Milt butted Nick from behind with the barrel of the shotgun, causing sweat to bead at the back of his neck. "Whatever Maloney's paying you," he said, hoping to keep Milt talking, "I'll double it. You can't pass up a sweet deal like that."

"Sure I can, mister—nobody double-crosses Mr. Maloney and lives to talk about it, something you're about to learn real good, ain't he, Will?"

"Shore thing," Willie said with an ugly laugh. "Besides, we cain't sample this sweet piece of sugar if we let her go, now can we, darlin'?" Rage boiled through Nick's body when Willie plucked several of the buttons off Alli's blouse with the tip of his knife.

Desperate to remain calm, Nick forced his breathing to slow, voice as relaxed as if they were taking a stroll down Market Street at noon. "I'll triple your take, Milt, and you and Willie can start over somewhere." His heart hammered as Alli neared the alley, not ten feet away. "I'll even bet Allison's family will match it, won't they, Allison. Go on, tell Willie . . . *Now!*"

Nick held his breath. In a surreal flash of motion that took only mere seconds, Allison executed a push-slide with near-perfect precision, just like Nick had taught her. She struck Willie's elbow so fast, he grunted when she thrust his arm in the direction of the knife. Her body was a blur as she spun to the right, sliding her left hand beneath Willie's forearm to thwart the attack. Two quick jabs of her right elbow, and she stomped on his foot and jerked from his grasp with a whirl. She plowed her right fist to his stomach, then left to the forearm that held the knife, clattering it to the cobblestones. Her foot to his groin doubled him over with a horrendous howl before she plucked Nick's gun from his pants.

Nick didn't waste any time. A heartbeat after Alli moved, he went into action with a spin to the left, escaping the line of fire. He jerked Milt's sleeve down hard, locking him in a rear choke that cut the air from the man's throat. With a strain of biceps, Nick obstructed his blood flow in a crushing squeeze until Milt dropped to the pavement like a sack of dung, out cold for several precious seconds. Nick lunged for the shotgun, stomach plunging when Willie wrenched Nick's gun from Alli's hand at very the same time. Eyes wild, Willie locked her in a chokehold while leveling the gun at Nick. "You best drop that shotgun right now, mister, or I'll squeeze the life out of this pretty little thing while I blow a hole right through you."

"Number six," Nick rasped, and in one violent throb of his pulse, Alli jerked Willie's arm down and head butted him before digging her chin into the crook of his arm. Slashing her right foot back, she trapped his, calf to calf, whirling 180 degrees to slam him flat on his back.

"Halt!" Nick shouted, but Willie lunged for the gun anyway, rolling on his back to take aim with a gleam in his eyes.

Kaboom! Alli's scream merged with the deafening roar of Nick's shot, the gleam in Willie's eyes fading with a blast that rolled him against the wall.

"Nick!"

He spun around, heart in his throat at the glint of a knife in Milt's upraised arm. "Alli—*drop!*" he shouted, pumping a round into Milt that launched him several feet in the air before both he and the knife sank to the ground in a bloody heap.

Nick's eyes shuddered closed. He barely heard the sound of Alli's weeping for the roar of blood in his ears. *God forgive me* . . .

Hurling the gun away, he dropped to his knees and swallowed Alli up, stroking her hair while she wept in his arms. "It's over, Alli." He rocked her slowly there on the dirty cobblestones now splattered with blood. Tears stung his eyes as he thought of how close he'd come to losing her . . . to losing their lives together. "Shhh . . . it's going to be okay," he whispered, "you're safe now." But his words buzzed hollow in his ears along with the sudden wailing of dogs and the faraway clang of the cable car, because deep down inside he knew it was a lie. It would never be okay again, not until he avenged his uncle and parents. And until he did, Alli would never be safe—not with him. Not now. His eyes trailed into a cold stare while her body shuddered in his arms.

Maybe not ever.

25

"How is she?"

Caitlyn jolted at the sound of Logan's voice, suddenly aware she'd been standing in the parlour doorway in a trance, body sagging against the Corinthian pillar beneath the wide, arched entryway. "What?" she whispered, legs shaky as she all but staggered across the room. Logan met her halfway and ushered her to the couch, and she immediately collapsed in his arms, clutching him tightly while she wept against his chest. "It's a-all m-my f-fault," she whispered, painful heaves stuttering her words.

Gentle fingers kneaded her back. "It's not, Cait," he whispered, the crush of his arms cocooning her in a place where she felt safe and warm. "It's simply life, with all its frailties. Allison is a far better, far stronger person for teaching at your school and so are you and every child privileged to attend."

"B-but . . . it's so dangerous there . . ."

"*Life* is dangerous," he said, drawing away to cradle her face in his hands. "Whether you're run over by a cable car on Nob Hill or trampled by a horse on the Barbary Coast. We can't live in fear of what each day may bring and we can't let fear stop us from doing the right thing." He grazed her jaw with his thumb. "You taught me that, Mrs. McClare."

"But it's no place for a school," she said, her voice nasal from grief over what had happened to Alli. "You tried to tell me that, and I wouldn't listen . . ."

His lip quirked. "True." He lifted her chin, the humor in his eyes giving way to a sobriety that quickened her pulse. "But that's only one of the many reasons I love you, Cait. Your fierce independence, your zeal for justice, and your beautiful heart of compassion. Which, much as I hate to admit, makes the location for the Hand of Hope School perfect."

"Not if it puts those I love in danger."

He cocked a brow. "So we take precautions. We hire a full-time handyman/guard to assist Mr. Bigley year-round, not just for a few months. We have Allison teach you and the others a few basic maneuvers in self-defense. And then we put our foot down with Allison, further restricting her working at the school past five or taking the cable car on her own."

Her lips wobbled into a faint smile. "We?" she whispered, not wanting to burden Logan further but painfully aware he was becoming more and more a part of her life every day—her decisions, her problems, her responsibilities.

And my heart?

He paused to study her, the potency of love she saw in his eyes making her want to weep all over again. "Yes, 'we,'" he whispered, trailing several fingers along the line of her jaw. "We're a team, Cait, you and I. We may not be a 'couple' in the true sense of the word, but we are two people in love with the same family, nonetheless. Which means your family is my family, and I will support and protect you—and it—until I take my last breath."

Her heart swooped when he leaned in to press a kiss to her cheek. The warmth of his lips on her skin caused her belly to quiver as tears misted her eyes. He pulled away and immediately she felt bereft of his touch despite the heat of his palms as they briskly rubbed her arms. "Is Alli in bed?" he asked, his businesslike tone surprising her, as did his behavior of late. Over the last few months, there'd been several situations where he'd held and comforted her over one family crisis after another, and yet never once had he taken advantage like he had in Napa. Not even when she'd kissed his cheek out of sheer gratitude the night he'd found Maddie. Cait suddenly realized her trust in Logan was growing, strengthening, removing the very barriers she'd constructed to keep her heart safe. Her cheeks grew warm when her renegade gaze flicked to his lips before she could stop it, and she swallowed hard, remembering all too clearly that offensive kiss in Napa. Offensive for one reason and one reason only—it had stirred her body far too quickly, making her want him far too much. *Like now . . .*

"Cait?"

She blinked, her gaze colliding with his and instantly her cheeks burned at what she saw in his probing stare. *He knows!* Knows I depend on him, need him . . . *want him.*

"Y-yes?"

There was a hint of a twinkle in those gray eyes and a tenderness that put her at ease. "I asked if Alli was in bed."

Cait buffed her arms, self-conscious over the fluttery way Logan was beginning to make her feel. "Yes, of course," she said quickly. "She seemed very upset and so did Nick, which leads me to believe they didn't tell us everything that happened."

A grunt rolled from Logan's lips. "An obvious character flaw when it comes to Barone, if you ask me, especially given how he bolted out of here before we could question him further."

"He said he was late for work, Logan," Cait defended, uncomfortable as always when Logan attacked Nick.

"Yes, well, that's a conversation for another day." He folded his arms and peered up, brows in a scrunch. "Did Alli shed any more light on what happened when you talked to her upstairs? Like how she got that bruise on her cheek?"

The malaise that had numbed Caitlyn from the moment Alli walked in the door returned in force, sagging her shoulders. "No, just that one of the attackers pushed her down. I'm just so grateful Nick was with her . . ." She hesitated. "Although Alli said something odd when she was trying to assure me it was an isolated case of two disgruntled vagrants asking for a handout."

"And what was that?"

Cait looked up, a pucker at the bridge of her nose. "She said one of the men mentioned another man's name, almost as if he expected Nick to know him. But Nick assured her it was 'nothing more than two drunks with a grievance.'" A shiver scurried down her spine. "But a grievance to me implies it might have been against Nick, which is a worry unto itself."

Logan's mouth thinned. "I'll tell you what, Cait—that man has skeletons in his closet, you mark my words, and I hope to prove it before Alli gets too serious."

"I hope you're wrong," she whispered, her respect and affection for Nick making it hard to believe the man would ever hurt her daughter. "I think she's falling in love with him."

"Trust me, I wish I were wrong for Alli's sake, but my source leads me to believe otherwise." His exhale was heavy. "But I'll wait for confirmation before I tell her."

Caitlyn released a mournful sigh, tears threatening all over again. "Oh, Logan—I'm not sure she can stand another heartbreak." She shuddered, prompting him to tug her back to the safety of his arms. "Nor can I." A fragile exhale feathered her lips while he gently stroked her hair.

"Don't worry," he whispered, "I plan to do everything in my power to prevent the risk of heartbreak for both you and Alli, so hopefully neither of you has to ever go through it again."

The risk of heartbreak, yes. A very real worry for a daughter who appeared to have already given her heart away.

And her mother? Cait's eyes weighted closed.

A distinct possibility, indeed.

Nick entered Miss Penny's darkened kitchen, void of all activity at the early hour of four a.m., and quietly set his two suitcases on the floor. Fumbling in the dark, he reached up to find the chain cord for the pendant light that hung over the sink, finally turning it on with a firm tug. The warm glow of the gas lamp quickly chased the gloom from a tidy kitchen that would soon be filled with the heady scent of cinnamon oatmeal and fresh-brewed coffee. But nothing could chase the gloom from his soul. Not when he'd just taken the lives of two men, men he'd led Alli to believe were only seriously wounded. *And* men who were hired assassins, forcing him to leave San Francisco to keep those he loved safe and sound.

The minute those two thugs said Maloney's name, Nick knew he couldn't stay. They were on to him, and although he'd taken down two of Maloney's men, he had no doubt more would soon follow. Which meant he needed to return to Chicago immediately to lead them away.

Reaching into Miss Penny's hodge-podge drawer, he pulled out paper and pen, then sat down at the long oak table that bore the happy scuffs and scars of meals and love served in ample supply. Within three short hours, laughter would reign among an equally hodge-podge family of ten orphans and the two elderly women who cared for them, minus one very cranky and very lonely fugitive on the run. The pen lay limp in his hand, but no more so than his body as he sagged in the chair, eyes trailing into a glazed stare. For the second time in his life, he was being cut off from the people he loved—first Mom, Pop, Gram, and his uncle, and now Miss Penny, Lottie, Mrs. Lemp, and the others.

And Alli. A sharp pain seared through him, and he laid his head on the sheets of paper, experiencing a grief and loneliness he hadn't felt in years. He had never intended to stay, but in the brief time he'd called San Francisco his home, it had become just that—a respite, a haven, and a place to learn how to love again. And although he hadn't a clue how it had come to pass, heaven help him, he loved Allison McClare. Her passion. Her drama. Her thirst for life and adventure. And her deep dependence on God—a dependence that had given him glimpses of what Mom and Pop had tried to instill in him. Stirring and stoking his own cold embers of faith until they had warmed his weary soul. Which meant he couldn't stay—not when his very presence put her and the people he loved in danger.

Please, God, if You're truly there like I've been taught to believe— protect them . . .

Lifting his head, he exhaled a cumbersome sigh and gripped the pen with purpose, saying his goodbyes, first to Miss Penny and the girls, then a separate note for Lottie. When he'd folded and pushed the missives aside, he turned his attention to the blank piece of paper before him, nausea churning in his stomach like the whitecaps on San Francisco Bay.

Dear Alli . . .

He stared at her name, loathe to leave her, yet reluctant to tell her why. Not when he wasn't sure when he'd be back. A chill shivered his body. And not when he wasn't sure if he even *could* come back.

"Can't sleep?"

His head jerked up. "Miss Penny." He swallowed hard. "What are you doing up?"

Her eyes flicked from the letters on the table to the two suitcases beside his chair before they narrowed on him. "I could ask you the same thing, Nicky," she said pointedly, "but I'd rather know why your bags are packed."

His mind raced as his gaze darted to the clock over the sink, biding his time to come up with a credible answer while Miss Penny went about lighting the stove. "Something's come up, and I have to return to New York," he said in the calmest tone he could muster given Miss Penny's piercing gaze over her shoulder.

"How long will you be gone?"

He watched as she filled the coffeepot with water, then methodically scooped coffee into the steel basket. "I . . . don't know, which is why I just wrote you a note. But rest assured the captain has another officer in mind to rent the room, so rent will remain intact."

She pulled two cups and saucers from the pantry and clunked them on the table so hard, he jumped. "I don't care about the rent—I care about you and why you're deserting us in the dead of night without even saying goodbye."

Her accusation jolted, and he shot to his feet, palms splayed to the wood. "That's not fair. You knew from the beginning my stay in San Francisco was temporary, so don't act like I'm deserting you." He sucked in a breath to help rein in his temper, releasing it in a steady exhale while he slowly reclaimed his seat. "And I'd appreciate if you'd keep your voice down. This is hard enough without having to say goodbye to the entire household."

"Never figured you for a coward," she muttered, jerking out a heavy spindle-back chair pert near bigger than she, as if it weighed nothing at all.

Releasing a noisy sigh, he thumped back in his chair, head in his hand. "Yeah, well, it's hard enough facing you, much less Lottie."

He heard her drop into her seat, saw the folded wizened hands on the table out of the corner of his eye. "And Alli, I suppose?"

A silent groan rose in his throat at the very sound of her name. "Trust me, Miss Penny—it's better I go," he whispered.

She grunted, a sound that any other time would have made him smile. "If heartbreak can be considered better."

The coffeepot began to bubble and brew, filling the kitchen with the nutty aroma of the Colombian coffee her nephew always gave her for Christmas, making Nick homesick before he ever set foot out the door. Silence hung thick in the air between them while Miss Penny bustled about, clattering dishes. She grabbed a knife and whacked off a thick slice of the cinnamon loaf Mrs. Lemp had prepared for breakfast. He jumped back when she slammed the plate and fork on the table before him, the saucer skittering across the wood, as twitchy as his nerves.

"And trust you?" she snapped, snatching the coffeepot from the stove. "Well, yes, until last night, when I found out you were running out on us." She poured his cup as ferociously as she glared, plops of steaming liquid scalding his hand. "From my nephew, no less, rather than you—the man I took into my home, loved like a son, fed until the pantry was bare—"

Guilt strangled his words. "Miss Penny, please—"

She sloshed coffee into her cup, then banged the pot back on the burner, returning to her chair with fire in her eyes. "Don't you 'Miss Penny' me, young man—there's something going on here and I want to know what it is."

His jaw ground tight as he snatched the pen and slid the paper close, determined to get Alli's letter written before he left. "I have things to attend to in New York, that's all I can say."

She slammed a palm to the table, shimmering the coffee in both of their cups. "No, that's not all you can say to people who love you. And now you're going to go and break that poor girl's heart too, aren't you?"

He bludgeoned the table, searing her with a heated look. "Blast it, Gram—" He froze, expelling a weary breath while he gouged the bridge of his nose. "I mean . . . Miss Penny." When he finally looked up, he didn't even bother to mask the grief in his eyes, his voice a painful rasp. "Don't you think I'm bleeding inside? Over leaving you—Lottie—the girls?" He looked away, fighting the sting of moisture as he lapsed into a vacant stare. "Over Alli." His eyelids felt like lead as they closed. "I love her, Miss Penny. Never wanted to, never expected to, never tried to." A fractured breath shuddered from his lips, voice barely audible. "It just happened."

"Then stay." Her frail hand lighted on his arm.

"It's not that easy," he whispered. "If I stay, the people I love are in danger."

"You're in trouble then?"

He looked up, seeing the tender love of Gram in those glossy blue eyes. "Yes, ma'am, I'm in trouble. Which is why I have to go back, and please believe me—I can't say any more."

"Will you return?" she asked, the grief in her eyes breaking his heart.

He stared. And then in a harsh catch of his breath, he swallowed her up in his arms, tears of his own burning his nostrils. "I hope so—someday." His eyes squeezed tightly over her shoulder. "No," he whispered, steel edging his tone. "I pray so."

"Good boy," she said with a gentle pat of his back, pulling away to cup his face in her hands. "Then I'll join you in that prayer, Nicky, because you've become the son that I lost, and I don't ever want to go through that again, you hear?"

"Yes, ma'am."

She nodded at the blank sheet of paper before him. "Are you going to ask her to wait?"

He expelled a wavering sigh, shaking his head. "I can't guarantee I'll be back."

She rose, palms flat to the table as she loomed over him with the same menacing glare Gram used to give. "Are you saying my prayers don't carry any weight, Nicholas Barone?"

"No, ma'am," he said with a cuff of his neck, the barest of smiles shadowing his lips. "But you and I both know God doesn't always answer prayers the way that we want."

Her frail chest expanded and released with a weary gust of air. "No, He doesn't, Nicky, but this time He will have two stubborn old women, ten relentless children, and one very pretty girl with a stick hounding Him to no end. So I suggest you tell that young woman you love her and intend to come back, understood? Because if our prayers have anything to say about it, Nicholas, you'll be back giving her a good dose of cranky in no time."

"Mr. Nick?"

His gaze darted to the kitchen door where Lottie stood in a pink flannel nightgown, rubbing her eyes. *No, please . . .*

"You didn't kiss me before I went to bed," she whispered, padding across the linoleum in bare feet. She crawled into his lap and laid her head to his chest, rosebud mouth expanding in a sweet, little yawn. "How come?"

He cuddled her close, his smile sad at the familiar scent of talcum powder and a hint of animal crackers he'd given her to stash in her drawer. "Sure I did, Lottie, but it was so late when I came home that you were sound asleep and never even knew."

"Really?" She tilted her head as if she were peeking up.

"Yes, ma'am," he said with a kiss to her nose, "and I just kissed you awhile ago too."

She pulled away to peer up intently, sky-blue eyes blinking. "Why?"

Heat singed his collar, and his gaze flicked up to see the pinched lips of Miss Penny before he wrapped his arms around Lottie to draw her close. "Because I'm . . ." He stalled, the prospect of telling her he was leaving every bit as difficult as he knew it would be. "I . . . have to go away for a while, Lottie."

She jerked back again, the sudden sheen in her eyes all but ripping his heart out. "Where?" she whispered, voice soft and frail like the little girl he held in his arms.

"Back home, sweetheart, to where I used to live."

"But why?"

Miss Penny hiked a brow and Nick blew out a shaky breath, tucking his head to Lottie's. "Because I have something I need to do, darling, and it'll probably take me awhile."

"How long?"

He glanced up at Miss Penny and expelled a weary sigh, taking Lottie's little hand in his. "That depends on your prayers, Lottie, and Miss Penny's." He tucked a curl over her ear. "Will you pray for me to come back?"

A pudgy hand to his cheek assured him she would, along with tender words that thickened his throat. "Are you and God friends again, Mr. Nick? Because Miss Penny and I have been praying for a long time that you would forgive Him."

Forgive *Him?* His heart wrenched. *No, sweetheart, I'm the one in need of forgiveness.* "Yes . . . yes we are, Lottie, so thank you for your prayers."

She patted his cheek. "You're welcome, Mr. Nick. And Miss Penny and me and the girls will pray every day that you come back, okay? Because we may be orphans, but we're all family now and you too—God's family." She turned to grin at Miss Penny. "Ain't that so, Miss Penny?"

The old woman's gaze glimmered with moisture as she swiped at her eyes. "Yes, darling, it is. God's Word says, 'I will not leave you orphans.'"

She turned back to Nick with a peaceful smile, tone patient as if she were the adult and he were the wide-eyed child in need of comfort. "See? He'll take care of you too." Scrambling to stand on his lap, she rested small hands on his shoulders. "So even though your mama and papa and Gram are gone to heaven, God gave you to us, Mr. Nick, to be in our family, so you just have to come back. 'Cause everybody knows God takes care of His family, okay?"

He nodded, unable to speak for the emotion clogging his throat.

She pressed a tender kiss to his lips, as soft and gentle as the wisp of an angel wing. "I love you, Mr. Nick." A tiny yawn escaped as she leaned her head against his. "Will you tuck me in? I'm sleepy."

"You bet," Nick said, voice gruff with tenderness while he bundled her in his arms. He ducked his head to Lottie's so Miss Penny couldn't see the sheen of tears in his eyes.

God's family. Which meant he was no longer alone. "*I will not leave you orphans,*'" Miss Penny had said, and somehow he felt the approval of Gram, Mom, and Pop from afar, assuring him it was true. He nuzzled his nose into Lottie's soft curls while he carried her up the stairs, the bong of the clock in the parlour matching the loud thud of his heart.

"He'll take care of you," Lottie had said with the utmost assurance, and at the thought, a warmth invaded his chest that had less to do with the small bundle of heaven in his arms than it did with the bright glow of a little girl's faith.

"Everybody knows God takes care of His family."

"I didn't," he whispered. Laying her back in her bed, he tucked her in and gave her a kiss before making his way from the room, the barest of smiles tipping the edge of his mouth.

Till now.

26

Alli stared through red-rimmed eyes, the rain-splattered panes of glass in the conservatory revealing a bleak, gunmetal sky that wept as much as she.

"Did he say why?" Her mother whispered, stroking Allison's arm, which now lay as limp on the cushion as the letter she held in her hand. The same letter Nick had couriered to her home early this morning, telling her he'd left for New York via train.

She shook her head, unable to fathom why Nick Barone would tell her he loved her, then just turn around and leave. "Unfinished business," she said in a nasal tone, handkerchief soggy. "Something he has to do in New York."

"If it takes my last breath, I'll find the slime who did it someday and gun him down too."

Her eyes wavered closed as a sob rose in her throat. *Oh, Nick...*

Loving arms pulled her close. "Alli, I'm so very sorry, but surely he intends to come back.

Alli sniffed and blew her nose. "Yes, he promised he would try, but he has no idea when. Said it could take six months or longer, maybe even a year ..." Her voice broke on a heave. "If at all."

"Oh, Alli ..." Her mother cradled her in her arms, rocking and soothing her like she'd done in all the tragedies of her life—

skinned knees, fractured arms, broken hearts . . . *Roger.* "Nick loves you, darling—I could see it every time you two were together this last month, and he told you so himself, didn't he?"

She nodded dumbly, recalling with painful clarity the intensity of his manner when he'd kissed her goodbye at the door after their awful ordeal last night. A mixture of sorrow and love in those gray eyes she wouldn't soon forget, and a desperation when he'd crushed her close, as if he never wanted to let her go . . .

"So, here you two are—why aren't you playing whist with the others?"

Alli's head jerked up at the sound of her uncle's voice. The pinch between his brows deepened as he squatted before her. "Alli? What's wrong—why are you crying?"

Her mother expelled a heavy sigh and patted Uncle Logan's arm as if to assure him everything was fine. "Nick's left town for a while for some sort of business dealing in New York," she said quietly before Alli could utter a word, "so understandably she's upset since he didn't tell her beforehand—just wrote her a letter." Caitlyn fanned loose curls from Alli's face, her smile shaky at best. "But I assured her he cares for her and will probably come back soon."

A heave shuddered Alli's body as she blotted her face. "Oh, Mother, I hope so."

"Alli," Uncle Logan whispered, his face a composite of grief and conviction that iced the blood in her veins, "please know how painful this is for me to say . . ." He paused long enough to engulf her hand in his own, his eyes locked on hers. "But I hope he doesn't."

She flung his hand away and sprang to her feet, almost toppling him in the process. "You have never given him a chance, Uncle Logan, not once, despite the fact that I'm in love with the man and he's in love with me."

"He's lying to you, Alli," he said with a sorrow she felt keenly. Gaze tender, he rose slowly, regarding her with a candor she'd come to respect and admire.

Until now.

"Which is exactly why I haven't given him a chance up to now—I sensed it in my gut. Believe me, Alli, after Roger, the last thing I want is for you to be involved with another charlatan, a man you can't trust."

"I *can* trust him!" she shouted, body quivering as she barricaded stiff arms to her waist.

"Logan, please . . ." Her mother intervened with a hand to his arm. "Allison doesn't need this right now. She needs our love and support."

"I agree," he said quietly with a firm squeeze of her mother's hand, "but she also needs the truth, because in the end, Cait, that's the greatest love and support we can provide."

Allison backed away, distancing herself from the words she didn't want to hear. "The truth is, Uncle Logan, Nick loves me and I love him, and you'll just have to get used to that."

"I can't," he whispered, grief bleeding into his words like fear was bleeding into her heart. "The man's a fraud, sweetheart. He lied on his police application. Led Captain Peel to believe he was on the force in Lower Manhattan for several years, but not only is there no Nick Barone on any police roll in the state of New York, but it appears he was a member of a gang. A con man who did a short stint in prison for manslaughter . . . right before he abandoned the woman who was carrying his child."

"Noooooo—I don't believe you!" Her voice edged toward hysteria, unable to fathom the man she loved was capable of anything so heinous.

"I'm sorry, Alli, but it's true," Logan whispered, tone thick with regret. "According to my source, Nick Barone is a wanted man who stole from his fiancée before he went on the lam. Supposedly the family is still looking for him."

Hands to her ears, Allison shook her head, refusing to listen. "No . . . you've hated him from the beginning, Uncle Logan, and you'd say anything to discredit him, but Nick will be back soon and he'll prove you wrong, I promise . . ."

Her uncle reached for her hand. "No, Alli, he won't . . . because he's not coming back."

"You don't know that!" she screamed, tears blurring her vision. She snatched the letter from the love seat and thrust it forward, eyes wild. "He promised, Uncle Logan, and he will . . ."

"Yes," he whispered, her pain reflected in his eyes, "but he promised his fiancée he'd return too, and yet he didn't—until now." He exhaled. "After I offered him money to leave, I might add, which I'll admit he refused at the time but I suspect will claim before long."

Her mother gasped while a harsh breath lodged in Alli's throat. The room swayed as blood drained from her face, bile rising along with a heave. *God, no, please, not again.*

"Oh, God help us." Her mother's rasp of horror echoed Alli's own.

"I didn't like Barone from the beginning, it's true, Allison," her uncle said quietly, "but Captain Peel vouched for him and he served a purpose in teaching you to protect yourself, so I ignored any misgivings I had. But when he made his intentions clear, I had no choice but to investigate and told Barone as much last week at your party, offering a tidy sum if he'd leave San Francisco—and you—forever, which it appears he did."

God, why? Tears spilled down Alli's cheeks as her eyes drifted closed, barely aware of her mother's arms enfolding her, tugging her back to the love seat.

"Oh, Alli . . . ," her mother whispered, and Alli collapsed into her hold with weeping so painful, she wanted to die. *Why, Nick . . . why?*

"Alli, forgive me, please," Uncle Logan whispered. "I love you, sweetheart, and this was one of the hardest things I've ever had to do."

She nodded against her mother's chest, pulling back to blow her nose on the clean handkerchief he pressed into her hand. "I kn-know you do, Uncle L-Logan," she whispered, her voice as broken as her heart, "and I love you too, you know that, but I'm in love with Nick Barone so deeply, that I'm not sure I'm strong enough to go through this again . . ."

With a low groan, he swept her up in his arms, voice fierce as he tucked his head against hers. "Oh, you are, Alli, and as God is my witness, your mother and I will see to it. You're not in this alone, sweetheart—don't ever forget that. We're family, and family is all the strength you need to get through." He eased back to take her hand in his while he gripped her mother's with the other, a sheen in his eyes conveying a depth of feeling she'd seldom seen in her uncle before. "That and God." He squeezed Alli's hand as he smiled at her mother. "Faith and family, Alli—an unbeatable combination that I learned about from a very wise woman."

"Oh, Logan . . ." Her mother gripped his hand before turning to Alli with tears in her eyes. "Your uncle's right, Allison—with God and family, weeping may endure for a night, but joy cometh in the morning." She caressed Alli's face with a tender palm. "Somehow, some way . . . God will see us through."

Alli nodded, a heave shuddering her body as she attempted to stand, legs teetering so much, Uncle Logan braced her with an arm. "I . . . love you both very much," she whispered, "but I . . . really need to be alone right now, if you don't mind."

"Of course," her mother said, shoring her up with a gentle arm to her waist. "You get some rest now, and we'll pray about this in the morning, all right?"

"Alli ..." Uncle Logan pulled her into his arms, the scent of lime flooding her senses with memories of strong arms and skinned knees. His words were quiet and warm in her ear, carrying an assurance she so wanted to believe. "You'll get through this, I promise—we'll see to it."

"Thanks, Uncle Logan—I hope so." She grazed his cheek with a kiss and then her mother's. "If you'd tell Cassie and the others I went to bed early with a headache, I'd appreciate it."

"Certainly, darling. How about some warm milk?" her mother asked, walking her to the door.

"No, thank you, Mother—just a warm bed."

"All right, then. Good night, Allison." Her mother gave her a tight hug.

"Allison."

On the verge of more tears, she turned at the sound of her uncle's call.

Love radiated from eyes resolute with a press of his jaw. "You're in love with something that doesn't exist, Alli, so trust me, the feelings will wane quickly, just like they did with Roger."

She stared, unable to do anything but nod before she turned away.

Something that doesn't exist.

Yes, she thought as she fled to the shelter of her room.

Except for the pain ...

"I'm worried, Logan," Cait whispered at the door, turning to face the man who had become her main source of strength when it came to family crises of late.

"Don't be, Cait—she's a strong girl—she'll weather this."

A cold chill shivered her body, and she buffed her arms, making her way to the love seat with a sick feeling inside over how wrong she'd been about Nick. She had liked him, come to respect him, and had even secretly hoped he might be the right man for Alli. And now this—a revelation so shocking, it left her depleted and depressed for what lay ahead for her daughter. She sat down and Logan followed suit, hunched with hands clasped over his knees and concern in his eyes. She quickly looked away, certain the tenderness of his gaze would tip tears ready to spill from a tide pool of emotions that seemed to drown her of late. Perching on the edge of her seat, she put her head in her hands, shoulders slumped and water welling beyond her control.

"Cait . . ." His gentle touch caused a heave to rise in her throat despite her most ardent attempt to ward it off, and when a sob broke from her lips, there was no stopping the pull of his arms. "It's going to be okay," he whispered, cradling her to his chest. "I promise."

She attempted to nod, but the heaves only came harder. Her arms slipped to his waist before she even knew what she'd done, clinging as if he were a lifeline while she wracked his body with tears. She could feel the strength of his arms as he held her, the warmth of his breath as he lay his head against hers, and she found she was no longer willing to battle life alone. The scent of lime and spice taunted, convincing her she not only needed Logan McClare in her life and those of her children, but she wanted him too. An unsettling revelation that left her as vulnerable and afraid as her daughter upstairs. This man was blood to her children and loved them as deeply as if they were his own, a powerful attribute that drew her as surely as his arms.

Her tears finally subsided, and the warmth of his hold flamed in her cheeks when she realized her body lay snug against his.

She jerked up with a start, apology in her tone while she awkwardly swiped at her eyes. "Goodness, this is becoming a habit, it would seem."

"One can only hope," he whispered, fingers caressing her face. "And pray . . ."

His gaze flicked to her lips for the briefest of moments, but it was more than enough, swooping her stomach so hard, she jolted to her feet, voice breathless. "Oh, Logan, I can't—"

With a gruff clear of his throat, he quickly rose. "No explanation necessary, Cait—I totally understand." Ruddy color bled up his neck as he adjusted the sleeves of his suit coat, his manner stiff. "I have an early train tomorrow for that weeklong conference in L.A. I told you about, so I best be going, but I'll see you when I get back."

He bent to give her his customary kiss on the cheek and she halted him with a hand to his arm. "No, you misunderstand me," she whispered, heart battering her rib cage as she skimmed her fingers along his jaw. "What I started to say was . . . I 'can't' thank you enough for all you do for us, but I'd seriously like to try." And with a hard swallow, she lifted to gently brush her lips against his, pulse surging at his sharp intake of air.

"Cait . . ." His voice was a strangled rasp as he searched her face, a glimmer of hope invading the clear, gray depths of his eyes. She heard his shallow breathing as he stared, Adam's apple ducking hard. "Don't do this to me," he said in a hoarse whisper, "not unless you're ready to take it somewhere."

She paused to scan his handsome face—more weathered and mature than when he'd first wooed and won her years ago, but the pull of attraction as strong as ever. An attraction emanating from eyes that seemed to be a window to his soul, revealing a depth of love and desire that made the tendons go slack at the back of her knees. Never would she have believed she could ever trust her heart to Logan again, and yet here she stood—on the threshold of doing just that, albeit tentatively so. But she wanted to. Oh, Lord, help her—how she wanted to! "To take it somewhere" where she could not only trust Logan as a man who cherished and protected her children, but trust him as a husband who would cherish and protect her as well. To be faithful and true to both her and to God all the days of their lives.

Her chest rose and fell with a shuddering breath as she made her decision, and with a skip of her pulse she cupped his bristled jaw with a shaky hand. "If God is an important part of your life now as you've led me to believe . . ." A muscle shifted in her throat. "Then I think maybe . . . just maybe . . . I'm ready to become an important part too."

A low groan rumbled from his throat as he scooped her up in a powerful embrace. "Oh, Cait," he whispered, his breath warm in her ear, "marry me now—*tomorrow*—and I will spend the rest of my life making sure you never regret it."

Breathless, she managed to pull away, determined to take it slowly. "Dear, sweet Logan . . ." Her lips curved in a tender smile. "As tempting as that sounds, I think it best if we took this one day at a time, don't you? Especially in light of Alli's heartbreak."

He exhaled slowly. "Agreed," he whispered, the gentle touch of his lips to her forehead causing her eyes to drift closed. Her stomach quivered when his mouth caressed each eyelid with the softest of kisses before grazing their way to her temple. "Besides," she whispered, her breathing as uneven as his, "I rather like the idea of courtship, Mr. McClare, just to make sure."

"Whatever you say, Cait." Heat skimmed her body when his mouth skimmed her cheek to nuzzle her lips. "But a little mercy, Mrs. McClare, please, in not making the wait too long."

"Excuse me, miss."

Caitlyn jerked from Logan's arms, heat engulfing her cheeks as Hadley stood staunch at the door. Never had she been more grateful for her beloved butler's disdain for the eyeglasses he seemed prone not to wear. "Mr. Andrew Turner to see you, miss."

"What's he want?" Logan snapped, his mood suddenly as heated as the blood in Caitlyn's cheeks.

"Thank you, Hadley," she called in a volume loud enough for the butler to hear. "Would you mind showing him to the study for me, please?"

Hadley gave a short bow with a click of heels. "Very good, miss."

"Blast it, Cait—if you and I are courting, I'd rather not have that letch around."

Caitlyn bit back a smile, Logan's jealousy over his ex–best friend surfacing once again. And with good reason, she supposed, given Andrew's persistence in asking her out, a persistence that had actually softened her stance toward him. Over the months they'd worked together, she'd begun to enjoy his company in a greater capacity, even playfully responding to his flirtations at times. And then weeks ago, he'd told her of his feelings, begging her to consider more.

"Promise you'll pray about it," he'd asked at the door after one of their many project meetings, which she took great pains to schedule on nights when Logan was not around. "You and I make a good team, Cait," he'd whispered, moving so close that her pulse had sped up. "We share a vision, a deep faith, and I pray that bodes well for sharing a life together as well."

"Pardon me?" Swallowing her shock, she attempted a step back, speechless when he'd stroked her cheek with his thumb.

"I'm falling in love with you, Cait, and I want to court you."

"Andrew, I . . ." She gulped. "I . . . I can't . . ."

He paused, his disappointment palpable. "Do you mind if I ask why?"

Her brain scrambled for an answer that wouldn't offend. "Because, I'm quite content with my life as it is. My family is everything to me, you see, and I want for nothing more."

He studied her with a keen eye, as if to decipher the truth of her statement before his mouth compressed in a thin line, a hint of hurt in his eyes. "It's because of Logan, isn't it?"

"Of course not," she said too quickly, ever in denial of her burgeoning affection for Logan McClare. "But you and he are not on the best of terms, Andrew, and I refuse to jeopardize that relationship further."

He gently gripped her arms, a plea in his tone. "Please . . . don't let Logan stand in the way of something God may have for us, Cait. At least promise you'll pray about it, all right?"

And so she had, and with all of her heart believed the answer was standing before her this very moment, scowling in that adorable crotchety way he had whenever Andrew's name came up. A smile curved on her lips as she reassured him with a gentle kiss. "I'll make it a short meeting, I promise, and perfectly clear that all future project discussions will be held at Walter's with him and other board members present, all right?"

Logan grunted and hooked her close. "I'd rather you kick him off the board, but since that isn't likely . . ." He bent to fondle the lobe of her ear with his mouth, tumbling her stomach when his lips slowly trailed to hers. "So, I'll just stake my claim before I leave." Cradling the back of her head with a firm hold, he consumed her with a kiss that all but melted her bones to the floor. Her breath caught as he skimmed the curve of her jaw to nip at the lobe of her ear before sinking to wander her throat, whispering his love against her skin. The warmth of his words coaxed a weak moan from her lips, adrift on raspy air. When he finally released her, the heat in his eyes matched that pulsing her body. "Kick him out, Cait—please? Then we'll continue this discussion when I get back." He deposited a kiss to her nose before striding to the door, turning to give her a shuttered gaze that made her mouth go dry. "I want you to forget about Turner, and the sooner, the better." He gave her a wink. "But don't you dare forget about the man whose heart you hold in the palm of your hand."

She blinked and he was gone, leaving her standing there with flushed cheeks and trembling limbs, mind racing and pulse even worse.

Forget the man whose heart she held in the palm of her hand? Sucking in a deep breath, she pressed a shaky hand to her chest with a quiver of a smile. *Good heavens . . . Andrew who?*

27

The grandfather clock in the parlour chimed midnight as Alli lumbered up from her bed, pillow soggy and cold, and her heart even worse. Chilled to the bone, she donned her robe and slippers, then pulled a fresh handkerchief from her drawer to replace the sodden one. Dabbing her eyes, she made her way to the door in search of the laudanum Rosie now kept on the top shelf of the pantry. Oh, how she prayed it would cure this horrific headache and lure her to sleep where she wouldn't have to think about Nick.

Nick. Mr. Nick. Detective Ga-roan. Mr. Cranky Pants. Mr. Pinhead.

And, apparently, Mr. Liar and Thief—the man who'd stolen her heart and so much more.

Her hope . . . her joy . . . her faith.

Opening her bedroom door, she padded down the hall and stopped, the light bleeding beneath her mother's door giving her pause. A sudden longing for the comfort of her mother's arms swelled in her chest like saltwater swelled in her eyes, and swabbing her face with the handkerchief, she darted down the hall to her room, hand poised, ready to knock.

A muffled sob leaked through the door, and Alli froze, fear

icing her skin. *Mother?* With two sharp taps, she eased the door open, stomach fisting when she saw her weeping on the bed. "Oh, Mother!"

"Allison?" Her mother jolted up, voice nasal as she quickly blotted a handkerchief to her eyes. "What are you doing up—are you having trouble sleeping?"

Alli rushed to hug her, snuggling into the familiar scent of Pear's soap and lavender. "Yes, Mother, I am, but what I want to know is why *you're* crying."

Ever the nurturer, Caitlyn McClare swept the covers aside to allow her in, then bundled them both back up and tucked her head to Alli's. "Oh . . . just a slight altercation with Andrew Turner," she said slowly, a thread of pain in her tone that Alli didn't miss. A levity that seemed a bit forced worked its way into her voice. "And an unhealthy dose of the change of life creeping in, I suppose, given how weepy I've been of late." She hesitated, hand gentle as she stroked Alli's hair. "I'm so very sorry about Nick, darling, and I grieve over your loss."

At mention of Nick's name, tears instantly stung. "I love him so much that I can't even imagine he did all those awful things." She peered into her mother's eyes, fear contorting her features. "How can that be? How can I have fallen for someone who deceived me so completely—not just once, but four times?" Her body convulsed in a sob as she collapsed in her mother's arms, heaves shuddering her words. "How will I ever be happy if I can't trust myself to fall in love with the right man?"

Her mother's voice was soft and low as she soothed Alli's back with a gentle massage. "I think, Alli, the answer may be . . . by *not* trusting yourself to fall in love with the right man, but trusting God instead."

"But that's just it!" Alli clutched her mother's arms to hold her at bay. "I *did* pray about Nick—over and over—with Cassie and on my own, but God let me down."

Sorrow etched her mother's face as she caressed Alli's jaw, voice bleeding with empathy. "No, darling, life lets us down, with all its sin and sorrow at the hands of humanity, not a loving God who died to redeem us from it all." She pulled Alli close, cheek pressed to her daughter's as she whispered a Scripture Alli had heard from her lips many a time before. "'In the world ye shall have tribulation,' He told us, 'but be of good cheer for I have overcome the world.'" She lifted Alli's chin, gaze tender. "He's overcome it, Alli, so that we can overcome it too, and you will." Her lips trembled into a sad smile. "As will I—the two of us together."

Alli swiped at her eyes, brows in a bunch. "What do you mean, Mother? Are you talking about your heartbreak over Father? Over losing him?"

———

Yes, darling . . . and over his brother. Caitlyn stared at her daughter, almost grateful she could share Alli's grief in a tangible way, like she had with Cassie a year ago when Jamie had broken her niece's heart and her trust. Her eyes drifted closed. *Just like Logan had broken mine.* A shiver skittered her spine. *And now he's done it again . . .*

"I'm sorry, Andrew, but the truth is Logan and I have decided to court . . ."

The shock in Andrew's eyes earlier tonight had calcified. "The truth? Really, Cait—and you have no qualms about marrying a man who doesn't have a clue what that is?"

The truth. The one thing she craved more than anything to shore up her trust in Logan McClare . . . and the one thing he couldn't seem to give.

"Open your eyes, Cait," Andrew had whispered. "Jamie Mac-Kenna is Logan's son."

She hadn't moved . . . breathed . . . blinked for several heart-beats, and then with a ragged rush of air, she'd listed to the side, hand to her eyes to hide a new tide of tears. A fresh wound over Logan's betrayal those many years ago. *In the flesh.* A betrayal all the more grievous given his sworn defense no intimacies had been involved.

"It was just an innocent flirtation, Cait, I swear," he'd told her at the time, "a minor indiscretion and nothing more."

No, not innocent, Logan—a deep-seated character flaw that will always stand in our way.

"Mother? Please—tell me what's wrong."

Caitlyn's eyes snapped open, Allison's frantic words shaking her from her painful reverie. Love compelled her to smile despite the excruciating ache in her heart and the tears in her eyes. "Nothing, darling, truly, that God can't overcome if we let Him." Desperate to hide her pain and deflect her daughter's concern, Caitlyn fluffed the pillows and lay back, drawing Allison to rest her head on her chest. "You can do this with His help, my love," she whispered, her voice strong and sure as she stroked her daughter's hair, her words shoring up her own spirit as well. "You can reap blessing from this betrayal of the heart and be set free at the same time."

"How?" Allison's voice quivered, frail and scared like when she'd dream of monsters in the attic as a little girl. "I love him, Mother, but I worry that my love will harden into bitterness and hate and fear before I can be set free."

Caitlyn's eyes blurred, the muscles in her throat constricting at the harsh reality of her daughter's statement. She now battled her own shock and bitterness over Logan's betrayal in lying about his son, and possibly Jamie's as well, denying her a truth she had every right to know, as did the family. Body numb, her mind still reeled from his deception. A deception that had slashed not only her heart, but any trust she might have developed for Logan despite the deep love that she bore, bleeding scarlet though it be. Eyes drifting closed, she knew that very love could harden and imprison her as well, and fighting a painful shudder, she held her daughter close, her whisper strong for all their frailty of heart. "'I hold that love, where present, cannot possibly be content with remaining always the same.'"

Allison peered up. "I don't understand, Mother—what does that mean?"

Caitlyn drew in a deep breath. "The words of Teresa of Avila, darling, a very wise woman with a true passion for God. It means, Allison, that true love—the unconditional kind God has called each of us to through His Son—must flourish. Whether it is met with joy or pain, it must grow and ripen into *His* love, the only kind of love that will ever satisfy." Her eyes lapsed into a faraway stare, fully aware that her love for Logan—her attraction to this man who haunted her soul—must transcend her own hurts and desires to achieve God's. A wispy sigh trailed from her lips. "The only kind of love that will change us for the better. Which means, darling girl," she palmed Alli's face with a tender smile, "that even this—a heartbreak so agonizing that it has stolen all peace and joy from your soul—God can use for your good . . . and Nick's."

Allison blinked, eyes glossy as she stared at her mother, echoing back to Caitlyn the very words she'd spoken to her children so many times. "'And we know that all things work together for good to them that love God . . .'"

Caitlyn swallowed hard, water slipping from her eyes. "Precisely."

Allison shook her head, her body shivering with the motion.

"I don't know, Mother, I have no idea how God can bring good from something so painful."

"No, but I do. Because I've done it before and I will do it again, only this time we'll do it together." Caitlyn sat up against the headboard, prompting Allison to follow. She looped an arm to her daughter's waist, tugging her close. "We're going to use this very love that has wounded us so deeply to heal our hearts and those of the men over whom we grieve. And it all begins with one of God's most powerful precepts—'to pray for them which despitefully use you.' We'll pray for God to bless them, heal them, and bring them to Him. Then we'll pray for God's grace and strength to forgive and love them as He does—unconditionally—expecting nothing in return except to see the touch of God in their lives."

"We?" Allison took her mother's hand in hers, brows tented in concern. "I don't understand, Mother—why would you need to forgive Daddy? He didn't mean to die."

Caitlyn felt the chill of a single tear as it slithered her cheek, bleeding from her eye like her joy was bleeding from her heart. "No, not Daddy." She squeezed her daughter's hand, her smile bittersweet at best. "His brother," she whispered. "Your uncle Logan."

Nick paid the carriage driver double fare, scarcely aware of the man's effusive thanks. His gaze lifted to the stone mansion before him—a house as cold and deceptive as the woman who resided within, the fiancée he'd deserted after she sold her soul to the devil.

"You're crazy," DeLuca had railed. "They'll gun you down before we even pull the trigger."

Not if I pull first. Nick's jaw compressed as he slowly mounted the steps to the carved wooden door, its arched entryway a focal point for the columned veranda where he'd once proposed to Darla Montesino. The rage carefully hidden for the last year pumped anew for the woman who'd made him bleed with her betrayal. He tugged at the collar of his camelhair coat, palm casually sliding his chest to feel the holstered Smith & Wesson. Well, now it was her turn to bleed—along with Lucifer's second. The family friend Nick had known nothing about.

Aiden Maloney.

Acid gurgled in Nick's gut along with two boxes of animal crackers that had no effect whatsoever on the hate that churned inside. Finger pressed to the brass doorbell, he waited, sweat slicking his hands while he adjusted the sleeves of the sack suit beneath his coat, where a Remington 1866 Derringer was also stowed, ready to extract revenge. The seconds ticked by like eons while memories flashed in a blur—Mom and Pop chatting with customers during happier days while Nick stacked the shelves with his buddies, the promise of penny candy watering their mouths. Or the twinkle in pretty Emmaline Heimann's eye as she worked with Mom behind the counter, her shy looks always directed his way. Weekends spent at his uncle's Edgewater estate, swimming, canoeing, building sand castles on the beach. Wonderful memories, all snuffed out by a fire and a Colt .45. Nick's eyes burned with vindication long overdue as the door opened wide, the woman he'd loved welcoming him home with open arms.

"Darling!" Darla shot into his embrace without a moment's hesitation, the scent of lilac water hitting him hard. Her body molded to his in that intimate way that had once roused his senses, quickened his pulse, satin-clad arms encircling his waist. Lifting on tiptoe, she brushed her mouth against his. "Oh, I've missed you so much—where on earth have you been? I've been a bundle of nerves since you called."

Jaw stiff, Nick carefully pried her arms from his waist and prodded her into the marble foyer with a none-too-gentle push. "Let's take this inside, shall we, Miss Montesino?"

She whirled around as Nick closed the door, a vision in lace and lavender satin, her honeyed hair glinting from the crystal chandelier overhead. Hurt furrowed her brow. "I don't understand—why are *you* angry? I'm the one you deserted for over a year."

"Don't play innocent, Darla." His tone was gruff as he scanned past the dimly lit library up the curved staircase to the darkened landing above, the house conspicuously empty. He took in the warm glow of the parlour where a fire crackled in the hearth, then seared her with a hard look. "You know exactly why I left, but what you don't know is why I came back."

"To marry me, I hope," she said with a strained smile. Preceding him into the parlour, she rubbed her arms as if she were cold.

To marry you? No, Miss Montesino, to bury you—and Aiden Maloney.

Ignoring her comment, he slipped off his overcoat and tossed it on a chair as he entered the room where he'd once indulged in chess with her father and cribbage with her mother. A tic flickered in his cheek. *And* courted their debutante daughter. He straightened the sleeves of his jacket, the weight of the derringer as heavy as his heart over the pain he would cause her parents, two people he'd respected and admired. Jaw stiff, he made his way to the candlestick telephone atop the cherrywood desk. He picked the receiver up and held it out. "Call Aiden Maloney."

"B-but . . . I don't understand."

"*Now*, Darla." The harsh tenor of his tone caused a lump to duck in her throat as she slowly made her way to where he stood, phone in hand.

Fingers trembling, she took the receiver and attempted to dial, fumbling the numbers several times before she got it right. Tears welled in her eyes while they waited for someone to answer, her gaze pleading with his. "He made me do it, darling, I swear—"

"I know." He steeled his resolve when tears trailed her cheeks.

She jolted at the sound of a voice on the line, her own fractured and frail. "Yes, M-miss Darla Montesino c-calling for Mr. Maloney, please."

A shiver traveled her body as she lifted her gaze. "I loved you, I swear," she whispered.

"Yeah." His lips clamped in a flat line. "Just not as much as an old family friend."

"Darla?" Maloney's voice came through loud and clear. "Everything go as planned?"

"Not exactly, Uncle Aiden," she said with a crack in her voice. "He wants t-to t-talk to you."

Nick snatched the phone, voice curt. "Hello, Aiden, missing any gorillas from your zoo?"

"As a matter of fact, I am—maybe you can tell me where they are?"

"Six feet under, Maloney, right where you're going to be when I'm through with you."

A malevolent laugh iced Nick's skin. "I think you have it backwards, *Mr. Barone*—you're the one in grave danger, pardon the pun, who will pay dearly."

"I've already 'paid dearly,' you bucket of slime. First with the fire at my parents' store and then with my uncle—another 'favorite employee' if I'm not mistaken."

"Ah, yes, my trusty lawyer, who turned my deepest secrets over to you. Not a smart thing to do, now was it?"

"Not when it earned him a bullet in the head, compliments of Aiden Maloney."

The laughter on the other end of the line turned Nick's stomach. "Indeed it did, and I would have gladly pulled the trigger myself had I not henchmen for that very mundane task." His sinister tone became amused. "But at least it was my money that put him in the ground."

"And my parents?" Nick's teeth clenched so tight, he could have ground them to dust. "Who did your dirty work there, Maloney?"

Evil incarnate crackled over the line. "Ah, yes, now *that* was my handiwork, I'm happy to say—a pipe bomb hand-delivered to educate your father that nobody defies Aiden Maloney."

Blood gorged Nick's face. "I'll see you strung up for this, you worthless sack of dung."

"Not before you, I'm afraid. If I'm not mistaken, two of my 'gorillas,' as you so rudely call them, should be waiting for you now."

Nick whirled around, sleet slithering through his veins at the sight of two of Maloney's henchmen at the door.

"Good night, Nick—or perhaps I should say . . . goodbye?"

The receiver clicked before it went dead, paralyzing Nick to the spot. His blood froze at the cock of a gun. One of Maloney's thugs sauntered over while the other fixed him with a slit-eyed stare behind the barrel of a Luger pistol. "Hands up, mister, nice and slow."

Nick did as he said, gut clenched when the one hoodlum frisked him and lifted his Smith & Wesson, cracking it against his head so hard, Darla screamed. Nick's vision blurred while the lowlife tucked the gun into the belt of his trousers. "Not real smart, mister," he said with a wicked laugh. The goon resumed frisking Nick, bypassing his wrists with a quick slide along the outside of his arms to pat down his legs. "He's clean, Roy."

Darla stood by the fire, arms tucked to her waist and face bleached white. "Uncle Aiden p-promised you wouldn't k-kill him," she whispered. "Just make sure he wouldn't talk."

Blinking to clear his vision, Nick kneaded his jaw, now sticky with blood.

Roy grinned. "Yes, ma'am—we'll make good and sure, won't we, Neil?" He pulled a length of rope from inside his jacket and tossed it to his partner. "Truss 'em up tight—don't want him giving us any trouble afore we teach him a lesson, eh?"

Neil snatched the rope and turned, and in one violent thud of his heart, Nick unleashed a frontal kick to the man's groin that doubled him over. Body-slamming him to the carpet, he jerked his gun from Neil's trousers and rolled to fire at Roy, winging his shoulder. A blood-curdling howl echoed in the foyer along with the clatter of Roy's gun as it skittered across the marble floor. Nick flinched at movement out of the corner of his eye, and pain seared him when Neil's foot bludgeoned his arm. Nick's gun careened against the wall with a loud crack. Deflecting a second kick, he yanked Neil's shoe, slamming him hard on his back. He jerked the derringer from the sleeve of his coat and aimed it at Neil's head. "Say your prayers, lowlife," he muttered, rising to his feet.

Click.

His heart seized at the cock of Roy's gun. A blast of fire scorched through him, and his derringer dropped to the floor when he slumped to his knees, a metallic smell filling his nostrils. His groan gurgled as he collapsed in a pool of blood. *Allison, forgive me, please . . .*

And the last image he saw was her face, before everything faded to black.

28

It had been a long, long time since Logan had felt this way—like a boy in college again, heart racing over the prospect of seeing his best girl. A grin spanned his face as he eased his Mercedes Phaeton up to the curb in front of Cait's house. *My girl*—Caitlyn McClare! Turning the engine off, he hopped out of the car whistling a tune and bounded up the steps two at a time. Sweet heavens, how he'd missed her in the week he'd been gone. He grunted as he rang the bell, his smile compressing a degree. Week? Try his whole sorry life. But . . . that was about to change, and the very thought curled his lips once again.

"Top of the evening to you, Hadley," he said when the butler opened the door, striding into the foyer like he lived there himself. The very notion caused him to grin all over again, a perpetual state, apparently, since Cait had agreed they could court. Handing his former butler his fedora, he shuffled out of his overcoat and draped it over Hadley's arm, cuffing the man's shoulder with affection. "Rosie treating you all right these days, I hope?"

A faint smile shadowed Hadley's mouth as he carefully hung Logan's coat and hat on the brass coatrack. "Most assuredly, sir. You might say the woman has had a change of heart."

"So . . . ," Logan asked with a broad grin, "she actually has one?"

A twinkle lit Hadley's eyes, barren of the umpteen eyeglasses Cait had purchased for the man. "It appears to be a well-kept secret, sir."

Logan laughed, palming a hand to his hair. "Well, she's certainly kept it from me." He squinted in the foyer, brow furrowing when he didn't see Cait. "Mrs. McClare home, I hope?"

"Yes, sir. She's resting at the moment, but she asked me to let her know when you arrived and to inquire if you've eaten?"

Resting? Logan glanced at his watch, a wrinkle wedging his nose. *At eight o'clock in the evening?* "Yes, Hadley, I had a bite at the hotel, thank you." He cocked his head. "There's nothing wrong as far as you know, is there? Mrs. McClare's not ill or anything?"

"Oh no, sir, not at all." With a nominal glance up the stairs, Hadley leaned forward a hair, the barest of smiles lining his weathered lips. "Although Miss Cait did mention she'd been having trouble sleeping this week, a comment coinciding with your absence, I believe, sir."

The grin returned full force. "Has she now?" he said, gaze flicking to the landing, where the ring of cue balls and laughter indicated Blake, Jamie, and Bram were battling as usual. He slapped Hadley on the shoulder again. "Thanks, Hadley—that's news I rather enjoy hearing."

"Yes, sir," the butler said with a secret smile. "I thought that might be a welcome report. Can I get you anything, Mr. Logan—coffee, tea?"

"No thank you, Hadley, just the lady of the house, if you will."

"Right away, sir," he said with short bow, shoulders erect as he ascended the stairs.

Entering the parlour, Logan rubbed his hands. His smile expanded at the sight of Cassie and Alli playing chess while Maddie drew at the cribbage table with the new Crayola crayons Logan had bought for her birthday. "So, who's winning?" he asked the two older girls, pretty sure it wasn't Alli, given the scowl on her face.

"Uncle Logan!" Maddie launched off her chair, squealing with delight when he swooped her up in the air and whirled her around. "We missed you!" she shouted, squeezing his neck.

"Did you, now?" He gobble-kissed her neck. "And how about your mother—did she miss me too?"

"I think so," Maddie said with a giggle. Her little nose scrunched as if she smelled something bad. "Although she's been crabby this week."

Logan laughed. "Good to know—I'll watch my step."

"Madelyn McClare!" Cassie jumped up to give Logan a hug. "Aunt Cait doesn't have a crabby bone in her body." She planted a kiss on his cheek. "She just wasn't herself, that's all, a little quieter than usual. But I suspect that'll change now that you're home, Uncle Logan."

Home. "One can only hope," he said with a chuck of Cassie's chin. He reached inside his jacket to produce a box of Cracker Jack that he tossed in the air, giving Maddie a wink. "Look what I found in L.A., young lady, but you'll have to share them with your cousin and sister."

"Gee whiz, Uncle Logan, that's swell!" Maddie tore into the treat. "I'll save some for Mama too, 'cause she ate half the box last time. Maybe then she won't be so crabby."

"Welcome back, Uncle Logan." Alli rose to give him a hug, her tone almost melancholy.

His breath hitched at the lack of sparkle in her eyes, prompting him to tease her gloom away. "Speaking of crabby—you aren't letting this Texas cowgirl whip you at chess again, are you? Where's your competitive streak?"

Alli sighed, looking up through doleful eyes that pierced Logan's heart. "I'm afraid it left when you did."

His eyes softened as he gently kneaded her shoulder. "You'll get it back, Al, I promise."

"I sure hope so," Cassie said with a smirk, obviously attempting to lift her cousin's spirits as well. "It's like playing pool with Jamie—no challenge at all."

Logan grinned. "You need to show that boy some mercy sometimes, Cass, and throw him a bone. You know, just so he feels like a man."

"Sorry, no ground given before the vows are exchanged, Uncle Logan—the boy's hard enough to handle now, this close to the wedding." Cassie plopped back into her seat, eyeing the board with a slant of her lips. "Can't imagine how cocky he'd be if I let him beat me at pool."

"Come on, Cass, have a heart," Logan said with a tweak of her neck. "Throw him a game of pinochle at least. I hate to see a grown man weep."

"Awk, read 'em and weep, read 'em and weep . . ."

"Logan McClare—are you discussing poker with my children again?"

He spun around so fast, Maddie giggled. "Cait!" Heat blasted his cheeks as a boyish grin stole across his lips. "No, ma'am—God's truth."

At his comment, the tease faded from her eyes, and his heart stuttered. Her gaze shifted to her daughter. "Maddie darling, it's almost bedtime, but I think Rosie has milk and cookies in the kitchen before you head up."

"Whoopee!" Cracker Jack in hand, Maddie darted out as soon as Logan set her down.

He grinned at Cait. "Don't suppose I can compete with that," he said on his way to the door, face softening as he gave her a tender look. His voice faded to a whisper for her ears alone. "Except hopefully with you . . ."

His breath stalled when she avoided his eyes, quickly turning toward the foyer. "Do you mind if we speak privately in the study?" she said quietly, face angled in profile.

"No, not at all." He followed her into the study, pulse jumping when she stepped aside to close the door and lean against it. He turned. "Cait . . . is everything all right?"

She appeared stiff, palms to the wood as if she needed its strength to hold her up. Her eyes focused on the paisley carpet at her feet. "No, Logan, it's not."

"What's wrong?" He took a hard stride toward her before her head shot up, the warning in her eyes fusing him to the spot.

"Not another step," she whispered, warding him off with a shaky palm. "Please."

His blood chilled. "Cait—tell me what's wrong. Why are you acting like this?"

He saw her chin tremble as tears welled, and he took another step forward.

"If you come any closer, Logan, I will ask you to leave."

He swallowed, heart pounding like a jackhammer. "Cait, I . . . I don't understand. Before I left, you kissed me—you led me to believe you love me as much as I love you and you said we could court. Was that all a lie?"

She shook her head, voice hoarse while rivulets of water trickled her cheeks. "No."

"Then why are you acting like this?" He leaned in, voice gruff and pulse erratic.

Her fingers trembled as she grappled to retrieve a handkerchief from the sleeve of her blouse. "Because I've had a change of heart," she said quietly, avoiding his gaze while she dabbed at the moisture that glistened her face. "About courting."

She may as well have slapped him—the effect was no less startling. "You can't be serious," he whispered. "I love you, Cait, with every breath in me, and I want to marry you more than I want anything in this world, and you're saying no? You're denying the love between us?"

A muscle shifted in her throat as she stared at the carpet. "I'm not denying the love, Logan . . ." Her voice broke before her watery gaze rose to meet his. "I'm denying the marriage."

He stared, heart racing at a hazardous rate. "For the sake of all that's holy—*why*?"

Her chin lifted as she blinked several times, voice frail. "Because I don't trust you."

A harsh word hissed from his lips before he could stop it, and he spun around, fingers taut as they gouged at the back of his neck. Head bowed, he forced himself to calm down with a kneading press at the bridge of his nose, chest pumping with ragged breaths. Reining his temper in, he turned to face her again, facial muscles stiff with a semblance of composure. "All right, Cait." He exhaled a heavy blast of air and bowed his head, hip slacked and hands moored loosely on his thighs. "I have kept the bonds of friendship for well over a year now since my awful blunder in Napa, and as God is my witness, I have not touched another woman since that night. I attend church with you and your family every single week, and my faith in God has been tried and tested until—like you—it's become a critical part of my life. I love your children like my own—they have my blood in their veins—and I all but worship their mother." He expelled another heavy breath, a nerve flickering in his temple while he seared her with a heated gaze. "So tell me please, Cait, if you will—what more can I possibly do to convince you that you can trust me?"

"Oh, Logan," she whispered, her body almost listing against the door as she clutched folded arms to her waist. "You could have told me the truth." More moisture spilled from her eyes as a trembling hand quivered to her mouth. "You could have told me Jamie was your son."

Paralysis claimed every muscle in his body as he stared, all blood siphoning from his face. "What?" His eyelids sank closed with the weight of his guilt, voice barely audible as he lowered his head, hand to his eyes. "Who told you?"

"Andrew—after I told him you and I were planning to court."

Fury snapped his head up. *So help me, I'll kill him . . .*

"He recognized Jamie's mother when he came to your office one day," she continued in a nasal drone, "claims you treated him abominably—"

"For decency's sake, Cait, the man is slime." He paced to the hearth, dread crawling within while his hope incinerated before his eyes, as dark and cold as the ashes beneath the flue.

"He's a brilliant attorney, Logan." The hint of defense in her tone infuriated him further. "He put two and two together."

He slammed a fist on the mantel, rattling the Venetian vase he'd given her for Christmas. "Blast it, Cait, he's nothing more than a toadying snoop, desperate to steal you away."

"No, Logan, he simply *cares* about me," she said with a firmer tone than before, as if defying another derogatory word. "Not unlike you with Alli and Nick Barone, I suppose."

Stomach sick, he shielded his eyes with a splayed hand, massaging his temples with forefinger and thumb. "Cait," he whispered, his voice a hoarse croak before his sorrowful gaze rose to meet hers. "I swear—I was going to tell you soon. Before Cassie and Jamie's wedding."

More tears sluiced down her cheek, sinking into the crevice of the shaky fingers at her mouth. "And how am I supposed to believe that? You lied about your 'minor indiscretion' years ago, an 'innocent flirtation' you called it, leading me to believe the most sacred of intimacies never took place." Her body shuddered as her head bowed in a near-silent sob, hand twitching when it slid to cover her eyes. "And then to harbor that same sin in silence all these years, denying your own flesh and blood for the sake of a lie—"

A painful heat scalded his neck. "No—I did *not* deny Jamie, I swear! I sent a monthly stipend until his mother married, even though I never believed he was mine."

Her eyes laid him bare with the depth of their sorrow. "And yet another lie," she said in a quiet voice laced with sadness. "You forget I know you, Logan—the shrewd businessman, the definitive lawyer—you would have *never* paid a cent if you truly believed Jamie wasn't yours."

The truth of her statement stabbed at his very core, where a wellspring of guilt and shame lay buried for far too many years. He hung his head, moisture stinging his nose, voice barely a whisper. "I was nothing more than a boy, Cait, a cocky kid too full of his own self-importance and lust to do the right thing and too shallow of faith to even want to."

She nodded, swiping at her eyes. "I know . . ." Her words trailed off.

"I've made amends with Jamie and we are well on our way to the father/son relationship I've craved since I fully realized he was my son at the age of twelve. He's forgiven me, Cait, and please know that both of us had our reasons for secrecy." He took a step forward, his agony over losing Cait's trust embedded deep in the furrowed ridge of his brow. "But I need you to forgive me too," he said, a plea bleeding into his tone. "Because I'm no longer that man."

"I know that too." Her words, as soft spoken as a thought, instilled a flicker of hope that halted the breath in his lungs. Her smile was sad. "And because of God, Logan—I do forgive you."

"Oh, Cait . . ." The muscles in his throat convulsed as he started forward.

Her raised palm halted him as effectively as the wall she seemed to have erected around her heart. "But I cannot marry you."

Her statement stunned like a blow, rendering him motionless for several shallow breaths before a horrendous wave of panic hit so hard, he felt like he was falling from the sky.

"Please forgive me," she whispered. "I know this is a shock . . ."

Shock? He stared, seeing nothing but the demise of his dreams. *No, Cait, this is the extinction of every hope, every breath I've taken for the last year . . .*

"Please know that I will always be your friend, Logan," she said quietly, "because I love you deeply, I do. But love like that must be gilded with trust—and an unwavering faith in God—in order to have the kind of marriage I hope to have." She paused, desolate eyes seeking his while she absently wrung the handkerchief in her hand. "Do you . . . do you understand?"

He shook his head, voice as listless as his gaze as it lagged into a cold stare across a paisley rug he barely saw. "I understand that you are a hard taskmaster, Cait, one whose trust I can never satisfy no matter what I do." His eyes rose to meet hers, an edge of anger creeping into his voice. "I guess I should be grateful it's only my heart that's captive and not my soul, lest I be a man lost forever."

"Oh, Logan—" She took a step in.

"Is that it then, Cait?" he said, cutting her off. "Your final word?" He rose to his full height with shoulders square, his shock giving way to an expanse of anger needed to walk away with his pride intact. "Marriage will not be an option—ever?"

"I . . . don't know," she whispered, brows puckered in pain, "but . . . certainly not in the foreseeable future."

A muscle jerked in his cheek. "I see." He adjusted his sleeves out of nervous habit, jaw stiff as he made his way to the door. "Well, you'll forgive me, Mrs. McClare if, in the 'foreseeable future,' I stay away to lick my wounds from a distance."

"Logan, please—"

He towered over her at the door, anger fairly shimmering off his body. "Please what, Cait? Smile and go on as before as if my heart hasn't been ripped out? Laugh and talk and dine with you and your family as if my hopes haven't just been crushed? Give you a lifeless peck on the cheek each time I leave when all I really want to do is make love to you night after night in a bed we share as man and wife?"

A flush swallowed her whole.

"No, thanks, Mrs. McClare," he said, bypassing her to fist the knob of the door. "You may have the power in dictating friendship over marriage, but I reserve the right to adapt in the only way I know how. Please tell the children I'll be tied up until the wedding, working on a difficult case, but I'll pick them up for dinner each Wednesday wherever they want to go." He opened the door, not even sparing her a glance. "Good night, Cait."

Cait's heart shot to her throat, cutting off all air when she realized just how much she'd wounded this man that she loved. Panic clawed in her chest at the painful thought of losing his friendship, his love . . . "Logan—wait!" She clutched his arm before he could leave, her words fractured by broken heaves. "Don't do this, please! My children need you here and I . . . I n-need you too . . . in m-my life . . . as m-my friend."

A nerve flickered in his cheek as he bowed his head, eyelids closed and jaw tight. "And I need time to regroup, Cait . . . and get over my anger."

Her sob forced him to look up while grief trailed her cheeks with tears. Listing against the door, her body quaked from the anguish searing her soul, her every syllable trembling at the prospect of losing this soul mate and friend. "God help me, Logan," she whispered, "but I'd b-be so very lost w-without you . . ."

His eyelids shuttered closed and in two ragged beats of her pulse, she heard his weary expulsion of air. "Blast you, Cait," he muttered, and when he turned to face her, she shot into his arms, clinging as if her very life depended upon the safety of his hold. Her body shuddered against his and as natural as breathing, his arms swallowed her in a crushing embrace, head tucked to hers as he eased the door closed. "Shhh . . . it's okay, Cait—I'm not going anywhere," he whispered, stroking her hair. His gentle touch and familiar scent calmed her body, eased her pain like the laudanum Rosie kept on the top shelf of the pantry.

With a gentle kiss to her hair, he led her over to the sofa and sat down, bundling her close while she wept against his chest. Her heaves finally faded into frail whimpers as he gently kneaded the nape of her neck.

Oh, Logan, I do love you and maybe someday . . . With a watery sniff, she pulled away to dab at her nose, her handkerchief as limp and soggy as she. The faintest of shivers traveled her body as she peeked up to meet his eyes, ashamed over her outburst of emotion . . . and ashamed just how much she needed him so. "Please forgive me for hurting you, Logan, because heaven knows that's the last thing I want to do to someone I love. And I do love you, you know, far more than I should." Her gaze was tender as she lifted a shaky hand to caress his jaw, her words quivering as much as the water that now welled in her eyes. "And I *need* you," she whispered, her voice frail and low, "far, *far* more than I should. I need your presence in this family and in this house. I need your affection, your wisdom, your strength . . ." Her voice faded to near nothingness as she studied his handsome face. "And above all, I need your friendship," she finished quietly, heart aching at the wounded love she saw in his eyes. She reached for his hand to entwine it with hers, a plea in her tone and an urgency in the press of her fingers. "Will you forgive me for hurting you, Logan? For dashing your hopes? And will you . . . somehow—" she swallowed hard, the fear of losing him thickening her throat, quivering her stomach—"find it in your heart to still be my friend?"

Friend. The very thought slammed so hard, he was tempted to break down and cry right along with her. *Not courting, not engaged, not married.* He exhaled slowly, most of his anger finally siphoning out on a surrendering sigh. *Friends and only friends.* The unwavering rock of friendship in every storm of her life. Like now—when fear had her in its grip, too paralyzed to proceed into a marriage that was always meant to be. And all because of her fear of betrayal. His heart constricted for surely the hundredth time over the damage he'd done to this woman he loved. *God, forgive me . . .*

And that's when it hit him. Caitlyn McClare was a strong and beautiful woman, undaunted and unafraid in most areas of her life—with her children, with the Vigilance Committee, with her faith. But when it came to him, she appeared to be that same tremulous and wide-eyed little girl he'd fallen in love with, starry-eyed at times, terrorized at others. And although he'd managed to put some of the stars back in her eyes over the last year, there loomed a fear so large—fear of his betrayal once again—that he realized she couldn't see past it to the future he was certain they were meant to have.

"All right, Cait," he whispered, his anger suddenly nowhere in sight. "Friends it is."

She pulled away, face swollen and mottled with tears, and yet still the most beautiful woman he'd ever seen. "You'll stay, then?" Hope flickered in her red-rimmed eyes like it was beginning to flicker in his soul. "You won't make me suffer by staying away?"

He took the crumpled handkerchief from her hand and tenderly wiped the remains of her tears. "No, Mrs. McClare, but be warned—I *will* make you suffer in a game of cribbage, where I vow to methodically grind you into dust."

She lunged into his arms again, clutching so hard, a silent groan lodged in his throat. "Oh, Logan, thank you so much! You're the dearest friend I have, and I never meant to hurt you." She stroked his jaw. "I love you," she said with a gentle smile, "and I'll make it up to you."

Oh, you bet. His lips took a slant. *But not on my timetable, apparently.* He rose and tugged on his coat, offering his hand to help her up. "Good. And you can start right now by letting me teach you how to play poker."

She balked, heels digging into the carpet as he attempted to usher her out. "Oh, no you don't—I abhor gambling and you know it."

A grin surfaced on his lips as he all but dragged her along. "I do, but seems to me this friendship has just shifted to my terms, wouldn't you say?" He latched a firm hand over her arm as he led her to the door. "Which means you're gambling already, Mrs. Mc-

Clare, but just to put your mind at ease—we'll play with Cracker Jacks instead of with money."

She halted midway, eyes flaring with interest. "Cracker Jacks, you say?"

He patted the left side of his vest. "Yes, ma'am—the very box intended for the woman I had hoped to marry, but since she's nowhere around, *you* will have to earn it."

Her eyes narrowed, the barest touch of tease in her tone. "You're taking advantage of this friendship, Logan McClare."

"You bet I am—get used to it." He turned the knob, his grin stretching as wide as the door as he prodded her through, deciding that maybe his hopes to marry Cait had not been obliterated after all, only stalled by a brick wall as stubborn as the woman herself. A wall that friendship and time and careful planning could certainly bring crashing down if he played his cards just right. He issued a silent grunt. And she could bet her bottom dollar the gamble wouldn't be for popcorn and peanuts this time. He steered her into the parlour, his resolve as firm as his grip. *Nope—it will be for your heart and your hand, Mrs. McClare,* he thought with a tight smile. *And winner takes all.*

29

"Alli, can I open just one present—please, please?" Maddie glanced up as she lay on her tummy beneath the ceiling-high Christmas tree in the parlour. Stubby legs wagged in the air while the twinkle of tinsel and colored tree lights sparkled as much as her eyes.

Alli gave her a sideways squint as she arranged the nativity scene amidst a mountain of presents, reaching to tweak her sister's neck. "Madeline Marie McClare," she said with mock horror, "Christmas is still a week away, you little minx. Of course not."

"But I'll die if I have to wait that long," Maddie groaned.

"You better not, you little stinker. Can't open my presents and yours too." Alli pounced and tickled unmercifully, unleashing a peal of little-girl giggles. "You'll just have to be patient."

"And this from the woman shaking every package under the tree this afternoon," Cassie called from the game table where she and Jamie were playing pinochle with Bram and Blake.

"Not to mention the brat who snuck downstairs at midnight at the age of five to open all the presents, *including* mine." Blake threw down a trick and shot Alli a wink.

"So I'm curious—file a lawsuit, why don't you?"

Bram chuckled. "Sorry, Al—Blake can't handle the workload he's got now."

Jamie tossed a trick down with an evil grin. "What are you talking about, Hughes—Blake can't handle work, period."

"You two are a regular vaudeville act, you know that?" Blake leaned back in his chair, studying his cards with a crooked grin.

"Up with you, Miss Maddie—your bath awaits." Rosie stood at the door, hand extended.

"But I'll miss Meggie coming home," she groaned, lumbering up with a tortured face.

Rosie's mouth edged up, her gaze narrowing on Blake. "At least you won't smell like sour milk sprayed from your nose when your sister arrives."

Blake grinned, offering a shrug of his shoulders as he gave Rosie a wink. "Come on, Rosie, can I help it if I'm so charming I make all the girls laugh?"

"Especially behind your back," Jamie said with a chuckle, tossing a trick down.

"Humph—oughta make *you* give her a bath," the housekeeper said with a mock scowl, snapping her fingers at Maddie who trudged forward with a heavy sigh.

"Gee, Rosie, I'm not sure he knows how." Cassie wrinkled her nose, giving Blake a sniff.

"Great—I'm playing pinochle with a bunch of clowns." Blake shook his head when Rosie actually cracked a smile on her way out the door.

"Yeah, but at least we smell good," Jamie said with a proud lift of his chin.

Laughing, Bram glanced at his watch. "So, when is our girl supposed to be home?"

"Any minute now," Alli muttered, strolling over to the front window to peer out into the dark. Meg's return was one of the few things that actually cheered her up since Nick Barone had disappeared from her life almost three months ago. Of course being surrounded by family at Christmas helped a lot, as did Jamie and Cassie's wedding two days away. And certainly her mother's advice to forgive and pray for the man who'd broken her heart had eased the malaise hovering over her life like a damp fog over the bay. Her gaze wandered into a glossy stare that blurred the street lamp into a surreal glow, reminding her that although she'd forgiven Nick Barone with the help of God, forgetting him was something else altogether.

Oncoming headlamps jolted her attention, and she blinked hard to stem her tears. "They're home!" she shouted, pulse jumping when Uncle Logan's Mercedes eased up to the curb. With a swipe of her eyes, she rushed into the foyer to fling the door wide, bounding down the steps to where Uncle Logan was helping Meg from his car. "Meggie—you're home!"

Glancing up, Meg shot into Alli's arms. "Oh, Alli, I missed you so much!" She pulled away with a worried look in gentle green eyes. "Are you doing okay?" she whispered.

"Better now that you're home." Alli hooked an arm through her sister's and flashed a smile over her shoulder. "I vote we have Cassie hog-tie her so she can't leave us ever again."

"Sounds good to me," Uncle Logan said with a heft of suitcases. "I don't cotton to my nieces being far away. Besides, Frisco is known as the Paris of the west, Megs, so we've got everything they do and more."

"Including a delinquent uncle who persists in teaching bad habits," her mother said easily, looping an arm through Meg's on the other side. Her lips squirmed with tease. "Like poker, for instance."

"News flash, Mrs. McClare . . ." Uncle Logan followed them up the steps, his tone dry. "Poker is a universal game enjoyed all over the world, even in Paris monasteries, no doubt."

Alli giggled and gave Meg an extra squeeze as she and their mother ushered her through the front door. "So, tell me, Megs, was it really as wonderful as your letters say?"

"Oh, Alli—more!" Meg's eyes sparkled as much as the cut-crystal tear drops in the chandelier overhead, her cheeks dewy with a blush that enhanced her soft, peaches-and-cream complexion. "The Rousseaus are so warm and wonderful—just like I'm one of their own, and Lily and I have gotten closer than ever. And, oh my—the sights I've seen!"

Alli bumped Meg's hip with her own, a devious smile tipping her lips. "Mmm . . . any of them tall, dark, and handsome, I hope?"

"Alli!" A pretty shade of pink promptly dusted Meg's full face as she slipped off her wrap, her shy grin displaying glints of gold from wire braces that matched her gold wire-rimmed glasses. She giggled while Uncle Logan hung her cape on the rack by the door, cheeks flaming to rose. "Well . . . maybe one or two," she whispered shyly, "but I think they may like Lily."

"Don't be too sure," Uncle Logan said in a brusque voice, swallowing her up in a hug. "That settles it, Cait." He cinched an arm to Meg's waist, gripping her to his side. "She's not going anywhere I can't keep an eye on her."

"I second that." Bram strode into the foyer ahead of Cassie, Jamie, and Blake, literally snatching Meg from Logan to hoist her up in the air in a joyous spin. He put her back down and stepped back. "Sorry, Bug, we've taken a vote—you're barred from leaving the city ever again."

"Oh, Bram!" Meg launched right back into his arms with tears in her eyes. "You have no idea how much I missed you!"

"Doesn't sound like it," he teased, voice gruff as he pressed a kiss to her hair.

"Hey, what am I—chopped liver?" Uncle Logan tickled Meg's neck, prompting a giggle.

"Perhaps," her mother quipped with a smirk, offering Uncle Logan a patronizing pat on the back. "After all, chopped liver *is* an acquired taste."

He slid her a thin gaze. "And considered a delicacy, I might point out, Mrs. McClare."

Everyone laughed when Caitlyn gave him an uncharacteristic pinch on his cheek. "Point out all you like, Mr. McClare, just don't make any of us eat it."

"Hey, don't hog the French girl," Jamie groused, nudging Bram out of the way to give Meg a hug. "Welcome home, kiddo—now maybe Bram won't be such a grouch."

"Ha! You ain't seen nothing till she leaves again after Christmas." Blake stole her from Jamie to press a kiss to her cheek, arm draped over her shoulder. "Thank God you're home—we need a little sunshine around here. I don't know who's been the bigger stick-in-the-mud—Bram or Alli—but we definitely missed your smile, kiddo."

"I'll say." Cassie gave Meg a tight squeeze. "Jamie and I can certainly attest to that."

"Oh, please, as if you even noticed anyone else is alive." Alli smirked, Meg's return lifting her spirits so much, she actually felt like teasing again. "These two have had their heads so far up in the clouds with the wedding so close, they don't know anyone else is in the room."

"Maybe that's because certain ones in the room have been a wee bit dull lately," Cassie said with a loop of Meg's waist, "but that's about to change with Meg home for the holidays."

"Hear, hear," Bram said with a grin.

"Speaking of the wedding." Her mother scooped Meg's waist, a slight pinch in her brow. "Have you lost some weight, darling? I'm worried your dress for the wedding may need to be altered."

A pretty shade of pink flushed Meg's cheeks as she nibbled on her lip. "Maybe a little, Mother, but only because the Rosseaus keep me quite busy, trekking all over the city. Certainly not enough to alter my dress, I'm sure." Her gaze roamed the foyer, settling on each and every one with a glow of love in her eyes. "Thank you, everyone, for such a wonderful welcome." She inclined her head to peek into the parlour. "But where's Maddie?"

"Upstairs wrestling with Rosie over a bath." Alli chuckled. "And Blake's next."

"Thank God," Uncle Logan said, strolling toward the parlour with a wry grin.

"All right, everyone, let's move the celebration into the parlour, shall we?" Mother's voice rose over the laughter, " Alli, darling, do you mind helping Hadley bring in the coffee and tea while I assist Rosie with Maddie? And, Meggie, we have a special dessert Rosie made just for you, sweetheart, and then you can tell us all about Paris." She kissed Meg's cheek before she made a beeline for the stairs. "We won't be long, so don't start without us, all right?" Her gaze flicked to Uncle Logan, humor sparkling in her eyes. "And I'd appreciate you keeping them busy in a respectable manner, Logan, until Maddie and I come down, if you will."

Uncle Logan rubbed his palms together with a decadent laugh. "You bet, Cait. Ante up!"

"Awk, ante up, ante up!"

"Don't you dare, Logan Beware!" Her mother whirled on the bottom step with a firm jut of her brow, but her lips twitched, indicating the threat of smile. "I do not want my children to gamble, is that clear? It's a vice we could all do without."

"Whatever you say, Cait." Uncle Logan shot her a wayward smile that belied his consent, striding into the parlour like a man who intended to do exactly what he wanted to do.

"May I escort you in, mademoiselle?" Bram extended his arm to Meg.

"*Oui*, monsieur," she said with a giggle.

Alli smiled, the lilting sound of her sister's chuckle buoying her mood. She watched her family file back into the parlour and released a wispy sigh. It had been so long since she'd felt any joy that Meg's homecoming—no matter how brief—was truly a blessing. A family like hers was a buffer against the heartaches of life, she suddenly realized, and moisture swelled in her eyes.

"Thank you, Lord, for the blessing of family," she whispered, her thoughts suddenly straying to a crotchety Italian she had hoped would be one of their own. Nick's absence left a gap so wide there were times she didn't know how she could hold on. Laughter filtered out from the parlour, prompting happier tears. *But I know now.* She turned toward the kitchen, gratitude thick on her lips despite the gaping hole in her heart. Her mother was right—gambling was a vice, especially for someone like her, so unlucky in love. But when it came to the love of family? She pushed through the kitchen door, promptly giving Hadley the soggiest of smiles.

She was the luckiest woman alive.

Signing the final letter with his usual scrawl, Logan handed it back to his young receptionist, his lips crooking into an affectionate smile. Without question, Patience Peabody was appropriately named. The shy granddaughter of one of the senior members of the Board of Supervisors had barely uttered a peep when he'd hired her as a favor two years ago. Today, she handled three senior partners, six associates, and two executive secretaries with nary a complaint. "Thank you, Miss Peabody, for typing these letters in Margaret's absence—excellent job."

"Thank you, Mr. McClare." A haze of pink braised her cheeks as she gave him a timid smile. Her classically pretty features reminded him of a grown-up Meg, which is probably why she evoked such a protective instinct in him. His smile inched into a grin. That and the fact she was totally immune to Blake's blatant efforts to entice her into any kind of relationship.

Letters in hand, she tipped her head in a playful pose he seldom saw, her usually reticent manner giving way to a twinkle in her eye. "So this is it, then," she said with a quick glance at the grandfather clock that registered five o'clock sharp, "the beginning of the weekend when Mr. MacKenna becomes a nephew as well as an employee."

Yes . . . and a son as well as a nephew. "Indeed," he said with a tight smile, shuffling a stack of papers into a manila file folder. "So now if I dock his pay, I answer to my niece."

He grinned at Miss Peabody's husky chuckle, which offered a rare glimpse into a private, young woman who was as professional as she was pretty. *And smart enough to stay away from rogues like Blake.* He released a silent exhale as he turned the folder over to her, his grin taking a wry tilt. *Like I used to be.*

"Goodness, Mr. McClare, I can't imagine how much fun it would be in your family, sir." She clutched the file to her chest with a hint of longing in her eyes. "With such colorful characters like Mr. MacKenna, Mr. McClare, and Mr. Hughes, you all must laugh quite a bit."

"We do." He reached for the family photo on the credenza,

thumb grazing the polished cherrywood frame as he studied it with deep affection. *Except possibly tonight.* He felt an immediate twinge in his chest over the dinner he'd planned at the Palace before the wedding tomorrow. The one where he'd reveal to Cassie's parents—his brother Quinn and his wife—that their daughter was not just marrying one of Logan's employees, but his illegitimate son as well. The forbidden union of two blood cousins, saved only by the fact that Cassie was adopted, without a drop of McClare blood in her veins. He glanced up, holding the picture frame aloft with a proud smile. "Tomorrow we'll have a new picture taken, and for better or worse, Mac will be in it."

"Definitely better," Miss Peabody said with a gentle smile. "Given the work ethic of Mr. MacKenna, Mr. McClare, and Mr. Hughes, I'd say you have a knack for hiring excellent staff."

"Present company front and center, Miss Peabody, I assure you."

The blush returned. "Thank you, sir. Is there anything I can get for you before I go?"

Yes, a bottle of Chivas Regal would be lovely, to steel my nerves. "No thank you—I'll be leaving shortly myself, so you have a good weekend."

"Thank you, sir, you too." Her smile was warm as she quietly closed the door.

"I certainly hope so," he whispered, wheeling around to stare out the window, the picture slack in his hand. Cait certainly hadn't taken the news of Jamie's paternity well, but then she had good reason. Jamie represented a twenty-six-year-old lie in the flesh, a betrayal of her love, and Logan bitterly regretted he hadn't told her sooner. It had been a stupid mistake, a moral error on his part, and a total lack of judgment. But his reluctance had been motivated by fear rather than insight and common sense, something that almost never happened, and he'd give anything if he could just take it back. If he'd learned one thing through all of this, it was that fear distorted wisdom every single time. Fear that she would have never given him a chance. He exhaled a weary sigh. And the same fear that kept her from trusting him ever again. He stared at the picture with Cait on one side of the family and him on the other, and a dull ache thumped in his chest. He had hoped by this time to be standing by her side in all pictures taken, but he knew now that it would be a good, long while before he could ease her toward the altar again. He set the photo back on the credenza, gently grazing her face with his thumb. But he'd do it—if it took every ounce of charm and prayer in his arsenal.

His finger absently glided across the glass of the frame, tracing each face in the picture until he paused on Alli's, heart cramping over the pain Nick Barone had caused. "We'll get you through this, sweetheart," he whispered, vowing to investigate any man in the future who even looked at her cross-eyed. "And so help me, if I ever get my hands on Barone—"

Whoosh! The door flew to the wall, along with Miss Peabody, face flushed and eyes as round as the knob gripped in her white-knuckled hand. "I tried to stop him, sir, truly—"

Logan shot to his feet. "What the . . . ?"

Nick Barone stormed in with his typical tight-lipped scowl, expensive suit rumpled and Italian leather shoes buffed to a shine. He tossed a ruler he'd obviously snapped in half onto Logan's desk, the jagged pieces as sharp as his tone. "What is it with women and sticks, anyway?" he muttered, hurling his Homburg onto one of two leather chairs. Slapping massive hands on Logan's desk, he leaned across with fire in his eyes. "I'd sit back down and get real cozy if I were you, Supervisor, 'cause you and me? We're gonna have a chat."

A tic pulsed in Logan's cheek. "So you're back to finish her off, are you? What—ripping her heart out the first time wasn't enough?" His cool gaze shifted to Miss Peabody with a stiff smile. "Thank you, Miss Peabody. If you'd be kind enough to call security before you go, I'd appreciate it immensely."

"Y-yes, s-sir," she stuttered, palms and back flush to the wood door as if she thought Barone might charge at any moment. "W-would you l-like me to call the p-police too?"

Barone whirled around, causing Miss Peabody to jerk so hard, the poor woman's body rattled along with the door. His glare pinned her in place, obviously cauterizing her to the spot. "I *am* the blasted police," he shouted.

"Yes, Miss Peabody," Logan said with icy calm, "please ask Captain Peel to send two officers over immediately to escort Nick Barone to a cell."

"Freeze!" Barone's command carried the weight of authority, paralyzing the terrified receptionist against the door. He jerked a badge from inside his jacket and practically rammed it at Logan. "Lieutenant Detective Ryan Nicholas Burke, Chicago P.D."

Logan's smile was as steely as the badge beneath his nose. "And just why should I believe you, Barone? Because you flash a tin badge you probably lifted from some cop?"

"It's Bur-kee," he snapped, enunciating both syllables through clenched teeth, "long *e*, you blasted bigwig, and after the bald-faced lie you told Allison, you can bet your sorry tail I have proof." He shoved the badge in his jacket and pulled out a folded letter, flipping it on the desk.

"M-Mr. McClare—do you still need me to call Captain P-Peel?" Miss Peabody hadn't moved a muscle except her lips, body pasted to the door like she was sweating glue.

Logan scanned the letter from the district attorney of Cook County and expelled a heavy breath, almost irritated that Barone was legit. "No, Miss Peabody, it appears our intruder, no matter how obnoxious, has credentials, so no police or security is required, thank you. Have a good weekend, and I'll see you on Monday. And close the door, if you will."

"Yes, sir, good night."

The latch clicked and Logan pitched the letter across the desk to Barone . . . or Burke—or whoever the devil he was—before leaning back in his chair, elbows propped and hands clasped. "It appears you have explaining to do, Lieutenant Burke, as to why you would lie to my niece, me, Captain Peel, and his aunt." He glanced at the clock before he pierced him with a cool gaze. "I have a prior commitment, so I will give you exactly five minutes before I throw you out."

Burke's facial muscles flickered, as if he were reining in a temper Logan knew all too well that he had. Massaging his temple, the detective finally released a weary sigh, an unexpected humility replacing the temper in his eyes. "Tell me, Supervisor," he said quietly, "have you ever kept the truth from someone you love to protect them as well as yourself?"

Logan froze, the query a bull's-eye as surely as if Burke had fired a gun. Drawing in a halting breath, he released it again slowly, the tension in his face relaxing along with it. *Unfortunately, yes*, he thought with keen regret, surprised that he and Burke shared any common ground at all. Giving a slow nod, he appraised the officer with a solemn gaze. "I repeat, Detective Burke—you have five minutes. State your case."

A long, tremulous breath seeped from Nick's mouth along with the rest of the anger he'd carried all the way from the station when Harmon had attempted to lock him up. And all because Logan McClare stuck his nose in where he didn't belong. Sucking in more air, he slowly expelled it again as he eased into one of the cordovan chairs, finally allowing his body to relax for the first time all day. He stared at the Supervisor's granite jaw and cold, slate-gray eyes and wanted to rail at Alli's uncle and call him every foul name in the book. For lying through his teeth about who Nick Barone was when no such person even existed at all. But the truth was, he couldn't. Not after the soul-searching he'd done while he lay in a hospital with a bullet in his chest, mere inches from his heart. Because had he been in Logan's shoes, he would have investigated Nick Barone too, and done everything McClare did and more to protect his niece.

His niece. Nick swallowed hard. *And God willing, my wife.* A connection too strong to continue a battle with Logan based on misconceptions and anger. Bitterness had skewed his perception of both Alli and her uncle from the start, distorting his mind and hardening his heart. But for all his wealth and political influence, Logan McClare was no more like Aiden Maloney than Alli was like Darla Montesino. Nick absently rubbed the side of his chest where the bullet had lodged, right next to an arsenal of bitterness just as hard. A bitterness that had prompted him to condemn both Alli and Logan on the spot. Grief pierced his heart. *Just like Maloney had with my parents and uncle.* He closed his eyes and kneaded the back of his head, where the gash from the butt of Neil's gun still throbbed as much as his guilt.

"You have three minutes left," Logan said in a dispassionate tone, and Nick peered up, hardly able to believe what he was about to do.

"I'm sorry," he said quietly. "I wish I'd looked out for my family half as well as you look out for yours. But the truth is, Supervisor McClare, I did too little, too late, and it made me a very angry man." Inhaling deeply, he sank back in the chair and started at the beginning in a low drone, from the murder of his parents to the robbery and subsequent murder of his uncle, a man who'd been a key cog in the corrupt and merciless hierarchy of the Irish mob.

He talked about his vendetta against Aiden Maloney and a political machine so corrupt that Nick had vowed he would make them pay as an officer of the law. Fueled by revenge, he'd risen in the ranks quickly until he joined forces with the district attorney to bring down as many of the Irish mob as he possibly could. They'd struck pay dirt when his own uncle—Aiden Maloney's attorney—had finally had enough and begun feeding Nick proof of Maloney's extortion. His uncle had meticulously duplicated file after file, one by one, willing to turn state witness against Maloney and other members of the mob. Until they silenced him.

"They murdered your uncle in his own house?" Logan whispered, his shock evident.

Nick nodded. "Gunned him down, right before they tore the place up, apparently looking for missing records they were tipped off about."

Ridges popped in Logan's brow. "By whom?"

Nick's jaw hardened to rock, the roiling of his stomach clear indication he still had some soul-searching to do. "My ex-fiancée, a scheming debutante my uncle introduced me to."

Logan leaned in, expression calcifying along with his tone. "Wait—she wasn't pregnant with your child, was she?"

"What?" Heat swarmed his neck like fire ants swarmed the bodies of dead rats in the sewers and alleys of the Barbary Coast. "What the devil kind of question is that?" he ground out, jerking hard on his ear.

"A legitimate one, considering the real Nick Barone abandoned a pregnant fiancée in New York's Little Italy." Logan's lips went flat. "Right after he robbed her blind."

Nick's jaw dropped. "Pardon me?"

Logan folded his arms on his desk, eyes in a squint. "Tell me, Burke—how the devil did you pick your phony name anyway?"

Nick's eyes narrowed to razor-thin. "DeLuca, the assistant D.A., wanted an ethnic cover, so I used my middle name with an Italian surname I picked from city records."

"And you never bothered to check if anybody owned it or not?" Logan's tone rose several octaves, suggesting Nick was clearly an idiot.

Blood braised Nick's cheeks, his lips as flat as McClare's face was gonna be if he continued this line of questioning. "The-city-records-confirmed-it," he bit out, "no Nick Barone, either in New York *or* Chicago."

Shaking his head, Logan sloped back with a chuckle. "Well, apparently Andrea Nicolo Barone—thief, murderer, and con man on the lam—preferred his middle name to his first."

Nick blinked, staring for several seconds before the faintest of grins tugged at his lips. "So that's who Allison thinks I am—some lowlife who'd abandon his pregnant fiancée?"

"In the flesh," Logan said with a flash of teeth.

It was Nick's turn to shake his head, the grin breaking free. "Well, then heaven help me if she has a stick in her hand when I see her."

Logan rested his head on the back of his chair, his smile fading as he studied Nick through pensive eyes. "What happened then—with the fiancée?"

Fiancée. The very word sucked the humor right out. "Seems she had an old family friend I didn't know about—a stinking sack of dung by the name of Aiden Maloney. Didn't discover she'd double-crossed me until one of my uncle's files disappeared—the one I'd been working on in my study, hidden in a secret compartment of my bookcase." He nodded toward the letter on Logan's desk. "DeLuca is a paranoid type who suspected a leak in both of our departments, so he didn't want the records stored either place. Especially since they required extensive decoding on my part based on a formula from my uncle. So I worked on them one at a time, hiding some beneath the floorboards in my grandmother's attic while DeLuca kept the rest at his place."

Nick sucked in a stabilizing breath and eased back in the chair like Logan, palms limp on the arms of the chair while his eyes trailed into a hard stare. "I thought I loved her," he whispered, the pain of betrayal still raw. "But right after the file disappeared, Maloney's thugs leveled Gram's house with a pipe bomb in the middle of the night, obviously hoping to destroy me and any files I had." A harsh laugh erupted from his lips while his vacant gaze wandered back to that night. "Blew me and the walls of the outhouse clear into the neighbor's yard, where I watched Gram's house go up in smoke." His voice sounded lifeless to his own ears. "Just like any love I thought I had for Darla, leaving me nothing but cold, dirty ashes and a shell of a house that smoldered as much as my hate."

"So you were forced to hide."

Nick peered up, facial muscles taut. "I didn't want to—I wanted to go after Maloney right then and there, but DeLuca was right—we needed time. The few records that had survived at his house were enough to maybe slap Maloney's hand, but not to cinch him up, and basically worthless without my testimony and translation. And it was pretty clear Maloney wanted me dead—the one man who could put him away forever if we could dig up even a shred of evidence linking him to the murders." He exhaled a wavering breath while he gouged the socket of his eye with the pad of his thumb. "So DeLuca wanted me as far away as possible. And since I'd promised an army buddy from San Francisco I'd pay a visit one day, it seemed like a safe bet while he scoured Maloney's district high and low for the one thing that could put him away."

"And did he find it?" Logan peered up with an intensity that told Nick he'd won an ally.

A hard grin curled on Nick's lips as satisfaction surged through his veins. "Oh yeah, got that arrogant son of a viper bragging about the murders in a phone conversation via wiretap, compliments of the D.A., who prewired Darla's parents' phone the night before. Led that scum right down the path to his own personal noose." His smile slanted toward dry. "Right before his thugs pumped me full of lead."

Surprise flickered in Logan's face. "And you survived?"

Nick grinned, rubbing the permanent knot on the back of his head. "I have a hard head, sir, and DeLuca had police swarming the place mere seconds after the first shot was fired."

A genuine smile eased across Logan's face as he stood. "Well, that's good, Lieutenant, because a hard head will come in handy if I agree to let you court my niece." He glanced at the clock before extending his hand. "If you hurry, you'll catch her at the school before she leaves, Nic—" He paused, a wedge between his brows. "I'm afraid this name thing won't be easy, Ryan."

Nick reached across the desk to shake Logan's hand. "I'll just stick with Nick, sir—it's my middle name and easier all around, and heaven knows I've caused you and your family enough problems." He turned to go.

"Uh, one last question, Nick." Head cocked, Logan stared, brows jagging low as he leaned forward with a sniff. "Do I smell animal crackers?"

Heat ringed Nick's collar. "Gastric ulcer," he said with an

awkward grin, "exacerbated, I might add, by you and your niece. They settle my stomach."

Logan nodded slowly, eyes in a squint as he issued a reflective grunt. "I'll have to give it a try. Her mother does the same thing to me."

Nick paused at the door, hand on the knob. "So . . . before I risk getting whacked with a stick, Supervisor, I need to know—do I have your blessing?"

"Hard head, guts, good taste in shoes, and Irish instead of Italian?" Logan slid his hands in his pockets. "Other than being a penniless cop, sounds like a match made in heaven to me."

"Uh, not exactly penniless, sir."

"No?"

Nick exhaled. "Sole heir of my uncle's estate, which is considerable, but I never wanted to touch it because it's tainted money." He peered up, his decision made. "But I think I may have a way to redeem both it and my reputation with Alli, her mother, and Miss Penny."

Logan's smile slid into a grin. "You're a shrewd one, Detective— I like that in a man."

"So I have your blessing?" Nick held his breath, suddenly wanting Logan's approval almost as much as Alli's consent.

The supervisor made him wait while he appeared to mull it over before finally expelling a weary breath. "After all Alli's been through, Nick, I'm sure you'll understand I need time to know you better before I make my decision. But at the moment, Lieutenant, it's not my blessing you need." He strolled around his desk to sit on the edge with a fold of arms, lips flat in a show of sympathy. "After four broken hearts, I wouldn't be surprised if Alli's written off all men."

"Good." Nick's smile was dry. "She won't be needing them

anymore." He opened the door and squinted at Logan, a mock scowl on his face. "And pardon my French, sir, but just when in the devil am I going to know if I have your blessing or not?"

Logan laughed and absently scratched the back of his neck. "When you find a huge crate on your front door, Detective."

"Yeah? Containing what?"

A twinkle lit Logan McClare's eyes for the first time since Nick had known the man. "Animal crackers, Lieutenant," he said with a faint smile, "and I suggest you use them wisely."

30

With a less-than-graceful hop, Alli boarded the California Street cable car, the shiny wood benches that once promised adventure leaving her surprisingly flat. "Thank you for the escort, Mr. Bigley," she called, turning to grip the steel pole. Several questionable men boarded behind her, the strong stench of alcohol almost enough to make her tipsy.

"You're welcome, Miss McClare." The school janitor fidgeted with a battered fedora, brows bunched in concern. "You're sure you don't need me to accompany you home, miss?"

"Absolutely not, Mr. Bigley. This is the only leg of the journey on which I need help, I assure you, especially with sunset still an hour away. And I actually enjoy the solitude to reflect on my day."

Her smile went stale. *Ha! Reflect on your miserable life, you mean.* Hand gripped to the pole, she flailed her reticule in a one-handed goodbye, its black-beaded fringe dancing with an excitement she'd once felt herself before Nick Barone. "Have a good weekend, sir, and my best to your family."

Digging in her pocket, she handed the needed fare to the driver, then made her way to the end of the outside bench, as far as possible from several seedy-looking men eyeing her with interest. She dusted the seat with her hankie and shimmied in with her purse on her lap, back square and eyes ahead, never seeing the faces milling on the street for the one in her head.

Nick "Pain-in-the-Brain" Barone. The man whose image followed her everywhere she went. She blinked to clear the sudden moisture in her eyes, jaw suddenly clenched as tightly as her fingers on the pole as the cable car pulled away. She hadn't heard from him since the night of the attack three months ago, but then she hadn't really expected to after Uncle Logan had divulged what a rat he'd turned out to be. She issued a shaky sigh.

Rats shouldn't be this hard to forget . . .

Eyes sinking closed, she found she was no longer interested in the sights along Montgomery that once fascinated her so. But that was the key problem with rats. Not only did they break your heart, they robbed you of the very essence of life itself—the passion to live it, the spirit to explore it, and the ability to enjoy it.

Her lips took a sad tilt. And the hope that true love would ever happen at all.

She sucked in a deep breath, and a whiff of body odor assailed her along with the idea that perhaps she wasn't meant to marry. Perhaps the Hand of Hope School was to be her husband and focus for the rest of her life. Surprisingly, the idea held appeal. At least she wouldn't have to go through this awful heartbreak again. Opening her eyes, she jutted her chin in resolve, deciding that the good her mother insisted God would bring from this unfortunate incident could well be the independence for which she'd always longed.

"Washington Street!" the grip man called, and Alli jolted to attention, determined to make the most of today's adventure on the cable car. Her eyes scanned up the fifteen stories of the Merchants Exchange Building, a brand-new skyscraper that now reigned as San Francisco's tallest building, stirring Alli's pride over the progression and beauty of her city.

Clack-clack-clack. The cable car groaned to a stop, admitting a number of passengers before it continued to chug along. The whir of the cables suddenly merged with the wheezing of some poor soul who sounded like he'd just sprinted all the way from Los Angeles. Fearful of eye contact with any man on the cable car, Allison peered straight ahead, ignoring a hulk of a person shuffling her way. He sat beside her, and she attempted to inch away without notice, his huffing and puffing worse than a cable car climbing Hyde Street with a cargo of elephants.

"Uh, I think you took a wrong turn, lady," a low voice intoned, its winded quality making it more of a rasp. "High tea is at The Palace."

For a split second she froze, body adhered to the bench like the varnish on the red-painted seat. And then with a gasp of air that literally choked in her throat, she whirled around, the hinges of her jaw sagging more than the cable.

"Out slumming again, I see," Nick Barone huffed, the green tinge of his face a nice holiday complement to the shiny red bench. He put a fist to his chest as if to ward off the rise of his lunch, then fixed her with a glassy-eyed stare that was more of a plea. "Can we get off this infernal thing to talk? I think I'm about to be . . ." He heaved, cheeks puffing with air as if to stop whatever wanted to come up. He swallowed hard, his face a tinge greener than before. "Sick."

She vaulted to her feet and jumped back, both to steer clear of the man and the contents of his stomach, her tongue unglued and ready to fire. "Ohhhhh . . . 'sick' will be the least of your problems, mister, if you think I am going to go anywhere with you!"

"Alli, please," he groaned, lumbering up to grasp her arm, "two minutes is all I need . . ."

She whopped him with her purse, disgusted that the rat even looked good in a green face peppered with stubble. "Two minutes?" she shouted, backing toward the exit. "I'd like to give you two decades, you pinhead—in Alcatraz!" Spinning around, she spotted a police officer strolling the sidewalk and quickly gripped the pole by the step, raising her voice over the clank of the rails. "Next stop, please."

The cable car jerked, and Alli glanced back, satisfied that the lurch of the car had left the rat staggering and slow. When it came to a halt, she hurdled the step in a near leap, making a beeline for the officer a half block away.

"Alli, wait!"

Darting a nervous gaze over her shoulder, she started to run. "Officer, please—I need your help." She panted to a stop in front of the gray uniform and pointed toward Nick, who was striding forward with a clamp of his jaw. A ruddy shade of Mr. Cranky Pants appeared to replace the green he'd worn on the cable car. "That man is attempting to accost me," she sputtered, ducking behind the officer just as Nick approached.

The officer's hand rested on the nightstick attached to his belt. "This young woman claims you are accosting her, sir—is she correct?"

Nick ground to a stop. "No, I'm not accosting her," he snapped, "I'm trying to talk some sense into her, which given our prior experience, might take till kingdom come."

"Prior experience?" The officer fixed Alli with a suspicious stare. "Is this a lovers' spat, ma'am?"

She faltered back with a hand to her chest, her horror evident in the gape of her mouth. "Good heavens, no! I'd rather be bound and gagged than associate with this . . . this . . ."

"Officer of the law," Nick supplied, producing a badge from his coat pocket for the officer to study. His gaze narrowed on her. "And it can be arranged, Miss McClare, trust me."

The officer nodded and returned the police identification. "My apologies, Detective, but do you mind if I ask your business with the lady?"

Nick replaced the badge, eyes locked on Alli. "Yeah, I'm trying to propose to the pigheaded woman, but she won't stop yammering long enough to hear me out."

"Propose?" Alli shrieked. "Ha! Right before you skip town again, I suppose."

The officer took a step back, palms up. "Look, folks, I'm sorry, but unless there's threat of bodily harm here, it's against policy to interfere in domestic disputes."

She glared at Nick. "I assure you, officer, the 'threat' is *very* real."

"Only if she gets ahold of a stick," Nick muttered.

Chin high, she continued undeterred. "Because if this snake-in-the-grass felon thinks—"

"Uh, ma'am, a little respect, if you will," the officer interrupted with a frown. "The detective is an officer of the law—"

"Ha! Law-breaking, is more like it," she said with a fold of her arms. "The man's not even a policeman, for pity's sake, and he probably stole that badge."

Nick huffed out a noisy sigh and shoved a letter beneath the officer's nose.

The officer let loose a low whistle. "The D.A. of Chicago, huh? You've got friends in high places, Detective."

"Yeah, enemies too," he said with a grunt, shoving the letter back into his suit.

Brows crimped in apology, the officer backed off with a tip of his hat. "I'm sorry, miss, but you and Detective Burke will have to hash this out between yourselves."

"His name is *Barone*," she shouted as the officer walked away, volume rising along with her desperation. "And he's obviously impersonating poor Detective Burke, whoever he is."

Nick grunted again. "Poor Detective Burke is right," he said, cinching her arm to lead her in the opposite direction. "And it's Burke, long *e*," he shouted. He blasted out a sigh. "What the devil am I getting myself into?"

"A jail cell, if I have anything to say about it." She slapped him away, bolting for home before he could weaken her defenses. "And don't you dare lay a hand on me, Nick Barone."

"Burke," he said through gritted teeth, hot on her heels. "It's Ryan Burke, long *e*."

She ground to a halt, pivoting with hands on her hips. "Oh, so you're not only a thief, murderer, and fugitive, you're an imposter as well."

Her breath snagged in her throat when he hoisted her up at the waist, his jaw grinding while her feet dangled in the air. "*Wit-ness*, Al-li-son," he bit out, giving her a little shake. "Not fugitive, not imposter, and not a criminal. An officer of the law forced undercover because his life was in danger for turning state witness."

She blinked. "I don't believe you," she said, voice draining along with the blood that coursed from her pale face to the tips of her suspended toes.

He blasted out another noisy sigh and dropped her, leaving her teetering while he reached for the letter again. With an abrupt brace of her arm, he steadied her before shoving it in her face. "Read it."

Gaze thinning, she snatched it from his hand, all anger seeping out as she scanned the piece of paper. "Oh, good heavens," she whispered, eyes blinking wide, "you almost died?"

"Yeah," he said, jaw clamped until the barest hint of a smile nudged at his lips. "Made sure he threw that in—figured it couldn't hurt."

"B-but . . . but . . . is it all true?" she asked, hand to her chest.

His gaze softened along with his jaw. "Yeah, but I couldn't tell you, Alli, because I took an oath." He moved in close with hands so massive, they shouldn't have been gentle, slowly caressing her arms with a touch so soft, she felt light as air. "Forgive me?" he whispered, those lethal gray-green eyes hypnotizing her with a half-lidded plea.

Her heart began to thud, barely able to believe Nick Barone was back in her life. "So you're not . . . engaged?" A lump bobbed in her throat. "Not a father who abandoned his child?"

A lopsided grin eased across his lips. "Nope—not engaged, not a father, and not a crook," he said in a husky tone, his smoky gaze bolting her to the sidewalk tighter than the cast-iron streetlamps. He slipped his hands to her waist and drew her near. "Just a man guilty of falling in love against his will . . ." He nuzzled the lobe of her ear, and her eyelids drifted closed, the caress of his mouth all but liquefying the tendons at the back of her knees. "*And* your uncle's."

Her eyes popped open. "Oh, Nick, Uncle Logan will never—"

Her words dissolved into his kiss, strong arms locking her limp body to his. "If you're going to talk, Allison," he whispered against her lips, "say something useful like 'I love you, Ryan Nicholas Burke, and yes, I will marry you.'"

"B-Burke?" she stammered weakly. "B-but, but how—"

"It's a long story, Princess, but then we have lots and lots of time." He skimmed her jaw to take her lips with his own. "Like the rest of our lives."

Dazed, her eyelids flickered open. "B-but does that mean you're Irish instead of Italian?"

He feathered her mouth with soft, little kisses, the scent of animal crackers making her heady. "It does—with a touch of English just to make it interesting."

"Ohhhh . . . I like that," she breathed. "Mrs. Ryan Nicholas Pinhead Cranky Pants Burke, long *e*." She perched on tiptoe to brush her lips against his. "Has a nice ring, don't you think?"

He laughed and deposited a kiss to her nose. "Yes, ma'am, it does," he said with a grin, hooking her arm to usher her home. "And you can bet your sweet stick on that."

Acknowledgments

To my incredible reader friends—when people ask what's the best thing about being an author, YOU are the very first answer that comes to mind. It's a privilege and joy to be both your friend and an author you read.

To Darla Montesion, Erica Hogan, Angi Griffis, Heidi Abbott, Shannon Murphy, Emily Reilly, and Kara Grant—winners of my newsletter contest to have a character named after them in this book—thank you from the bottom of my heart, not only for your boundless enthusiasm and support, but your precious friendship.

To my agent Natasha Kern and my editor Lonnie Hull DuPont—two of God's many (and most patient) touches in my life—thank you for your faith in me.

To the great team at Revell, true professionals all—thank you for all you do. A special hug to Michele Misiak for her kindness and patience, to Cheryl Van Andel and Jones House Creative for their great covers, and to the best copy editor in the world, Barb Barnes, and her very thorough sidekick, Julie Davis—you guys make editing an absolute pleasure.

To my precious prayer partners and best friends, Joy Bollinger, Karen Chancellor, and Pat Stiehr—I would be lost without you.

To my sisters, Dee Dee, Mary, Rosie, Susie, Ellie, and Katie, for your love and prayers, and to my sisters-in-law, Diana, Mary, and Lisa—family just doesn't get any better than you.

In loving memory of my sister, Pat, and my mother-in-law, Leona—we love and miss you more than we can say.

To my daughter, Amy; son, Matt; daughter-in-law, Katie; and precious, *precious* granddaughter, Rory—along with God and my husband, you are my life.

To Keith Lessman, the man I love with every fiber of my being—never in all my dreams of romance did I ever believe I would feel so cherished and loved. I've said it before, babe, and I'll say it again—I don't deserve you.

And to the God of Love who taught me that love is never a dare when HE is involved—I will love You and worship You all the days of my life.

Award-winning author of the Daughters of Boston and Winds of Change series, **Julie Lessman** was American Christian Fiction Writers 2009 Debut Author of the Year and voted #1 Romance Author of the year in *Family Fiction* magazine's 2012 and 2011 Readers Choice Awards. She has also garnered 15 RWA awards and made *Booklist*'s 2010 Top 10 Inspirational Fiction. Her ebook *A Light in the Window* is an International Digital Awards winner, a 2013 Readers' Crown Award winner, and a 2013 Book Buyers Best Finalist. You can contact Julie and read excerpts from her books at www.julielessman.com.

Stay in Touch with

Julie Lessman

Visit **www.JulieLessman.com**

to learn more about Julie, sign up for her
newsletter, and read reviews and interviews.

Connect with her on

 Julie Lessman

 julielessman

Don't miss book 1 in
The HEART of SAN FRANCISCO series!

"*Love at Any Cost* will not only soothe your soul, but it will make you laugh, stir your heart, and release a sigh of satisfaction when you turn the last page."

—**MaryLu Tyndall**, bestselling author of *Veil of Pearls*

"*Love at Any Cost* is the start of an unforgettable series, certain to win a place on your keeper shelf!"

—**Laura Frantz**, author of *Love's Reckoning*

"Guaranteed to satisfy the most romantic of hearts."

—Tamera Alexander, bestselling author

Full of passion, romance, rivalry, and betrayal,
the Daughters of Boston series will captivate you
from the first page.